They Stood in the Moonswept Ruins of an Ancient Castle. . . .

Aidan drew her into his arms, his mouth seeking hers, supplicant instead of hungry, reverent instead of carnal, asking for response instead of demanding it.

She gave him her very soul.

A cry of surrender shuddered through her, and she clung to him as he kissed her cheeks, her eyelids, her throat. He threaded his fingers through her hair, crushing the gardenia petals in his fingers, releasing their rich scent to mingle with the light tang of mist, the slight salt whisper of the sea.

"I want you, Norah," he groaned, low in his throat. "Want you more than I've ever wanted any woman. Need you to touch me, angel." She could never know what that admission had cost him. "Let me take you back to Rathcannon, to my bed. Let me love you."

"No," she breathed, her fingers tunneling beneath his cloak, trailing up the hard plane of his chest.

Aidan's jaw knotted, and he started to draw away, but she caught at him with pleading hands, her eyes making him captive. "Aidan, please. I want you here . . . here with the magic all around us. . . ."

Please turn the page to find praise for Kimberly Cates's previous novels. . . .

STEALING
HEAVEN

Books by Kimberly Cates

Stealing Heaven
Crown of Dreams
The Raider's Bride
The Raider's Daughter
To Catch a Flame

Published by POCKET BOOKS

KIMBERLY CATES

STEALING HEAVEN

POCKET **STAR** BOOKS

New York   London   Toronto   Sydney   Tokyo   Singapore

This book is a work of fiction. Names, characters, places and incidents are products of the author's imagination or are used fictitiously. Any resemblance to actual events or locales or persons, living or dead, is entirely coincidental.

An *Original* Publication of POCKET BOOKS

 A Pocket Star Book published by
POCKET BOOKS, a division of Simon & Schuster Inc.
1230 Avenue of the Americas, New York, NY 10020

ISBN: 0-671-89745-4

Pocket Books printing May 1995

POCKET STAR BOOKS and colophon are registered trademarks
of Simon & Schuster Inc.

Cover art by Jacqui Morgan; stepback art by Pino Daeni

Printed in the U.S.A.

This book is dedicated with love:

To the Old Ones in Rathinane who welcomed me home.

To Eileen Dreyer, Pathfinder, who shares Celtic blood and druid magic, and in whom bard-songs whisper to another generation.

To Karyn Witmer-Gow, Navigator, who climbed to the top of the world and taught me about sea-magic on a rocky shore. Thank you for understanding.

To Liz and Kieran O'Driscoll, and John and Kathleen Selman for taking us into their homes and letting us see a side of Ireland we never would have discovered on our own.

And with special thanks to The Ghost.

The Irish Fairy Tour, September 1993.

CHAPTER
1

Only a madman would have dared to ride the night-darkened road alone, with just the moon to guide him. Any sane traveler would have barricaded himself in the relative safety of a sturdy coach, outriders armed with blunderbusses mounting guard along the way. Lanterns would have blazed at the coach front, peeling back the shadows that could hide lurking danger.

But never in the years Sir Aidan Kane had traveled the labyrinth of roads that led to Castle Rathcannon had he hidden from the night.

He craved the darkness, the wind, the wildness. He embraced the haunting beauty of a land he could never truly understand.

As if possessed by madness, he spurred his stallion down the road, his mantle billowing behind him like the wings of a dark angel, the planes of his face hard and reckless and wild.

The night coiled about him, its chill breath whispering beneath his collar and through the mahogany waves of his hair. It mocked him with the shadows of the denizens of night—desperate rebels and soulless thieves seeming to leap out from behind every tree and rock.

But Aidan wouldn't have given a damn if Lucifer's own army were clawing at his heels. He'd been destined to be the devil's own before he'd taken his first step, bedded his first woman. And Aidan Kane was being hunted by darker ghosts this night—the spirits of the poor bastards who had been betrayed by various Kanes of Rathcannon for five long centuries.

Doubtless, those disinherited by the Kanes would have been thrilled at the prospect of sending Aidan to join his ancestors in hell, but he already suffered a far worse agony. An eternity of waiting, a grinding sense of impending doom that grew more painful with each beat of his stallion's hooves on the road to Castle Rathcannon.

Rathcannon. Spoils of war. The reward for the countless betrayals and traitorous plots that were the only rightful legacy Aidan Kane had inherited from his ancestors.

For five hundred years, the Kanes of Rathcannon had been the slender blade the English held to the throat of western Ireland.

But if those unquiet Celtic spirits wanted vengeance against the Kanes, Aidan was certain they must be pleased, since even now he fought to secure the future of the only person he had dared to love.

Aidan leaned close to his stallion's neck, trying to drive back the images in his mind. A rosy-cheeked little girl with silver-gilt curls, a small hand clutching at his, dragging him to see a nest of kittens or a thrush's speckled egg. A fairy-bright child urging her pony to soar over fences, never once imagining that she might crash to the ground.

Cassandra.

Child of all that was bright and beautiful, so brave and strong and lovely that nothing could dull the magic that surrounded her. Nothing except the darkness that consumed her father's soul.

Aidan reined in the pain with practiced savagery. No, there had to be some way to help Cassandra, to shield her. To keep her safe, as he had from the moment he had brought her to the Irish castle beside the sea.

Aidan leaned into the wild sea-sweetened air as if it could banish the stench of the city from his skin, brush away the traces of his mistress's hands.

The wildlands had always seemed the gateway to another world, another life. And when he went there he was a different man, a better one, what few fragments of decency that still remained in his jaded soul polished bright for just a little while.

But it was a cruel enchantment, for it made him pay for that brief span of time with the knowledge that the man who rode through the stone gates of Rathcannon was an illusion. And that the girl waiting for him in Rathcannon's tower chamber believed with her whole heart that he was real.

Aidan raised eyes gritty from lack of sleep to the magnificent turrets of Rathcannon, which were bathed in the soft light of dawn. The surge of triumph he usually felt at winning his race with the sunrise was dulled by an insidious sense of dread. A dread that had crept more and more often into his consciousness for the past year. A sense of unease that told him that this tiny island of beauty in a sea of madness was slipping through his fingers forever.

He reined Hazard to a halt outside Rathcannon's stables and was greeted by a short bowlegged man, Gibbon Cadagon. The aged head groom was already busy with his morning task of brushing out the impossibly long manes of an exquisite pair of perfectly matched ponies Aidan had imported from Spain for Cassandra's eighth birthday. Aidan didn't want to think about how many years ago that had been.

"Welcome home, sir!" Cadagon exclaimed, lifting one hand from Lancelot's glossy gold flank, while Guenevere eyed Aidan's stallion with an expression of ill-disguised feminine admiration. "I know one young lady who will be pure delighted when she opens her eyes this morn! She's been stewing and stewing over whether or not you'd come."

Aidan dismounted, tossing Hazard's reins to one of Cadagon's underlings. "I received the child's royal summons, didn't I?"

Cadagon gave a hearty chuckle. "Miss Cassandra is not a child anymore, as she'll be telling you soon enough in that lofty way of hers! An' she's been worrying herself to a fever over whether or not you'd come. After all, you've been busy of late. We haven't got to see you near as much as we like, if you'll pardon my saying so."

Aidan's cheeks stung, and he averted his eyes from the keen gaze of Cadagon. It chafed at him when he heard the edge of defensiveness in his own voice. "I visit when I can."

Color flooded the pixyish Irishman's face. "I know that, sir, but Miss Cassandra, she . . . well, that daughter of yours grudges every day you're gone like a miser payin' out gold coins. I was tellin' Mrs. Cadagon just last evening that I never saw a girl adore her da more than our Princess does."

If the elderly groom had plunged a pitchfork into Aidan's chest he could not have wounded him more deeply. Aidan's fists knotted unconsciously, and he wondered when the knowledge that his daughter loved him had become so painful. Perhaps it was when he had realized that time and truth would drive that hero worship from her eyes. Or when he began to picture just how bleak his life would be when she had left him behind.

"Aye, Miss Cassie's got the whole castle in a pelter over your birthday. Why, the little termagant even bullied Coachman Sean into making the trip to Dublin to fetch up the gift she's got planned for you. Not that it was any surprise that she bent poor Sean to her will. She's been ordering the man on mysterious errands for months now, in her efforts to arrange things."

"She sent Sean all the way to Dublin? What the blazes could this be about?"

"I don't have the slightest idea, sir. But it must be something grand. The girl was acting right fairy-kissed, she was, threatening to run off to the city herself if we didn't send the coach. She would've done it, too. You know the Princess when she gets in one of her states. And *then* what would the lot of us have said to you?"

Aidan knew he should be filled with parental wrath, or at least an appropriate measure of vexation at his daughter's antics. Instead, he felt a raw tenderness squeeze his heart. "The girl is incorrigible. Mrs. Brindle always said she would be."

"Mrs. Brindle! Sometimes I think she's the worst o' all of us! Acting so stern and all prunes and prisms, when she's as soft on the girl as any of us! She's the one who finally surrendered to the girl. The surprise seemed to mean so much to Miss Cass, it did. And well, sir, no one understands how persuasive Cassandra can be better than you do. You've never been able to say no to her yourself."

"I've never been able to say no to one last roll of the dice either, Cadagon, but throwing them has usually gotten me neck-deep in trouble. Give Hazard an extra measure of oats once he's cooled down."

Aidan strode up to the castle, and a footman scrambled to open the heavy door still emblazoned with the crest of the family the Kanes had disinherited generations before. But Aidan barely returned the youth's greeting. He hastened through the corridors of the glistening haven he had built for his daughter, then took the stairs two at a time, unable to quell the strange tightness in his throat as he hurried up to his daughter's room. When he reached the landing, the door was ajar, and he flattened his palm on it and gently pushed it wide.

Sunbeams filtered through the wide windows he'd had carved out of the castle's old defenses, brilliant diamond patterns of stained glass setting the exquisite chamber aglow.

If the weavers of legend had set out to fashion a fairy bower, it would have mirrored this suite of rooms at Rathcannon. The walls were warmed with tapestries stitched by the holy sisters in France ages past. Unicorns laid their heads in maidens' laps, knights tested their courage against dragon fire. Trees spilled gold and silver fruit into children's hands while blossoms grew in exquisitely sewn fields.

Even the furniture that filled the chamber had been patterned after the fanciful stories Cassandra Kane adored: Nymphs and woodsprites danced across the rosewood armoire, dainty fairies with gauzy silver wings adorned the candlesticks. The four posts on her huge tester bed were wound about by garlands of flowers, so delicately wrought it seemed that when one touched them their fingers should come away wet with dew. Curtains—which Cass had insisted were the impossible blue-green of a mermaid's hair—draped the bed, the velvet hangings embroidered with winged horses that seemed so lifelike the mere brush of a hand should make them take flight.

But to Aidan the most miraculous creature in the room had always been the girl who drowsed among coverlets sprinkled with gold-flecked stars.

Cassandra, half angel, half imp—a treasure that fate had foolishly thrust into a rogue's awkward hands. The most intense battle Sir Aidan Kane had ever waged had been his struggle not to destroy her.

With a stealth acquired by years of practice, he slipped across thick carpets from lands of spice and mystery, and his throat felt oddly tight as he saw a gilt chair drawn close to the bed. A blanket had been draped across its seat, and a small satin pillow placed atop it, small luxuries he knew Cassandra had set out the night before in an effort to make him more comfortable when he took up his customary vigil.

He could remember the first time she had devised the chair, heard her child's plea echo in his memory. She had been seven years old, still reeling from her mother's death in

6

the disaster that had nearly cost Cassandra her own life as well.

She had grasped his hand, tight in her own, and stared up at him with wide blue eyes.

Papa, when it's time for you to visit, I wake up and wake up and think you are here, and run to your room again and again until I'm quite fractious indeed and my feet are very cold. If you slept in the chair, when I woke up I could reach out and touch you and make certain you are real.

Aidan would have walked through fire for his daughter. It had always seemed a small sacrifice to please her by taking up a vigil in the chair on the nights he arrived at the castle. What he hadn't expected was that those night watches would become the most precious moments of his life.

Times when he could watch Cassandra's little face, soft, rosy, content, her lashes feathering across her cheeks. He could know that she was safe, that she was happy, and that, for a brief, precious space in time, nothing could hurt her—not even Aidan himself.

Slowly, he reached out, to draw back one of the bed's embroidered curtains, his gaze taking in the tumble of silver-blond curls tossed across her pillows. For an instant, he pictured her cuddling the doll he'd bought her in London, imagined his daughter's rosy little mouth sucking on two fingers, the way she had when she was small.

He had spent countless hours worrying that she would ruin the shape of her mouth, but as he looked down at the girl now, he would have been grateful for such a minor concern. There were far more painful dangers drawing inexorably nearer to Cassandra with every day that slipped past.

She was growing up. Aidan's heart lurched as the morning light revealed the face of a girl on the verge of blossoming into a woman. Even in slumber, there was an expectancy in those features that were so familiar and yet suddenly so changed.

A splinter of pain pierced Aidan's chest at the sudden

awkwardness he felt—the knowledge that he no longer belonged here, keeping vigil. It was time the chair and blanket were tucked away forever.

It was inevitable, Aidan knew, this letting go of childhood games once cherished. But that knowledge didn't dull the ache of knowing it would not be long before Cassandra abandoned him as well, leaving him behind the way she had the ragged doll she'd finally outgrown.

Aidan closed his eyes, hearing the echoes of her chatter on his last visit.

Was my mother beautiful when you first saw her at General Morton-Syffe's ball?

Aidan had tried to keep the bitterness from his voice. *Yes, she was beautiful.*

Beautiful and cunning, selfish and greedy for pleasure. A foolish, spoiled, brainless girl who threw herself away upon the rogue most likely to send her family into apoplexies. . . .

Mrs. Brindle says that my mother was the belle of the season, with a dozen beaux fighting over the privilege of bringing her a cup of ratafia. And when she eloped with you, three of her suitors went into such a deep decline they had to be sent to the seashore, and another nearly shot himself in desperation. Do you think that I will have as many beaux when I have my season in London?

It had been difficult enough to speak of Delia, costing Aidan untold effort to keep his hatred of the woman from spilling into his voice or revealing itself in his eyes, where it could wound the one decent thing that had come out of his union with Delia March.

But when dreams of London—balls and theaters, waltzing and flirtations—had crept into his daughter's conversations, Aidan had finally understood the depths hell could reach.

My season in London . . .

How many times had those words seared through Aidan the past three years, more painful than the pistol shot a disgruntled duelist had driven through his shoulder?

He had reeled at the realization that Cassandra had spun out fantasies that could never come true, and his own responsibility for her inevitable disillusionment had festered inside him, a wound that wouldn't heal.

Since she was five, he had kept her safe, happy in her castle beside the Irish Sea—a princess running about her private kingdom in a gilded pony cart, begging for presents, hurling herself into his arms, laughing, laughing. He had marveled at her, a miracle of goodness in a lifetime ill spent.

The only peril he had never reckoned with was the one overtaking them now: his bright-eyed imp changing into a restless spirit, anxious to fly; a young woman with no understanding of the word *impossible,* and no inkling that a scandal from a decade past still had the power to harm her—that the sins of her father and mother were emblazoned like some hideous brand upon her breast.

Aidan would have given the last drop of blood in his veins to spare her pain, but he'd been too selfish, too arrogant, too unthinking during that brief span of time when he might truly have fixed things for her. And now it was too late. There were some wrongs that couldn't be righted, some wounds that couldn't be healed. No one knew that better than Aidan Kane.

He reached out a fingertip to trace the scar usually hidden by the curls that tumbled across her brow, the faint white arc a poignant reminder of how close he had come to losing her forever.

At his touch, Cassandra's lashes fluttered open, revealing wide blue eyes, so like her mother's. But instead of the vanity, the deceit that had characterized Delia Kane, delight shone unabashedly in his daughter's face. She scrambled out of bed in a flurry of nightgown and flung her arms about Aidan's neck with no thought to her jealously guarded adolescent dignity. "Papa! You've come! If you hadn't, I would've been quite desperate!"

Aidan gave a strained chuckle. He gathered her close, his heart wrenching at the realization that she nearly reached his chin. He buried his face in her curls and breathed in the scent of milk and cinnamon and innocence. "Desperate? That sounds rather alarming, Princess. Is there something amiss?"

"No!" she said rather too hastily. "It's just that . . . it's been forever since I saw you last!"

"Three months only," Aidan corrected. *But when I left, you were still a child. . . .*

She drew away, looking up at him with eyes suddenly far younger than her fifteen years. "You used to think that three months was forever too. Remember, Papa?"

Wistful. Wide. Her questioning gaze slayed Aidan, left him bleeding. *But that was before, when I didn't have to face how I've hurt you, simply by being your father. When I didn't have to feel this grinding guilt.*

"Perhaps I stay away to save myself the embarrassment of making a disaster out of your presents, girl. Last time I came, I brought a length of muslin for a gown and, when I saw how tall you'd grown, was forced to face the fact there was scarce enough fabric to fashion a petticoat for you!"

A heartbreakingly beautiful smile tugged at her lips. "It is *my* turn to surprise you with a present this time! After all, it's not every day that a gentleman turns . . . How old is it? Eighty? Eighty-one? A great doddering age."

"Thirty-six, minx," Aidan said, pinching her cheek. "And seeing you is the best present I could receive. Except . . . perhaps one. Pray, tell me you have *not* baked me a cake again. The last one nearly poisoned me, if I remember rightly."

"I have a much better gift this year," she said loftily. "I worried over it until my head ached. But it was worth the agonies. It is absolutely perfect."

"You perceive me positively agog with curiosity." Aidan made a great show of searching the room. "You know, it *is* officially my birthday. When do I receive this paragon present?"

Cassandra swirled about to grab up her dressing gown. "I

10

don't know *exactly.*" There was an over-bright quality to Cassandra's voice that set alarm bells rattling in Aidan's head. "Sh—I mean, *it* is arriving by coach."

"Ah hah! You nearly said *she!* Let me make a guess! When last I was here, I told you that Squire Phipps was going to breed that delectable pointer bitch of his. I'd wager a hundred pounds you've sent for one of the pups from Dublin!"

"Dublin? I don't know what you mean."

"You needn't dissemble, girl. Cadagon already told me how shamelessly you tyrannized over them, sending the coach clear to town to fetch it! You knew that I was in the city. If you'd just have written, I could have scooped her up and—No, you needn't put on such a sour face. I'll have her trained to my hand before the week is out! Make her the most devoted female ever . . ."

Cassandra went quite pale. "It's not a dog! It's something ever so much more—more . . . exciting."

Aidan raised one dark brow. "Why does that particular adjective suddenly make me nervous?"

"Because you are far too stodgy and set in your ways, and you need someone to shake you up royally, sir," Cassandra said, with a most disquieting gleam in her eyes.

"I see. And you are just the imp to reform me, eh?" Aidan laid one finger alongside his beard-stubbled jaw. "Come to think of it, I passed a coach on the road a ways back, but between the darkness and the crazed pace I was setting, I didn't even realize it was my own! Perhaps I should roust out Hazard and go make a search of it." He started toward the door, but Cassandra lunged for him, grabbing his arm.

"No!" She glanced at the window as if expecting the king himself to come racketing up to the door. "You should carry yourself off to make yourself quite handsome."

"I should, eh? Since when did you become so particular about my appearance?" Aidan peered into the gilt-framed mirror that graced one wall. His mouth tipped up in a rueful grin. Cassandra was right: He was looking even more

11

disreputable than usual. Stubble shadowed his square jaw, his hair wind-tossed and wild about sun-bronzed cheeks. His eyes were reddened from a shortage of sleep and an overabundance of liquor. A spectacular bruise stained his left cheekbone where he'd been struck by a vase his mistress had flung at him when he'd not tarried in her bedchamber. His cravat had been mangled by impatient fingers, while his breeches and boots were dulled by a fine layer of travel dust.

"Your coat is deplorable," Cassandra insisted with a graceful toss of her head. "And your whiskers nearly burned my cheek raw when you kissed me!"

He rubbed at the offending stubble with one long-fingered hand. "I should hope these will be a minor irritation, since I doubt I'll be tempted to kiss my present!"

Cassandra choked, sputtering. "Y—you could make yourself presentable for me. A gentleman . . . Well, I— Papa!" Her garbled scoldings vanished in a vexed cry. "What on earth have you done now!" Accusation was edged with worry.

Aidan frowned, confused. "I don't have the slightest idea."

"Your eye! Don't even attempt to tell me you ran into a stable door again, for I shan't believe it! Tell me you haven't been indulging in fisticuffs at that awful boxing salon again!"

"I haven't even been to London!" He raised his fingers sheepishly to the place Stasia had bruised him and groped for a plausible lie. "When I was riding out of the city, I was set upon by . . . by a pair of brigands who tried to relieve me of my purse."

"Brigands? Oh, Papa!"

"Yes, there must have been four big, burly fellows." Aidan paced to the window overlooking the castle drive, warming to his story.

"I thought you said 'a pair.'"

"Well, I was much confused. It was dark, and after all, I'd taken the devil of a blow to my head. I . . ." Aidan paused,

12

nearly sighing aloud in relief as a reprieve came in an unexpected form—that of a coach rumbling toward the castle.

"It seems as if I will have to regale you of my adventure some other time," he said, tugging at Cassandra's curls. "My gift seems to be coming up the drive."

"Wh—what?"

"The coach!" Aidan said with diabolical glee. "I'll beat you to the door!"

With a squawk, Cass started to dart out ahead of him. Aidan caught a handful of her dressing gown, reeling her in. "Cassandra Victorine Kane, you are still in your nightgown. A young lady shouldn't parade in front of the servants *en dishabille.*"

"I won't if you'll wait for me! Papa! Papa, no!"

Aidan had never been able to resist teasing her. He raced down the stairs, making a deafening racket, while he heard Cassandra scrambling to get dressed. He had no intention of spoiling her surprise, of course, fully planning to wait for her in the grand entry to Rathcannon. But at that instant the door flew open, revealing the face of Rathcannon's coachman, Sean O'Day, the burly Irishman looking as distraught as if he had just set fire to the stables. Ashen faced, he railed at the footman, Calvy Sipes.

"Jesus, Mary, and Joseph, you won't believe what Miss Cass has done. The master is going to flay the hide off every one of us, and I vow I'll hand him the knife to do it with!"

Aidan stepped into the coachman's line of vision, and Sean looked as if he was about to be judged at the seat of Lucifer himself. "Come now, man, don't be so hard on the girl!" Aidan soothed. "I promise not to resort to violence unless I'm severely provoked."

O'Day's wild eyes slashed to Aidan, his big hands clutching at the front of his travel-dusty livery. "Sir . . . oh, sir," he mourned, "I was hopin' you weren't here yet. That there'd be time to fix things somehow. But we wouldn't be able to right this in a hundred years! You have to believe me,

13

sir, I had no idea what Miss Cass was about or she couldn't 'a dragged me off to Dublin bound with chains! But if I hadn't gone, what would have become of *her?* Didn't know what the divil to do once I had her . . . didn't dare to tell her . . ."

"Tell who *what?*"

O'Day blinked, looking even more dazed. "Why, the lady, sir! There she was, standin' at the dock plain as the wart on Cadagon's nose, with a letter in her hand and her thinking you wrote it. But I knew the truth the minute I saw it."

O'Day's rattling was stirring up the dregs of gin in Aidan's head, starting a painful throb in the base of his skull. "You're blathering like a half-wit!" Aidan bit out. "Just tell me what mischief the girl has kicked up, and we'll sort it out somehow. You're acting as if she committed murder, for God's sake!"

"It's *you* who might be tempted to murder, Sir Aidan, when you see what lurks out there!" O'Day waved one hand toward the open door, as if some horrendous monster lurked beyond, waiting to devour them.

Fists on hips, Aidan stalked to the threshold, glaring out at the scene before him. Slivers of light drove beneath his burning eyelids, and he swore, rubbing his fingers impatiently across his suddenly blurry gaze.

He didn't have the slightest idea what he expected to see as the mist cleared from his vision—the hounds of hell tied to the coach wheels, a tribe of gypsies setting up camp on the front lawn, or the horsemen of the Apocalypse kicking up their hooves in an effort to separate old Cadagon's few remaining teeth from his gums.

However, one thing Aidan didn't expect to see was a footman unloading a spanking new trunk, while a lone woman stood beside the coach, looking on.

Aidan took in wide brown eyes, dusky curls peeking out about a heart-shaped face that looked rather pale under the shelter of a bonnet brim. A rich blue pelisse that should have

14

seemed the height of fashion and elegance flowed about her slender figure, but instead of setting her charms off to advantage, the garment made the woman look, for all the world, like a child caught dressing up in her mother's finery.

Even the object caught in her arms seemed designed to accentuate that impression, for she was holding onto a child's doll with white-knuckled fingers.

Yet when she looked up at him, there was something about her—that stiff-necked English propriety, that sense of control—that had always set his teeth on edge. His face twisted into a black scowl as he stalked down the stairs.

"What the blazes is going on here! The coachman's raving like a cursed Bedlamite!"

The woman raised those melting-dark eyes to his, and Aidan was stunned as they were transformed into a rare loveliness by her nervous smile. "He's been acting quite strange since the moment I met him. As if there is some sort of—of confusion. If you could just take me to your master, I'm certain it can all be untangled."

"My master?" Aidan echoed.

"Yes. I'm looking for Sir Aidan Kane, of Rathcannon Castle. If you could . . . find him for me?"

He eyed her warily. "What the devil do you want him for?"

Color flooded her cheeks. "It's a personal matter, rather difficult to explain. But I can assure you, he's expecting me."

"The devil he is! I mean, the devil I am. I'm Kane."

The revelation seemed to cast her into dismay, and Aidan was excruciatingly aware that he looked like absolute hell. The sensation irritated him beyond belief.

"Who the blazes are you?" He cursed himself, unable to keep his hand from creeping up in an instinctive effort to straighten his tousled hair.

"I'm Norah Linton." She looked at him as if the name should explain everything. But Aidan just watched her, tension coiling at the back of his neck.

"I—I answered your letter of advertisement," she stammered out. "The one you intended to place in the *London Times.*"

Aidan folded his arms over his chest in challenge. "I never entered any advertisement."

Disbelief streaked across features that were far too waiflike for beauty. "But of course you did. I have your letter right here in my reticule, and you . . . you arranged my passage from England—"

"I didn't arrange a damn thing!"

At that moment, a whirlwind of tumbled curls and sweet muslin frock bolted out the door, Cassandra still fastening the buttons at her throat.

"Miss Linton!" Cassandra cried, rushing up to the woman, beaming. "I'm Cassandra. It's so wonderful to meet you at last!"

The Englishwoman looked astonished.

"Cassandra . . . but I thought—thought . . ." A flush stained her cheeks. She looked down at the plaything in her hand.

"You thought I was younger, didn't you?" Cassandra trilled, her smiling gaze fixing on the little lady rigged out in primrose-hued satin. "Did you bring this for me?"

Aidan gaped as his daughter—of late so determined to guard her dignity—reached out to accept the toy then stroked the doll's tiny feathered bonnet. "It's adorable! I shall save it for when I have a little sis . . . ahem!" She dissolved into a fit of theatrical coughing.

"You know this woman?" Aidan interrupted, pinning his daughter with a glare. What he saw made his stomach knot. "Cassandra, what is this? Some sort of crazed joke?"

"Joke?" What little color had stained the woman's cheeks drained away. "You can't mean you had no—no idea. . . ."

"It's not a joke, Papa," Cassandra said breezily, linking her arm through that of the stunned Englishwoman. "Miss Linton is the present I told you about."

"My present?" Aidan choked out, casting a wild glance

16

from his daughter to the woman standing in his carriage circle. "What the devil is she supposed to be? A maid servant? A governess?"

"Don't be ridiculous, Papa." Cassandra gave a fluttery laugh. "You don't need a governess."

"You drag some strange woman from God knows where, and tell me she's my goddamn present, and then say *I'm* being ridiculous?" He sucked in a deep breath, battling for inner balance. He knew damn well he shouldn't ask the question Cassandra was so obviously anticipating, but he couldn't help himself.

"If I don't need a governess, what in the blazes *do* I need?"

The girl who was the mirror image of Delia raised her chin with a pure Kane recklessness that always presaged disaster.

"What you need is a *wife.*"

CHAPTER
2

"A *wife?*" Aidan bellowed, feeling as if the earth had split beneath him. Anger flooded through him. He couldn't move. Didn't dare. Because if he did, he'd be tempted to thrash his daughter for the first time in his life.

Aidan let fly a string of oaths. The coachman dove for cover. The sturdy footman who had unloaded the trunk tried to hide behind the lead horse in the coach's traces.

The Englishwoman looked as if Aidan had snatched O'Day's whip from the coach seat and lashed it about her head and shoulders.

Only Cassandra stood her ground, her face twisting in a formidable scowl. "Papa, if you'll just stop and think for a moment, you'll see that it's the most perfect gift in the world."

"Why not snap a foxtrap to my leg and call *that* my present? Better still, shove my boot through the stirrup and have Hazard drag me a dozen miles! A wife? My God, Cass—"

"Stop it right now!" she hissed between clenched teeth. "You're going to ruin everything!"

"There's nothing to ruin!" he snapped. "I need a wife like I need a cup of hemlock, Cassandra! There is *no way in hell* that I'm marrying *anyone*. Especially some brainless female so desperate she'd marry a man she'd never set eyes on before! By God's blood, she must be mad!"

"You're right, of course." The woman's voice startled Aidan, and he wheeled to glare at her. Something about her reminded him of a wildflower crushed beneath a careless bootheel. Those dark eyes were bleak in a pale face, and in them he could see just how much hopefulness she had packed up along with her polished trunk and her flower-decked bonnet. But it was the set of her shoulders that tightened the cinch of tension about Aidan's chest. For they were squared beneath the blue pelisse with the air of someone who had withstood withering blows before.

Why the devil did that make Aidan feel like the most vile tyrant who'd ever breathed? He was just an innocent bystander. Cassandra was nothing but a reckless girl. But Norah Linton was a grown woman who should have some notion that this whole scheme was insane!

"It was rash of me to come here," she admitted, sounding so reasonable that Aidan wanted to wring her neck. "And it was wrong of your daughter to—to concoct such a drastic scheme without telling you. But there's no need to rage at the child. She made a simple mistake."

"There's nothing simple about this disaster! There never is when Cass is involved! I'll have to find some way to get you back to wherever you came from."

"It's not a disaster unless you make it one!" Tears quivered just beneath the stubborn tones of Cassandra's voice. "Papa, you should read her letters, they're so kind. She's lonely just as you are and wants someone to love. She didn't say it in exactly those words, but I know—"

"Please," the woman interrupted, a little desperately. "I

know you didn't mean any harm, but it's obvious this has been a mistake. There's no need to—to make it worse by repeating what was in those letters."

"Do you mean to tell me that you set up a correspondence with Miss Linton?" Aidan roared.

"I didn't. *You* did. I said everything I knew you would say if you dared let your true feelings out."

The notion of a fifteen-year-old girl whose head was stuffed with romantic nonsense penning a letter in Aidan's name made his head spin. He hadn't blushed since he was sixteen and his father had taken him 'round to his current light o' love to rid his son of the troublesome burden of virginity. But as Aidan looked from his daughter to Norah Linton, hot blood surged into his cheeks.

"My true feelings?" he said through gritted teeth. "Let me make this very clear, Cassandra: *I do not want a wife.*"

Cassandra cast Norah Linton a pleading glance. "He rode all night," she attempted to explain. "He doesn't have the slightest idea what he's saying. If you would pardon us for a moment."

"Devil burn it!" Aidan protested. "I know exactly what I'm—"

Cass grasped Aidan's hand, dragging him off behind the carved griffin bearing the Gilpatricks' heraldic device.

"You may not want a wife," Cassandra raged at him in scathing undertones, "but I *do* want a mother!"

Aidan reeled at her impassioned words. "Cass . . ." He tried to gentle his voice, but it was roughened by her pain. A secret pain he had never suspected. An empty place he thought she'd long since forgotten.

"Don't you see, Papa? When I go to London, I want to be like everyone else." Her words sliced deep into Aidan's soul, exposing stark impossibilities. *You're not like everyone else. You never can be.*

He winced, remembering that adolescent desperation to fit in with the hordes of young people who would descend upon London with their dreams in their hands, ready to discover their futures.

But she was continuing, so earnestly it broke his heart. "Papa, I want a mother who will help me pick out gowns and explain so many things I don't understand."

Aidan felt as if she'd ripped away something indescribably precious. Something he hadn't even noticed was slipping through his fingers. "You've always said you can tell me anything."

She caught his hands, squeezed them, hard. "Papa, I love you more than anyone in the whole world. But you're a man! You can't tell me about things like—like when to let a beau kiss my hand, or how to be certain that I'm in love."

"I *can* tell you that I'll thrash the daylights out of any whelp who dares come near you." Aidan closed his eyes against the image of his proud little Cass suffering through her first heartache. Because even with her beauty, her wit, her courage, Aidan knew the odds were high that she'd suffer more than one disappointment. Romantic youths were quick to abandon their infatuations with "ineligibles" when they were confronted with the harsh reality of the haute ton's disapproval. And there was no doubt that those interfering snobs who had nothing better with which to occupy their minds than gossip and ridicule would have a veritable feast of scandal to feed on when it came to Cass.

He sucked in a steadying breath, groping for the right words, as he had so many times in the past. "Cass, we'll figure out how to deal with all that when the time comes, just the way we always have before," he said, stroking back one tangled silver-blond tress. "I understand that you feel the loss of your mother." Aidan looked down at the ringlet that clung to his finger, knowing that the one thing he had learned in his marriage to Delia was that it was possible to grieve for something you never really had. "The one thing I'm certain of is that dragging Miss Linton into our lives isn't going to change the ache you feel."

"Why not?" Cassandra's lashes were wet with tears, her eyes shining with belligerence. Belligerence, all the more heart-wrenching because Aidan could see beneath it her absolute faith that he wouldn't fail her, that he would deny her nothing.

"Papa, I want a mother more than I've ever wanted anything in my life. And soon it will be too late. I'll be grown up. From the time I first came to Rathcannon, I've watched the Cadagons with their babies and Mrs. O'Day with her little ones. And I would have traded all my pretty things if just once I could run to my own mother when I was sad, or sorry, or hurt."

Aidan winced at the memory of how many scraped knees and bumped elbows he'd soothed. But there had been far more bumps and bruises that he hadn't been at Rathcannon to heal. He'd done his best to make certain Cassandra was surrounded with people who adored her: Mrs. Brindle, the Cadagons, the O'Days, everyone from the head butler to the lowliest stableboy.

He'd told himself it didn't matter that no one carried the official title of Mother. In fact, if he was brutally honest, he'd thought Cassandra well rid of Delia, since the woman had possessed about as much maternal instinct as the stone griffin. But the lack of a mother had obviously mattered to Cassandra. Just one more bruised place in her spirit she'd kept hidden from him.

He looked from his daughter, now holding that ridiculous doll, to the woman who still stood silhouetted against the side of the coach, ash-pale, agonizingly quiet.

Was it possible that this stranger could give Cassandra something he could not? A confidante to initiate Cass into the rites of becoming a woman? A protector if her father should fail her?

"No, damn it," Aidan muttered more to himself than the hopeful girl standing beside him. "Hellfire and damnation, I would be mad to even consider . . . Cassandra, for the love of God, girl! Think!"

"I *have* been thinking! Thinking and thinking until my head ached!"

"That's enough! God's teeth, Cass! You're acting like a spoiled child!" Aidan snapped. If only she had been. Instead, she was facing him with the aura of a most determined young woman.

"If you don't marry her, I'll never forgive you for taking this chance away from me!" Cassandra said, her eyes shimmering with tears she was fighting not to shed. Never." She wheeled as the first tear fell and ran up the stairs.

Aidan swore. When had his daughter—his willful, strong, adorable little Cass—become prey to those wild, hysterical vapors the fair sex seemed given to? When he'd left her last, she'd seemed so blasted rational, reasonable . . . asking him such sweet questions: Are you happy, Papa? Do you ever get lonely, Papa? This visit, were she to query him, the question would be *Do you mind if I ruin your life, Papa?*

He would be willing to promise her the moon if it would make her dry her eyes. But *marriage?* Bind himself until death to a woman?

He shifted his gaze to where the woman stood—what the blazes was her name? Lyndon? Mitton? Something as unremarkable as her face. The name Linton finally came to his mind.

Still, he could hardly leave her standing out here. He walked toward her, his arms folded across his chest. Why did she suddenly look fragile? Forlorn?

"Well, I suppose there's nothing to do but take you inside," he allowed grudgingly. "I can hardly leave you standing in the carriage circle until I figure out what to do with you."

"I am not your responsibility, sir," she said in that frosty way Englishwomen had that had always tempted Aidan to try to melt them. "I'm certain there must be an inn nearby."

"There is. Fifteen miles away. But the only way you are going to get there, madam, is to walk, and it's a damn sight too far for you to try it."

There was just enough fire under that icy voice of hers to taunt him. "Sir Aidan, you have made it absolutely clear what you think of me. If you think I would consider inconveniencing you any further after you've bellowed at me, humiliated me, and maligned everything from my intelligence to my appearance, you are much mistaken."

She was making him feel like a bastard. It infuriated him. Mainly because she was right.

Aidan set his teeth. "Madam," he said very carefully, aware of a bevy of servants who had heard the ruckus and gathered to peep out the door. "I think we've both made fools of ourselves long enough for one morning, don't you? If you don't march yourself up to that castle right now, I am going to throw you over my shoulder like a common tavern wench and haul you inside myself."

Her eyes widened, and she took a step backward. "You wouldn't dare!"

"Wouldn't I? I rode all night half drunk in an effort to get here from Dublin. I've got a daughter who has some demented notion that she wants you for her mother. And whether I want to deal with you or not, the truth is that my daughter's mischief is what brought you here in the first place, so I *am* responsible for you. At least as responsible as a man can be for a scatter-brained . . ." He bit down on the words, cutting them off, battling for control of his badly frayed temper. "In other words, Miss Linton," he said carefully, "it's not even nine o'clock in the morning, and already it's been one of the worst goddamn days of my life. To top the whole thing off, it's supposed to be my birthday." It sounded ridiculous, even to Aidan's own ears.

"I'll offer you my felicitations when I leave this disaster behind." Nothing she could have said would have made him feel more the fool.

"Don't worry, madam," Aidan said. "No one is in a greater hurry to hasten your departure than I am. But until then, we'll just have to limp along as best we can." He

24

signaled the footman. "Put the lady's trunk in the Blue Room."

He saw the footman's jaw drop open.

"Is there some problem, Sipes?" Aidan shot the youth such a glare the boy flushed scarlet.

"Of course not, sir. It's just that no one has stayed there since—since, well . . . I'm certain it's not prepared for occupancy."

"Then prepare it."

"Aye, sir. I'll make certain Rose does so right away, sir." The footman heaved up the trunk.

"Is there something amiss about the room?" Norah asked, unease flickering in her dark eyes. "I'd not want to inconvenience anyone."

"You're a damn sight too late to be worrying about that," Aidan grumbled. "As for the chamber assigned to you, it's perfect." Aidan flashed her a diabolical smile, possessed by an unholy need to unnerve her. "It belonged to the last Lady Kane—a fitting place for you, since you were so eager to take her place. If I should change my mind, and become tempted to matrimony, I figure it would be best if I were within easy reach of you so I can sample what you've offered so prettily."

It was a damnable thing to say, but Aidan believed he would have said far worse to assure that he dashed the last of any romantic notions this woman had woven about her mysterious bridegroom.

The woman's face went scarlet. "I cannot imagine anything that would induce me to marry you now. And unless you want your other eye blackened, you had better not attempt to sample anything."

Aidan reached up his fingers to touch the bruise he'd all but forgotten and fought not to heave an audible sigh of relief. "Perhaps my birthday can be salvaged after all. Sipes will show you to your room." He watched Norah disappear through the door through which a tearful Cassandra had fled, and it seemed as if an eternity had passed in that brief time since he'd charged out into the sunlight, laughing with his daughter.

Barely a heartbeat later, here he was, with Cassandra crying her eyes out and a woman he'd never seen before taking up residence in the Blue Room.

Perhaps he had acted like a bastard, thrusting the Linton woman into the chamber adjoining his own. And yet, it seemed the perfect location for this "bride" Cassandra had dredged up for him.

Every time he looked at the Englishwoman he would remember the nights Delia had hurled out her contempt of Rathcannon—the servants, the castle, and everything Irish. Most especially Aidan himself.

Surely, if he ensconced the woman in the middle of such relentless reminders of his disastrous first marriage, even Cassandra couldn't tempt him to slip his neck into the matrimonial noose again.

Could she?

His gaze flicked to the door where the Englishwoman had disappeared, and Aidan battled a sudden urge to race after her and haul her back outside. To stuff the woman back into the coach and send her careening off to God knew where— anywhere, away from him.

The man who hadn't quailed from charging hordes of Napoleon Bonaparte's Frenchmen swallowed hard, reaching up a hand to wipe away the beads of sweat suddenly dampening his brow.

There was only one thing to do, Aidan resolved: He would have to get that woman away from Rathcannon as soon as possible.

Norah trudged in the wake of the footman, her stomach churning with hopelessness, the sick, wrenching futility of it all. She had failed, miserably. Completely. She'd made a total fool of herself before this hard-eyed Irishman she'd dared to weave dreams about for such a brief and precious time.

She winced at the image of herself, straining for a glimpse of Ireland's shore from the ship's rail, and shuddered at the memory of the fluttering of her heart as she'd seen the turrets of Rathcannon.

But most of all, she was sickened by the soaring sense of hope that she had felt from the moment she'd first taken up the letter from Sir Aidan Kane. She hadn't paused to question the oddly rounded, elegant penmanship, so unlike a grown man's. Instead, she'd drowned in the poignant beauty of the words, words that had convinced her—just this once—to take a chance. To dare dream of happily ever afters, and of a man who needed someone to love him.

A mate who hungered as desperately as she had for a family.

How many years had she bottled up the love inside her, kept it hidden away, knowing it would be unwelcome in the house of her cold stepfather? How many years had she pretended it didn't matter that she was isolated, so very much alone?

But the soul-deep need to love and be loved had surged up inside her, battering her like a raging river against an ancient dam, until a fistful of letters had shattered all her defenses, and she had taken her heart in her hand to offer it up to a man. A man who didn't want her any more than her stepfather had, any more than any of the high-brow beaux in London society had.

Crippling disillusionment tightened its grasp about her throat, making it burn with tears she would not shed.

She tipped her chin up high, her face aching with the effort it took not to betray the turmoil inside her as she made her way up the exquisite staircase, then passed through the curious throng of servants that seemed to peep at her from every doorway.

It should have been simple enough to barricade herself

behind the wall of icy dignity that had been her retreat since she was a wary child, wandering into her stepfather's domain for the first time.

Never once in the years that followed had she allowed Winston Farnsworth to see past her pride into her pain. And yet, the feelings roiling through her now were far more daunting than anything she had endured before—a churning mixture of self-loathing, despair, exhaustion, and hopelessness.

Dear God, what had she done? Charging off to Ireland like a dream-struck fool to marry a man she'd invented in her imagination. Emerging from the coach—not with the sense of calm acceptance that would have been sensible, considering the circumstances—but, rather, with a thousand fragile dreams clutched, like that ridiculous doll, in her hands. A doll that had been intended as a gift for a gap-toothed little cherub with skinned knees and plump baby hands.

Dreams of a man, a lover, a husband, Norah hadn't dared to admit she'd had, even to herself, until Sir Aidan Kane had stormed out of the castle's massive doorway and dashed those secret fantasies to bits on Rathcannon's stone stairs.

Sir Aidan Kane—no solemn hero scarred by battle, no lonely father, wanting to share his life with a woman.

Rather, Norah's worst nightmare. A raging, arrogant beast with the hard glitter of dissipation etched in a handsome face and a mocking edge of cruelty in a voice roughened with a sensuous burr no woman could help but understand. Exactly the kind of male who had been casting dismissive sneers at Norah Linton since she'd been in short skirts.

Most humiliating of all, Aidan Kane hadn't made the slightest effort to hide his reaction toward her.

Horror.

Disbelief.

Utter contempt.

Kane had looked as if the mere word *wife* were anathema to him, and she had set out singlehandedly to ensnare him in the jaws of marriage. No, not singlehandedly, Norah thought, exhausted. There had been two other parties involved.

Her stepbrother, Richard, so earnest, so hopeful as he pressed the mysterious Irishman's letters into her hands, wanting to save her from the hideous marriage his father had arranged for her. Richard, showering her with a trousseau so lovely it stole her breath away, with no notion that his attempt to help her had merely plunged her into an even more calamitous disaster than the one she was leaving behind.

And second, Cassandra Kane, penning letters in her father's name, plotting to give him the "gift" of a bride, never suspecting that her father would be horrified by the mere suggestion.

A tight ache knotted in Norah's chest, a sense of loss spawned by a child who had never existed. Cassandra. Not the winsome little waif Norah had been led to anticipate, a bright-eyed angel rushing over to cradle the doll her new mama had brought her. A child she could lavish with all the affection Norah herself had never experienced.

Rather, Cassandra Kane was a headstrong girl on the verge of womanhood, who had recklessly plunged both Aidan Kane and Norah herself into this maelstrom of disaster.

A budding beauty Norah could never have hoped to be an adequate mother to.

Norah raised her fingertips to the dusty curve of her cheekbone, wincing inwardly. No, even if Aidan Kane had welcomed her with open arms, she would not have been a proper mother to his daughter. She wouldn't have known how to begin to deal with a lovely, bright, confident little beauty who would never spend her adolescence as Norah had—staring at her reflection in a mirror, trying not to regret the ivory pallor to her cheeks, the plain shape of her nose, the solemn mouth that was far from ripe and kissable.

Not even the swan's down pelisse Richard had given her could fire color into Norah's cheeks. Not even the glorious bonnet he'd tucked over her brown curls could spill beauty into features that were ordinary as any chambermaid's in Farnsworth House.

Farnsworth House.

The name alone was enough to make bile rise in Norah's throat, her fingers tremble.

I can hardly leave you standing in the carriage circle until I can send you back to wherever you came from, Aidan Kane had snarled.

Yet the very idea of dragging herself back to her stepfather's household, rejected, humiliated, was more than Norah could bear. She could imagine Winston Farnsworth gloating over her blunder, certain he would rejoice in his proud stepdaughter crawling back to his doorstep, placing herself under his control once more. Likely, the man wouldn't even allow her in the door.

How very gratifying he would find it to stand like some villain in a Cheltenham tragedy, driving her into the streets.

The thought alone made Norah's jaw tighten until it seemed the muscles must snap. She would never go back. Never afford Farnsworth that kind of satisfaction. She'd starve first.

No. That would give him pleasure too. Imagine his pompous delight, waving that thick finger of doom over her corpse, pontificating about the justice the fates exacted over an ungrateful child.

But if she wasn't returning to Farnsworth House, where else could she go? Richard couldn't help her. It was no secret his father had planted servants willing to spy upon his son, to assure that he be kept aware of his heir's behavior. Generous as Richard had been in providing her with a trousseau for this unorthodox marriage, there was no use entertaining grand delusions of rescue from that quarter.

Yet, was it possible that her mad dash to Ireland might have freed her to do as she'd wished in the beginning?

Before Winston Farnsworth had made her feel the full reach of his power?

Could she find a position of employment for herself somehow, somewhere her stepfather would never find her? She might even be able to enlist Sir Aidan Kane's help in finding a situation.

Norah grimaced. There was more chance of Sir Aidan Kane coming to her chamber and falling down on one knee, begging her hand in marriage.

Norah grimaced as an apple-cheeked servant in a charming white cap came barreling out of a chamber, a bunch of linens clutched in plump white arms.

"Rose!" the footman called out. "You'd best drop whatever you be doin' and take yourself off to the Blue Room directly. The master wants it buffed up right smart now."

"Tell 'im it's plenty buffed up for them that stays there!" The pert Irish girl tossed Sipes a smile that must have broken a dozen hearts. "I much doubt a haunting ghost would have need o' clean bedding."

"Maybe not, but this lady will." Sipes set down Norah's trunk with a bang. "She be visiting at Rathcannon, and Sir Aidan ordered she be put in that very chamber."

"I don't believe it!" The maid gaped at Norah. "Has the master waxed mad?"

At that instant, a precise figure dressed in black swooped from another door, keys jangling at her waist. "Even if Sir Aidan has taken more leave of his senses than usual, it's not for you to be gossiping about, Rose. Follow his orders at once, or—heavenly days!"

The older woman slammed to a halt, pressing one hand to her breasts as she stared at Norah. "What in the world—"

"It's a lady come all the way from England." Sipes scurried over to the woman, relating the debacle in the carriage circle in hushed tones.

By the time he was finished, the woman looked quite pale, and Norah braced herself for another bout of recriminations for her foolishness. "Don't tell me that wicked girl dragged

31

you all this way," the woman blustered, "and Sir Aidan, without so much as a notion you were to come here. What kind of female would do such a rash thing as to—"

"To come to Ireland to marry a stranger?" Norah's cheeks burned as she interrupted Mrs. Brindle's disjointed tirade. "I don't know. But I would say that she deserves whatever disaster befalls her, wouldn't you?"

She looked away from the older woman, hiding the sudden, sharp sting of tears.

The words seemed to take the woman aback. She drew closer, and Norah smelled a comforting scent of lavender swirling up from dark skirts.

"Now, now," the woman tsked. "Whatever brought you here, 'tis obvious you're a lady. And not a hard one either, with the soft look to your eyes. I'm Maude Brindle, Sir Aidan's housekeeper and, once upon a time, Miss Cassandra's nurse. Though if the child's been up to the kind of mischief Sipes is prattling about, I'm ashamed to own her."

Norah forced her lips into a tremulous smile. "This was all a terrible mistake, Mrs. Brindle."

"Anything where men are involved is like to be one, child," the housekeeper observed with a shake of her head. "I buried my husband nigh thirty years ago, and I can tell you right off that men are nothing but trouble, especially men the like of Sir Aidan."

"I can't argue with you about that. I intend to leave the moment I can arrange it."

The woman's face pursed up in a formidable scowl. "I'm certain if I bundled you into a coach this instant you couldn't be quit of the two of them soon enough! Of all the inexcusable mischief!" Outrage streaked across an ageless face. "Oh, and I shall take them to task for this, I promise you! You look tired to death, miss, and us not expecting you! Put the trunk in that room there, Calvy Sipes, and tell Noddie and Claire to bring up a bath for the lady. And cook can wet her up a bit of tea, and put some cakes on a plate. Poor thing looks like to fade clean away, she's so pale."

It seemed as if it had taken forever to traverse the maze of corridors and stairways of Rathcannon. But in a heartbeat, Mrs. Brindle had swept Norah into the mysterious Blue Room, enthroning her before a freshly started fire, with a hartshorn pillow at her back and a heartening cup of tea warming her hands.

The irrepressible Rose and three other lively maids rushed about, spreading exquisite sheets on the four-poster bed, dashing blue-velvet draperies back from windows that hadn't been opened in so many years that their frames were warped shut. But if they could have been thrown open, Norah doubted even the sweet-smelling Irish breezes could drive back the mustiness that thickened the air in the chamber, or the shadows that seemed to press themselves into the painted wallpaper and huddle in the corners. Shadows that seemed to lodge cold and dismal in Norah's own breast.

As a child, she'd been tormented by the oddest notion that at night her stepfather had torn away the floor outside Norah's room, so that if she set foot beyond that door to seek her mother she would plunge into a black abyss, filled with snarling monsters.

She'd told herself a hundred times to go, to open the door. Certain that if she raced very fast across the chasm, she'd be able to reach the other side and find her mother again.

Of course, she had never dared and had spent the solitary nights trembling beneath the coverlets, listening for the scritch-scratching of the monsters' claws and the soft, hungry growls of their stomachs.

Tonight she felt as if she had finally dared the chasm, outwitted the monsters, only to find herself at the edge of an even deeper chasm, populated with monsters far fiercer than the ones she had faced before. And there was no way she could turn back.

If only she had realized it before it was too late.

"Miss Linton." The sound of a voice at her shoulder made Norah start, shaken from her memories. The redoubtable Mrs. Brindle patted her hand. "I didn't mean to startle you, my dear, but I thought it best to warn you that Sir Aidan likes his dinner promptly at six."

The idea of descending those stairs again to confront Aidan Kane was more than Norah could endure. If there was a God, she would be able to creep away from Rathcannon without ever having to look on his face again.

"I don't think I could eat a bite. I'm very tired. I think I will just . . . just go to bed."

"And so you shall, lamb, if that is what you want. And if either of those two miscreants dares disturb you, they shall answer to Maude Brindle, they shall. Of course, if it's the master's temper you fear, well, you needn't. Got the fury of the Irish in him, true enough—but he blazes up in a right spectacular show and then it burns itself out."

The woman patted her hand. "If you'd like to have a comfortable chat later, Miss Norah, I'm a good listener. Lord knows, I've had enough practice with Miss Cassandra. She can out-chatter even her mama at that age. . . ." Mrs. Brindle stopped, just a tinge of pink on her cheekbones. "But here now! I'm being as tiresome as can be. You say you need some rest, and I chatter the ears right off you, instead of tucking you up nice and cozy. Why don't you let me play maid to you, get you out of these things and—"

"That isn't necessary," Norah interrupted hastily. "I can manage on my own."

Shrewd blue eyes seemed to peel away Norah's protective layers of pride and stubbornness, probing to places that were raw. "From the look of you, you've been managing on your own far too long already."

With that, Mrs. Brindle swept out of the room, shooing the other servants before her like a nettlesome brood hen. Norah heard the click of the latch, and with a sign of relief, she allowed her shoulders to sag.

34

"Oh God," she whispered, "how has everything gone so wrong?"

She let her lashes drift shut as the memories flooded through her, carrying her back to the London shore, a sky churning with storm clouds, a heart raw with dreams.

Sea spray. It stung her nose, bit color into her cheeks, while wild anticipation mingled with wariness in Norah's heart. Her fingers trembled as she clutched at her reticule, her dilapidated trunk beside her.

She was the only passenger waiting alone; the others, from the lowliest sailor to the most exalted grande dame, were lost in throngs of well-wishers, drowning in hugs, words of love and caution.

It wasn't as if Norah had expected anyone to see her off this morn. Her mother had been stricken with a bout of hysterics, her stepfather a study in grim satisfaction, sending her off to a future he hoped would prove to be a fitting punishment for the ungrateful child he'd been saddled with these many years.

Norah tried to tell herself it didn't matter that no one would care if she tumbled from the edge of the earth the way the ancient sailors had believed.

But as she stood with rain spattering her bedraggled cloak, her hands trembling as they straightened the brim of a much-abused bonnet, a wrenching sense of loneliness shivered through her, blending with the tiniest sliver of dread that this mad plunge into Ireland might be just another mistake, another disappointment, when she had already been battered by far too many.

She caught her lip between her teeth, wishing for just a moment that she had someone else to lean on. But showers of embraces, tender farewells were not for Norah Linton. She should have learned that long ago.

"Norah?"

The sound of her name made her jump, and she spun around to see the slender figure of a man limping toward her from a sleek black coach. He was hatless, and his golden hair clung damply about his cheeks. His greatcoat was all but hidden by a mountain of parcels caught in his arms. He was the most welcome sight Norah had ever seen.

"Richard!" Norah called out to her stepbrother, tears of gratitude and alarm nipping at her eyelids. "You shouldn't have come!"

"You think I would send my baby sister off to the wilds of Ireland without saying goodbye?" Richard asked breathlessly, ducking beneath the shelter of the eaves.

"But your father . . . If he ever found out that you had dared—"

"Defy him?" Even in the flickering light of the lantern suspended from an iron hook in the eaves, Norah could see her stepbrother's handsome features darken. "Devil take the coldhearted bastard! Would God I could fling his ultimatums back in his face and call him what he is—a villain, an arrogant tyrant who dared condemn you to this."

"He didn't condemn me to anything. I chose this fate. Willingly. Thanks to your kindness."

"Chose marriage? To some stranger in that godforsaken wastela—" He broke off, his jaw knotting as he dumped his bundle of parcels atop her trunk. "I curse my own weakness, that I could not come up with a better way to aid you. When I think of my father's cruelty, I could—"

"No, Richard. You mustn't anger him any further. You've already risked far too much on my account. No matter what awaits me in Ireland, I will be far happier than I would have been here in England."

"I don't doubt that! What Father did was abominable! Trying to marry you off to a pimple-faced cub, seven years your junior! I swear I could have called the sop-nosed brat out myself, the way he attempted to paw you at Filderland's soiree!"

"But you didn't call him out, Richard. You did something so much more helpful. You helped to find me a way to escape forever. Escape your father and Purcival Wither-spoon."

"By offering you up to some Irishman like a virgin sacrifice? Sometimes I curse myself for even bringing that infernal letter to you. It's possible this man will be as bad as either of them." Richard raked impeccably gloved fingers through his hair. "It's possible he'll be worse."

Norah tried to muster a smile. "And it's possible that he will be everything I've ever dreamed of. Perhaps you are sending me into the arms of my own true love."

Richard looked at her as if he wished very much it were so. "I just don't want you hurt anymore, Norah."

Her heart squeezed at his concern, astonished by the man who had of late been peeking past her brother's spoiled facade. Richard, as shallow as a child's footprint filled with new rain. Whoever would have dreamed that he could shine so brightly? Her deepest regret was that this closeness between them had come so late, when she was leaving.

She reached out impulsively, taking her stepbrother's hand. "It will be all right. I'm not a foolish chit with her head stuffed full of happily ever afters," Norah lied. "The reality of my marriage will probably be like all others—somewhere between perfect bliss and Armageddon. Contentment is all anyone can truly hope for." Norah turned her face away from the light, trying to hide from her stepbrother's eyes her hopes for her future. Her gaze alighted on the parcels mounded on her trunk.

"What on earth are these?" she queried, overjoyed to have something to focus his attention on other than her upcoming marriage.

Richard started, as if he'd forgotten, then he beamed at her. "I thought that a bride should have a trousseau."

Hot tears spilled from Norah's eyes, hot and fast and unexpected. "A—a trousseau?" she echoed, disbelieving.

"I know that Father said he'd not buy you so much as a handkerchief if you went through with this mad plan. And the clothing you have—well . . . ," He squirmed, a little uncomfortable. "I have eyes. I've seen how drab and threadbare your things have grown. I just thought that if you insist on running off to marry your Irishman, you should dazzle him. The first time he sets eyes on you, you should steal his breath away."

"Oh, Richard, as if I ever could! I've never been a beauty, but . . ." How had he known the secret tears she had shed over her trunk, when there was no one to see? How had he discovered how disheartened she had been as she attempted to mend frayed seams and replace faded ribbons?

Guilt made her cheeks burn as she remembered how often she'd thought Richard was spoiled and self-absorbed, unable to see the misery of others because he was too engrossed in indulging his own pleasures. No, she'd not waste time in regret, only accept this new Richard with an open heart.

Delighted with his surprise, Richard scooped the largest package from the bottom of the stack, only Norah's quick movements keeping the other parcels from tumbling to the wooden platform below.

"The first thing we hurl into the rag basket is that—that thing you're wearing." He gave her mantle a scornful tug, discarding it. Then, before she could protest, he ripped open the paper wrapping as enthusiastically as a child at Christmas.

The lantern light spilled across a pelisse of Prussian blue trimmed in swansdown, the combination impossibly beautiful, like mountain snow pillowed in the center of a sun-kissed summer sea.

Norah couldn't speak as her fingers stole out to touch the garment, make certain it was real.

But Richard was already sweeping it about her shoulders. She stood like a moon-struck child as he fastened the exquisite pelisse about her. "There is a bonnet too," he said, retrieving a confection of blush-colored lace and myrtleblossoms from another box. He settled it on Norah's curls, his brow furrowing in concentration as he tied the bow beneath her chin.

"Richard, how can I ever thank you?" Norah ran trembling fingers across the cloud-soft down.

He flashed her his most dazzling smile. "Virtue is supposed to be its own reward, is it not? Just go off and bewitch your Irishman, Norah. Your marriage . . . and happiness will be reward enough for me."

At that moment, Richard's coachman and postilion staggered over, hauling a shining new trunk twice the size of Norah's battered old one.

Norah gasped. "More? Oh, Richard—"

"Mr. Piggle, you may take Miss Linton's old trunk and dispose of its contents as you will."

Norah raised a hand to her throat, dismayed. "No! I, oh, I don't think—I mean, it's not that I'm not grateful—"

"I'll brook no argument on this point, sister mine. I know how your devious feminine mind works far too well. You'd want to *save* the new things—keep them pristine, for God knows what reason, and wind up 'making do' with your old ones. I want you to wear the pretties I bought you. Enjoy them."

"But I—" She started to protest again, but he looked like a small boy she'd deprived of a sweet. She surrendered with a laugh. What else could she do? Especially when he was right? "Abominable boy!" she said. "At least let me take out my treasure box."

She opened the trunk and removed a hatbox in which she'd tucked her few treasures: one stray earring of a set that had belonged to her great-grandmother and the doll her father had given her the Christmas before he'd died—a doll garbed in refurbished finery to delight a new little girl, the child who would be Norah's daughter.

There had been few physical demonstrations of affection in Winston Farnsworth's house, but Norah flung her arms around her stepbrother nonetheless. Her voice caught on a sob. "I shall miss you so much. I cannot believe I'm losing you now, when we've finally grown close."

"It's dashed unfair, I know. But it's not as if we'll never see each other again," he said, awkwardly patting her on the back. "Why, I'm certain you'll come to London from time to time. And I shall see to my brotherly duty and make certain that all is well with you. In fact, I have already arranged for a friend of mine to stop by your castle to make certain this Irishman realizes what a treasure I've entrusted to him."

Norah felt blood rush to her cheeks, and she pulled away from him, beseeching her brother. "No! It's not necessary." But her dismay only increased as Richard laid his gloved fingertips against her mouth.

"I will be the judge of what is necessary to fulfill my duty where my own sister is concerned. The Honorable Philip Montgomery has already offered to see how you fare."

"Philip Montgomery?" Norah's dismay increased a thousandfold. Anyone but him! She had cherished a schoolgirl's crush on Montgomery since she was scarce fourteen—and she couldn't count the number of times in the ensuing years the elegant aristocrat had caught her staring at him like a love-sick ninny. "Oh, Richard, please tell me you did not confide the circumstances surrounding my betrothal to Philip Montgomery!"

Richard looked genuinely hurt. "I'm not quite the insensitive dolt people think me! I made your engagement sound quite romantic, as if this Irishman had swept you off your feet. Of course, Montgomery was positively surly when I told him the story. But then, he is suspicious of anyone possessed of a drop of Irish blood. They've had an estate near Sligo for two hundred years, and I vow it's been nothing but agony for them. Ungrateful devils, those Irish. Never appreciative of the lengths we English go to to save them from themselves."

Norah pressed a hand to her cheek, her skin hot despite

the chill of the wind. There had been a time she might have taken some pleasure in Montgomery's apparent unhappiness over her betrothal, daring to attribute it to some secret flight of passion. But she had long before abandoned any foolish girlish dreams about the handsome aristocrat. Great beauty might overawe a suitor into excusing a meager dowry, or a generous dowry might prove an irresistible ornament to plainness. Norah had never deluded herself that she had either to attract such a matrimonial prize.

"Richard, it will take some time for me to become—become accustomed to my new surroundings. My bridegroom, his daughter. I would rather not have to do so before an audience."

"I hardly think Montgomery is planning to move into a room beneath the castle stairs." Richard clasped her hands with an affectionate chuckle. "You cannot spend your entire marriage hiding from former acquaintances. What better way to have news of your happiness carried to the witchy chits who snubbed you?"

"A lovely plan, assuming there is happiness for Mr. Montgomery to carry tales *about.*" It was the closest she could come to confessing her fears.

"There will be, sweeting. I'm certain of it." Richard turned as the doorway opened, passengers beginning to file out, bending their bonnets and the brims of their hats to shield their faces from the dampness.

Norah watched the parade of travelers make their way toward the ship, and a sudden fear of the unknown shivered in her breast. She reached out, grasping Richard's hand and holding on tight, her gaze sweeping the storm-darkened sky. "The weather—it seems so—so wild."

"Yes, but they say that a voyage begun in storm will end in bliss."

"I'll be certain to repeat those words of wisdom to the other shipwreck victims when we sink to the bottom of the sea." Norah gave a strained laugh, but despite her resolve to

41

plunge into her future bravely, she couldn't help waving one hand toward the sullen sky. "Do you think this is an omen, Richard?"

"No, I think this is a storm. We've had them before, you know."

"Those were someone else's omens. This one is mine." Norah worried her lower lip with her teeth. "I don't know, Richard. I just wish that I—I had some idea what he is like. This Sir Aidan Kane."

Richard heaved a long-suffering sigh. "I only know what I found out before I gave you Kane's letter—and, I might add, I've recounted my discoveries to you a dozen times. Aidan Kane is a war hero who saved his entire regiment in some deliciously noble fashion during the Peninsular War. His wife died in a tragic accident. Since then, by all accounts, he's been a reclusive widower, living at his Irish estate of Rathcannon with his daughter—quite broken-hearted, I daresay. He needs you, Norah."

He needs you. . . . Norah had clung to those words, knowing all the while that it was probably the most dangerous of all feminine delusions—the irresistible desire to heal a man whose spirit had been wounded.

Richard's soft laugh jarred her from her thoughts. "Of course, unless you hustle aboard that ship, you may never be wed at all."

Norah cast a helpless glance toward the ship, the last of the passengers trailing up the plank that led to it. Richard called out to two sailors nearby.

"You there, take Miss Linton's trunk to her quarters."

There was something terrifyingly final in watching the two burly men heave Richard's gift up from the platform and carry it away. Raw panic swept through every fiber of Norah's being.

"I can't—I don't think I can . . . Oh, Richard, you *do* think I'm doing the right thing?"

"I am certain of it."

Norah flung herself into her stepbrother's arms, embracing him fiercely one last time. "I'll never forget your kindness, Richard. Never. I pray God will reward you for it."

He smiled. A glittering smile, vaguely disturbing, like a solitary ripple disturbing a glass-smooth stretch of lake.

"I hope I won't have to wait long enough to receive a heavenly reward, my dear. You see, I've just struck three wagers that should make me a very wealthy man, little sister. And the first . . . the first is well on its way to being won."

A log blazing on the marble hearth fell apart, crackling, snapping, yanking Norah back from memories of the storm-swept wharf to the quiet bedchamber that mocked the dreams she had held for such a brief time.

It was as if an eternity had passed since she'd mounted the gangplank, and watched Richard wave goodbye to her as she left behind everything she'd ever known, sailing into an uncertain future.

A future that now seemed almost as bleak and far more dubious than the one she'd left behind.

Norah was exhausted. Disappointment more bitter than any she'd ever known made her eyes burn and her spirit ache for the foolish young woman who had stood outside in the English rain such a brief time before, her head stuffed with dreams, her heart daring to hope for the first time since she could remember. Hope—not for happily ever afters and miracles. Not for the grand passions that were legend spun. But, rather, for contentment, peace.

Someone to need her.

But there was no one here who could fill that place for her. There was no sweet miracle awaiting her within Rathcannon's stone walls. Only a deeper echo of the loneliness that had tormented her from the time her father had died. Only an underscoring of a hundred shortcomings that had made her stepfather despise her. Only another empty, aching place with nothing to fill it but Norah's own most secret tears.

CHAPTER

3

Richard Farnsworth stared down at his father's wife, her
face pale, her eyes dark with the shadows that rarely left
them. He could even pity her at times. God knew he'd been
every bit as beaten down and awkward years before, bludg-
eoned into submission by Winston Farnsworth's relentless
will. Yet staring into Corabeth Linton Farnsworth's face
always made him damned uncomfortable too. Maybe because it forced him to remember. . . .

"I don't mean to disturb you, Richard, dear," she
breathed in a tremulous voice, one thin hand clinging to his
coat sleeve. "I know that you are very busy entertaining
Viscount Cirlot and Lord Millhaven." She cast an apologetic glance toward the drawing room in which his friends
awaited him. "But I had hoped that perhaps you might have
received a letter—"

"Are you worried about Norah?" he inquired, his face a
mask of concern.

The woman's sallow cheeks flushed, as if he'd caught her
with a lover. "Your father would be most displeased with me

for asking. He insists Norah should be dead to me. Yet a mother cannot help but worry. Ireland is such a wild place. And to go there, intending to wed a man she's never seen before—" A shudder racked Corabeth's slight frame. "It is so dangerous, Richard, to surrender complete power over her life to a total stranger. What if this man is cruel to her? A monster?"

Richard was more than aware why his stepmother viewed the state of marriage with such dread. It was a kingdom Winston Farnsworth had always ruled with the same petty tyranny he'd ruled his son and heir, ruled everyone that touched his life. Only Norah had never buckled under to his tyranny. Proud, honorable Norah, with her unbreachable Linton dignity.

"Norah is fine," Richard insisted. "I'm certain of it. You must not allow yourself to get so overwrought. You know how impatient Father gets when you do." He pressed her hand so hard she winced a bit. "Didn't I tell you I had looked into this Irish knight's background to make certain he was suitable? Didn't I promise to take care of her? Surely you don't think I would have sent her off to be chained to some monster?"

Corabeth pleated a fold of her skirt, her eyes downcast. "Of course not! I cannot thank you enough for your kindness to my poor girl. I'm a fool to worry, and you must think me the most abominable nuisance."

"You know exactly how much I adore you and my little sister." He patted the woman's shoulder with studied gentleness. "In fact I have already arranged for a friend of mine to visit Norah, to make certain all is well. But if it would ease your mind, I would go to this Irish castle myself, to see that this Aidan Kane is treating my sister as she deserves."

"You would do such a thing? For my Norah?" Tears welled up behind thin lashes.

"Of course I shall, the instant I can afford to." Richard looked away, pensiveness stealing across his face. He gave Corabeth a boyish smile, full of embarrassment and regret.

"I'm afraid I have had a rather bad run at the faro table of late. You won't tell Father?" He gave his cravat an anxious tug.

His stepmother regarded him with abject worship. "Poor boy, was it so very bad? Perhaps I can help you. I have a most generous sum set by for a lovely necklace I saw in the shop window, but it would please me so much more to help you."

"How could I allow you to make such a sacrifice? No. It was my own recklessness that brought me to this point, and I should have to pay the price for my mistakes. Even if I should be scooped into a sponging house, I could not take your coin."

"You shall indeed!" Corabeth insisted with more forcefulness than Richard had ever seen her expend on her daughter's behalf. "I insist. And if you do not allow me to do this for you, I shall . . . shall . . ." She was searching for a suitable threat, Richard knew. "I shall tell your father about your financial difficulties so he can aid you."

"No! No, you cannot!" Richard stalked away.

"I can and I shall," she insisted with a resolute nod. "Now you must go off to entertain those dear boys in the drawing room, or they will think you quite rude. After all, with Lord Millhaven just back from the Continent, I'm certain you have much to talk about."

Richard chuckled and pinched Corabeth on the cheek, watching her face brighten until he could see the faintest impression of the beauty she had once been. "You are so very good to me," he said. "I cannot imagine that my own mother could have been sweeter, may God rest her soul." His mother . . . haunted eyes, nervous hands, and dread pressing down on her until it suffocated her. As a boy, he'd been certain she'd died of it. He shoved the thought away as tears sprang once again to Corabeth's eyes.

"We shall take care of each other, dearest boy," she said, patting his hand. "I love you, you know."

Love him? Richard thought with a swift flash of bitterness. She didn't even know him.

He turned and entered the drawing room, drinking in the subtle scent of tobacco and leather that clung to the cream-colored plasterwork walls of his private domain. The two men lounging about the green baize gaming table glanced up at him with drink-bleary eyes, sated by Winston Farnsworth's finest brandy and by the attentions, this past afternoon, of London's most elegant courtesans.

"Cirlot wagered a hundred pounds you fell into the privy," Millhaven observed with a smirk.

Richard chuckled. "You'd best collect on your wagers now. By Christmas Cirlot won't have two coins to rub together. After I win my wager with him, he'll be forced to wed some dough-faced heiress just to keep himself out of debtor's prison."

"A new wager?" Millhaven perked up, rattling his dice box with interest. "One penned down in White's betting book, or one exclusively for our own entertainment?"

"Gawd, but Farnsworth wouldn't want this bit dragged out all over London!" Cirlot scoffed. "It's a masterpiece. And damn me if I can imagine either of us will ever be able to top it."

Millhaven licked his lips, his eyes glowing with greed. "Show me, Farnsworth," he demanded. "By damn, I cannot wait to see it."

Limping to the bookshelf in the corner, Richard reached for the small leatherbound volume on the topmost shelf and opened the pages.

"I cannot think you've been in town long enough to hear my family's momentous news, Millhaven," Richard said. "My stepsister should be making her way up to the altar even as we speak."

"The devil you say!" Millhaven snorted with a ribald laugh. "What poor sot is getting leg-shackled to her? Surely Montgomery didn't come up to scratch! His family would never stand for it."

"Montgomery? Marry a woman without a dowry or a title? Not for a king's ransom, though I have sometimes detected a certain wistfulness about him when he sees Norah across a room. I'm afraid the most Norah could hope for from that quarter is a brief liaison—and only then if someone else had the cunning to arrange it for her. No, my esteemed Millhaven, I have provided my dowdy little stepsister with a far more intriguing bridegroom. Sir Aidan Kane."

Never in their long, notorious association had Richard seen Millhaven so stunned. "You *are* a heartless bastard," the nobleman breathed. "Sacrificing your own sister to a man whose lust for women is outstripped only by his lust for the gaming tables? By God, they even claim he murdered—"

"You, above anyone, should know better than to heed idle gossip," Richard said, returning to the table. "I have provided Norah with a husband; as her brother I could do nothing less." He trailed one fingertip along a gold-embossed leaf bedecking the book's binding.

Cirlot splashed more brandy into his crystal goblet. "Just show Millhaven the book and be done with your infernal gloating."

Richard extended the volume to Millhaven. The drunken nobleman snatched it from him and scanned the lines penned on the page. Millhaven's face went still with awe.

"A thousand pounds, Farnsworth!" Millhaven exclaimed with stunned fascination. "I'll pay you a thousand pounds if you carry these wagers to the bitter end."

"Oh, I shall see them to the end, I assure you," Richard said evenly. "And when I do, I will achieve what I have desired for so long: Sir Aidan Kane's destruction."

There was nothing like a wedding to give a man indigestion. Even attending a ceremony in which another man put his neck in the matrimonial noose had always been enough to make Aidan lose his appetite for a week. And the threat of a prospective bride under his own roof was positively nausea-inspiring.

He sat at the head of the long table in Rathcannon's dining chamber, the candles guttering in the sconces, the remains of his solitary dinner long since swept away. Time could more easily be measured by the number of times the glass of Madeira in Aidan's hand had needed to be refilled than by the ticking of the clock on the mantle.

The celebratory birthday meal had—predictably—been a disaster. Wan and tragic as any beleaguered heroine upon a London stage, Cassandra had dragged herself to the table long enough to see if Miss Linton had come to dinner. When informed that the lady had begged to be excused, Cass had drooped back out of the room. Aidan hadn't had the energy to stop her.

Cassandra had spent the entire rest of the evening fortressed up in her tower chamber, waiting, no doubt, for the sound of her father's step on the stone stairs so that she could enact a truly spectacular bout of theatrics.

But Aidan wouldn't have dared that chamber tonight if every cutthroat in Ireland had been charging at his heels. No, Aidan thought, slinging back another fiery gulp of the liquor. There was no way in hell he was giving his daughter a chance to incite him to madness. A madness that could all too easily end at an altar with him trussed up as a human sacrifice.

Aidan grimaced. If he'd stayed in Dublin, right now he'd be sampling the charms of the beautiful if temperamental Stasia. He would be playing at hazard or faro or piquet with a convivial tableful of men whose most dastardly intention toward him might be a simple sword thrust over a bad throw of the dice, or a swift, merciful pistol shot through some insignificant part of his anatomy.

He could be barreling down the road in a curricle race, grazing the wheels of passersby and listening to their curses with great relish. But no. Here he sat, his daughter in high dudgeon and some woman he'd never seen before setting up housekeeping for the night in the room adjoining his bedchamber.

Well, she wouldn't be inhabiting the chamber for long, by Triton's beard. He'd sent a rider off to make arrangements to hurtle Miss Dora—or was it Laura?—Lytton off to London post haste. By this time tomorrow night, the Englishwoman would be on her way, and he could set himself to important matters, like finding something to distract his daughter from her disappointment. Perhaps a new gown or a trinket, or that lovely little mare Adam Dunne was breaking over at Ballylaire. If Aidan could just convince him to part with it . . .

Damn, he was doing it again! Rewarding the rebellious chit for her mischief! How many times had Mrs. Brindle warned him that such a practice would only make the girl incorrigible. He'd brushed off the admonition as he had so many others. But now, confronted with the coil Cassandra's headstrong ways had embroiled him in, Aidan couldn't help but wonder if the Old Battle Axe was right.

Aidan's jaw clenched. Maybe it was time to take the girl in hand. Teach Cassandra some discipline. Oh, yes, and Aidan Kane would be such a perfect one to preach propriety to his daughter! The very notion made his head ache. Far better for him to light out for Dublin, maybe even London, and leave the taming of Cassandra to Mrs. Brindle. She needed a woman's touch, and the only women Aidan consorted with were of an ilk totally unsuitable to be held up as models for a proper young miss.

I don't want a wife, Cassandra. Aidan's words echoed in his mind, and he could see his daughter's face, determined and yet vulnerable, suddenly so infernally young.

I do want a mother! Cassandra had cried. *Someone to teach me so many things. . . .*

"Papa?"

For a heartbeat, Aidan thought that the soft query was just one more whisper of his own imagination. He angled a glance over his shoulder, to see Cassandra framed in the doorway. A cozy wrapper with tiny bluebirds wreathed about the collar flowed to the tops of her insteps. Her pale-gilt hair was tangled, and her eyes had that heavy look Aidan knew was the result of a bout of tears. Her fingers plucked at a ribbon tied about whatever she clutched in her hand.

She hovered in the doorway for long seconds, looking uncertain, more than a little lost, as if wondering what kind of reception he would give her.

A wiser man might have remembered his sense of caution and steeled himself against her. Instead, Aidan opened up his arms.

Cassandra ran and flung herself into them, and Aidan cuddled her close, as he had when she had been barely an armful of ruffles and hair ribbons.

"Papa, I'm sorry you didn't like the surprise. I truly thought that once you thought about it, you'd come to like her."

Aidan stroked the girl's hair. "I'm certain you had the best of intentions, sweeting. But you can't just go about arranging other people's lives to suit you."

Cassandra sniffed, and Aidan rummaged in his pocket for a handkerchief. Grasping her chin gently between two fingers, he turned her face up to his, dabbing at her cheeks as he had when she was small. A forlorn sob shuddered through her.

"I know, Papa. I know it sounds childish, but I wanted her for me. I kept thinking and thinking, and I couldn't get it out of my mind."

"Get what out of your mind, sweeting?"

"That the worst thing in the whole world was to be all alone."

"I'm not going to leave you alone." His own voice was unsteady, and he reached out a hand to cup her cheek.

"But what would happen to me if—if you died?" The tremulous question struck Aidan with the force of a Celtic broadsword.

"How did you get such a crazed notion in your head? There's nothing to concern yourself—"

"You could get sick, Papa. There could be an accident. I'd have no one."

"Despite my advanced age, I'm scarcely at death's door. I'm not planning to die for a very long time." He touched the tip of her nose with his finger. "The angels wouldn't have me, and the devil would be afraid I'd take over his domain."

"It's not funny, Papa. My mother didn't plan to die either. It just . . . happened."

Happened? No, Aidan thought with a flood of bitterness, it hadn't just *happened*. Delia Kane had put herself into danger on purpose, not giving a damn what the consequences would be as long as she could get revenge on the husband she hated. When the carriage had overturned, she'd had no one to blame but herself. She'd been reckless and foolhardy, courting disaster the way she had wooed countless lovers.

Aidan froze at the thought of revelations he didn't want to face. Truths about himself that were sobering.

Wasn't that what he did every time he rode away from Rathcannon? Dash himself into a hundred different situations where the mere flick of a sword blade, the blast of a pistol barrel, the wild charge of horse or curricle could send him catapulting into hell?

He'd made certain Cassandra would be cared for in the event of his death. His solicitors had enough money in trust to allow her to live in the luxury she was accustomed to. But as to who would protect her, shelter her . . . *love* her . . . he hadn't dealt with that. It was too painful. But it was obvious from the expression on Cassandra's face that she had thought about it enough for the both of them.

"Oh, Princess . . ." Aidan stroked her cheek, aching for her.

She was peering up at him through tear-spiked lashes, contrite, chastened, in a way that made Aidan suspect he'd do anything to see her smile.

"Papa, I'm sorry that I didn't warn you before Miss Linton arrived." A tiny crease appeared between soft blond brows. "I know it was . . . was probably a silly idea. But if you didn't want to marry anyone else, I guess I hoped you wouldn't mind very much if I asked you to marry her. Her letters were so wonderful. So . . ." She pulled the beribboned bundle from where it had been half hidden by the folds of her wrapper. "I brought them to you. I thought—thought you might want to read—" Her voice caught. "Never mind. I love you, Papa. I'm sorry I ruined your birthday."

With that she slipped from his arms and started toward the door, leaving the bundle of letters in his lap.

"Cass," Aidan called after her. She paused and looked over her shoulder, her lips trembling.

"You know, you could pull the whole castle down on my head, and I would still think you were the most wonderful creature ever born. I would do anything in my power to make you happy, Princess."

"Would you, Papa?" It was the softest of questions, the most moving of pleas.

Aidan turned toward the stone-carved fireplace and stared into the flames. He was dead certain he would walk through fire for his beloved daughter.

The question was, did he have the courage—no, the stark insanity—to risk a far more dangerous hell? To repeat to another woman the wedding vows he had exchanged with Delia so many years before? Vows that had sent them both upon their separate paths down to perdition?

Blast it, that was too much to ask of him. Too much even for Cassandra.

Papa, I don't want to be alone. . . .

His daughter's words wisped back to him, curling deep into his soul where his own most painful secrets lay, shattering him more deeply than any other words could have.

They pulsed there inside him as the night wore on,

tugging at him the way Cass's tiny fingers had when she was small, insistent, compelling, the only thing that could move Sir Aidan Kane's jaded heart.

Twice he nearly threw the bundle of letters into the fire. When he finally pulled the ribbon free, and the first pages fell into his hands, he cursed himself for a fool.

I understand the pain of searching for a kindred spirit, needing someone to banish the loneliness. I have often felt the same. Ghosts of the past can be a horrible burden, yet so can a future without children, a home, a husband. Perhaps, as you said, we can find a way to heal each other.

As *he* had said? Aidan's cheeks flamed, a sick churning in his stomach. Pain? Loneliness? Goddamn kindred spirits?

Sweet Jesus, what had Cassandra written to this woman, that Norah Linton would send such a reply? What ridiculous caricature had Cass painted of him? Some hero spun of her fairy stories? Some Galahad or noble knight-errant? Even more alarming, what had she told this Englishwoman about the past, and the ghosts that still stalked Rathcannon?

Aidan ran his fingers through his hair, fighting back a stab of panic. He was getting himself in a blather over nothing. The girl could not know of Aidan's secret hauntings. Cassandra had no way of discovering the truth of what had happened the night her mother died. He had made certain of that, because he'd suspected from the first that such knowledge would destroy her.

No. It was far more likely Cassandra had been overdramatizing matters in the letter, playing things out like some melodrama upon a stage, the way she had every trial she'd faced from the first blot on her copybook to a tumble from her horse.

And heaven knew, the girl had inherited her ancestors' gift of persuasion. The gift that had made enemies raise their portcullises in battle could hardly have faltered at such a simple task as luring some lonely woman to journey to Ireland.

Especially when the method of convincing the woman to

take such an insane risk was by making her intended bridegroom sound like a wounded hero, tormented, despairing. What the devil was it with women that they should be obsessed from the cradle with healing such a man?

Aidan grimaced. He had long since quit trying to understand that suicidal feminine impulse and had merely enjoyed the benefits of such tender passions in the beds of the women who hoped to tame his demons. Demons he had joyfully embraced so many years before.

Never once had he gilded his own wicked nature, his dissolute ways. Never once had he been anything but honest about his lack of honor, of the noble impulses women seemed to set such ridiculous store by.

But it was obvious that Cassandra had had no such scruples when writing to the woman she'd chosen as his bride. If the Englishwoman's reply was a reflection of the kind of romantic rot Cassandra had penned in his name, it was no wonder the idiotic female had shown up on his doorstep all starry-eyed and hopeful.

Lord, what a shock he must have been to the damnable woman! No fairy-tale prince. No hero. No knight to kneel before her and offer up his heart.

Aidan flinched at the sense of feeling exposed, vulnerable in a way that infuriated him. He thrust the letters in his pocket, unable to read another word. Damn both of them!

His mouth compressed in a hard line, but in the end there was only one thing he could do. With an oath, he stalked to the table and drained his Madeira in one gulp. Hoping that the liquor would dash away what little common sense still reigned in his head, Aidan grabbed up a branch of candles and stormed out of the chamber. He stalked up the castle stairs toward the room where the woman lay sleeping.

CHAPTER

4

The fire was dying. The candles left about the chamber had long since flickered out, but still Norah couldn't bring herself to return to the tumbled coverlets of the four-poster bed. It seemed as if every time she stirred, she could feel the ghostly imprint of another woman's body in the feather ticking, imagine another woman's scent still filtering through the air.

A woman beautiful enough to have given Cassandra Kane the face of an angel, the hair of a fairy queen. A woman Norah could only pity because that woman had been wife to Aidan Kane.

What had she looked like? Cassandra's mother? How had Delia Kane's life ended? Had the tragic accident changed her loving husband into this rogue of a man? The letters Norah had received wreathed the woman's death in mystery. Cassandra Kane's knowledge of her mother's death was obviously vague, hidden by the mists of time and the lies adults told children in an attempt to soothe them. Had Aidan Kane broken his wife's heart?

He had the face of a man fashioned to lure women to their own destruction, sweeping them into his sensual spell.

Had he loved this mysterious woman? Loved her so deeply that her death had left him shattered? So shattered that his daughter had wanted to ease his pain with some misguided notion of providing another woman to love him?

Love: It was a word that seemed foreign when linked to Aidan Kane. It was all too easy to picture the man, his blood hot with a passion unbridled and dark, addictive and deadly sweet as opium. Yet to imagine Kane in love—supplicant, adoring, worshiping a woman with his eyes, with his fingers —was as futile a fantasy as smoothing a storm-tossed sea with the touch of a hand.

Norah struggled to imagine those hard, sensual features gentling into adoration, those hands—long fingered and strong—initiating a lover into rites of pleasure Norah couldn't even begin to understand, while his mouth seduced a woman to taste the recklessness in him, the passion. The promise.

Promise . . . of what? Norah wondered. Heartbreak? Pain?

Why should it even matter to her?

She'd be gone long before she could begin to unravel the enigma that was Aidan Kane. But even if she did stay in this castle forever, she was not the sort of woman who could manage to unlock whatever secrets Kane guarded beneath the relentless green fire in his eyes.

No, she could only pace the chamber of his first wife in an agony of sleeplessness, listening to the whisperings of Castle Rathcannon, wondering about the woman who had occupied this chamber years before and the man who had given her his child.

She might even have been tempted to satisfy her curiosity about the first Lady Kane by asking one of the numerous maids as they fluttered in and out of the chamber from time to time, except that the servants continued to regard her as if she were some strange creature brought back from a gypsy fair.

In any case, even if she'd been rash enough to question someone about Aidan Kane's first wife, it was too late to do so tonight.

The chatter of servants had long since died down to silence, and not a sound had come from the other side of the door she was certain led to Sir Aidan's bedchamber.

Norah pressed one hand to the window, wishing with all her heart that she could surrender forever to her own loneliness and hopelessness—a bleak existence that had seemed to be her destiny from the day her father died.

Her ineffectual efforts to change her fate had all been in vain. She had defied her stepfather, braved the sea to reach a man who didn't want her.

And so here she stood in the darkness, garbed in a lovely bridal nightgown, the blush of her skin shining through the fabric, whispering of wedding-night secrets that she would never come to know.

Her fingertips toyed with one primrose-hued ribbon, and she flushed with the knowledge that Richard was the one who'd ordered the gown for her. It touched her heart that her feckless brother would think to make her a wedding gift of the kind of gown any bride would dream of—one that would turn a bridegroom's eyes to hot pools of need, make his hands tremble as he reached out to trace the delicate latticework of blossoms that trailed across her breasts.

She would have given anything to be able to put on one of her old worn nightgowns—prim and plain as she was—a gown that didn't seem to have impossible fantasies woven into every thread.

But those garments were heaven only knew where, disposed of by Richard. Richard who had sent her off from England with such high hopes, such fierce determination that she should be happy.

Happy.

Poor Richard would be appalled if he knew what had befallen her.

Tears stung her eyelids as she pictured her stepbrother's face when he'd brought her the letter that had sent her on this crazed journey. He'd been ecstatic. Eager. So certain it was the right thing to do. And she had dared to believe it too, because she'd had nothing else left to believe in.

She dashed away the moisture on her lashes, then stiffened as she heard the sound of footsteps in the corridor—resolute masculine steps that reminded her of a soldier marching off to war.

A servant? No. She was certain it must be Kane himself. She could feel his presence even through walls of stone and the door's heavy-carved panel. She could feel the restless energy in him, like a pulse in the castle's floor.

Her heart hammered against her ribs, and she held her breath, waiting for him to pass—impatient, no doubt, to put an end to this hideous day.

Nothing prepared her for the crash of a fist on the oak door to her own chamber. She started to call out, to protest, but the panel was already being wrenched open, and light poured into the bedchamber from the branch of candles clutched in one of Sir Aidan Kane's hands.

Norah's first instinct was to dash for the coverlets, to find something—anything—with which to cover her, but her legs wouldn't obey her commands. Her mind was too overwhelmed by the image of the man framed in the doorway.

He was every woman's nightmare—or secret dark dream.

Broad shoulders strained against a white shirt, which was open at the throat to reveal a vee of sun-bronzed chest. Breeches of midnight blue clung like a second skin to powerful legs and lean hips. Ebony waves of hair, tousled as if by the fingers of a lover, tumbled above eyes fired with such savage resolution, Norah had to grasp the back of a gilt chair to keep her knees from buckling.

His mouth was set in the grim, determined line of a man who had decided what he wanted and would not be denied.

The Blue Room was my former wife's chamber, Kane had taunted her. *The perfect place for you in case I am tempted to sample . . .*

Norah's throat went dry and she groped for something she might defend herself with, but he was already striding into the room, shoving the door closed behind him. Her fingers curled about the base of a silver unicorn. "Wh—what are you doing here? I told you I'd blacken your other eye if you dared—"

"Dared what? Ravish you?" Kane raked his fingers distractedly through his dark hair. "If it was only that goddamned simple. But no, I can't charge in here on a mission of pleasure. I have to make an absolute ass of myself, laying out ridiculous maxims, to untangle this impossible mess."

Norah stiffened her spine. "On the contrary, you're not required to come charging in here at all. As you can see, I'm hardly prepared to entertain visitors. You have no right—"

He slammed the candlestick down on a table, then turned to glare at her. "A man driven to the brink of insanity isn't particularly concerned with the rights of the woman who is responsible, Miss . . . whatever the devil your name is."

"Linton."

"Yes, that's it, God curse it. Well, you can leave off your maidenly protests, Miss Linton. I might have been tempted to plunder a lady's charms before, but I have no desire to do so to yours. Now, or ever. No offense, you understand. It's just that my taste in women runs to something a trifle more . . . ah . . ." His emerald gaze skated from the loose cascade of her dusky curls past the delicate embroidery upon her breasts to where her bare feet peeked out beneath the garment's hem. ". . . more ripe and rosy," he finished.

She should have been grateful for his dismissal, comforted that he posed no threat. Instead, Norah's skin burned beneath the thin shielding of fabric, Kane's words sizzling in a painful path to the very core of her. Her chin held high, she left the meager protection of the gilt chair and crossed with arctic dignity to where she had laid her silver satin wrapper upon the foot of the bed. With her back to Kane, she drew the garment on.

"Since you've no desire to plunder my charms, Sir Aidan, you can leave this chamber before you ruin my name."

"No, damn it to hell, I can't. There's no help for it. Might as well settle this now, get it over with as expediently as possible."

She turned to face him, outrage and hurt laced with confusion. "Get *what* over with?"

"Deciding what to do about this mess Cassandra has trussed us both up in."

"There is nothing to decide. I'm leaving tomorrow."

"That's how I saw it too, until my daughter came downstairs, to beg me . . ." Aidan scowled. Shoving his thumbs into the waistband of his breeches, he began ranging about the chamber like some wild, captive beast. "Miss Linton, there is no easy way to say this, so I'm going to just fling the dice onto the table and see what the devil you say about the roll. In case you failed to notice, my daughter is a damnably stubborn, willful, determined little female. She is also the only family I have. For some strange reason, she's got it into her head that she needs a mother."

Norah closed her eyes for a moment, remembering her own painful longings at Cassandra's age, the need to be so grown up, yet still be able to bury her face in a loving mama's skirts and sob out her heartaches, her fears, her confusion. True, Norah's own mother had only been separated from her by the length of a corridor, but the distance hadn't mattered. Corabeth Linton Farnsworth had still been as unattainable as if she'd been a sky's breadth away in heaven.

"Cassandra's longing is not so strange. She must miss her mother very much. Were she and your wife close?"

"Close?" Kane blasted away Norah's own poignant musings with a bitter snort. "Cassandra's mother was a cold-

61

hearted bitch who did her best to forget she'd ever borne a child."

Norah gasped, stunned by his loathing-filled words. "You sound as if you hated her. Surely you must have—have cared for your wife!"

"Cared about Delia? Oh, I was quite besotted over her in the beginning—the way her breasts filled out the bodice of her gown, her lips all tempting red, and, of course, the fact that half the men in London would have joyfully slit my throat to get her in their bed. Then there was also the entertainment factor: Her dragon of a mama regarded me as if I were the blackest-hearted serpent ever to be spawned of Eden, an Irish demon trying to seduce her precious daughter into sin. The woman hadn't a clue that Delia was one of those women destined to incite men to madness, a woman with insatiable appetites for *amours.*"

He had painted an all too vivid image—the devastatingly handsome rogue, the exquisite beauty and the carnal magic that blazed between them. Norah remembered a time when she had dreamed of being transported by the same fierce passion. She'd almost believed it would be worth the anguish that came after if she could just taste of that intoxicating wonder.

But men—especially men like Aidan Kane—couldn't be moved to madness by someone whose only claim to beauty was her generous fall of curls and eyes that looked far too large and dark and haunted in her pale face.

Norah's fingers clenched the silvery satin tight at her breast, her chin lowered in an attempt to hide the fiery blush he'd raised to her cheeks. "I had no right to ask. I only . . ." Have only spent the past hours racked with curiosity about her, wondering . . .

Kane waved one hand in dismissal. "I volunteered the information. That may be my only virtue: I never make the least attempt to gild the ugly truth about myself. You needn't ever fear I'll attempt to dupe you into thinking me some noble hero."

"Whatever you are, it's not my concern."

"It damn well is if you're going to marry me."

"M—Marry you?" Norah took an instinctive step backward, gaping at him as if he'd run quite mad.

"That's what you came here to do, isn't it? Enter into holy matrimony? Exchange all those empty promises? Become my bride? When you and Cassandra stirred up this insane scheme—"

"It wasn't a scheme," Norah insisted. "I thought you wanted a wife. That you were anxious to marry."

Kane raised one sardonic brow, his lip curling. "Marriage is like the plague, Miss Linton. You can hardly blame a man for being reluctant to contract it again once he's survived the malaise from hell. But I've been racking my brain over this mess, and I've decided that there might be a way to end this satisfactorily for all concerned."

"Sir Aidan, I—"

"Just quit your blasted arguing and hear me out. This isn't easy, you know. Proposing marriage to a total stranger. God, I should've had at least three more glasses of Madeira before I came up here, but it's too late now."

"You're drunk?"

"Not drunk enough, by all appearances. But it's a situation I intend to remedy the instant I get this over with." He crossed his arms over his chest and glared at her. "I have a proposition to lay out for you."

"Wh—What kind of proposition?"

"Cass thinks she wants you to stay—not that girls of this age have the least idea what they want from one minute to the next. But I suppose it's possible that the girl really will form an attachment to you. If she does, I'll cast the devil to the winds and marry you, even if it kills me."

Norah gaped at him. "What woman could resist such a pretty proposal?" She groped for the words every girl of marriageable age was schooled in before their entry into society. "I—I am aware of the honor you—you bestow, but I cannot—" Norah stopped abruptly. The man hadn't honored her. He'd insulted her, raged at her, embarrassed her beyond bearing.

Kane hurled out a disgusted oath. "Don't tell me they're still stuffing girls' heads with that ridiculous rubbish! There's nothing pretty about this, nothing romantic, and the sooner you dash away any fool notions you may have in that regard, the better for both of us. I'm offering you a business proposition, plain and simple. One for which you'll receive a generous compensation."

"Business?"

"Yes. But before we enter into it, I want to make certain the terms of any such agreement are clear."

"I . . . see."

"Any union between us will be in name only. I have no desire to exercise my conjugal rights, nor do I want any more children. I want to go on with my life exactly as it is now—no recriminations, no complications."

"And exactly how is your life now?"

"When I am with Cassandra, I am her father. I protect her, love her, spoil the blazes out of her. When I leave Rathcannon, I am a wholly different man."

"Different?"

"Would you like me to spell it out for you, Miss Linton?" His eyes blazed with defiance, and a fiercer emotion Norah couldn't begin to name. "Last night at this time, I was at a gaming hell, fleecing a seventeen-year-old boy out of his inheritance." He held his fist to the candlelight, an emerald flashing on one finger. "This ring had been in that boy's family since the reign of Henry VIII, and when he wagered it in an effort to regain his fortunes, I took that from him as well."

Norah recoiled, sickened. "I don't—don't need to know—"

"The bruise beneath my eye is from an opera dancer who threw a vase at me in a temper because I would not tarry long enough to warm her bed. I would have been delighted to accommodate her, except for the fact that I had promised

Cassandra I would arrive at Rathcannon before the morning of my birthday."

"The way you choose to spend your evenings is none of my affair."

"I beg to differ. If you intend to be my wife—"

"I don't!" Norah flung out. "How can you even think I would—"

"*Defile* yourself by linking your future to a man like me?" he finished for her. "I can't imagine why any woman would. But you must have had some reason to come all the way to Ireland in search of a husband. You must have been desperate. Or foolish. Or both."

Norah felt as if he had struck her. "I wanted a place for myself. A home."

"And so you shall have one. As my wife, you will be mistress of Rathcannon until Cassandra is grown and gone. Then I will set you up in an establishment of your own, if that pleases you."

"But we would still be married in the eyes of God and the world. Linked forever."

"Countless marriages end in amicable separation. You need never fear that I would bother to end it with the scandal of divorce. I don't give a damn if you carry the dubious honor of the title of my wife to your grave."

Norah paced the chamber, feeling as if the walls were suddenly pressing in on her. "This is insane. I don't even know you."

"A fact that didn't seem to concern you overmuch when you thought me some pathetic beggar desperate for a soulmate. I shall make it simple for you. Put it in terms I am certain that even one of your innocence can understand. You would be wise to heed anything reprehensible you hear about me. The worse the accusation, the more likely it is true."

"But your daughter . . . she obviously adores you."

"Don't shore up your opinion of me by using my attachment to the girl. A child's heart is often blind. She regards

65

me as some kind of hero now, but the truth is that I had nothing to do with Cassandra until she was five years old, and neither did her mother. We were both so caught up in gambling and drinking and stirring up scandal that sometimes we forgot she even existed. It's a testament to Cassandra's own strength of spirit that she survived at all."

"But it's obvious you love her."

He shrugged one broad shoulder with a studied negligence. "As much as I'm capable of loving anyone. It's because I love her that I'm considering making this marriage. It seems she's worried about what will happen to her if I die. She's afraid of being left alone."

The words echoed in the secret places in Norah's own heart. "There is nothing more frightening in the world," she allowed softly. "But she'll soon be grown and gone, with a family of her own. With her beauty and wit, the instant she enters society she will be swept away."

"The instant she sets foot on the haute ton's threshold, every door will be slammed in her face," Kane cut in ruthlessly.

Norah started, stunned at the quicksilver emotion that flashed into those cynical eyes. Anguish, devastating in its power. Norah could feel the force of it even after Kane shuttered it away.

"You see, the one legacy Delia and I did manage to bequeath to our daughter during those first years of Cassandra's life was to make certain that no decent family will let her within a mile of their door."

Norah knew she shouldn't probe any further, shouldn't ask Aidan Kane about things that were none of her concern. There was no need to understand him, to touch whatever place in his soul had been illuminated for such a fleetingly raw moment in those bedeviling green eyes. She was stunned to hear her own voice. "It was all a long time ago. Whatever happened was not Cassandra's fault. Perhaps all is forgotten."

"Forgotten? Surely you must have some idea how cruel society can be, Miss Linton. And how unforgiving. The stigma of dishonor can't be sponged away by beauty or wit or a fortune in ill-gotten gains."

"No, I suppose that is true." Norah turned away from him, crossing to the window to stare out into the night. "Society would much rather you starve nobly in the gutter than demean yourself by attempting to make your own way in the world. They prefer to commiserate and sympathize with you, admit you into their gilded halls so they can whisper behind their hands how desperately threadbare General Linton's granddaughter appears."

"General Linton?" A measure of awe and astonishment crept into Kane's voice. "Don't tell me you're one of the Lintons of Stanwycke!"

"We lost Stanwycke years ago." Norah gave a bitter laugh. "Honor is the only thing my family managed to hold on to through the years, though we lost everything else."

"Why the blazes would a Linton of Stanwycke be running off to the wilds of Ireland to marry a stranger? For God's sake, every door in London must be open to . . ." Kane stopped, those predatory eyes of his suddenly burning with a quiet intensity Norah found more unsettling than any bout of rage. He paced toward her, and one strong hand caught her chin.

The callused warmth seeped into Norah, making her tremble, excruciatingly aware of the way Aidan Kane towered over her, close, so close she could see the tiny scar on his left cheekbone, she could catch the scent of him—wild Irish winds, night mist, and recklessness, all overlaid with the subtle tang of Madeira.

When he spoke his voice was rough, low, as if he were making some effort to gentle it. "What the devil are you doing here, Norah Linton? Halfway to hell, with no one to keep you safe? Your family must be crazed with worry."

Norah knew she should tear away from his touch, tell him

her affairs weren't his concern. But he held her, pinned with that probing gaze, a devastating uncertainty clinging about lips far too compelling.

"My family?" she echoed with a broken laugh. "I am quite certain they are relieved to be rid of me."

Kane's dark brows lowered, his eyes suddenly free of their lazy cynicism. He was searching for some clue, some reason for her flight to Ireland. She could see it in features that bespoke a keen intelligence buried beneath the shadows left by decadence. She knew the moment he reached a possible conclusion. "Norah," he said with astonishing gentleness, "are you with child?"

"W—With child?" she choked out, stunned. "I—"

"Before you answer, know that it would make no odds with me. No man knows better than I do the kind of siege unscrupulous bastards can lay against a woman's virtue."

There was contempt beneath those rough-velvet words, a contempt not for the fallen doves society scorned but rather for the men who used them so badly. Norah was astonished, set off balance by this Aidan Kane, the one without the hard cast to his features, the devil-take-the-world attitude in his eyes.

She swallowed hard and drew away from him, shaken to the core. "There is no child. I'm not in disgrace. I'm just—just in the way."

"In the way?"

"An inconvenient reminder of my mother's first marriage. An unwelcome burden in my stepfather's house." She struggled to keep the pain from her voice, to capture a little of Aidan Kane's careless sarcasm and use it for her own. "It would have been much simpler if I had been a hound or a horse left behind by my father. I could have been disposed of most expediently, thrown in a pond with a rock tied round my neck, auctioned off at Tattersalls. But the only way one can dispose of female children is to wash your hands of them in a marriage."

"Your family is responsible for sending you here?" Outrage thrummed beneath Kane's liquor-warmed voice. "Damn the thoughtless bastards to hell! For all they knew, I could've been some kind of monster!" His mouth twisted, grim. "Hell, I *am* a goddamn monster."

Norah couldn't help but smile a little. "True, you are not exactly what Cassandra's letters led me to believe. But no man who loves his child as you do could possibly be such a beast."

"I—blast, we are discussing how the devil you got abandoned on my doorstep, Norah. I want to know what could possibly have driven a lady the likes of you—a lady of damn fine family—to such rash lengths."

"My stepfather had arranged a marriage for me with a mere youth, the most odious, disgusting . . ." She shuddered. "If I refused to wed him, my stepfather intended to turn me out into the streets."

"I shall be most anxious to make your stepfather's acquaintance," Kane snarled with velvet menace. "Teach him his duty by you."

"The truth is, I wanted nothing more than to escape his house forever. If anyone else had offered for me, I would have bolted headlong into marriage and my stepfather would have happily palmed me off on another man. But, as you observed earlier, I am not . . . *ripe and rosy* enough for most gentlemen's tastes. Add that to my lack of fortune, and you can imagine how I fared upon the marriage mart."

Kane winced, a sweep of crimson appearing on his high cheekbones. "By 'ripe and rosy,' I only meant that you are a different sort of woman than—than my first wife. In truth, that's the highest compliment I could give you," he explained hastily. "God's teeth, it got so I thought I could walk through Delia's bedchamber and see her with a dozen men between the coverlets, and merely caution them not to let the cat slip out the door when they took their leave. You, on the other hand, are obviously a lady of quality. . . ." He stammered to a halt, his jaded face twisted in evident dismay at the words that had tumbled from his mouth.

"Don't distress yourself," Norah said, holding up one hand. "I know exactly what you meant by your comment, Sir Aidan. I became resigned to the fact I'm not a beauty long ago." Then why was it that here, now, with this man staring down at her, she suddenly felt the fierce pangs of regret she'd thought packed away with the slippers and fan from her first disastrous ball? "As you said, even if we—we enter into this arrangement, it would be purely a practical one. Not an affair of the heart."

"No. It would not be an affair of the heart. But I would do my best not to cause you pain. I would . . . But then, there will be time to hash the rest of this out later, if there is, indeed, a wedding. In any case, you are welcome here for as long as you need safe haven."

"Kindness? From you, sir?" She looked up at him, and for a heartbeat she thought she saw a flicker of shame, almost self-loathing in his eyes.

"Don't deceive yourself. I only indulge in the most selfish pursuits, madam. If they benefit someone else, it is purely accidental, I assure you. As for my motive in allowing you to remain at the castle, well, it's possible I only want to give Cassandra time to grow tired of this notion she has of making you her mother. Perhaps I simply don't give enough of a damn about your presence to trouble myself to get rid of you at the moment. Rathcannon is a huge castle, the grounds extensive. I could house a dozen runaway Englishwomen and not even know they were here."

He hesitated for a moment, and a shiver skated beneath Norah's skin as that emerald gaze locked with hers. "It's also possible that I'm such a bastard, I have already figured out a way to use you to my advantage, Miss Linton. I shall see about procuring a special license at once, so that if we do choose to marry no time will be lost scrambling around crying banns and other such nonsense."

"But . . . but I thought we—that marriage . . . I still cannot believe you would want to wed—"

Shadows melted across Kane's face, deepening the hollows, darkening his compelling eyes. "Miss Linton, do you know why I have such luck at the gaming tables?"

"I've not had much experience with games of chance," she answered warily.

"I excel because I play fast and dangerous. Once I choose a course, I never look back. If I choose to marry you, the wedding will take place the same way."

He turned and crossed to the door, then paused one lean hand on the brass latch, the emerald ring glittering wickedly on his finger. "There is one other thing I do that you should be made aware of."

"What is that?" Norah asked faintly.

"I shift the rules to suit me, Miss Linton. I cheat. It's a family legacy. Bred in the bone."

Norah's throat felt parched, her lips suddenly tingling, as Aidan Kane's sensual gaze flicked across them. She expected him to leave, to close the door behind him. But instead, he turned and paced toward her, his eyes suddenly narrowed, his lips parted.

Norah took a step backward. "What is the matter?"

"The most damnable thing. It just occurred to me that I've never been betrothed before. Delia and I raced off in a fit of impulsive passion. It seems as if a man should kiss the woman he is bound to."

"But we're not bound! I mean, we probably won't be . . ." Her voice vanished, stolen away by the overwhelming aura of Aidan Kane. He was a whisper away from her, his eyes smoky, a sulky cast to his lips, as if her protest had robbed him of something sweet.

"I suppose we are not bound—yet," he allowed, his breath warming the curves of Norah's lips, heating places far deeper. "However, a betrothal kiss is something to contemplate."

With that he slipped through the door. Norah pressed a hand to her racing heart, taken aback by the knowledge that

71

there was a part of her that had wanted Sir Aidan to close the space between them, to fit that beguilingly sensual mouth to hers.

Her experience in kissing had been limited at best. There had been the snipe-nosed Mr. Lambeth to whom she had allowed the liberty in a fit of simple curiosity, and there had been the sickening, overly enthusiastic groping of the lustful youth her stepfather had chosen to be her husband.

Never had she suspected that a man like Aidan Kane would kiss her. Never had she imagined tasting the power, the passion that would be in the Irish knight's mouth, in hands so skilled that a dancer hungered for them.

Never had she imagined such an experience, except in her dreams.

She pressed her fingertips to her lips, trembling. No. Aidan Kane was no dream-spun hero, no lover born of mist and magic and fantasies ages old. He had made it glaringly clear that he was no man for a woman to build dream castles about.

He was selfish. Ruthless. Dangerous. He was a man at one with vice and greed and dark pleasures.

When I leave my daughter, I am a wholly different man.

Norah paced toward the tumbled bed Aidan Kane's first wife had slept in and wondered if he had always been a man lost in the darkness, or if Delia Kane had driven him to wander the path he embraced.

She crossed to the dressing table onto which he had slammed the candlestick he'd forgotten in his haste to quit her chamber.

The mahogany surface was still littered with woman's things: a cut-glass scent bottle, a half-open fan depicting the seduction of Venus, a silver jewel case with the initials D.K. etched in elegant letters. And a . . . note?

The folded square of paper was propped against the looking glass, a gobbet of sealing wax glistening red, as if defending the missive from prying eyes.

Norah stared at it long moments, her gaze taking in the freshly inked inscription:

Lady . . .

She caught her lips between her teeth, confusion and curiosity warring inside her. The servants had made it clear this chamber had rarely if ever been used since the demise of the first Lady Kane. Was it possible that this note was yet another relic of the dead woman, like the jewel box and the fan? Could this be some impassioned letter from one of Delia Kane's lovers? A missive left behind by the woman who had once possessed the dark-haired man, the fairy child, and this lovely, haunting room?

No. Sir Aidan said Delia Kane had died when Cassandra was five. The ink would be faded, the paper yellowed with age if it had belonged to that time so long ago.

Then who could this missive possibly be intended for? One of the servants? Or . . . most unlikely of all . . . could it be for Norah herself?

Norah took it up, a sense of foreboding, a whispering of unease prickling at her nape.

An unease that multiplied tenfold as she broke the wafer of sealing wax and read the verse inscribed on the bit of paper:

> *Three tragedies has Rathcannon,*
> *cursed from a rebel's grave—*
> *A princess, imprisoned in a tower,*
> *A mistress, murdered by her husband's hand,*
> *A woman, straying near hell's flame.*
> *Flee, before it consumes you.*

Norah's heart fluttered, a thick knot of fear lodging in her throat, and she glanced about the room, half expecting to discover some phantom there, ink stains on transparent fingers, a cryptic warning on death-cold lips.

Hatred. Bitterness. Norah had heard those emotions, raw

in Sir Aidan Kane's voice. *Cassandra's mother was a coldhearted bitch. . . . Believe anything reprehensible you hear about me. . . . It's probably true. . . .*

But this?

Norah shivered. If she didn't know better, Norah might believe that this note was warning her . . . of what?

That Aidan Kane had murdered his wife?

CHAPTER

5

Nights at Rathcannon had always been miserable—silent eternities chafing Aidan. During the hours when Cassandra was filling the castle with laughter and temper tantrums, mischief and magic, he was able to forget at least a little, subdue the constant litany of regrets that warred inside his head.

But after his daughter had trailed up to her tower chamber to lose herself in sleep, Aidan had always ranged about the castle with the restless tension of a condemned prisoner listening to the carpenter's hammer strokes on the gallows that would be his destruction. A man tormented with the knowledge that the trapdoor would be sprung beneath him eventually, though unsure exactly when the fates would hurtle him to his doom.

He retaliated against that sense of powerlessness the only way he knew how: by riding the night until he could return to Rathcannon too tired to think, too numb to dream, too exhausted to peer into a future that only looked bleaker and more dismal with each passing year.

But as he plunged his stallion over countless Irish hills this night, he knew that his future had been altered forever.

Altered by a dark-eyed woman with sorrow, softness in her ivory face, and quiet courage drifting in a veil about her, as subtle as the gossamer nightgown that had hidden her most intimate secrets.

Redemption.

She had offered it to Aidan with one slender hand, as certainly as any angel come to give him pardon from heaven.

Her name.

Linton.

It was the key that could unlock the most noble doors in London, gain entry there, even for the daughter of an infamous scoundrel like Aidan Kane. It was a passage through darkness into the light.

The salvation of Cassandra's future. Yet this miraculous pardon could only be bought by the ultimate act of selfishness, villainy. The price? What little decency remained in Aidan's own soul. That, and the future of the innocent woman who had strayed too close to the beast's den.

He reined his stallion up the rise to where the ocean crashed against the cliffs. As dastardly as he might have been—dissolute, decadent, jaded—he'd never yet stooped to taking advantage of a woman like Norah, using her for his own purposes.

The prospect of doing so now twisted something deep in his chest, sickened him to the point that he was nearly tempted to thrust her into the coach and drive her away from Rathcannon as quickly as possible—not to save his own neck this time, but, rather, to save hers.

And yet he hadn't sought her out, hadn't intentionally drawn her to him. She had come to Rathcannon wanting a husband. He was merely going to grant her wish. At Rathcannon she would be out of reach of her bastard of a stepfather. She would have a home.

Cassandra would have someone to chatter with about

dresses and hair ribbons, someone to go to during dozens of balls and soirees, in search of a pin to catch up a drooping flounce. In search of consolation when the young gentleman who had caught her eye failed to sign her dance card. And Aidan—Aidan would never have to suffer the hell he had been dreading for so many years—seeing his daughter rejected because of his own sins.

He drew rein, barely halting Hazard at the edge of the cliff, sending a spray of pebbles and turf cascading down into the water. He stared down at the moonlight melting over the waves, heard the violent music of the sea, felt the rush of certainty in his heart.

He would take what Norah Linton had so innocently offered. He would bind her to him forever, not out of love, or even affection, not to build some sort of future. But to use her for this small space in time. For Cassandra.

Self-loathing pulsed through him, mingled with fierce resignation, as he remembered the great dark pools of Norah Linton's eyes, that determined lift of her chin that had been intended to assure him that she had entered into this adventure with only the most practical of intentions. That she had not spun girlish dreams of fairy tales and love about this marriage she had sought.

But it had been a lie, a lie exposed in the lines of the letters she had written him, words that whispered through his memory like the haunting strains of a ballad, revealing secret, tender places inside her soul that a man like him could never touch, never heal.

Beneath Norah Linton's quiet strength and stiff-necked English pride, he recognized the remnants of the emotions he had seen so often of late in his daughter's eyes. A kind of breathless anticipation, a waiting, a hoping that Norah had not yet fully extinguished from her soul.

Hope that could never be realized once she was Aidan's wife. Dreams she could never fulfill in his bed.

Aidan grimaced. Damn, what a heartless bastard he was.

For he had promised Norah Linton that he would not demand his conjugal rights only two hours before, but already he could almost feel the satin-ribbon tie of her nightgown between his fingers and imagine what it would be like to slip the bow free, taste the ivory-satin skin along her delicate collarbone, the hollow of her throat—a far different sensual flavor than the wanton fare he had become accustomed to.

Aidan swore, disgusted with himself, berating that part of any man's nature that allowed him to be led about by what was tucked beneath the flap of his breeches.

He had always enjoyed women—all women—buxom and bonnie, temperamental and passionate, exotic beauties and giggling little idiots, the size of their busts far outstripping the size of their intellects. He'd had females clambering after him even before his father took him to lose his virginity—and he'd been offered more than his share of trysts in the ill-spent years since.

But the only temptation he had faced when confronted by a woman of Norah Linton's mold was the devil-inspired craving to drive them to distraction, to break through their proper facades with the hot whispers and teasing suggestions that had sent them fleeing in the opposite direction whenever they laid eyes on him. Surely it should be easy enough to keep himself distant from such a pale, solemn slip of a thing as Norah Linton. Surely he wouldn't be tempted. . . .

A sudden sound, barely audible over the voice of the sea, made Aidan stiffen. He wheeled Hazard about. Aidan's eyes narrowed, searching the tumble of stone and heather, gorse and rowan that spangled the hills around him, searching the faint track of bare turf that couldn't be described by any term so grandiose as "road."

Night sounds. Wind whispered in the leaves, rustling creatures skittered beneath hedges, concealed by the darkness. He had heard those sounds on a hundred different rides. He had felt the prickling at the nape of his neck, the sensation of someone watching him, waiting—for what, he'd never been certain. To watch him plunge down into hell, perhaps, or to send him to the devil with help.

Never had Aidan cherished any delusions about the danger that lurked beyond Rathcannon's boundaries. If hate-filled looks were daggers, the country folk who dwelled among the wild Irish hills would have put him in his grave years before. His death would be a fitting blood price for his family's nefarious deeds throughout the years.

But his demons drove him to dare their wrath, to plunge into their territory, their havens, and challenge them.

It wasn't until tonight, with Cassandra's fears still reverberating through his mind, that he had considered what might happen if he pushed the Irishmen too far. If one night he had not ridden back to Rathcannon's stable, exhausted, exhilarated, but rather been hauled there on a litter, past the ability to hold his daughter or shield her ever again.

His fingers moved to the butt of the pistol he had shoved into his boottop before setting out on his ride. He spurred Hazard toward the road, but the horse reared, nearly unseating him, when a crouched shadow appeared nearly beneath his nose. Eyes flashed in the moonshine, wide and defiant by the silvery light—the face of a zealot beneath a shaggy tangle of hair, something unwieldy cradled in his arms. A boy who looked to be Cassandra's age was crumpled like a child in the larger man's arms, a man whose rugged features seemed strangely familiar to Aidan despite the darkness.

No, it was not the man who was familiar, Aidan assured himself. Rather it was the scent that filled his nostrils, a metallic mixture of blood and gunpowder and desperation that still haunted his senses from a dozen different battlefields.

Yet these two figures had been silent, still as rabbits cornered by the ravaging fangs of a fox.

"What the devil!" Aidan started to dismount.

"Ride out now, murdering English bastard, or die!" the man snarled.

"Your boy there needs help. Let me—"

"He'd rather have his last drop of blood soaked up by Irish soil than have his wounds bound up by a thieving Kane of Rathcannon! Leave, before I have to kill you!"

Aidan was stunned that the man had recognized him in the dark. Yet in a heartbeat Aidan understood the situation as the sound of hoofbeats approached at breakneck pace from down the road. They were being hunted, the man and the wounded boy. For what crime? God only knew. Yet their helplessness chafed at Aidan as the two huddled there, helpless, awaiting certain doom.

He shielded his eyes with one hand, trying to peel back the veil of darkness. He caught a glimpse of scarlet, a flash of gold, heard the unmistakable tones of an English soldier.

"Certain . . . can't have gotten far, sir." The assurance drifted toward them. "At least . . . one bullet . . . hit the boy. Sure of it."

"Perhaps you managed to kill him, Denny. Save the Crown the cost of a new rope to hang him with, though the hangmen'll be fighting over who gets to stretch the neck of the other bastard."

A hanging offense. Whatever these men had done, they were to pay for it with their lives.

Aidan glanced down at the Irishman, just in time to see the man lunging toward Hazard in an effort to grab the horse and make an escape. With the barest shift of his knees, Aidan sent the stallion bolting out of the man's reach, leaving him defenseless.

How many times had Aidan known that sensation of helplessness in the years he'd battled under Wellington's command? How many times had he felt the blind panic, the wild surging of fear through his veins as his enemies charged toward him? How many times had he been certain he was about to die?

Blast it, these men were no one to him. Aidan attempted to rein himself in savagely. For all he knew, they could've been plotting villainy against Rathcannon, destroying his own fields.

But at that instant he heard the wounded lad whimper, felt his desperation like a living thing in his own chest. Damnation, could he really abandon them to the soldiers' vengeance?

Cursing himself as a fool, he spurred Hazard toward the contingent of soldiers bearing down on their prey. If he hadn't consumed so much Madeira hours earlier, he was dead certain he would have pointed the way to the idiots' hiding place, or at least ridden on, not embroiling himself in affairs that were none of his concern. Instead, he felt a wave of pure stupidity unfurling in his gut.

"Halt! Who goes there!" Alarmed commands rang out as Aidan cantered from the shadows, to find the whole bevy of soldiers bristling with pistols and muskets aimed squarely at his heart.

With a reckless laugh, Aidan reined his stallion so that it blocked the narrow breach in the road. He held his hands aloft. "Don't shoot! I surrender! Only tell me my crime! Attempting to steal the moon? Disturbing the peace of the sea gulls? Or something truly heinous, like trampling the fairy folk dancing in the raths?"

"How would you like your words rammed down your throat at the point of my sword?" one of the soldiers growled.

"It might be a novelty. Last acquaintance I had with a sword, His Majesty was laying it atop my shoulders, knighting me for heroism. I vow it was one of the most chilling confrontations of my life."

"His Majesty—knighting—who the devil . . ." The portly sergeant sent his mount trotting toward him, and Aidan turned so that his profile was angled into the light.

"Sir Aidan Kane, your obedient servant."

"Sir Aidan!" The man glared owlishly at him, obviously

disgruntled. "Please remove yourself from our path! We're on a mission of the highest importance."

"But of course you are!" Aidan said, as if to a petulant child. "How diverting for you. Just what is this mission?"

"Hunting down a pack of Irish rebels who set Magnus MacKeag's barn afire."

"MacKeag?" Of all those who dwelled around Rathcannon, there was no man Aidan loathed more—a pompous, self-righteous fool with a penchant for petty cruelty.

He chuckled. "Doubtless the brigands considered it a mission of mercy to destroy MacKeag's stable. You know—end the horses' misery in one fell swoop instead of leaving them to MacKeag's whiplashes. The Irish always did have the most infernal attachment to the beasts. I wish you happy hunting, gentlemen. What, pray tell, do these brigands look like? Of course, I'll excuse you if you don't know. After all, it's dark."

"There was one of their infernal whelps—they teach them murder and thievery from the cradle, I vow. Can't say I'd recognize him except for the bullet hole in his gut. But I'd know the leader's face if I saw it in hell! Donal Gilpatrick, may he be damned by Lucifer himself."

Aidan averted his eyes for a heartbeat as a blinding flash of images jolted through him: pain, confusion, and two boys who for a moment in time hadn't realized that they were destined to hate each other. The night-shadowed image of the man hiding in the shadows shifted into focus, fueled by Aidan's own relentless memory. A memory already scoring Gilpatrick's face with a twisted scar. It took immense force of will to school Aidan's features into their usual mocking sneer.

"And here I always thought that the dubious honor of damning the Gilpatricks had been usurped by my ancestors, Sergeant." Aidan flashed his most beatific smile, cursing himself for a fool, knowing the price he could pay for his sudden bout of insanity. The Crown was brutal to those foolhardy enough to shelter fugitives. Still, Aidan couldn't seem to help himself. He *tsked* condescendingly. "Of course, I dare say it is no wonder you haven't apprehended the scoundrel yet."

Even in the moonlight, Aidan could see the soldier's cheeks puff in outrage. "What do you mean by that, sir?"

"Just that you are going the wrong way."

"What?"

"I nearly trampled two men fitting your description five miles north of here, near the ruins of Castle Alainn. Dashed ugly wound in the whelp, I must say. Fed me some nonsense about his being gored by a bull while trespassing on someone's field."

"Are you quite certain?"

"You have my solemn oath as a gentleman that it's the God's truth! Damned annoying, the way the bastards trespass! By the way they act, you'd think the island belonged to them!"

"I'm not speaking of that, you f—" The commander choked off the words.

Aidan raised one brow and examined the tips of fingers encased in the butter-soft leather of his riding gloves. "If you don't mind me mentioning it, you're speaking a good deal too much. I fear that your quarry may be getting away. Of course, if you care to continue your search in this direction, by all means do so."

"Sir Aidan." A whey-faced little private with hero worship in his eyes kneed his mount forward. "I fear that Gilpatrick and his cohorts have been making things quite uncomfortable hereabouts. In fact, it's rumored that they are planning some vile skulduggery. Not that they'll ever get a chance to carry it out."

Aidan's hands tightened on his reins. Damn, what if the Irishmen were plotting some dark deed and he were allowing them to escape? "What exactly are they plotting?"

"We don't know exactly. We've only heard rumors and such. The vaguest of whisperings."

The vaguest of whisperings weren't enough to hand a man a death sentence, Aidan reasoned grimly.

The soldier was smiling at him, adoration in his eyes. "If you should hear of anything that might be of help in bringing him to justice, Sir Aidan, I am certain your loyalty to the Crown will be as devoted as it was during the Peninsular campaign."

"I assure you, the depth of my . . . *loyalty* never wavers. Please, do inform me if you arrest the miscreants. I should so loathe to miss the spectacle of a hanging."

"Never fear. We'll run the bastards to ground. We know how to deal with traitors to the Crown." The sergeant shot Aidan an insolent salute, meant to convey exactly what he thought of the infamous wastrel who had so shamed a hero's laurels.

Aidan affected a bored grin until the sound of hoofbeats disappeared; then, with an oath, he wheeled his stallion and set it at a run toward the place where the Irishmen had been hiding.

He was out of the saddle the instant he reached the makeshift shelter, wondering how the devil he was going to get the wounded lad to safety, wondering why the devil he should even attempt it.

"Gilpatrick, the soldiers are gone," Aidan snapped, stalking toward the shelter. "You can swallow your goddamn Irish pride for once and let me hel—"

He slammed to a halt, stunned as moonlight drifted over the clump of brush, illuminating nothing but tangled branches, a dark void. Swearing, Aidan thrust his hand into the center of it, his skin scratched by bits of bark and thorn, gritty dirt dusting his fingertips. Dirt, and something wet, clinging to his skin.

Blood.

But there was no other sign that anyone had taken shelter in the copse of underbrush.

"Damn your eyes," Aidan snarled into the darkness, his gaze slashing about him, seeking some hint of where

Gilpatrick and his wounded compatriot had fled to. "Let me help you! The boy will never last."

But only the wind whispered an answer, mocking Aidan, taunting him. Damn the Irish, they could melt into the hills themselves when they wished it.

Aidan stood up, furious, feeling as if he'd been trapped there forever, caught between the English soldiers at his back and the Irish cupped in the palm of the sheltering night. He belonged to neither, was loathed by both, held in contempt.

Nearly as much contempt as Aidan had for himself.

He swore as he grasped the reins of his stallion and swung up into the saddle. The devil take them all, then. Just as the devil was bound to take him.

Aidan tightened his knees about Hazard's sides and urged the stallion into flight. He plumbed deep to the hard, reckless part of himself. Let the whole lot of them plunge into the sea. He had more important matters to tend to.

He had to prepare for a wedding.

He grimaced.

Unless he had already convinced the bride that allowing Sir Aidan Kane to slip his ring on her finger would be the biggest mistake of her life.

CHAPTER

6

How did one greet a suspected murderer over a plate of scones and clotted cream? The absurd question tugged at Norah as she hovered outside Rathcannon's breakfast parlor.

I see that you are reading the London Times, *Sir Aidan. Are there any edifying pieces on the most propitious time to bury corpses beneath the rosebushes? Or, better still: I received the most intriguing message last night. I do believe the droll fellow was attempting to tell me you killed your wife. Do confess if you did!*

It was insane, absurd. The perfect coup de grace in an entire night of madness. Madness or the most ridiculous bout of melodrama Norah had ever indulged in.

She grimaced, berating herself for the all-too-vivid imagination she had nurtured as a lonely child. Hour after hour last night, she had lain in the huge bed that had belonged to Aidan Kane's first wife, her gaze flicking time and again to the silver jewel box where she had stashed the mysterious note, her heart hammering.

Norah had even considered attempting to move the armoire in front of the door joining her chamber to Kane's in an effort to block his entry, but she'd doubted she could move the heavy piece of furniture alone, and she'd supposed it would be a trifle awkward to roust up the irrepressible chambermaid and ask for assistance.

Pardon me, Rose, could you help me barricade myself in this bedchamber? You see, I suspect that your master might be a murderer.

The thought of such a ridiculous scenario had finally driven Norah to clamp her eyelids resolutely shut. After all, Aidan Kane could hardly murder her on the first night, could he? Cassandra would be bound to ask questions if the bride she'd provided her father were found dead. Besides, Norah had reasoned with grim optimism, even if he *were* a murderer, Kane had been married to his first wife a long while before he'd done her in. Norah had barely known him a day—hardly enough of an acquaintance to be worthy of homicide.

And yet, as slumber had overtaken Norah, she'd been forced to admit that it wasn't the specter of some murdering fiend that danced upon her nerves like a razor's edge. It was the image of a man with a far more subtle weapon, one more dangerous than anything Norah had ever known.

Eyes that taunted, that challenged, that seduced. A mouth cast with a blatant sensuality that made promises to the secret wanton who lurked in the heart of every woman.

She had been haunted by dreams of that dangerous, beguiling face, cleansed of dissipation by the touch of loving hands. She had been mesmerized by the image of the hard, cynical light in those green eyes shattering, exposing the man who lay beneath Aidan Kane's dissolute facade.

She had awakened with her skin damp and excruciatingly sensitive beneath her nightgown, her nipples tingling as if the fingers of her dangerous lover had left their spell on her forever. She'd sprung out of bed as if she could shed those sensations as easily as the bedclothes. Then she had attempted to put some small mark of normalcy on the morning by crossing to Delia Kane's escritoire.

There, she had penned the letter she had promised Richard what seemed an eternity before, her throat aching at the memory of his earnestness and concern as he'd pleaded that she let him know when she arrived safely at her betrothed's home.

It had been too painful to imagine his distress over the disastrous situation she had fallen into, so she had merely written that she was safely at Rathcannon and that he was not to worry. She had sealed the missive and grimaced, certain she would be doing enough worrying for both of them.

She doubted she'd have come downstairs at all, were it not for the necessity of posting the letter. She ran nervous fingertips over the paper's edge, excruciatingly aware of how silly she must appear, hovering outside the door.

Even with sunshine spilling across Rathcannon's corridors and Cassandra's excited chatter echoing from the breakfast room, Norah was appalled to feel a heavy warmth spread across the tops of her breasts as Sir Aidan's deep chuckle rumbled from the chamber. Her tongue stole out to moisten lips that were suddenly trembling.

No. This was absurd, she struggled to reassure herself. Even when she confronted Aidan Kane face to face, the man wouldn't have a clue about the cryptic warning she had received, nor about the scandalous things she had dreamed of: his hands stripping away her gown, his mouth searching out the dips and hollows of her naked body, where heat pooled, an untamable need to be tasted . . .

"So are you going to join us, or should I have your breakfast served here in the corridor?" The deep male voice made Norah nigh jump out of her skin. She glanced up to see Aidan Kane lounging in the doorway, one tanned hand braced on the door frame, a bedazzling grin turning his face into a study in raw masculine beauty.

A quotation from Shakespeare's *Hamlet* whispered

through Norah's mind: *One may smile, and smile, and be a villain.*

Her eyes widened, and she took an instinctive step backward, as if to avoid a shower of sparks. Dazed, Norah struggled to form a coherent reply, but once again Kane had taken her completely off guard.

"You're late for breakfast, Miss Linton," he observed. "You must've been sleeping like the dead." An unfortunate choice of words. Norah caught her lips between her teeth in an effort to keep another bubble of melodrama from washing away her hard-won sense of logic.

Kane seemed oblivious to her unease. He stunned her by capturing her empty hand in his and raising it to his lips. He chuckled as she snatched her fingers away from the moist silk of that mouth that had invaded her dreams. "I do hope you found your chamber comfortable."

"Comfortable?" Norah choked out. With whisperings of murder clinging to the shadows? With her own indecent imaginings taunting her?

She would have had a far more restful sleep if he'd bound her to a bed of thorns.

"I—I slept just fine," Norah lied hastily, stuffing both her hands behind her as if half expecting him to take possession of them again. The letter crinkled in her hand, and one of Kane's diabolically dark brows shot up.

"I hope that is not intended for me? A letter of farewell?" He seemed genuinely concerned as he drew the missive from her hand.

"No! I wrote to my stepbrother to let him know—know I had arrived."

"And that you'd been met in the carriage circle by the castle ogre?" He leveled a self-deprecating smile at her, one purely dripping with potent male charm.

"No, I . . . there seemed no need to . . . to—" To what? a voice jeered inside her. Tell Richard that she was under the roof of a man who might be a murderer? A man who wanted nothing to do with a wife?

"I intend to make certain that you will have a great deal to write to your brother in the future." There was husky promise in that honeyed voice.

At the slight sound from the far end of the corridor, he angled a glance to where the bright-eyed Rose was industriously polishing the marble toes of a statue of Perseus.

"Rose?" Kane beckoned to the chambermaid. The girl's saucy smile froze as she glimpsed the object in his hand. Unease tickled the back of Norah's neck as the cheeky girl hung back a little, wary, her fingers twisting the buffing cloth.

"Sir Aidan?"

"Have this letter posted for Miss Linton. It seems her brother is anxious to know she has arrived in one piece."

"But I—I know nothin' about such like, not bein' able to read. Calvy Sipes could do it."

"As long as someone does. At once."

Rose took the letter and bobbed a curtsy, then hastened away.

"There. That should ease your stepbrother's mind. Do you think it would help if I penned a letter myself?" The timbre of Kane's voice dropped just a whisper, roughening just enough to set Norah's pulse racing. "A man likes to know a woman he cares about will be well taken care of when she leaves his protection."

Norah stared at Kane, unnerved, confused. The man acted as if yesterday's disaster had never happened. He had never stood in the carriage circle bellowing at his daughter, hadn't raged at Norah for her rashness, then stormed into her bedchamber to lay out a most indecent proposal.

That angry, sullen, sensual man with his hot eyes and rumpled clothes had been replaced by an Aidan Kane whose dark hair fell in silken contrast to the hard lines of a clean-shaven face, whose impeccable breeches were molded to his thighs and whose dark coat fit his broad shoulders to perfection.

But it was the flashing smile that made Norah feel even more disoriented than she had when he'd nearly kissed her in the bedchamber last night. It was a smile that reminded her of tropical plants she had read of, so beautiful they lured the unwary to touch their petals, but deadly dangerous beneath that exotic allure.

The image was brushed aside by a vision in white dimity and angel-gold curls as Cassandra darted out of the breakfast parlor.

"Miss Linton!" she cried. "You will never guess what a wonderful day we are to have! Papa has agreed to take us on an outing to the Tinmartin fair, so that the two of you can become better acquainted! We're to have a picnic, and if we see something pretty he shall buy us both presents."

Norah glanced from the girl's face to Kane's. The man's eyes were all innocence, but his mouth curved with a knowing expression, one that set all Norah's instincts on edge. "A fair?"

Kane shrugged one shoulder with lazy amusement. "The child has always been diverted by them. Nothing Cass likes better than gorging herself on pastries, robbing my pockets to buy herself ribbons and hovering around the gypsy carts, sniffing their musty herbs and begging for tales of their witchery."

"The gypsies have the most wondrous things of all. Bright ribbons and magic herbs, potions and balalaikas that make the most lovely music."

"They're thieves, every one of them. I can't imagine why I continue to allow them to strip me of my coin. But perhaps this time I shall find something useful in their carts."

"What could you possibly want from the gypsies?" The question tumbled from Norah's lips of its own volition.

Kane's gaze caught hers with an intimacy that made her quiver with a pulsing heat that reminded her all too clearly of the feel of Kane's breath, hot and filled with dark promise against the tingling curve of her lips.

"What could I want from the gypsies?" he echoed, in a seductive voice. "Perhaps a love potion to enchant my betrothed."

"I'm not your betrothed!" Norah cried, flinging a dismayed glance from that meltingly sensual grin to Cassandra's brightening face. "Sir Aidan, I thought we'd discussed—" She pressed cold fingertips to cheeks hot as fire, angry and discomfited, confused and infuriatingly prey to the shivers of attraction sizzling through her veins. "It's not necessary . . ."

Those green eyes skated over her face with a caress so sensual she felt as if she'd been touched by Kane's fingertips. "I'm quite certain Tristan and Isolde didn't think a potion was necessary either, before they mistakenly sipped the cup that was to bind them," he said.

"Bind them? Or send them to their doom?" Norah barely knew the words had escaped her, so stunned was she that the cynical knight even knew of the star-crossed lovers. But then she supposed that to be a successful rakehell, a man would have to know the secrets of feminine hearts. And there were few things more likely to put a woman in a sentimental mood than a tale of love so beautiful it had clung to people's imaginations for generations.

She was jarred from the thought by Cassandra clasping her hands together in girlish delight. "Oh, but Tristan and Isolde shared the most wonderfully romantic doom, Miss Linton!" the girl enthused, proving Norah's theory about the effect of such tales on the feminine sex by heaving a dazzled sigh. "They both fought so desperately not to love each other, struggled not to betray Isolde's husband, but the potion was so strong they could not fight it." The girl's face shifted to an odd expression, bemused, a little eager, as she echoed, "They could not fight it."

Norah turned away.

The ancient story of impossible love had haunted her from the first time she'd heard it. Honorable Tristan, escorting his liege lord's intended bride to Cornwall. Isolde, the Irish princess whose mother had so wished for her daughter's happiness in marriage that she had secretly sent a love potion along with Isolde's maid. The servant had been instructed to slip the potion—a potion destined to meld the lovers' spirits in a fiery passion unbreakable even by death —into the bride and bridegroom's cup when the party reached Cornwall.

But tragic Isolde had not shared that cup with the husband her family had chosen for her. Instead, she and Tristan had unknowingly partaken of its sweet poison, condemning them forever to a love so fierce, so tragically beautiful, that the tender-hearted still wept over it though thousands of years had passed.

Norah looked away, a quiet sorrow closing about her heart at the memory of herself as a child, dreaming of such soul-deep love. But she'd learned since that such love was for other girls, not for her.

"Cass, if I intend to woo the lady, I suppose I would have been wiser to choose a different tale," Sir Aidan said, his voice tinged with soft amusement and some other more subtle emotion she couldn't name. "One with a happy ending. After what happened to those two poor unfortunates, the mere suggestion of love is enough to send one fleeing into the night. Is it not, Norah?"

Norah.

Her name. Just her name. She had heard it spoken a thousand times, a plain name and simple. But it slipped from Aidan Kane's tongue like silvery moonlight, lilting, liquid.

Norah's fingers clenched as she drew back from that secret, beckoning warmth. She didn't understand him. Didn't know what he was attempting to do. When she had arrived at Rathcannon, he made no secret of the fact that he would have happily tossed her atop a donkey cart bound for Dublin if he could have gotten rid of her.

Last night he had come to her, belligerent, angry, trapped by his daughter's pleading. He'd all but dared her to be fool enough to wed him.

Now here he was, spinning out love stories and teasing her in a way designed to make feminine hearts melt.

If I intend to woo the lady . . .

The mere thought of Sir Aidan Kane turning that soul-searing charm upon her was the most terrifying prospect Norah had ever faced. Terrifying because she wasn't certain any woman who breathed possessed defenses against such a dangerous weapon. A weapon in a game Aidan Kane had obviously played many times before. A game in which Norah could only lose, come away bested by him, embarrassed past bearing—or, worse still, with an aching heart.

Norah's chin tipped upward. "I do not require wooing, if you remember, Sir Aidan. Even if we do enter into an agreement, it will be a practical one. A business proposition."

Cassandra's brow wrinkled in confusion. "A business proposition?" Heat flooded Norah's face, but Sir Aidan remained almost beatific.

"Cass, run and get the basket that Cook prepared and meet us by the carriage." Kane gestured toward the door.

The girl started to protest, but he only said, "If we don't get there early, all the prettiest things will be gone."

Cassandra turned in a flutter of hair ribbons and excitement and hurried from the room.

"I'm sorry," Norah stammered. "I didn't mean to say that in front of Cassandra. There's no need for her to know that this is a purely practical arrangement. I mean that we agree that—"

"That was before," he cut in softly.

Norah blinked. "Before what?" Before he'd been dazzled by her beauty? Before he'd seen past her pale face and into her soul? No, more likely he'd taken an unexpected blow to the head that had left his brain addled.

She watched one bronzed hand slip into his coat pocket, a

smile melting onto his face, slow and sweet as fire-warmed honey. "Before I read these."

Norah stared in horror as he withdrew a packet of letters bound up in ribbon. Letters written in her own careful script, penned to a dream-love who didn't even exist.

From the moment Norah first entered her stepfather's house, she had learned to hide her feelings. Winston Farnsworth had no patience for a child's tears, shed over the father she had lost. Farnsworth said that any such display was one of weakness, and Norah knew instinctively that showing weakness to this great, scowling man who so disliked her would be a mistake. And now, to allow Sir Aidan Kane to see the tender places tucked beneath her defenses would be the worst mistake she could ever make.

Instinctively, she lunged at him in an attempt to snatch the letters from his hand, feeling as if he held the tenderest secrets of her heart in that careless clasp. Kane whisked them out of her reach.

"Give them back," Norah demanded between clenched teeth. "They're mine."

"I'm afraid I have to disagree," he said, reaching beneath the flap of his blue coat to tuck the letters into the pocket of his gold-and-sapphire-striped waistcoat. "They are clearly marked with my name: Sir Aidan Kane, Castle Rathcannon."

"You *know* they were not meant for you! I mean, you weren't the person who wrote . . . I was penning a reply to someone who—"

"Regardless of how they came to my hand, I've found the contents most . . . illuminating."

Norah was appalled to find her eyes stinging, her throat tight. But this man had already seen her too many times, vulnerable, lost. She forced her chin to bump up a notch, fighting back with the only weapon she could find at hand. "As I recall, my letters are not half so *illuminating* as the ones written in your name."

Kane winced as if she had slammed a hammer down on a

particularly sensitive tooth. His silky-dark brows collided, a good measure of his charm vanishing. He shrugged, and Norah sensed he was attempting to adopt that aura of devilish arrogance he wore so often. But the stain of red along aristocratic cheekbones betrayed him.

"It's obvious I didn't write the letters. You should thrust the damned things in the fire. Now, the carriage is being brought 'round, so if you're hungry, scoop up a scone or currant bun, something to munch on our way. What is it to be, my love? A nibble of one of Mrs. Cadagon's sugar buns?"

"I am *not* your love, we are *not* betrothed, and I am not about to subject myself to an afternoon trapped with you anywhere! Especially when you're acting like a candidate for Bedlam!"

"Bedlam? Blast it, I haven't come down to breakfast attired in nothing but my nightshirt and riding breeches again, have I?" He made a great show of examining his attire, from the polished leather of his Hessian boots to the impeccable sleeve of his coat. "No," he observed, "all seems to be in order. And it was no mean feat, I might add, since I barely slept all night."

Norah glared at him. "If lack of sleep always has such an improving effect on your disposition, I suggest you give up slumber altogether."

"But you are not impressed by the change."

"Sir Aidan, at the moment I would not trust you if you said the sky was blue."

"Very astute. A desirable quality in a woman, though there are men who want their wives mutton-headed and docile."

"*And* ripe and rosy," Norah snapped, then flushed, furious that she had allowed him to hear how much his careless comment the night before had stung her. It wasn't as if she'd wanted him to find her attractive, was it? A man like him? A rogue? A scoundrel?

She silently damned him to a torturous death as he

reached up and caught her chin in his fingertips. Jerking away, she intended to storm down the corridor, but in a heartbeat Kane had trapped her in the sinewy prison of his arms, his palms flattened on the wall, his thumbs entangled in the wild curls of her hair.

"Norah, have you ever strolled in a garden?"

"You are mad! What could that possibly have to do with—with anything?"

"Humor me for but a moment. When you first stroll through the gate, what do you see?"

"Weeds that the gardener hasn't bothered to pull."

His lips quirked in that disarming way, and he chuckled just a little. "Why doesn't that surprise me? But flowers, Norah. Which ones do you notice first?"

"This is insane. I don't—" The futility of arguing with a madman bore down on her, and she snapped out, "I suppose, the roses."

"Yes. And why is that?"

"They have the brightest colors. They're the most beautiful."

"Not necessarily. I suppose that on first glance one would say that was so, but if you wander about, with a watchful eye, there will be other blossoms even more lovely, tucked away beneath the rose's shadow."

Wonderful, Norah thought with a grimace. She now had a murdering parental rakehell horticulturist holding her prisoner in his dead wife's bedchamber. "I'm sure I haven't the slightest idea what this has to do with anything."

"Have you ever seen heartsease growing in a crack between stones? There is nothing more delicate, more fragile; and yet I think they are far stronger, even braver than the rose that grows in the walls of your garden. A man could crush one beneath his heel and not even know it. He could pass it by without seeing the way sunlight turns golden on the petals."

What was he trying to say? she wondered a little desperately. Norah swallowed hard, excruciatingly aware of the hard plane of that masculine chest brushing the tips of her breasts.

But it was his eyes that suddenly held her, impossibly green, starred with thick, dark lashes. Eyes in which she had seen so many conflicting emotions since her arrival at this castle by the Irish shore, so many warring revelations about a man whose soul seemed as tangled as any enigma woven of a sorcerer's spell.

"I—I don't understand what this has to do with—"

"With you? With *us?*" The timbre of his voice roughened just enough to make a shiver of heat wash through her. "I just think that there might be a chance I have . . . heedlessly passed over something beautiful."

She didn't know why his words hurt so badly. "I wish you wouldn't."

"Wouldn't what?"

"Say things that are ridiculous."

"You mean it isn't possible that I have nearly cast aside a treasure? You forget, I lost the first five years of my daughter's life because of that same blindness. Anything is possible, Norah. Just ask Cassandra."

Cassandra, beloved, indulged in every whim. Cassandra, who had not yet found herself pitted against the real world, its harshness, its ugliness, its cruelty.

Anything is possible. . . . Kane's words echoed through Norah, vibrating in the fragile threads of her own storm-battered dreams. She closed her eyes, remembering the cryptic message tucked in the silver box in the bedroom of a woman who might have been murdered. She shuddered at the memory of Kane ripping back the darkest part of his soul, ruthlessly exposing the throbbing anger he dulled with gambling and women.

But even as she tried to cling to those memories, another image shuddered to life in her mind: the fleeting flash of anguish, the self-loathing, the helplessness that had shone so briefly in Aidan Kane's eyes when he spoke of his daughter's uncertain future.

What was illusion?

What was real?

Norah shivered as the questions tugged at her with chill fingers, teasing her with an even more daunting enigma.

What fate might befall any woman who tried to find out the answer for herself?

Sunlight glinted off new tinware, turning pots and pans, spoons and ladles, into shimmering ornaments of silver. A crowd of Irish crofters already thronged the rows of booths, bickering over prices, laughing over gossip, chattering about the latest news. Bright shawls and kerchiefs were splashes of brilliance, as voices cried out their wares, trying to conjure up the coins from the pockets of passersby.

It was a perfect day for a fair, as Cassandra had pointed out at least a dozen times. And, greedy little baggage that she was, the girl had spent hours dashing about gorging herself on the sights and sounds, the wonderful smells and the bright trinkets that had delighted her since childhood.

Aidan watched her hold up her wrist so that the sunlight could sparkle on the little coral bracelet he had bought her at the last booth. Her fingers were sticky from candies, and her bonnet hung by its ribbons down her back.

He might have been able to pretend she was a child again, caught back five years in some delightful enchantment, if it weren't for Cassandra's continued attempts at matchmaking. And if it weren't for the fact that half a dozen village lads kept stealing up to Cassandra to present her with necklaces woven of wildflowers and dainty sweets to nibble on. The smile she flashed in gratitude was one that would break the poor lads' hearts. Of that much, Aidan was certain. God knew, it was slowly demolishing his own.

Aidan swerved around a vendor's cart, tempted to scoop up a bright-skinned orange, hoping the sweet sting of the fruit would distract him from his thoughts, but Cass had uttered a squeal of pure delight and was off, hastening toward the cluster of bright painted carts at the far edge of the fair. Aidan grimaced as he noticed which campsite had lured his headstrong daughter.

"Trust Cassandra to single out the most disreputable gypsies in the entire fair." He grumbled beneath the brim of Norah's bonnet as he regarded the two gypsy women bickering over their goods.

Herbs were bundled up on gossamer veils spread across boards between two wagon tongues. Cards bearing the strange figures of the Tarot were scattered out to lure the curious to peer into their future. Sinister-looking vials were lined up in a rainbow of mystic colors. Aidan didn't even want to guess what they contained—distilled lizard's blood and spider's legs, or warts scraped from an old woman's nose.

From the looks of the older of the two crones, the caravan needn't fear running short of that particular ingredient for some time to come, Aidan thought in wry amusement. The unsightly blemishes clustered about the gypsy woman's nose like bubbles in a washerwoman's tub. But Cassandra seemed to see no further than the bright black eyes of the woman.

Aidan could only be grateful for that girlish oblivion, for neither did Cassandra notice the way the crowd of fairgoers melted away wherever Aidan chose to wander. But he sensed that Norah was aware of the arctic glances, the way the lowliest crofter's wife snatched her children from his path, as if afraid he bore some fatal disease, some wickedness that could be passed to another by the mere brush of his hand.

He had scanned the crowd for hours now, searching for some sign of the Irish rebels he had encountered the night before, wondering which, if any, of these people were hiding a wounded, frightened fugitive from the king's justice somewhere in their pathetic little cottage.

It wasn't his affair.

That stubborn bastard Gilpatrick had made that clear enough last night. And God knew, it should've been a lesson Aidan had mastered long ago, when he was ten years old.

He had done his damnedest to dismiss thoughts of wounded rebels and arrogant soldiers, burning stables and a gaping wound in a boy the age of his own cherished child. He had plunged into the fair determined to focus on Cassandra's pleasure and that of the woman who sat so quietly, so strangely solitary, beside him.

But from the instant they had drawn in sight of the bustling crowd, a restlessness had stirred in Aidan, a chafing sensation deep in his gut that had left him edgy and off balance.

Guilt. That was what he attributed it to, plain and simple. A few loose scruples rattling around somewhere in his psyche that he hadn't managed to pickle in gin or stamp out like embers drifting across dry tinder. That was the trouble with tendering even the most minuscule of scruples: Left unattended, they could flare up into the most uncomfortable brush fires. And before a man knew what he was about, he was taking insane risks—interfering in arrests, surrendering fortunes fairly won at the hazard table.

Aidan shook himself inwardly. No, there was only one table he should be focusing on at the moment, and that was the one full of gypsy wares that his daughter was poring over with unabashed delight.

Cass leaned over the collection of herbs and flowers, her nose poked into a bunch of dried yarrow, until she dissolved into a fit of sneezes.

"Miss Linton, did you ever hear anything so amazing?" Cass cried, turning to where Norah stood and thrusting the bundle into the Englishwoman's hands. "Madame says that if you stitch this into your clothes it can ward off all manner of sickness. And if you distill this nightshade and a person drinks it up, they will believe whatever you tell them."

"How convenient," Aidan muttered. "Perhaps I should

lay in a supply for the next time you get into one of your stubborn fits and won't stop arguing with me."

Cassandra laughed, tossing her curls. "Better to put it in your own porridge, Papa. That way you would know that Miss Linton is the perfect bride for you."

"Cassandra." Norah set the yarrow down hastily, color creeping along her cheekbones. "I really wish you would not discuss this."

Aidan caught Norah glancing at the keen-eyed gypsy women, felt her gnawing discomfort. "You had best prepare yourself, my dear," he warned. "When Cassandra desires something, she is like a dog on a bone. She'll gnaw on your nerves, give you no peace until she gets her way."

Those great dark eyes peered up at Aidan from beneath the sweet curve of bonnet brim, eyes too serious, a mouth too soft. "We do not always get what we want most. It's a lesson Cassandra will learn someday, whether you will it or not."

The warning made Aidan wince, not in resentment, but rather because it was true. His eyes shifted to his daughter. Cassandra had darted over to finger the glass vials, holding them up to the sun so that the light glinted through the strange mystic colors trapped beneath the glass.

"What is this one for?" she demanded, holding up a rose-colored liquid.

Madame hobbled over, squinting at the vial. "Ah. Powerful, is that one. Very powerful. To heal the heart that is bleeding inside."

"You mean if someone is having palpitations, it can cure them?" Cassandra asked. "Why, I think that Mrs. Cadagon's grandmother has a weakness in the heart. Miss Linton, do you think I should take this to her?"

Aidan felt Norah stiffen, her discomfort rippling over him in waves. But he cut in, "Absolutely not. I'll not have you poisoning poor Granny Cadagon, Cass."

"He is right, your papa," the gypsy said. "Is not heart

bleeding from wounds of the flesh, but from a far more savage knife blade."

Cass gave a delicious shudder, her gaze flicking again to the vial. "What knife blade is that?"

"Love." The woman hobbled toward Norah, scrutinizing her with those strange eyes, and Aidan felt the brush of Norah's skirts against his thighs as she edged a trifle closer to him.

"Do you know the bite of that knife, me lady?"

"N—No. Of course not."

"Pah! You have the look of a wanderer about your eyes."

"A wanderer?"

"One who journeys through time, searching. . . . Would you like me to see if this journey is the one you find him?"

"Him?"

"The sea to your storm, the sun to your moon. He who is crystal-blue water to the thirst that burns inside you."

"No. I had very much rather not."

"Oh, please, Miss Linton!" Cassandra begged, her eyes sparkling. "Let Madame conjure over you! It gives me the most delicious shivers!"

"Your hand, me lady. Give it to me."

Norah glanced from Aidan to Cassandra, and he could tell she was loath to disappoint the child. He took possession of her hand.

"It might be amusing," Aidan allowed, unbuttoning the glove at the fragile pulse-point of her wrist. "After all, it's just so much nonsense. A mere parlor game." With feather-light touches, he stripped the delicate kid away from each of her fingers—fingers suddenly trembling. He could only hope from his seductive touch, and not from her nervousness about the whisperings of the occult that clung about the carts.

He would have caressed Norah's hand a moment longer, but the gypsy captured Norah's fingers in bony claws, turning her palm to the sunlight. The hag bent so close her coarse mane of hair obscured that tender palm from Aidan's sight, and he could almost feel Norah squirming with discomfort as those gnarled fingers traced the lines that marked her hand.

"You have journeyed far," the woman said, "far and alone, sent off by an ill wind from the isle across the waves."

"She guessed you are from England!" Cassandra enthused breathlessly.

"She knows I am English by my accent," Norah protested resolutely. "It would be obvious to anyone who heard me speak."

"Would it now, doubter of the mysteries? And perhaps your accent would also have me knowing that your papa died when you were . . . four?"

Norah gasped, and Aidan felt a strange prickle at the back of his neck.

"'Twas as though your heart was torn from your breast, dearie. Gone. Everyone gone. Alone." The gypsy clicked her tongue, shaking her head. "Poor little one . . . abandoned in a room of . . . blood?"

Aidan's brow furrowed as a sick feeling stirred in his stomach. The gypsy was speaking about Norah Linton's past—*her* past, not the chamber Aidan had put her in the night before. Yet could he ever walk through that door and not wonder if indeed he had blood on his hands?

"You will be torn by the thorns of three great trials," the gypsy continued. "Great love. Great pain. That and . . . betrayal at the hands of . . . of a man."

Aidan stilled, the words seeming a portent of doom—a whispered warning about the price to be paid should he wed this woman. Love—she would never have it as his wife. Pain—that she could suffer in plenty. Betrayal—in that the Kanes of Rathcannon were masters.

"Pah!" The other gypsy shouldered her compatriot aside. "She thinks she tells the fortune, she does! See into the future, handing down a sentence that the poor bonnet lady will be betrayed by a man? And what woman hasn't been, a dozen times or more? You, my fine sir, give me your hand, and you shall see true into tomorrow."

Aidan felt an absurd urge to jam his hands into his pockets, to walk away, laughing, scorning the gypsies' arts. But a niggling fascination stirred inside him. Silent, he stripped his own glove from his hand, then held it out to the conjurer as if he half expected the old woman's touch to burn him.

"Tragic is the babe born on Whitsuntide, fine sir." Aidan hated the chill that crept down his spine at the woman's quavering purr.

"He was born on Whitsuntide!" Cassandra gasped. "Miss Linton, he was! Mrs. Cadagon told me so! How remarkable!"

"'Tis nothing to rejoice in, *cailin,*" the gypsy warned. "A fatally dangerous time to be born is Whitsuntide. The babe born on that day is destined to die a death o' violence, or"—the woman's voice fell, hushed—"to send another dancing into death's arms before 'tis their time."

Cassandra's cheeks lost their bloom. "Dancing into death? What does that mean?"

"Murder, child. The babe born on Whitsuntide is destined to kill another."

Aidan felt his blood chill, heard a tiny sound from Norah—the merest breath, as if the gypsy had touched a place that was raw.

"My papa wouldn't hurt anyone!" Cassandra exclaimed, most put out by such dire predictions. "He's brave, and good, and—and he was a hero in the war!"

Aidan shoved aside his own discomfort, forced his voice to be light, teasing, in an effort to soothe his daughter. "Cass, I'm certain Madame Gypsy doesn't want to hear tales of my exploits. Besides, my nurse made certain she broke the curse."

"Your nurse?" Norah was gazing up at him with wide eyes—eyes a little frightened, as if someone had just walked over her grave.

"She was stuffed to the top of her kerchief with superstition. Warned my mother that I was foredoomed, and that there was only one way to break the spell."

"What could it possibly be, Papa?"

"Dig a grave and lay me in it."

"Merciful heavens!" Norah gasped.

"Oh Papa, how awful," Cassandra said, wide-eyed.

"My mother was understandably hesitant about the whole procedure, but considering the tendency to devilment already cast upon me by my ancestry, she thought it wise to take the precaution. So Nurse Dunne whisked me out when I was but three days old and made her magic over me. Of course, it remains to be seen if I was saved that night or if all I got was an extremely dirty backside. Now, it seems to me we've all had enough of this deviltry. I saw some lovely pastries down the way—"

"But 'tis not all I saw upon your palm, sir," the gypsy said, barring his path. "'Tis a devil pact I see marked upon your skin. A wager with Mephistopheles himself that you entered into long ago."

Aidan looked into those dark eyes, strangely transfixed, and tried to infuse into his voice a lightness he didn't feel. "That wager has already been lost."

"Or perhaps the battle is just being joined, the prize to be won your immortal soul."

Aidan forced a laugh. "And I suppose, Goodwife, that you have some cure amongst all this rubbish that will prove my salvation? Some posset—at a very dear price, of course. No, I must insist on no more graveyard visits, no rowan branches over my cradle—or, er, bed. Dashed uncomfortable when the things begin to shed their leaves. I'm afraid the devil and I shall have to wrestle this out alone. And if it's hell I'm bound for, well, I am certain that the Kanes will have a torture chamber set aside in Lucifer's palace for their exclusive use."

He gently but firmly took Norah's arm. "Come along, Cass. We can't tarry here all day."

"But Papa, she—she hasn't read my palm yet." There was a note of doubt in the girl's voice, as if she were no longer certain she wanted those glittering black eyes to peer into her future.

"We are leaving, Cassandra. *Now.*" Aidan dug into his pocket and removed a few guineas. "I'm not certain what the going rate is for predicting a man will go to the devil," he said, dropping the coins into the gypsy's withered hand, "but I assume you think some payment is due. However, if you would allow me to give you a bit of advice?"

The crone nodded.

"I would suggest that from now on you foretell wealth and happiness, true love and great honor, no matter what the scribbles on a person's palm say. I am quite certain your grateful patrons would be much more generous with their pay than if they walked away feeling a cloud of doom hovering above their heads."

"I say what I see. The truth. 'Tis no gift to mock, having the sight. You would do well to heed my warnings."

Aidan merely laughed, yet whatever luster had been on the day seemed to have evaporated. Taking Norah's arm, and shooing Cassandra before him, Aidan tried to tease away the strange shadows that had circled about them beside the table of the gypsies' mystic wares.

It was nonsense. Absurd. The gypsy could have plucked any generality out of the air, given such broad meanings to her predictions that any fool could twist happenings about until it seemed they had come true.

Then why was it that each time he looked at Norah Linton's face he heard the whispered warning? Why did he see the reflection of her betrayer every time he peered into her eyes?

CHAPTER

7

Aidan drove like a madman. Norah gripped the brace of the carriage seat as the tension that had coiled her stomach into knots during the hours since breakfast tightened even more ruthlessly inside her.

Every muscle in her body ached with the effort it cost her to keep from bumping that hard masculine shoulder bare inches from her own, the steely length of thigh stretched out with suicidal negligence beside her.

The insane pace Kane set would have been terrifying enough on its own, the spirited team of grays seeming bent on hurtling the carriage to its destruction. But more disturbing still was the sight of Sir Aidan Kane's face—his eyes intent on something she could not see, hazed with secrets she couldn't begin to guess at.

He had barely spoken after they'd left the gypsy fair, and even Cassandra seemed strangely preoccupied, restless, a disturbing light in those angel-blue eyes, as if the gypsy magic still hovered about them in an iridescent haze of gloom. Even the arrival of Gibbon Cadagon and his mischievous brood of children hadn't been able to restore the gloss to the day. When Sir Aidan had suggested it was time to leave, Cassandra's mood had shifted with the swift fury of a summer storm, the sunshiny girl displaying a formidable stubbornness, the fierce determination of one unused to having her wishes denied. She had insisted that if Sir Aidan and Miss Linton were weary, she was not, and there was no reason her fun should be spoiled when she could remain behind with the Cadagons.

Norah could think of a dozen reasons why the girl should not be given her way. Not the least of which was her suspicion that Cassandra was up to something—an instinct Norah had honed during the years she had helped with the younger children while attending Miss Valentine's Academy for Young Ladies.

There had been something in the girl's face that Norah couldn't help but mistrust, and yet, when bolstered by the pleas of a dozen little Cadagons and the troll-like groom himself, Aidan had finally given his grudging consent.

It was none of her concern, of course, how he chose to discipline his daughter. Yet Norah couldn't help but feel he would come to heartily regret giving in to Cassandra in this instance.

By the time she and Sir Aidan had reached the carriage, it seemed he already did regret his actions. He guided the elegant equipage onto the road with skilled hands. But it seemed as if he had left the last bright pieces of himself behind, in Cassandra's care. It was as if he were yet another man, another enigma, far too complex to be unraveled.

Here, with the soft, moist breeze tousling his dark hair, his eyes misty, and his mouth strangely vulnerable, the hardened scoundrel who had come to her bedchamber the night before seemed to have vanished. The bedeviling tease of that morning had also melted away, leaving a man who looked daunted, not dangerous. Lonely, not reckless. Angry, yes, still angry. But mostly at himself.

Norah had tried once or twice to comment on something

in the ever-changing landscape but at last had lapsed into silence, sensing that a battle was waging inside Aidan Kane. She knew that he was not a man to share his pain. No, she thought with sudden insight. He would not share his pain, only his darkness, his flaws, his shortcomings.

He had made certain she'd witnessed every one of these the night before.

She pressed one hand to her bonnet, as the strings had come loose yet again, and tried to gauge exactly how far it was to Rathcannon. But none of the landmarks were familiar. It seemed as if they were going astray somehow, listing to the west.

"Is this the way we came?" Norah cried above the wind when she could bear her confusion no longer.

He slowed the carriage just a bit, his stormy gaze slashing to meet hers. "No. This isn't the way we came. I thought I would take you someplace where we can be alone."

Alone? Norah felt a shiver of nervousness and glanced up into that implacable face. "Surely Rathcannon has a dozen rooms—"

"A dozen rooms stuffed with servants whose wagging tongues cannot be trusted," Kane cut in. "Every man jack of them doubtless with their ears pressed to the wall. Nothing quite so entertaining as watching the grand folks make fools of themselves, you know."

"But I don't know—I don't understand what this is all about," Norah said helplessly. But then, did she truly understand anything anymore?

It seemed that Kane was in no hurry to enlighten her. That sensual mouth merely hardened, the lines carved at its sides deepening as the carriage crested the hilltop.

In that instant, Norah's questions were swept away by a glory beyond imagining as the sunset's magnificent paintbox spilled into the valley below. Red, orange, gold, the impossibly vivid hues glittered on hedges and piled stone fences and dyed the wool of sheep nibbling on green grass. The land tumbled, vale over stone, a symphony of lushness, of untamable majesty melting down to where the sea cast foam upon its shore.

These beauties alone would have elicited a gasp of pleasure from anyone who saw them, but it was the structure that stood in the valley's heart that made Norah's fingers loosen their grip on the seat brace, numbed with awe.

Gray stone battlements soared in stark majesty against the sky. War had shattered the front of the castle ages before, but time had healed the ugliness of the wound with the tenderness of a lover, until it seemed as if a fairy's hand had peeled back the wall to reveal what lay within.

Empty windows shaped the light into gingerbread patterns. Stone stairs spiraled through lovely archways, their landings high above the ground seeming like jumping-off places to the stars. The floor on the upper stories and the walls that had sectioned the castle into chambers were only ghostly imprints in the stone, but the fireplaces remained, lovely carvings surrounding them.

Encircling the base of the entire ruin was a wreath of grass, darker green than any other, a ring of ancient stones showing beneath, as if the site had been marked somehow, blessed by the Old Ones from the mists of time.

Norah had seen so little of Ireland. In Dublin and on the journey west, she had been so anxious about the meeting with her prospective bridegroom that she'd spent the whole trip rehearsing what to say to him, trying to imagine his face, his form.

On the trip to the fair, she had been unnerved by the sudden change in Aidan, continually glancing over at him as if he were a wolf that might decide at any moment to turn about and snap off her head.

But as she stared at the desecrated loveliness before her, her throat closed, her eyes stung.

Magic and mist, soul-deep sorrow and heart-shattering beauty—was it not the lifeblood of this fey and lovely land?

Where the ravaged dreams that clung to the hillsides in gray stone ruins seemed more searingly beautiful than dreams come true anywhere else on earth?

Yet trapped within the beauty were skeins of tragedy, of simmering violence, of passions dark and bright, just as the same wild traits were caught in the man beside her.

"What is this place?" Norah breathed, as Aidan drew the carriage to a halt beside the vivid cascade of a fuchsia hedge.

"In Gaelic it's called *Caislean Alainn.* Castle of Beauty."

"It *is* beautiful. It seems almost . . . enchanted." Norah's cheeks stung with embarrassment at words that might have come from Kane's starry-eyed daughter.

But he was already leaping down from the carriage, and his strong hands were tying the team to a branch bowing under the fragrant weight of magenta and purple blossoms. "Enchanted, is it? No wonder Cass was taken with you. From the moment Cassandra first discovered the castle, she populated it with fairy folk and dragons. There were times I could almost see the fairies through her eyes." His fingers were still for a moment as an unaccustomed wistfulness clung to Kane's careless words.

Norah looked down at him, attempting to picture this devastatingly handsome rogue watching his daughter cavort among a myriad of playmates only she could see, bright-winged, beautiful playmates painted by her imagination.

How many pretend worlds had Norah created for herself as a child? Safe places, protected from the bitter winds of reality that buffeted the tender hearted too harshly.

What would happen when Sir Aidan's princess stepped beyond the boundaries of her dream castle and into the real world? It was a world Sir Aidan had already admitted would be waiting for her, not with the praise and love and open-hearted kindness she was accustomed to, but rather with cruel talons, clutching at scandal a decade old, long lists recounting the sins of her father and mother.

The knowledge broke Norah's heart all the more, for she understood what it was like to step from such a haven into a cold realm where no one could help you, not even the papa you believed was invincible. The empty ache was an aftermath she remembered all too well.

She was jarred from these troubling thoughts as Sir Aidan circled the carriage to help her down. She stood up and started to step down, but he caught her about the waist, his hands hard and hot pressed against her, his fingers so long they nearly spanned her waist. For an instant, that hard, sun-bronzed face was so close to her that she could see the lines carved about his eyes and mouth. A shiver skated through her at the realization that this Sir Aidan could be far more dangerous than the angry man who had charged into her bedchamber the night before.

She started to protest, but before she could pull away, he lifted her high into the air, then drifted her to the ground, as if she weighed no more than a flower blossom plucked from the hedge.

Of course, it was only gentlemanly that he should aid her. But did she imagine it, or were those hands clinging a heartbeat longer than necessary? Were those eyes clouded with an odd uncertainty?

Unable to bear the weight of those compelling eyes another moment, Norah whisked away from Sir Aidan's grasp and started toward the castle ruin, searching for something, anything, to fill the sudden, pulsing silence. "Who did this place belong to?"

"Cassandra would tell you it belongs to the Tuatha de Daanan, the fairy folk who made the circle of stone. The fortress itself was built many centuries later, an Irish chieftain's gift to his bride in the years before Strongbow and his Normans came to conquer Ireland."

"The chieftain must have loved her very much to give her such a beautiful gift."

"I'm afraid their tale is about as cheery as that of Tristan and Isolde." He shrugged one broad shoulder. "But then I suppose it would have to be when the lady in question was called Maire of the Ten Thousand Tears. They claimed she was both the most beautiful and the most virtuous woman ever to set foot upon Irish soil."

"Why was she so unhappy? Because the castle was destroyed? I can see why that would have broken her heart."

"No. Caislean Alainn withstood the tragedy that befell Maire and her chieftain. It wasn't until Cromwell scourged Ireland that the place was destroyed." He grimaced.

"The tale of Maire of the Ten Thousand Tears," Norah found herself prodding him, alive with curiosity about the woman for whom the Castle of Beauty had been built.

"Legend has it that my ancestor Eremon of the O'Caighans made a wager with the chieftain's enemies, claiming that he could make the queen swell with bastard seed. If he succeeded, he would receive a hundred cattle and a torc of gold. The legend says Eremon used Druid arts to shape-change into a likeness of Maire's husband, then slip into the bed of the chieftain's wife in the darkness. She welcomed him into her body, for it is said she loved her husband more than life. But apparently the Druid arts did not shift Eremon's touch into that of the chieftain, and Maire suspected something was amiss.

"She tried to ignore her doubts, and when she bore a son nine months later, there was great rejoicing through the land. But as the years passed, the child grew up not to resemble the chieftain she so adored but became the mirror image of my kinsman—a man as notorious for chasing skirts as I have been. For ten years, Maire had been beloved of all, especially of the chieftain, but nothing could protect her from the whispers, the constant speculation about the child's birth. After all, she had been barren as the chieftain's wife for so long."

"But she couldn't have known . . . couldn't have guessed," Norah breathed.

"No," Aidan allowed, a pensiveness in his voice. "She couldn't have known that she had already met her doom. In an effort to cleanse the stain of scandal from her name, the good lady prayed to the Holy Mother to give her some means to verify the truth of her child's birth. The Blessed Mother answered her in a dream. Maire of the Thousand Tears gathered the entire sept at the Hill of Night Voices, where there was a standing stone that supposedly had magical powers. Then she had my kinsman brought there. She begged Eremon to swear to the king upon the holy rock that she was a true and faithful wife and never had they joined their bodies in bed."

"What happened?"

"My kinsman laid his hand upon the stone and attempted to lie. Something—supposedly whatever power was trapped in the stone—flung him to the earth and killed him."

A chill shivered through Norah. "It must be just a—a story. A stone couldn't possibly have—"

"Whatever power defeated my kinsman's lie—whether it was the Stone of Truth or the fact that Eremon couldn't resist gloating and finally revealed what he had done to someone with an unguarded tongue—the lady did realize the truth at last. The knowledge that she had unwittingly betrayed her husband would have been agony enough to that gentle lady. The knowledge that her son was a bastard, born of that unholy union, was torment. But the most hellish torture of all was the fact that the chieftain she adored would never forgive her this slur upon his honor. His fierce pride demanded that he set her aside. The grief ate at Maire until she flung herself from the top of the castle wall. Sometimes, the peasant folks say, you can still hear her crying."

"What a tragic story," Norah said, stepping through a narrow space in the fairy rath and into the castle's enchanted circle.

"Any tale involving a Kane is likely to be. There is a saying hereabouts that the only way a Kane could ever get into heaven is to steal the key." Aidan gave a noncommittal shrug. "As for the legend of Caislean Alainn, aren't most tales tragic when the players are foolish enough to give away their hearts?"

Norah picked her way through fallen rubble overgrown now with wildflowers and pressed her palm against the pitted stone of Caislean Alainn's wall. Her palm tingled with an almost painful awareness, as if she could feel the pulse of the people who had lived here, loved here, died here. As if their grief and joy, hope and fear, had been trapped forever, preserved inside the fairy ring. "Cassandra would say the stories were romantic," she said softly.

"Damnably depressing, that's what they are. It's enough to make a man swear off women for all time," Aidan insisted, levering himself up to sit on a ledge of stone and leaning back against the wall. A myriad of glistening sun drops tumbled across his dark hair as he drew up one breechclad knee and rested his arm lazily upon it. "The blasted things never turn out happily. Think about it for a moment. Do you remember Tristan and Isolde trotting off to their castle to play bed games and eat sweetmeats once their tale was done? Or Orpheus and Eurydice cavorting through fields of flowers in eternal bliss? No. The poor bastards always end up the same: in absolute agony, until they die—heroically, of course." He grimaced. "As if that is supposed to make up for everything they've gone through. Miserable and dead. That is the end result of these epic love tales you women get all dewy eyed over."

There was all the gruff disgust of a boy in those unremittingly masculine features, a boy who had long since given up believing in Father Christmas but who very much wished that he still did.

Norah was stunned to feel her lips tugging into a wary smile. "Surely there must be one or two with a happy ending."

"Not a one that comes to my mind." His face stilled, his eyes intent beneath thick lashes. "I wonder how our tale will end, Norah Linton."

Norah turned away from that probing gaze and went to a window that let in a keyhole-shaped block of light. "Sensibly, I would hope," she said with forced lightness. "There is

116

something to be said for avoiding jealous passions, ill-fated love potions, and such like. The one certainty in the matter is that it *will* end. And considering the circumstances, the sooner it does the better."

She heard the soft crunch of Aidan's boots on the rubble that littered the castle floor, the sound of Aidan coming near her. She stiffened, aware of him—every line and sinew, every dark angle and coiled muscle—even before his shadow covered her.

"You are ready to be quit of us already, then?" His voice was like aged whiskey, warm and intoxicating. "I wonder if I could change your mind."

She started as those sinewy hands closed on her shoulders, turning her gently to face him. His touch sent sizzling awareness racing through her veins, whispering of the danger in him, the perilous allure. His eyes burned her with a glittering intensity.

"Norah, do you believe in fate?"

"Fate?" The echo came out in a breathless whisper.

"That some things are preordained, no matter how we carry on about having free will."

"Of course not. I . . ." She gave a sad laugh. "No, that's wrong. I *must* believe in fate. I'm sure I do. Look at my mad actions when I got the letter advertising for a woman to be your bride."

"How did you come to receive Cassandra's letters?" he prodded gently.

"My stepbrother has a friend with connections at the *London Times*. When the letter came, his friend was making a jest of it, showing it around his club."

"Perfect." Aidan winced, and Norah could guess just how uncomfortable that notion made him. "Bloody perfect."

"Richard saw the note, and he was certain the position was ideal for me," Norah hurried on. "He knew how desperately unhappy I was. He gave it to me, and I—I thought . . ." She stopped, her cheeks burning, her gaze dropping to where the crisp white of Aidan's shirt was edged by his dark green waistcoat. But he forced her to meet his gaze, curving one palm against her cheek, tipping her face up toward his with warm, callused hands, suddenly almost tender.

"What did you think, Norah Linton?" he encouraged, more gently than she would have imagined possible.

"I thought you were my destiny. Isn't that absurd?"

"If you had asked me that question yesterday, I would have agreed. But I'm not so certain anymore."

Norah's heart fluttered in her breast, her fingers trembled. He was confusing her—utterly, completely, disarming her.

"Did you ever stop to think that we need each other?" he asked. "Badly?"

Need—hadn't that been what Norah had wanted when she'd set out for Ireland? Some purpose in her life, some direction? Somewhere to belong? Someone who needed her? *Loved her?*

She hadn't admitted it even to herself, how much she wanted someone to cherish her, just a little. The admission alone made her draw back, wary.

"I need a home, Sir Aidan. And from what you said yesterday, what you need is to be left in peace. Your life is arranged just as you like it."

"What would you say if I told you I was drowning, and that you—you may be the one person in the world who could reach out a hand, pull me back to shore?"

Norah winced inwardly at the echoing of her own secret dreams, her most dangerous fantasies. "Now I know where Cassandra inherited her flair for the dramatic, Sir Aidan. I cannot imagine what I could possibly do to . . . how did you say it? Pull you back to shore? Especially since it's so evident you are swimming with all your power in the opposite direction."

Aidan's eyes darkened, earnest, almost . . . supplicant. "You could open the doors to society for Cassandra. Your name could restore to her everything I threw away."

Her heart tripped. It was as he'd said: The honor of the Linton name had been the one legacy her father had managed to leave her.

"With Cassandra's beauty, my wealth, and the name Linton to lend her respectability, I know Cass could weather whatever snubs are directed at her. You know how winning the girl is. Within weeks, she would have the old dragons at Almack's eating out of her hand."

"You think a triumph at Almack's will guarantee her happiness? Did your time among the haute ton bring you such joy?"

Tempests swirled in the green mist of Sir Aidan's eyes, a muscle in his jaw working. "Cassandra is different. Special. If you would only marry me, she could rise above Delia and me—be what we never could be. Something wholesome and good, strong and happy . . . She deserves to be happy."

There was such passion in his words, a catch of desperation in the husky tones. Norah couldn't help but feel a tug in her heart.

He raked one hand through the tumbled ebony of his hair. "Norah, I'm asking you—no, begging you—to help us."

For all his attempts to paint himself a villain, there was a fierce pride in the chiseled handsomeness of his features that allowed Norah to see exactly how much that plea cost him.

For a heartbeat, she felt a mad urge to reach up and lay her hand against that stubborn jut of jaw, smooth back the lock of dark hair that fell across his brow. But she reined herself in harshly. It would be all too easy to succumb to Sir Aidan Kane's entreaty. The man was intoxicatingly dangerous, as compelling as a siren's song.

She didn't dare forget the perilous bargain he wanted her to make. How could she enter into such a cold and loveless marriage? Agree to the terms Sir Aidan Kane had flung out at her like a duelist's glove the night before?

A marriage that was no marriage. A husband who would

slip his ring upon her finger, then do his best to forget she even existed.

A business arrangement, he had called it; and yet what would it be like to watch her husband with his lights o' love? Knowing that those were the women whose company he would delight in, who would see him laugh and feel the power of his kiss?

The instant Cassandra was launched into her own life, Norah would once again be a stranger in a house that did not belong to her. A useless appendage that her "husband" would cast away with no more thought than a waistcoat whose color he had wearied of.

Why did that stark reality make her suddenly feel so desolate?

She sucked in a steadying breath. "Sir Aidan, I know you are fearful for Cassandra's future, but to enter into marriage —to take holy vows—knowing before we even begin that the promises have no meaning . . ."

"You lied to me then when you said you wanted a comfortable home? You hunger after the *grande passion* instead? As one who barely escaped its fires with my life, I can assure you, the experience is highly overrated."

Norah cast her gaze away from him, a troubled churning in her breast at those careless words, and the ease at which she could picture this man—so gloriously sensual, so wild and reckless, indulging in such earthly pleasures, such savage passions—passions Norah couldn't even begin to understand or hope to possess for herself.

The pain, the loss, in surrendering hopes that had once fluttered in her heart surged again inside her, and she raised her chin a notch, clinging to the legendary Linton pride. "You want me to marry you to ease your daughter's way. To shield her from the humiliation a scandal tied to your past might cause her, do you not?"

"Exactly so."

"And yet, if I were mad enough to wed you, wouldn't my

fate be exactly that which you are battling so hard to spare your daughter?"

Dark brows lowered over a patrician nose. "What do you mean?"

"You fear that your daughter will become the target for cruel jests and mockery because of your actions."

His face whitened, that flash of anguish and self-loathing burning in the fierce green lights of his eyes. "You need me to say it? Yes. That is exactly what I fear. Damn it, there is no justice on God's earth if that girl has to suffer for my sins."

"On that we both agree. But if I *do* decide to aid you . . ." Her voice trembled just a whisper. "If I were to become your bride, what will happen when Cassandra is safe? What possible use will you have for me?"

"Your task will be done. I would grant you any wish within my power, to the last drop of my blood."

"Anything," Norah said softly, "except honor."

Aidan stared at her, his voice low, roughened with earnestness. "If you spare my daughter pain, you will be honored by me above all other women."

"I suppose I should be flattered. After all, from our previous conversations, I gather that the annals of your regard is quite overflowing with those of the gentler sex."

"What are you saying?"

"Just that I saw enough of my stepbrother's friends to know the way of men like you. They lavish gifts and entertainments on mistresses who are bright and beautiful, bold and dashing. When they are forced to think of their wives at all, they make sly mockeries of them, often within the wife's hearing, as though a wedding ring upon a woman's hand deadens her to all feeling."

Aidan's features darkened, his mouth tightened. "You think that is how I would repay you for sparing my daughter pain?"

"You wouldn't have to make jest of me. Others would be happy to do so for you."

"Norah—"

She raised one hand in protest. "Can't you imagine what they would say? How they would speculate about our marriage?"

"Why the devil should they?" he demanded, stalking away a few paces.

"Because—look at you," Norah exclaimed helplessly. "At everything you are. Then look at me."

He turned, his arms crossed over the hard plane of his chest, the Kane belligerence she had seen in Cassandra carved much more formidably in her father's aristocratic features. "I see nothing but a man and a woman who both need what the other can provide."

"Society will see a desperate spinster and a man who could not possibly love her. They'll see you with women battling for your favors, and believe that you are trying to wash away the sour taste of a night in my bed." Norah's cheeks flamed, her voice faltered, but she plunged onward with brutal honesty. "That is, if they believe you ever seek my bed at all."

Green eyes clashed with hers, and she felt as if the mere weight of his pulsing intensity were crushing her, making it impossible to breathe. "Do you want me in your bed?"

Norah gave a pained laugh. "And if I did? Are you saying you would accommodate me in exchange for my services to Cassandra?"

"Norah, I've attempted to be honest with you. As honest as I know how to be. You be honest with me. If you want me as your lover, I'm certain we could do well enough."

The words poured hot acid into the most vulnerable place in Norah's battered heart. "What? Would we make consummation part of the bride price? Perhaps we could get it written up in the marriage contract: 'Herewith, Sir Aidan Kane does solemnly swear to perform his husbandly duty every month on the last Tuesday—'"

"Blast it, what do you want me to say?" Aidan roared with a helpless gesture. "That I'm madly in love with you? We'd both know that was a lie. Truth to tell, after what happened with Delia, I'm not capable of loving any woman, ever."

"You made that quite clear already."

"Do you want me to promise that I'll never look at another woman?" he demanded. "Or that I'll duel every ton bastard who dares make mockery of our marriage? Why should they stand in judgment? When it comes to marriage, society has always set far more store by practical considerations than anything so fleeting and ephemeral as love. And as for your fear of being scorned because of my infidelities, you needn't worry. Taking lovers is as common a practice among the ton as sipping ratafia at a rout party. You might even find a man who strikes your fancy one day—and you can be sure I would wish you both a most pleasurable dalliance."

The words bit into Norah like a lash, and rippling fire shot through the tattered remnants of her pride. She groped for something to say—something with which to wound him, to make him feel the desolation drowning her in crushing waves. But the slightest movement, the tiniest breath, and she feared she would disgrace herself by bursting into tears of exhaustion and soul-deep disappointment.

Sunlight and shadow pooled on that harshly masculine face alive with restlessness and impatience, his burning gaze clashing with hers. "Blast it, don't look at me that way—as if I were some blackhearted villain who dragged you here by your hair! When you left England it was with every intention of—" He cut off the words, pressing his fingertips against the hollows of his eyes.

"Of what?" Norah demanded with icy dignity.

"Of marrying a man blindly." His hand fell away to reveal eyes glittering with a recklessness already too familiar. The heat of his anger fired hotter still with a darker intent that stirred raw panic inside her—panic and something more.

"Perhaps that is where I have erred in my wooing of you, Miss Linton. Perhaps I should give you a taste of that which you seem to crave."

Norah took a step backward and collided with solid stone. "No!" she said, fighting desperately to hide her alarm. "You're mistaken if you think—"

"If I think what?" Aidan purred, flattening his palms on either side of her. "If I think you came here to taste of a man's passion before it was too late?"

Norah swallowed hard, her heart hammering, her pulses racing. "Whatever I came here seeking, I'm certain I haven't found it."

"You should fall down on your knees and thank God for that. Love is poison when compared to simple passion. Love blinds you, seeps into your marrow like the most insidious venom, weakening you until it strips away everything— your strength, your honor, your pride."

She was shaking under the force of those bitter words, words that made her question his callous dismissal of the woman who had once been his wife. Words that made her wonder just how deeply Delia Kane had wounded him— this man who despised himself, everything he was, everything he stood for, except when his life brushed that of his cherished daughter.

"Let me show you, Norah," he breathed. "Let me show you how much sweeter passion tastes than the poisonous bond you think you desire."

Norah stared into that starkly handsome face, her lips parting to protest. But at that instant, Aidan Kane lowered his mouth to hers.

His breath heated her tingling lips for just a whisper, those thickly curled lashes dipping lazily to half mast, until all she could see was a mesmerizing glimpse of emerald green. Then that hard, reckless mouth mated its sensual contours to her own, hot and moist and insistent. Fire sizzled through Norah's veins—wild, terrifying, as Sir Aidan Kane's mouth seduced hers with a mastery that left her knees weak and her spirit shaken.

Rocked to her very core, she grasped for something, anything, to anchor her in the maelstrom his kiss released in her. Her fingers clutched at his coat, the scent of him musky and dangerous, touched with the tang of salt waves and wind-battered moors.

As if her touch signaled acquiescence, Aidan moaned low in his throat. His tongue, hot and skilled and sweet, traced the crease between her own lips, starting a shuddering pleasure blossoming in that secret forbidden place between her thighs.

A tiny sound of pleasure and despair rose in Norah's throat, and her lips parted to allow it to escape. Aidan caught it in his own mouth and answered the longing plea Norah didn't even understand by entering her mouth with his tongue.

Once the lecherous youth her stepfather had bade her marry had attempted such liberties, and she had been so sickened she had all but retched after breaking away from him. But the wet, stroking roughness of Sir Aidan's intimate kiss unleashed in Norah something wild and frightening in its power. He shifted, the stiffened joints of his elbows softening, buckling, so that the length of his forearms met the stone, bringing the virile plane of his body tight against hers. The masculine ridges and hollows imprinted themselves on her until the folds of her gown and petticoats seemed no more shielding between his flesh and hers than the last veil of mist, burned away by a too hot sun.

Her nipples were afire, abraded by the buttons on his coat. Her thighs were melting where his long, sinewy legs molded against hers, her senses spinning, wheeling dizzily into madness.

She whimpered in quiet anguish when Aidan broke the kiss, trailing his questing mouth down her cheek to the vulnerable curve of her throat. Those straight, impossibly white teeth nipped at her with an exquisite artistry that made a sob shudder through her. A sob of need, of despair, born of longings that could never be fulfilled. Never, by any man. Especially this bitter, anguished, reckless Irish knight.

"See, ladylight?" Aidan murmured against her heated

flesh. "I can give you what you crave, though I can't give you love. I *can* give you this." His hand swept up to capture the fluid weight of her breast, his thumb circling the pearled bud of her nipple. "And more . . . there's so much more, Norah. I can show you. The moment my ring is on your finger."

The words were icy water, drowning the flames he had ignited inside her with his consummate skill as a lover, a skill Norah knew with agonizing certainty he had learned in the beds of countless other women. Women who had offered him only the lush bounty of their bodies, the sating of mutual desires, not the striking of some cold bargain that had brought him to their bed.

The thought tore an anguished denial from her throat, and she flattened her palms against him, shoving with all her might. "No! I can't—you can't make me—"

Aidan staggered back a step, the unfathomable green of his eyes clouded with a strange light, his mouth reddened from taking hers with such fervor. "I can't make you what?" he grated, his breath rasping, a raw uncertainty about his mouth. "Can't make you want me?" he demanded, low. "By God, Norah, I already have."

The truth seared Norah's shattered nerves as nothing else could have, and she choked out, "You think I don't know what you're trying to do? Use me? Bend me to your will by—by—"

"By kissing you until your goddamn knees are weak? What? You expect me to regret that you responded to me? Or would you prefer a *gentleman,* who would attempt to lure you with soft promises and honorable deference? One who would beg for your help, and yet never dare to look beneath all your pretty tales of desiring contentment, a home, to be useful—*useful,* for God's sake? A man who would never once delve beneath your pretty protestations to what is revealed in those goddamn eyes of yours? That you, my dear, spinsterish, honorable Miss Linton, need a man."

Tears were stinging Norah's eyes, humiliation rushing in

to fill the void left by Sir Aidan's broken kiss. "How dare you?" she quavered.

"You'll discover there isn't much that I won't dare. I may be everything you've named me," he bit out roughly. "A villain. A heartless bastard prepared to use you for my own devices. But I am also a man who knows a woman's body better than you do, my sweet innocent—places that the merest brush of my fingers, the softest touch of my lips or tongue, will hold the power to make you lose every one of your high-brow principles and beg for more."

He had wounded her so deeply she couldn't breathe, ripped out the desperate secrets inside her, leaving her naked, vulnerable to his arrogance, his mockery. She groped for any weapon to drive him away.

"If that is so, then I cannot fathom why your wife would have sought consolation in so many other men's beds."

All color bled from Aidan's face, as if she had suddenly driven a knife in his chest, and for an instant his eyes were unguarded in all their wild anguish and self-doubt, all their fierce recriminations and regrets.

She expected him to rage at her, let fly the fury she must have unleashed with her calculated blow.

But Aidan only drew away from her, his lips curling, his voice bitter and soft. "Touché, madam. That was a thrust even Delia would have been proud of."

With that, he turned and strode away from her, across the floor of the ruined castle, through the break in the fairy ring, an exile from Caislean Alainn's sweet enchantment.

With her whole body trembling, Norah stared after him, hurting and angry, confused and raw. He had insulted her in every possible way, mocked her with his sensual arrogance, tried to bend her to his will by taking shameless advantage of her inexperience where the ways of pleasure were concerned.

He had wounded her, bullied her, humiliated her by reaching into the darkest recesses of her heart and ripping out the fantasies she had once held, exposing them to the harsh light of reality.

In the end, he had left her no choice but to fight back in the only way she knew how. To retain some tiny grip upon what frayed remnants of pride he had left to her.

Then why did she suddenly want to go to him, to soothe him? Heal that wound she had glimpsed for such a fleeting moment in his eyes, assuage the hunger she had sensed in his mouth, his hands? It was not the carnal desire he had spent in the bodies of so many other women, but a hunger of the spirit he didn't even know that he possessed.

Or had Sir Aidan been right when he'd cast out his accusation? a voice whispered inside her.

Was it Norah's own hunger she wanted to ease? The ache of emptiness Sir Aidan Kane's impassioned kiss had just begun to fill?

CHAPTER
8

The study at Rathcannon was as grim as Aidan's mood. Heavy burgundy draperies were drawn tight over the windows, and the dark wood paneling that rose halfway up the walls cast the lower section of the chamber in pools of dismal shadow. The pale plaster above seemed alive with phantoms whose macabre robes bled through the ornate frescoes on the walls. Aidan knew the specters well. Spirits of Kane ancestors, blackened by devil fire and the reproachful wraiths of those they had betrayed.

But tonight they were accompanied by a far more disturbing apparition: that of a determined seventeen-year-old boy who had stormed away from Ireland and his family's dark legacy, determined to rise above the scurrilous past he'd inherited. A boy who had only found that destiny was far stronger than the will of one reckless fool who dreamed of becoming a hero.

A fool who had had the dream dust clawed from his eyes by the savage talons of war, and by a girl as heartless as she was beautiful. A huntress who had used him and thrown away whatever goodness he'd struggled to dredge up from his soul in her name.

Aidan swore, stalking over to where a cut-glass brandy decanter caught the last fragments of light from the dying fire. Grasping the delicate glass piece by its neck, he sloshed yet another measure into the goblet that hadn't left his hand in the hours since he and Norah had disembarked from the mud-spattered carriage, each ominously silent, melting into the depths of Rathcannon to tend the wounds each had been dealt by the other.

Aidan had come to this room to forget, to drown his regrets, his fury . . . and, yes, damn Norah Linton to hell, his pain, any way that he could. But he had only found more specters stalking him, felt the fingers of regrets decades old clinging to his coat sleeves like beggar children.

And for some reason—his own crushing guilt, or the haunting memory of the wounded brown eyes that had gazed into his amidst Caislean Alainn's shattered beauty— he could not free himself of his demons tonight.

Aidan crossed to the desk in the center of the room and sank down into the leather chair behind it. He set the glass onto a surface bared of the usual ledgers and correspondence, tallies of livestock and business dealings that would have littered that of any industrious landowner.

Aidan had long before delegated all such affairs to his man of business. God forbid the notorious Sir Aidan Kane be distracted by an outbreak of hoof-and-mouth disease when he was at the gaming tables, or that he inadvertently muddle up some dealings with his tenants. He didn't understand a blasted thing about farming, and the people who lived on Rathcannon land already regarded him with a loathing deepened through generations of conquering Kanes. Besides which, he had wanted to devote himself to Cassandra whenever he set foot on Rathcannon land.

Yet tonight he would have been glad of the distraction of a mountain of paperwork to wade through. He would have been grateful for anything that could divert his thoughts from the scene that had played out in the exquisite ruin of Caislean Alainn.

Christ, what had he done? Last night, upon the moon-dark moors, he had decided to wed Norah Linton, to use her for Cassandra's sake, and for his own.

He had vowed to himself that he would woo the Englishwoman any way he could, with empty promises or hot kisses, with pretty lies he should have been able to utter without so much as a twinge from the deadened reaches of his conscience.

God knew, that was why he had arranged the outing at the fair, and afterward taken advantage of Cassandra's absence to bring Norah to the castle ruin. That was why he had plied the Englishwoman with romantic drivel, softening her with his words, his touch, like a master violinist, preparing a familiar instrument to play the tune he desired.

Even the kiss had been planned, the finishing stroke to drive away any doubts, to mold her to his will, to make her want him. Because that was one gift Aidan knew he possessed: the ability to bend a woman to his will by the use of his body, the sensual talents that had been but another facet of the Kane legacy. It was an ability he'd cultivated ruthlessly in the years since Delia's betrayal.

It had seemed so simple in those moments when he'd exited the breakfast parlor to find Norah hovering in the corridor, big eyed and uncertain. But somehow, within Caislean Alainn's fairy ring, the carefully plaited strands of his plan had come unraveled, and there had been no way that he could stop himself . . . from what? From showing her exactly how ruthless he could be? From exploiting not just the secrets he'd gathered from the depths of her eyes, but stripping bare any pretenses, exposing to her exactly what he was doing.

Then, worse still, he had taken her when she was fragile, uncertain, and forced his kiss onto her trembling lips, forced her to drink from a sudden and soul-wrenching river of passion he had not even suspected existed in himself.

Aidan's fingers trembled, his pulse thudding in his chest at the memory of those sweet lips.

Do you want me in your bed? he'd demanded, already imagining the far different flavor of passion he would taste in this reserved woman, one that titillated his imagination, made his sex harden and throb.

Never in all his planning and manipulating, plotting and arranging, had Sir Aidan Kane suspected that the kiss of this gentle woman would undo him so completely, confuse him so utterly.

Never had he suspected that he would want her.

Not that it mattered anymore. He grimaced. He had made damn certain he would never be Norah Linton's lover now.

She was doubtless in Delia's chamber overhead, gathering up her belongings, intent on escaping his evil clutches even if she had to walk the entire way back to Dublin.

She had to be horrified at what she had seen in his face at Caislean Alainn, and she was thanking the saints that she had discovered she'd nearly betrothed herself to the devil before taking marriage vows.

She'd be insane to wed him now that she'd looked into the darkest places in his soul, now that he'd let her see . . .

Aidan dashed the thoughts away, uncertain why they should pain him so deeply. To banish them completely, he clung to a far more familiar misery.

He had failed Cassandra. Condemned himself to a hell beyond even Lucifer's torturous imaginings. And in the process, he had somehow managed to rise above the orgy of decadence and gaming, drinking and wenching, that had been his life these past fifteen years, to sicken even himself.

Aidan closed his eyes, remembering Norah's face in stark contrast to the crumbling gray stone of the castle wall.

What kind of woman would cross a sea to marry a man she had never met, he had demanded to know. Now his conscience whispered the answer: a desperate woman, a hurting one, one wounded by the harshness of those duty-bound to protect her.

Friendless. Alone.

Just as his own innocent Cassandra might one day be, despite all his efforts to protect her.

A knife blade forever buried in his soul wrenched savagely, making him grip the edge of his useless desk with white-knuckled fingers.

No, he raged inwardly. Cassandra was worlds different from Norah Linton. He'd raised his Cass to be brave and bold, confident in her ability to challenge anyone who dared cross her. If she had to, Cassandra Kane would damn well be able to defend herself.

And yet, Aidan reasoned, downing the last of his brandy in a single fiery gulp, hadn't quiet Norah Linton dealt him a blow that had paralyzed him for long seconds? Chilled him with its deadly accuracy?

I am also a man who knows a woman's body better than you do, my sweet innocent, he had claimed in his arrogance. *Places that the merest brush of my fingers, the softest touch of lips or tongue will hold the power to make you lose every one of your high-brow principles and beg for more.*

And she had gazed up at him, with those haunting eyes that seemed to reflect condemnation of all the evil he had ever done, and said, *If that is so, then I cannot fathom why your wife would have sought consolation in so many other mens' beds.*

He'd deserved that verbal riposte, after all that he had done and said to her. But that hadn't dulled the brutal surge of uncertainty, the terror of his own inadequacy that had been Delia's parting gift to the brash youth who once would have conquered all the world's kingdoms for her sake if she had only taken a moment to . . . to what? Aidan thought bitterly. To love him?

His chest aching, he buried his face in one hand, exhausted by the inevitability of it all. Disgusted with his failures—with Rathcannon, with Delia, and with the

Englishwoman who had been set adrift by the fates and landed on his doorstep, like the most capricious of salvations.

If there were a shred of decency in his jaded heart, he would go to Norah this instant and apologize, give her whatever aid she required to leave Rathcannon, Ireland, and most of all himself.

If he had a lick of sense, he would arrange for her departure before Cassandra got more deeply attached to her, or he sank deeper into the strange fever Norah's innocent kiss had inspired in him.

But he'd spent a lifetime taking up the dice when all seemed lost, to cast them one last time. . . .

A soft knock at the door made Aidan straighten, dragging one hand through his hair in an effort to neaten the unruly tresses. His pulse quickened, and he bid the person enter, half expecting it would be Norah, wrapped up in pelisse and bonnet, ready to leave Rathcannon.

But when the door opened, it was a rosy-cheeked Cass who peeped her head in. Aidan's brows lowered in puzzlement. God knew he couldn't remember the last time the chit had bothered announcing herself before she came careening in to greet him.

"Papa, whatever are you doing?" she demanded. "We've been waiting and waiting to start dinner! Do you want Miss Linton to think you're always late?"

"Miss Linton?" Aidan echoed, dazed. "She can't mean to dine with . . ." *With the bastard who'd humiliated her, who'd taken advantage of her.* "I was certain that after what happened, she . . ." He bit the words off abruptly as his daughter shoved the door wide.

"After *what* happened?" Cass queried, her eyes lit with that unpredictable light Aidan had long before learned to mistrust. "Papa, what on earth did you do?"

"Why are you so certain *I* did something amiss?" Aidan said in an effort to deflect her curiosity. "Isn't it possible your precious Miss Linton—"

"Did what?" Cassandra repeated with a laugh. "Ravish you on the trip home from the fair?"

Aidan's cheeks burned, and he looked away, scowling. "Cass, you dumped this woman in my lap, for God's sake. From now on, can you please let *me* handle the infernal courtship?"

Cassandra tossed her curls, candlelight picking out an adorable smudge of flour on her regal nose. "If you're already sulking in here, you cannot be doing a very good job of it. And even though Miss Linton *did* come down to dinner tonight, she's not exactly chattering madly about what a lovely drive the two of you had back to Rathcannon this afternoon. Even with my very best wheedling, I could scarce pry out a single word."

The idea of Cass badgering Norah was more than Aidan could endure. Hadn't he made enough of a mess of the afternoon without a nosy fifteen-year-old digging around the whole incident with that single-minded determination of her sex?

"Hellfire and damnation, Cass, let it be!" he roared. "The woman is under my roof, isn't she? I took her to the goddamn fair, didn't I? What the devil did you expect? That the instant she stepped out of the coach we would fall into each other's arms in abject devotion?"

His daughter's eyes sparkled with an aura far more ominous than storm clouds edging the rim of the sea. "It seems to me that you could make a bit more of an effort. If you would only—"

"Take your infernal little nose out of my courtship, blast it!"

"Your . . . courtship?" Cass's eyes sparkled, triumph emanating from her in waves.

"Don't make more of it than there is, Cass. Just because I've decided to tolerate the woman doesn't mean you should begin to call her 'Mama.' She may very well decide that we don't suit."

"But you *do* suit. Perfectly! You don't think I would have

135

gone to the trouble of finding a bride for you without giving the candidates serious consideration, do you?"

"Candidates? Plural?" Aidan said with a sinking heart. "Don't tell me there are a dozen other women floating about who are privy to my entire life story à la Cassandra."

"Well, actually, Miss Linton *was* the only one who answered the advertisement, but she was so wonderful I was certain it was fate."

"Fate." *Do you believe in fate, Miss Linton?* The words reverberated in Aidan's mind. *I see two people who need each other. Badly. . . .*

"Oh, Papa! Don't you see, I'm certain I can help—"

"I've had all the help from you I can stomach, thank you very much. *No more meddling!* Do we understand each other? I want your word on it, Cassandra Victorine."

She batted her lashes, thrusting her hands behind her back. "I swear, Papa! From this very instant, I will not—"

"Not interfere," he prompted in steely accents.

"I'll try my very, very hardest, but—"

"No 'buts.' Now let's not keep Miss Linton waiting any longer."

"Wonderful, Papa! I just have to dodge back to the kitchen to make certain all is well. I helped Cook stir up your favorite dish tonight, Papa! A most delightful chocolate cake, with raspberries atop it."

He didn't even have the energy to fall into one of their favorite teasing games regarding Cass's culinary disasters of the past as he watched his daughter dart out of the room shining with optimism. Optimism Aidan was certain he would one day destroy.

His tread was decidedly slower as he exited the study door. He paused before a gilt looking glass long enough to make an attempt to straighten his cravat, but the limp folds were mangled beyond repair. Aidan's features twisted in disgust. Not that it would matter what he looked like. After what had transpired by the castle ruins, he doubted Miss

Linton would be impressed if he turned up in full court dress.

He sucked in a deep breath as he approached the dining room, hoping to hear Cass's chirrupy voice emanating from the room, a buffer in the first awkward moments when he and Norah were forced to confront one another. But there was only silence.

He heaved a weary sigh. Of course Cass would be contrary enough to be absent when he would actually have been grateful for a little of her "interference."

But perhaps it would be better if he and Norah got this first uncomfortable meeting over with, minus the all-too-keen scrutiny of his daughter.

By force of will, Aidan attempted to drain the tension from his features, then stepped into the room. He'd thought himself prepared to see the woman again, having pictured the countless feminine facets of behavior one could anticipate after the type of scene that had taken place at the castle ruins. But Norah Linton was neither defiant nor petulant, scornful nor wounded, teary eyed nor stonily silent.

She stood before the window overlooking Rathcannon's hills, one delicate hand pressed against the mullioned panes. Her slender body was veiled by muslin the color of a dove's breast, devoid of any ornament save a single amber ribbon that tied at her throat. The gown would have seemed stark on any other woman, and yet it provided the perfect foil for Norah, not overpowering the purity of her profile, but picking out elusive streaks of dark gold that threaded through hair that glistened unexpectedly lustrous in the candlelight.

At the sound of footsteps, she raised her gaze to his, and Aidan was stunned to see—not censure, not loathing, not disgust, but a soft apology, an understanding that made him want to take her by the arms and shake her, remind her how badly he had treated her, and warn her not to trust his motives even now.

The only thing that betrayed her nervousness was the smudge of pink upon her cheekbones and the smile she gave him, tremulous and uncertain. Was it possible she had decided to forgive him?

"I can't accustom myself to how green everything is here," she said. "After the dullness of the city, it makes one so thirsty to drink it in."

"Sometimes when I'm away too long it is like a hunger inside me, that yearning to drink in the greenness. It's as if I can't truly breathe anyplace else." He felt like a fool—a raw lad who had bungled his first kiss and come, penitent, to beg pardon. The sensation irritated him, and he brushed it away, impatient with his own odd vulnerability.

With long strides, he crossed to where she stood and grasped her hand, raising it softly to his lips. "I feel honored that you've chosen to dine with us tonight. Honored, and . . . somewhat surprised."

Lashes astonishingly thick swept down over her dark eyes, not coquettishly but with regret. "It seemed to mean so much to Cassandra that I . . ." She stopped, her gaze flicking up to his for a heartbeat. "She is going to be so disappointed when . . ."

She didn't finish the sentence. She didn't have to. Norah Linton had endings written all over her innocent eyes.

Aidan was stunned at the wrenching sensation in his chest. It was time for him to charm her, beguile her, the way he knew so well how to. It was time for soft pleas and honeyed promises. Instead, his fingers tightened on those slender fingers, so cold, so small in his own. "You're leaving us, then?"

"The sooner the better—for Cassandra's sake. It wouldn't do for her to get her heart any more set on things that are impossible."

He nodded, uncertain why those quiet words made him feel so bereft. "I don't suppose there is anything I can say that would make you reconsider?"

Her gaze fluttered up to his, and there were no lies in his eyes as he peered down at her.

"Norah, I know we've not begun right. And this afternoon . . ."

Her cheeks went scarlet, the hue making an almost startling change in that face that had been far too solemn and pale.

"Please! It's already forgotten," she protested, so hastily Aidan was certain she had relived that kiss in the ensuing hours as many excruciating times as he had.

His lips curved into a wry smile. "I'm not certain whether to feel shriven of my sins or bruised in the ego, milady."

"I—I'm sure it would have been a very lovely kiss. I mean, as kisses go, I've not had a great deal of experience. But had circumstances been different, I . . ." She raised a hand to her cheek as if to cool it. "Please. I just wish to get through this dinner and then go in peace."

Peace. Had Aidan ever known what that was? He wanted to plead with her, rail at her, coerce her into staying. He wanted to kiss her again, to melt his mouth into the pliant warmth of hers.

But he only reached out to squeeze her hand.

At that moment a hurricane in hair ribbons came bounding out the servants' door. Norah jerked away from his clasp, but not before Cassandra's bright eyes had caught a glimpse of their joined fingers. Pure elation shone in her gaze, and Aidan knew—in a sudden, aching instant—just how crestfallen the girl would be when Norah Linton went away.

CHAPTER

9

"Come to the table," Cassandra enthused. "Everything is *perfect,* despite the fact that *some* people were inexcusably late." Aidan tucked Norah's hand into the crook of his arm and escorted her to the seat beside him that had been empty for so long.

He'd thought the endless ride home from Caislean Alainn had been abysmal, the hours in his study interminably long. But this supper so carefully planned by Cassandra, this eternity of looking into his daughter's hopeful face, was by far the worst punishment he could endure. Unless, of course, it was his agonizing awareness of the woman picking at the food upon her plate as Cass shamelessly grilled her about her life in London.

"Miss Linton, did you ever have a London season?" Cassandra asked, her eyes shining expectantly.

"Yes. I had one."

"Was it magical?" Cass asked, taking a bite of Cornish hen. "Did you go to breakfasts and balls, and Almack's, and dance and dance with the most handsome men?"

"Actually I spent most of my time hiding behind pillars, wishing heartily that whatever entertainment I was attending was over," Norah said, sipping at her wine. "And as for my dancing partners, they were . . ."

Aidan was amazed to see a dimple appear in one cheek.

"They were not exactly the sort to inspire flutterings in feminine hearts."

"You mean they were oafish? Did they—did they attempt to lure you into the gardens and steal a kiss?" the girl asked with an eloquent sigh.

"Cassandra!" Aidan snapped, all too aware what the fate of a young woman like Norah must have been upon the marriage mart. "For God's sake, let poor Miss Linton eat her dinner in peace!"

"I don't mind. Really."

"You see, Papa? She is most amenable! Didn't I tell you that she was the most perfect—"

"Cass!"

The girl desisted, but Aidan's gut twisted as she charged into an even more unwelcome subject. "My mama had bushels and bushels of suitors, Mrs. Brindle says. She was the belle of the season, she was so beautiful and witty, and—did you ever meet her? Miss Cordelia March?"

"No. I'm certain even if we had been out at the same time, I would hardly have moved in the same circles as an acclaimed belle." Norah said it so gently Aidan felt guilt gnaw him afresh.

"Oh." A flush spread onto Cassandra's cheeks, and Aidan was certain she had just realized how she'd blundered into a subject that must be painful for the woman she so desperately wanted to please. "I'm sorry. I didn't mean to—to . . . Papa's forever telling me I shouldn't go poking about other people's business, but I just can't seem to help it. He says I am terminally curious and is constantly barraging me with hopeless clichés about cats being killed and such like."

Norah blessed the girl with a smile of pure understanding. "Don't distress yourself. I've long since gotten over any disappointment I felt. In fact, I have actually succeeded in regarding the entire affair somewhat in the light of a diverting farce."

"A farce?" Aidan repeated, trying to conceal the hollow sensation he suffered at the knowledge that Cassandra's dreams of such a season were slipping from his fingers forever, to be lost the instant the coach wheels carried Norah Linton away. "I cannot think of a better analogy for the madness that possesses London society at such times."

"Papa, you just don't understand how wonderful it seems. I am quite certain I would adore—" Cassandra bit off the sentence, casting an apologetic glance at Norah. "But maybe I am mistaken. From what you say, Miss Linton, it must have been terrible."

Norah laughed, a subtle, musical sound that sank into Aidan's very bones. "I cannot imagine you hiding behind pillars as I did. Even if you tried, I'd imagine that enterprising gentlemen would come to roust you out." She had meant to comfort the child, Aidan knew, but the instant Norah recalled what he had confided to her regarding the bleakness of his daughter's prospects, he could see the unease ripple to life in her eyes.

Oblivious to the undercurrents between the adults, Cass rushed on. "Surely you must have had *some* gentlemen attend you. Your eyes are lovely. Especially when you smile. You're *so* comfortable to be with, and you have the most cunning sense of humor."

Aidan winced at the reminder of his own callous estimation of Norah's appearance the night before, the flash of pain he had seen in those expressive eyes. "Cass, what a thing to say!"

"You can't fault the child for telling the truth, can you, Sir Aidan?" Norah asked, looking at him in a forthright manner that made him tug at the disreputable folds of his neckcloth.

"Actually," Norah continued, "I did have a few feathers in my cap. The first was an earl."

"An earl!" Cass clasped her hands to her breast. "Why, that would be a marvelous match! I'd wager all the beauties you spoke of were green with envy!"

"Not for long, I'm afraid." The dimple danced again. "You see, Lord Lavensby had the ill manners to die before he came up to scratch."

"How tragic! No wonder you were heartbroken! Did he die a hero? My papa was one—a hero, I mean. At Badajoz in the Peninsular War. You know, I wrote you the tale in my letters."

"Battle tales are hardly appropriate fare at the dinner table, Cass," Aidan said, dashed uncomfortable at the reminder of those infernal Banbury tales Cass had used to lure this woman to Rathcannon.

As if she sensed his discomfort, Norah jumped in. "Lord Lavensby's demise was nothing quite so noble as your father's heroics. Nor was his death surprising, considering the circumstances."

"The circumstances?" Aidan couldn't help himself, the barely suppressed laughter in those dark eyes intriguing him.

"His lordship was eighty-six years old."

"Oh! Oh, how disgusting!" Cassandra shuddered, revolted. Aidan, on the other hand, felt a swift stab of empathy for the girl Norah must have been, forced to endure the lecherous advances of a wizened old man.

"My next suitor was the Honorable Fiddlestone Biltmore. He had the most unfortunate resemblance to a toad." At Cassandra's gasp, Norah laughed. "It's true, I'm afraid. He had a prodigious belly he covered with the most garish waistcoats imaginable, and he was cursed with an uncommonly wide mouth that split huge, round cheeks. And when he laughed, it came out in the most amazing croak."

"Not truly! You're teasing!"

"No. I vow it is the God's truth. Fortunately for me, his mama brought him to heel before he was overcome with passion for me. In the end he married an heiress with a rabbity face. I always wondered what their children would look like."

"There must have been *some*one more—more appealing. Just one dancing partner. Anything but a withered old corpse and a toad-person."

Those dark eyes lowered for an instant, and her smile softened in a way that made Aidan frown. "Actually, there was one. He wasn't my suitor, exactly. He was . . . one of my stepbrother's friends. He rescued me from behind my pillar on one occasion."

"Was he quite handsome?"

"Half the belles were in love with Philip, the others just refused to admit it. He was handsome and gallant and—and he saw me in the light of a rather grubby little sister, I'm afraid. But I will always be grateful to him for dancing with me that night."

"Why should you feel grateful?" Aidan felt compelled to demand, inexplicably irritated with this high-brow gallant. "Did you tread upon his toes? I doubt it could have been much of a hardship to drag you about a ballroom for a little while."

The laughter was gone from her lips, leaving them vulnerable, shadowed with remembered pain. "For some reason I had earned the enmity of the reigning belle, and I'm afraid she was quite pointed in her disdain of me. Philip overheard some rather cruel remarks, and—"

"He came to your rescue?" Cass enthused. "Just like a hero in those delicious French novels?"

"Damme, girl, if Mrs. Brindle has been allowing you to read those things, I'll have her head!" Aidan snapped, but he was all too aware of the cruel phenomenon Norah had described. He had seen Delia and her set ruthlessly carving to ribbons girls with less claim to beauty or wealth, girls without that killer instinct more virulent than any he had ever witnessed upon a battlefield.

"I read the tales at Lila Matterling's, Papa. Her parents

aren't so hopelessly old fashioned! Now tell, Miss Linton: Did you both fall madly in love?"

"If we had, I would hardly be here now, would I, dearling?" She dismissed the girl's query, but Aidan couldn't help but notice the darting of shyness that clung about those dark-lashed eyes, the fleeting pensiveness that tugged at the corners of her lips. Why the devil such variations in her expression should bother him was beyond Aidan's comprehension.

I haven't had much experience where kissing is concerned. . . . Her stammered words echoed in his memory. Had her charming, gallant Philip felt duty-bound to kiss her as well as dance with her?

For some reason Aidan was damned reluctant to find out the answer. With grim determination, he changed the subject, firmly withstanding his daughter's efforts to probe more deeply into Norah's past.

Yet the whole revelation had left a decidedly bitter taste in his mouth, one that conspired with the inevitability of Miss Linton's departure to rob him of his appetite and leave him decidedly raw.

By the time Cass flew out to help serve up this mysterious dessert she had aided Cook in concocting, Aidan would've been glad of a fire in his own fields if it meant he could escape this grindingly uncomfortable scene.

But Cass breezed out in the wake of a footman bearing two plates with chocolate cake, drizzled over with a raspberry syrup.

"Cass, I'm really not that hungry," Aidan said, eyeing askance the plate-cracking portion she had presented him with. Then he muttered, "Especially after the journey into indigestion your last culinary experiment led me on. Remember how you forgot the sugar?"

He had only meant to tease, but she affected such a wounded expression he cursed himself roundly.

"Papa, how could you bring that up now?" she asked, casting a pointed glance at Miss Linton.

"How could I not? It was almost the end of me."

Cassandra's chin gave a little quiver. "I made it especially for you. But if you don't want it . . . well, I'll not cram it down your throat, even though I did burn three fingers baking it up for you." She displayed the tiny blisters with the artlessness of a six-year-old.

"Sir Aidan, surely you can at least taste it." Norah Linton's voice was as censorious as if she'd caught him plucking the wings from a fairy princess. "I only wish that I could eat it."

Cassandra looked at her with woeful eyes. "You can't eat at least a little?"

"Not unless you want me to break out in the most dreadful scarlet spots," Norah explained.

Aidan eyed his own plate fatalistically, knowing that between Norah's refusal and his own fatherly transgressions he would probably have to lick the crumbs from his plate.

Manfully, he dredged up a forkful of cake fairly oozing with raspberry sauce and put it in his mouth. It was all he could do not to go into fits of choking. Horrendous, bitter, he was reasonably certain that scum-covered dishwater would've tasted more appealing.

He glanced at Norah, hoping that somehow the Englishwoman would say something, do something that would allow him to forgo poisoning himself with Cassandra's latest brew. But Norah was gazing quite wistfully at her untasted portion. When she nibbled at a bit of plain chocolate cake and smiled at Cassandra, saying how wonderful the stuff must taste, Aidan was convinced that Norah Linton must be a runaway from Bedlam.

Cass was positively radiant at her praise. "Papa is always tormenting me when I help Cook. When I baked him a birthday cake last year, he was abominable! He even said he dared not feed it to his dogs, lest they turn their toes up dead."

"Cass, even you couldn't eat the stuff," Aidan protested, aware of Miss Linton's quelling stare.

146

"But I've been practicing, and Cook says this is the most delicious raspberry sauce she's ever tasted. Miss Linton, couldn't you just take the tiniest taste?"

"I'm afraid not, but it looks delicious. Whatever did you put in this?" Norah asked, with what could only be genuine interest.

Cassandra cast him a baleful glare, then preened. "Why, lots of sugar, and berries, of course. Fresh-picked. And then, well, there were some other ingredients." She gave a most unsettling smile. "But I promised to keep them a secret."

Whatever they were, Aidan was damned sure he didn't want to know. He took another forkful, swallowing it with all the haste of a child taking codliver oil. To keep from gagging, he washed it down with a gulp of wine. The footman scurried over to refill his glass, and Aidan was tempted to ask him to leave the bottle. God knew he was going to need it.

He must've devised a dozen schemes of slipping the horrendous confection off his plate and into the oblivion where it belonged, but it seemed as if Cassandra watched every mouthful, prodding him unmercifully with wistful comments about his former rejections of her efforts, bolstering her demands by drawing countless compliments from Norah.

By the end, Aidan was certain he would've betrayed his own mother to spare himself one more forkful of the dish he'd already christened Cassandra's Curse.

But when he saw the look of absolute delight in his daughter's eyes when he was finished, he was almost tempted to ask for more. He would have, had he not been prey to a serious wish to survive the night.

His insides were already markedly unamused. He could only sincerely hope they wouldn't fly into outright rebellion. But in truth, he couldn't be certain exactly what was leaving him so on edge: Cass's concoction, or his own sense of guilt as he watched Cassandra catch Norah Linton's hand, bubbling with enthusiasm as she led her into the drawing room.

What worse torment could he have endured than listening to their laughter as Norah expounded on her shortcomings in the accepted feminine accomplishments of needlework, music, and drawing, describing in detail the samplers that had been relegated to dust cloths, the watercolor landscapes that had all the pastoral tranquillity of Armageddon, complete with rampaging sea monsters instead of swans.

It was as though the knowledge that she would soon be leaving somehow freed the woman, left her at ease, and the demonic fates were determined to show Aidan exactly how perfectly she was suited to deal with his daughter.

He lounged in his chair, listening to Cassandra's chatter and Norah's replies, their subtle wisdom hidden in drolleries that left Cass gasping with laughter. The same comments left him sullen and resentful, angry and aware, for the first time, how insular his nights with Cass had become. How this woman's laughter blew like spring's fresh breezes through the room.

He listened as Cassandra cozened Norah into singing, despite protestations that she couldn't carry a tune if it were nailed inside a keg. And then he was furious to find her off-key warbling more endearing than any of the practiced solos he had heard in the finest drawing rooms of London.

The only time a shadow fell across features illuminated by candlelight was when she hazarded a glance his way. Then a shyness darted into her eyes, an uncertainty that made him want to cross the room in three swift strides and press his lips against hers to remind her—and remind himself—that she would be leaving in the morning. He needed to still the sound of her laughter, her voice, to banish it, the way he wished he could banish the delicate scent of milk of roses that drifted from her hair to tantalize his nostrils.

He gritted his teeth, assuring himself that it was not desire for this woman that he felt, but the residue of the encounter he'd had with his mistress before he left the gaming house two nights before—the fact that he hadn't taken the time to fulfill the sensual fantasies Stasia had been whispering in his ear from the first roll of the dice. Those were the pent-up tensions that set him on a blade edge of awareness with this woman whom he'd thought boasted little claim to beauty. Until he had seen her lips reddened from his kiss, felt her gasp with astonishment and pleasure as his tongue had slipped into the sweetness of her mouth. Until he had found her with her hand pressed against the window, her incredible eyes filled with sorrowful dreams.

And now she sat, smiling with his daughter, as if she would be at Rathcannon forever, acceding to Cass's every plea, her hand sweeping out to stroke his daughter's fairy-gold hair with a heartbreaking tenderness, a sense of loss buried so deep in those dark eyes, Aidan was certain he was the only one who could see it. It was a genuine tenderness, not the careless caresses Delia had so rarely given to their daughter—as if Cassandra were a pretty little pug, whose mistress sadly neglected her, yet refused to part with her plaything.

The realization ate inside Aidan like poison, coiling inside him with the raging tension that had been building in him from the moment they had left the dining table.

"Papa!" He was startled from his dark thoughts by Cassandra's plea. "You're being a far worse boor than Norah's toad-person! You've barely said a word all night. Whatever is amiss?"

It was as if his daughter's petulant question shattered something inside him. The sight of Cassandra, an angel in white muslin, clasping Norah Linton's hand made reality crash down about Aidan's shoulders.

"Cass, there's something you need to know," he said, his stomach knotting painfully. "Miss Linton is leaving Rathcannon in the morning."

"What?" Cassandra shrank back, her face even more stricken than Aidan had feared it would be. "But things have been going so—so wonderfully. She—Miss Linton, you—you like Rathcannon. . . . You think it's beautiful. I know that you do! And me . . ." Her voice trailed off uncertainly, questions welling up in her eyes. Aidan could see the uncertainties were breaking Norah's heart.

"I think you are charming, sweetheart," Norah said. "But . . ."

"Is it Papa, then? I know he was reprehensible when you arrived, but he's promised that he'd court you now. And he must be good at it, because all the housemaids sigh over how—how handsome he is, and how dashing. I'm not supposed to know that, but I can hardly help it."

Those dark eyes flicked to Aidan's, distress and confusion warring in their depths—that, and just enough accusation to put Aidan's teeth on edge. "Cassandra, the simple truth is that your father doesn't want a wife. He loves you very much, and I know how much he wants to make you happy. But you cannot force people to . . . to fall in love."

"You don't have to fall in love right away," Cassandra insisted. "Oh, it would be lovely if you did, but you don't have to in order to marry. Tell her, Papa. You and Mama, you didn't love each other."

Aidan reeled at Cassandra's words, sick with the certainty that she must have some memory of the vile mockery that had been her parents' marriage. "Cass, your mother and I . . . we cared about each other at first. We lost each other as time passed. The difference is that we had you to bind us together."

"I'm certain in time you and Miss Linton can have more babies, little brothers and sisters for me to spoil quite abominably. That would make you happy, Miss Linton, wouldn't it? In your letters, you said how much you wanted children. With Papa, I'm certain you'll have the most beautiful little green-eyed babies."

Scarlet spilled onto Norah's cheeks, filling Aidan with images that were far too painfully sharp and clear, images of what it would be like to fill her with his child.

Christ, didn't every man picture such a thing? His woman, glowing, blossoming with the fruit of his passion, a soft, secret bond that could never be broken?

No. He'd learned the hard way exactly how much sentimental rubbish such dreams were.

Aidan's jaw clenched at the memory of Delia's reaction to the joyous announcement that she was going to bear him a babe: hysterics, fury, loathing, as if he'd planted a monster inside her instead of a helpless, fragile new life.

"There will be no babies. There will be no wedding."

"But you said you were going to court her! I don't understand."

"Cassandra, it's too late. I . . . made mistakes."

"Mistakes? What did you do, Papa? To make her unhappy? Why did you—"

"Cassandra." Norah's voice was sharp yet strangely bracing. "Listen to me. This is not your father's fault. It's not anyone's fault."

"Then why are you running away? Running away like my mother ran away?" The girl wheeled on her father, tears streaking her cheeks. "Papa, why are you making her run away?"

Agony ripped white-hot through Aidan's veins. Oh, God. Had his little girl believed that all along? Blamed him for Delia's defection and death in some secret part of her soul?

"Cass, after what happened with—with your mother and I, surely you must see Miss Linton deserves far better than marriage to a man who cannot love her."

"You *could* love her if you'd just put forth some effort! I already do! Papa, she doesn't have anywhere else to go!"

"Damn it, Cass, she doesn't want to stay here! Ask her, for God's sake!"

Cassandra cast a desperate glance at Norah. What she saw made her face crumple, a sob tearing from her throat. "It's not fair! I already lost one mother! How can you make me lose another one?"

With that she spun and ran from the room, the sound of her desolate sobs knifing through Aidan's vitals, leaving in their wake the most savage regret he'd ever known.

Silence pulsed in the room for long seconds, Cassandra's

desolation seeming to have a life of its own. Slowly, Aidan turned to where Norah stood white-faced, her own eyes glistening with tears.

"I'm so . . . so sorry," she said, in a quavering voice. "Should I go to her?"

"Why? So she can become even more attached to you?" Aidan lashed out in his own blinding pain. "Just get the devil out of here before you make it any worse."

The tears shivered on her lashes, but Aidan was too far gone in his own pain to care. He turned his back on her as Norah ran from the room.

CHAPTER

10

Norah rushed about the Blue Room, flinging her belongings into her trunk as if to hasten her escape from Rathcannon and the hard-eyed man who had kissed her to madness and the fairy-like girl who had wanted a mother so desperately it broke Norah's heart.

Leave, before you make things even worse, Aidan Kane had ordered her. Had it only been hours before in the drawing room? Even the harshness of his words had not concealed the anguish he was suffering, the scathing wound his daughter's words had raked in his spirit. Norah had known her inevitable departure would be difficult for Cassandra. And despite the shortness of her acquaintance with Sir Aidan, she had realized how difficult it would be for him to upset his only child. A child he adored in a way that wrenched Norah's heart, a child who, she was certain, could easily break Sir Aidan's own—that vulnerable heart the Irish knight tried so hard to deny he possessed.

What had she been thinking of, letting her growing

affection for Aidan Kane's willful, delightful daughter show? She had only wanted to drive away the nagging uncertainties of her own future for just one night and enjoy the daughter she would never have. She had wanted to forge a memory to take with her from the ashes of the dreams she had dared to spin during the days after she had received the first precious letter from Ireland.

But she had only tantalized the girl with things that could never be, pointing out with ruthless clarity empty places, not only in her own life but in Cassandra's as well.

Norah placed the last garment into her open trunk, then brushed one hand across the traveling costume she had put out for the morning journey.

No, there was no question she needed to leave Rathcannon. The only uncertainty was where to go when she did so. Was it possible for her to throw herself on Richard's mercy? Did she dare embroil her stepbrother any further in her difficulties, knowing the possible consequences should Winston Farnsworth discover his son was harboring the disobedient stepdaughter who had publicly shamed him?

Even if she did go back to London, she could hardly remain dependent on Richard forever. The idea of living on someone else's charity once again was more repugnant to her than ever, now that she had escaped that fate even for such a short time.

The notion of acquiring a position as governess and devoting herself to other people's children could hardly be expected to hold any delight when she had been foolishly spinning out daydreams of holding her own babies in her arms.

Babies who had acquired unruly dark hair and flashing green eyes in the days she had stayed at Rathcannon, babies with a softer version of Aidan Kane's bedazzling smile.

She closed her eyes against a wrenching sense of loss. No, there would be no emerald-eyed lover filling her with his seed. No delight in splaying a hard masculine hand over her belly, to feel the first miraculous flutterings of a life they had created together.

She would never lie in a bridal bed, her veins singing with that primitive thrill she'd tasted in the dizzying moments when Sir Aidan had mated his mouth with hers.

Not that she would want to surrender herself to Aidan Kane now, Norah hastened to assure herself. Or would she?

It would have been so easy to answer that question two hours ago. Dismiss Sir Aidan Kane as an arrogant libertine, a cad. But now?

Norah hesitated an instant, her eyes shifting to the door that joined her bedchamber to his own, the agitated sounds of movement beyond that carved oak panel rasping against her nerves.

Yet instead of the intricate carvings, she saw Sir Aidan as he had been in the ruin of Caislean Alainn, so certain of his carnal power over her, disdaining love even as he introduced her to the heady power of passion. She remembered him as he had appeared in Rathcannon's dining room, his eyes dark and aching, subdued when she told him she was leaving.

Is there anything I can do to make you reconsider?

Why had he suddenly made such a plea, sincerity glimmering beneath that usually rakish gaze?

He had looked at her as if she were something precious that was slipping from his grasp.

And when she had asked to go in peace, he had enfolded her hand in his warm, strong one, that touch conveying a far more eloquent apology for his behavior than words ever could.

She had watched him undergo a transformation a dozen times. From the debauched scoundrel to the doting father. From reluctant hero to a man with loneliness hidden beneath his scoundrel's facade—a loneliness every bit as bleak as Norah's own.

A loneliness that had almost given Norah cause to hope . . . for what? That they could somehow forge a bond on shared misery? That they could weave their futures together in the patterns of one of Cassandra Kane's fairy tales and live happily ever after?

Happy, when so much pain, so many questions and dark mysteries, still lay between them?

Norah's gaze flicked to the silver box in which the cryptic note still rested. She shivered, Cassandra's distraught face rising in her mind; the girl's cry was that of a hurting child as she'd accused her father of making her mother run away.

Sir Aidan had looked sick, stricken, at his daughter's accusation, guilt tearing with brutal evidence across his features. Guilt, and a hideous sense of shock, as if the girl had unconsciously ripped away a meager covering on a festering wound.

Norah couldn't help but recall the sinister hints buried in the mysterious note. What had happened the night Delia Kane had died? Had she been running away, as Cassandra had claimed? If that was so, she had bolted headlong to her own doom.

It seemed impossible. And yet, was she being naive—no, positively foolish—in trying to dismiss such grim charges? Sir Aidan had made no secret that he'd despised his wife, a woman who, from what Kane had confided, had committed transgressions that would have driven more than one man of Norah's acquaintance into a fit of murderous rage. And even Cassandra had obviously known her parents' desperate unhappiness, despite the fact that Norah sensed Sir Aidan would have shielded his daughter from any such ugliness, even if it cost him his last drop of blood.

Norah nibbled at her lower lip. If Aidan Kane were responsible for his wife's death, would his face have taken on that gray hue at the girl's accusations? Would his features have twisted so grimly, like a man in abject agony, battling to get a handle on his pain?

If Aidan Kane's soul were blackened by such a heinous sin, why would she have felt the almost unquenchable need to reach out to him in that moment? To comfort, to heal wounds she doubted he even knew were hidden inside him?

Blast the man, he was an enigma. If only he were not as mesmerizing as he was incomprehensible. If only he hadn't reached out to her so fleetingly with those aching eyes, that strange vulnerability clinging to lips that would have been far easier to dismiss had they remained only blatantly sensual, filled with mockery.

If she had not been able to picture all too clearly what it would be like to brush his mouth with hers—not in the courtesan's kiss he had treated her to in the castle ruins but, rather, a healing kiss, one that would take away his pain.

Norah felt a lump rise in her throat and burn there, born of her own regret as she pictured Cassandra Kane, likely sobbing out her misery into her pillow. Aidan Kane's bond with his daughter was obviously shaken. "Why did it have to turn out this way?" Norah breathed the words aloud. "It hurts so badly."

A cry of regret rose in Norah's breast, but before it could find voice, it was echoed by a sound of such anguish it rocked her to the marrow of her bones.

She stilled, as that muted sound rippled forth beneath the oaken doorway, the restless noises that had drawn her attention before more disturbing than ever.

She took a tentative step toward the tightly closed door, then stopped to listen. She stiffened as she heard a guttural groan, then the shuffling noises of someone tossing and turning.

Sir Aidan? Norah pressed her fingertips against her lips. Who else could it possibly be?

She listened a moment longer, expecting Sir Aidan's valet or one of the other servants to hear him and come to help him, but there was no sound except Sir Aidan's muffled groans.

Norah's lips compressed in a white line. What if he were

really ill? She could hardly leave the man to suffer in the next room. Yet could she charge into this man's bedchamber demanding to know what was amiss?

Excuse me for the impropriety, Sir Aidan, but I heard you moaning just a moment ago.

Her cheeks flamed. Surely he would summon up his servants if he needed help. Wouldn't he? She had all but resolved to stalk to her bed and pull the pillow over her head to drown out the sounds when another groan rent the quiet of the night. In that instant, she made the decision.

Resolutely, Norah rummaged her wrapper from the still-open trunk. Flinging it about her, she paced back to the door.

Her fist trembled, but she gritted her teeth and rapped on the panel. "Sir Aidan?" Norah called through the doorway.

A spate of tortured curses singed her ears, mingled with the thrashing sounds of hard male flesh against bedclothes, a thud of feet against the floor.

"Leave me . . . the hell . . . alone." That deep voice that had once taunted her rasped miserably. "Can't . . . god-damn man die . . . in peace?"

Before she could think, Norah had turned the doorknob, pushing experimentally against it. She was surprised to feel the panel give way.

The room was huge, with heavy, dark furniture generations old. A Jacobean bedstead stood in ornate glory, hangings of forest-green velvet flowing from its carved posts. A branch of candles in a silver holder blazed on a stand beside the bed, illuminating it in waves of flickering orange and red shadows, casting the white sheets and tumbled coverlets into stark relief. But Sir Aidan was not among them. He stood before the wide-flung windows, and moonlight turned the sweat-limned sinews of his bare back. Stripped to nothing but his breeches, he leaned out into the night, his dark hair clinging to his neck, the corded muscles of his body standing out alarmingly, like whipcords so tight they were about to snap.

"Sir Aidan?" Norah queried softly, a flutter of panic bubbling in her throat at her own boldness.

"Go away!" Kane bellowed. Norah might have fled if he hadn't gripped his stomach with white-knuckled fingers. "Ah, sonofabitch!"

Sweat beaded his brow, his glazed features contorted.

"What is it?" Norah demanded, rushing to his side. "What's wrong?"

"Insides on fire." Agony vibrated deep in his voice. "And didn't even . . . have the pleasure of drinking myself into . . . oblivion to start the flame."

"Where is your valet? We need to summon help."

"Tried. Probably off drinking the champagne . . . supposed to be polishing . . . Hessians with."

She put her arm around him, attempting to brace his weight. Ever so carefully, she struggled to ease him back toward his bed, but the distance seemed interminable, her alarm fueled by the deep trembling in his rigid muscles, the strange, clammy chill to the skin pressed so close to her own. He stumbled, groping for something to steady himself, his large fist knotting in the front of her dressing gown, tearing the loosely tied knot free. The silk of the wrapper fell away, and he buried his face against the swell of Norah's breast, his ragged breath singeing her through the meager shield of her nightgown, his lips taut, twisted, dampening the place where they had fallen.

If the man had not been in such a hideous state, Norah would have been mortified. As it was, she tightened her own grip about him, praying she could make it the dozen steps to the bed.

She banged into a table, something breakable shattering on the floor.

Sir Aidan swore again. "Crazy. Whole house . . . going to hear—"

"I hope to God they will. You've got to get help."

"No! Can't—find you in here."

She was stunned at the realization that this self-proclaimed villain, supposedly jaded beyond redemption, was trying to shield her honor, despite the fact that he was in such horrible condition.

"Be . . . all right," he gasped. "Just give . . . a minute." But at that instant, his lean body was gripped by another shuddering wave of pain that shook Norah to her core.

"Help!" she shouted. "Somebody!" She heard footsteps racing toward the suite of chambers, heard them stop at the door that led from the main corridor into the Blue Room. An urgent knock sounded and a male voice called out.

"Miss Linton? Is there aught amiss?"

"Help! In here!"

She heard the distant door swing open, bang against the wall, heard the heavy tread of what could only be one of the male servants racing into the other bedchamber.

"Miss?" She could hear the man slam to a halt, and she called out again.

"In Sir Aidan's bedchamber! Help me!" At that instant, Aidan's long legs tangled with hers. Norah gave a helpless cry as they crashed to the ground, Aidan wrenching to one side in an effort to spare her his weight. But he didn't release the nightgown, and the flimsy fabric tore with a sickening sound. The chill air teased a generous scoop of her breast as she and Aidan slammed to the floor in a wild tumble.

A heartbeat later, a blinding flash of livery filled the doorway, the footman slamming to a halt bare inches into the room. Calvy Sipes's jaw dropped open, the youth's gaze flooding with horror as it locked on the scene before him. A horror matched by Norah's own. Sir Aidan, all but naked, sprawled over her scandalously clad body, his fist still clenched in the nightgown he'd ripped from one shoulder, his face pillowed against her half-bared breast. She wanted to cry out and explain, but the fall had knocked the breath from her lungs, and all she could manage was a frenzied croak.

"Jesus, Mary, and Joseph!" the footman cried out, indecision warring with alarming ferocity in his honest features for a frozen moment. Then his youthful face hardened, the pugnacious jut of his chin belied by the cracking of his voice. "Sir, I can't—I mean, you can't be . . . be doin' that to— Me mam didn't raise me to sit by an' twiddle me nose while you . . . She'd beat me, certain sure if I let you. Not that I could face the priest hisself in confession if I ever turned away."

"Hell with . . . your priest an' your infernal . . . mother!" Aidan growled.

Norah made another effort to choke something out, but the impossible man had buried his elbow in the soft swell of her stomach and was trying to lever himself up. "Stop!" she managed to beg. "You're hurting me!"

At that instant the fire of pure Irish temper lit the young footman's eyes. Norah shrieked as he grabbed his master by one arm, wrenching Aidan around, one fist connecting solidly with Sir Aidan Kane's aristocratic chin.

The knight flew backward, the back of his head slamming into the overturned table, an animal cry tearing from his bare chest. Glazed green eyes rolled back beneath trembling lids.

"My God! You've killed him!" Norah railed, scrambling toward him on her hands and knees. "Aidan? Aidan, say something!" she pleaded, dragging his inert form into her lap. His head lolled back against her, his face ice-white.

"Deserves to be flayed, so he does, even if he does be master here," the youth insisted. "Beggin' me pardon fer sayin' so, but you should take a few whacks at the villain yourself, miss! Even if I did stop the bastard afore he finished his wicked deed."

"Wicked deed?" Norah demanded. "What in the world?"

Hot color surged into the boy's cheeks. "Ravishing you, milady. He's ruined you, sure as you're born, the devil take him! Heard all the stories whispered 'bout his dealin's with the ladies, but never thought he'd bring his debauched ways here, with Miss Cassandra about!"

Shock jolted Norah, and she gaped at the footman, suddenly excruciatingly aware of what her encounter with the notorious knight must have looked like when the youth came charging in. As if that weren't bad enough, a ripple of a breeze from the window whipped in to chill bare flesh no other man had ever seen before, while from the corridor beyond, the alarm had obviously been raised throughout Rathcannon. Norah could hear with heart-sinking clarity the sound of others racing toward the scene of the scuffle.

She tussled desperately to drag her wrapper up around her, without dropping Sir Aidan's bruised head unceremoniously on the Axeminister rug, but the garment was pinned beneath her. "N—No!" she protested. "It's not what it appears!"

How it "appeared" was much too evident as a bevy of wide-eyed servants poured in, followed by Mrs. Brindle. Norah thought it couldn't possibly be any worse, until suddenly a slender, golden-curled figure plunged through the door.

Cassandra Kane stared at them with horror-filled eyes.

"Oh, no!" the girl cried out. "It wasn't supposed to work that fast! I didn't think it would—would make him— Oh, Papa! Miss Linton, I'm so—so dreadfully sorry!"

"Sir Aidan is sick," Norah explained with a firmness she wished would steady the erratic beat of her own heart. "Sick."

"No, Miss Linton! I'm certain he would've behaved with the utmost propriety if I hadn't—hadn't fed him the . . . It's not his fault! Oh, Papa!" The distraught girl fell to her knees, grabbing up one long limp hand.

"I wanted you to fall in love, Papa. Not—not fly at Miss Linton like this!"

Norah shook her head, trying to decipher the girl's garbled babble. "Cassandra, stop talking madness! Your father did not fly at me. He needs a doctor."

"A doctor?" Mrs. Brindle echoed, shaking away the last vestiges of confusion.

"Yes, as quickly as one can be summoned! It's as if Sir Aidan has been . . . I don't know, stricken with some strange illness. We have to get him into bed."

Mrs. Brindle bustled off in search of cool cloths. The sound of footmen racing to do her bidding was drowned out by Cassandra's heartbroken wail. "But I didn't mean to hurt him. It wasn't supposed to hurt him."

Sir Aidan expelled a ragged groan as he was lifted off of Norah and borne over to the bed. "Poison." Aidan grasped Norah's hand with bone-cracking force as they rolled his long frame onto the unkempt coverlets. "Help me. Poison . . ."

"Don't be absurd," Norah said softly. "You're just ill. We're fetching the doctor. You'll be better in a trice."

"Don't understand." The effort the words cost him terrified Norah. "Feels like . . . last time."

The last time? Norah's mind whirled. What in heaven's name could the man mean by that? That he'd been poisoned before? No. He must only be talking about the hideous nausea ripping through him. That he felt *as if* he'd been poisoned.

Cassandra was sobbing with a wildness that raked Norah's nerves, the girl clutching at her father. "Papa, please don't die! I can't have killed you!"

Heartbroken, Norah wheeled on the girl, grasping her by the arms. She shook her, just enough to jar the glassy expression from Cassandra's eyes. "Stop this! You can't help your father by—"

"I did this to him! I did! With the sauce—the raspberry sauce."

"Cassandra, don't be ridiculous! Of course you didn't. Your father was only teasing when he made jest of your cooking."

"You don't understand! I put love potions in—in the sauce."

"Love potions?" Norah echoed, a sudden stark suspicion taking hold of her.

163

"I bought them after you two left the fair. The gypsies couldn't make up their mind which was the most powerful, so I got all three. Then I stirred them into the raspberry sauce."

Norah remembered Cassandra's protest when she'd refused her portion. She wrenched her gaze back to the masculine figure writhing in the bed, his sweat-soaked hair almost black, a frightening contrast to his ice-white skin.

Oh, God. Fear lunged in Norah's breast. Was it possible that Cassandra had inadvertently poisoned her beloved father in her quest to see him marry? What deadly ingredients might have been in the potions she had bought with such innocence and optimism? Once those ingredients had been combined with two other mysterious mixtures, the most horrendous of outcomes were all too possible.

"Cassandra, what were in those potions? Surely the gypsies must have told you?"

"It was a secret! They said if they revealed the magic they'd be stricken by the evil eye."

Norah flung a frightened glance at the cluster of terrified servants. "Someone has to go to the gypsy camp, find the women who sold Cassandra the potions, and bring them back here. There must be some kind of antidote, some way to help him. We have to know what he's taken."

"But the evil eye—the young missy said—"

"It's the only way to help your master! Now go!" Norah ordered.

"I'll go!" the boy who had dared strike Sir Aidan volunteered as he barreled out of the room.

Norah turned back to the man who lay on the bed, writhing with pain.

"Poison," he squeezed the word between parched lips. "She . . . she's dead . . . how could she . . ." That deep voice that had been laden with such sensuality, such arrogance, shattered on a groan. Sir Aidan clawed at Norah, and she caught his hand in her own.

"Help her . . ." he rasped. "My baby . . . don't let her take—"

Norah held his hand tightly, her worried gaze skating from Sir Aidan Kane's tortured face to that of his daughter, so terrified, so young. Stricken with guilt far too harsh for such a fairy child to endure.

With trembling hands, she stroked back a lock of sweat-dampened hair from Sir Aidan Kane's brow.

"Don't leave her . . ." he rasped, in a final, shuddering breath. "Promise you won't leave her . . . alone."

"I won't," Norah said, her heart breaking for this man suffering so deeply, tormented by fear for his child. "I'll help you both." But as she stared at his anguished face, she prayed that Sir Aidan wouldn't be the one leaving his daughter, starting on that deathly journey to a place Cassandra could not follow.

CHAPTER
11

"Miss Linton, I must object to a lady remaining in Sir Aidan's quarters when he is . . . en dishabille," the dour-faced valet insisted. "I am certain he would be appalled at the prospect."

Norah gritted her teeth, trying to restrain herself from insisting the valet tally up the number of "ladies" who had likely seen Aidan Kane in such a state of undress—to the man's indubitable delight.

"You must depart with the rest of them." The valet gestured to the door through which the other members of Rathcannon's staff had been banished—a frightened Mrs. Brindle, a teary-eyed Cassandra, and the bevy of other servants who had been gaping, horrified, at Aidan's condition.

"Much as I hate t'agree with this pompous windbag, ye shouldn't be stayin' in here with the master all undone," Cadagon said, bustling over with a carefully pressed nightshirt. "A lady the likes o' you shouldn't be exposed to a gentleman in this condition, miss. 'Tis most improper. I'm certain the doctor will be here soon enough."

"And I will be here when he arrives," Norah said firmly. "Sir Aidan asked me to look out for things while he was ill, and I intend to do so."

The valet choked in horror, his gaze flicking to his master's half-naked state. For an instant, Norah feared the fool would fling himself across Aidan to shield him from her maidenly eyes.

"I'm hardly going to ogle Sir Aidan's unmentionables when he's at death's door!" Norah snapped. "We must make him as comfortable as we can."

"We?" The valet went red as a fresh-baked brick. "Oh no, miss. You don't understand. It just isn't fitting for you to—"

"Stop arguing and help your master, or stand aside." Norah exploded, her patience frayed beyond a thread. "I vow I'll get him out of those breeches myself if I have to!"

Cadagon went scarlet, and the valet uttered dire predictions about the fate that awaited interfering women. But to Norah's abject relief, they did as they'd been ordered.

She rushed about, gathering whatever she might need: a mound of fresh cloths, a cool basin of water from the pitcher on a stand in the corner. She only caught glimpses of a hard, masculine chest limned with a smattering of dark curling hair as the two other men fought to strip Aidan of his clothing on the huge bed. Long muscular legs lashed out and Cadagon grunted as a knee caught him in the stomach.

In a dozen secret fantasies Norah had pictured Sir Aidan without the gilding of elegant clothing. But she had never imagined she would catch her first glimpses of him this way, tossing and turning in an agony not only of the body but of the soul.

It was horrible, shattering, to watch him fight against the poison, not knowing if it was a battle that he could win. The valet attempted to wrestle Aidan into a nightshirt, but those white-knuckled fingers fought to tear it away, as if it were some sort of hellish snare of thorns trying to entrap him.

The idea of tending a man who was stark naked beneath the coverlets set discomfort blazing inside Norah. Yet she couldn't bear the thought of Aidan suffering any more than he was already.

"Leave it off." Norah bit out the command, averting her eyes. "It is only upsetting him even more."

Aghast, the valet sputtered in protest, but Cadagon waved him to silence.

"Miss Linton is right, 'tis only makin' him wilder. Always did when he was sick, from the time he was a wee boy. 'Sides, the doctor'll want to be having a look at him anyway. Jest draw up the covers an'—"

"I'll not be party to this . . . this improper—"

"Then get the divil out, ye crack-brained fool!" Cadagon roared.

Norah couldn't have said it better herself.

The groom caught Aidan's fist just as it thrashed out, narrowly missing Cadagon's chin, that gravely old voice gentling as the valet rushed from the chamber.

"Easy there, Aidan boy. 'Tis all right, me fine little man." Norah paused to watch the groom tend his master as if Sir Aidan were his own son, so far gone in suffering. Her throat closed at that gruff tenderness as the older man drew the tumbled coverlets over Aidan's restless form.

"There ye be, missy. He's all tucked up, an . . ." Were there tears in the old man's eyes as he turned away? She never knew for certain, because the groom swept up an armful of Aidan's cast-aside clothing. "That flea-bitten city fool won't be pestering you further," he said as he exited the room. "Ye have Gibbon Cadagon's word on it."

With that he shut the door. Norah turned back to the bed, now alone with Sir Aidan, this man so desperately sick. This man who unnerved her, entranced her, infuriated her, and inspired her with secret dreams far too dangerous, too ephemeral to admit, even to herself. She looked down into his rugged features.

The white sheets were a startling contrast to the broad

expanse of his bare chest, his dark hair tossed against the pillow. Pain had robbed his handsome face of all cynicism, stripping it away until his very soul seemed torn open, exposed in his sweat-limned face.

Saints above, what was she supposed to do with him? Norah thought with a quiver of alarm. She didn't have the slightest idea how to tend someone who had ingested poison. She didn't know what to say to calm him the way old Cadagon had done. If she had a lick of sense she'd leave this chamber and put Aidan in the capable care of his servants. She wouldn't bow to a promise dragged from her by a man half out of his mind with pain.

Catching her lower lip between her teeth, she approached the bed warily, a bowl of water in her hands, a fresh cloth floating in the cooling liquid.

She set it on the table beside him, then reached out tentative fingers to touch his fevered face. He stilled for a heartbeat, turning toward that feminine touch, as if he knew . . . knew that she had stayed, as she had promised.

Gently, she stroked back his hair.

"De—Delia," he choked out the name, shuddering violently. "De—Delia, please, God . . ."

He was calling out for his wife? The wife he swore he didn't love? Had never loved? The realization twisted inside Norah's heart like a knife.

"Oh, God . . . Delia, don't . . . don't do this!"

Agony. It vibrated through the broken words, laying bare wounds in Sir Aidan Kane's soul.

Norah took Aidan's hand and lifted it to her lips. "I won't do anything you don't want me to," she whispered, knowing he was hearing another woman's voice, another woman's promise.

"Don't kill . . . my baby . . ."

"I won't." Norah comforted him, but her mind reeled. What was he saying? What was he pleading for? Had there been other children born to his wife? Or had Cassandra been in some kind of peril? What in God's name could it mean?

"Delia . . . bitch! Hate . . . won't let . . . hurt. Kill—"

The sound of the door opening startled Norah, tearing a tiny cry from her throat. She looked up to see Cassandra.

Tear-stained cheeks flushed with regret, red-rimmed eyes brimming with guilt, Cassandra clutched a blanket tightly against the front of her pale cambric gown. She looked like a child, a child who was desperately hurting. A child who, Norah was certain, would hurt even more terribly if she were to catch any of her father's tortured whispers, his rasped, agonized cries.

"Miss Linton, I—I came down to sit with Papa," she said, fighting the tears brimming on thick lashes. "He always sits with me when I'm sick, even while I'm sleeping. He holds my hand and—and tells me stories, and I feel better just knowing he's there. He'll feel better too, if I'm with him."

Norah regarded the fifteen-year-old, her heart aching with the image of the accustomed myriad of childhood illnesses that must have trooped through Rathcannon, dulling Cassandra's eyes, making her fretful, restless.

It was all too easy to picture Aidan standing sentry beside her sickbed, plying her with tales and pretty toys, tenderness and treats, until the bloom returned to her cheeks. His daughter's earnest desire to stay with him now was silent testimony to the special relationship the two of them shared. One Norah envied. One whose rarity she understood enough to treasure.

But the thought of this innocent, impressionable girl remaining here while his fever raged was unthinkable. The thought of Cassandra overhearing the incoherent cries Norah had just listened to was appalling.

Norah was certain that would be the last thing Aidan Kane would want. And, Norah thought with a painful tug, sparing Cassandra his anguish might be the only gift she could give this man who lay even now fighting for his life.

"Cassandra, I know that your father loves you with all his heart," Norah began, groping for some logical reason she could bar the girl from the bedchamber. Something beside the torment that was tearing broken words from her father's fevered lips, words that could cripple this sheltered, headstrong girl as deeply as they had her father. With fierce gratitude toward the quarrelsome valet, Norah latched on to another excuse. "Your father would be the first to tell you that a gentleman's sickroom isn't a proper place for a young lady."

"Not proper?" The fair brow creased. "Don't be silly. Papa and I have always . . . I mean, he's my papa, and he's sick, and—"

"I know how difficult this is for you, sweeting. But try to understand. You need to be quite grown up and do as your father would wish you to. What he needs you to do."

Resentment simmered in the girl's blue eyes. "He needs me here! He needs me beside him!"

"No, he needs to be able to work through this—this illness without sensing that you are hovering over him, all white-faced and half sick yourself."

Norah saw the girl gape at her, hurt and a fierce stubbornness firing in her eyes. "How do you know what he needs? You're barely acquainted. You don't even like each other."

"Cassandra—"

"You're supposed to be leaving Rathcannon altogether, Papa said. So don't trouble yourself to tarry here. Papa and I have been getting along on our own ever since my mother died. We will work through this . . . this disaster as well."

The proprietary tone left no doubt that young Cassandra Kane was setting up boundaries, building some enchanted circle around parent and child, banishing Norah from that special place.

Cassandra tipped her chin up in regal dismissal. "I am quite certain you're anxious to be on your way."

Norah realized, with a tug in her chest, that it was now Cassandra who was eager to see her leave. But Norah remembered all too clearly Sir Aidan's broken pleas, his desperate need to know she would not leave his daughter alone. "I intend to stay here until your father is well again," she said, gently but firmly.

"Well, I'm staying too."

A groan tore from Aidan's chest, muttered words falling from his taut lips. Words barely intelligible, for now. Words that could become brutally clear in a heartbeat, rending Cassandra even more savagely than they had Norah minutes before.

"Cassandra, you have to leave. Now," Norah said as Cadagon returned through the doorway.

"No! You can't make me leave!" the girl cried, outraged. Her piercing voice drove Aidan to claw at the coverlets with increasing restlessness.

"Mr. Cadagon! Tell her she's not in charge here! Make her leave!"

"You're the one who needs to be leavin', sweeting," the old groom said quietly. "Come along with ol' Gibbon here, an' I'll take you down to the cottage where you can play wi' the little ones."

"The cottage? You can't mean you'd take her side!" Betrayal. It filled the girl's tear-reddened eyes and paled her cheeks.

"Miss Norah is goin' t' take care o' things, just as your da asked her to. Now don't get yourself all blathered, sweetheart, just come along, an' 'twill all come right in the end."

"No! You can't make me leave him!" A sob broke from Cassandra, and she bolted over to her father's side, clambering onto the bed as if she were small. She clutched at Aidan's restless hand. "Papa, wake up! Tell them not to make me leave you! Papa!"

"Hurts . . ." Aidan groaned, groping for something he couldn't see. "Delia . . . for the love of God . . . don't—"

The child's face was stricken and pale. "Mama? Why is he—he talking to Mama?"

"Mr. Cadagon, we have to get her out of here now," Norah insisted. But Aidan's garbled words had been enough to galvanize Cadagon into action. He grasped Cassandra by the shoulders, pulling her into his arms despite the girl's struggles.

"Don't! Please, you can't do this!"

"Come along, girl," the old groom crooned, as Cassandra broke into shuddering sobs.

"When my papa awakes, you'll be sorry for this," the girl cried, casting Norah a glare filled with loathing and searing hurt. "He—he'll make you sorry!"

Fighting back her own tears, Norah smoothed her hands across Aidan's brow in a desperate effort to soothe him, to quiet him.

At the doorway, Cassandra almost broke free. She clung for a heartbeat to the wooden frame. "The blanket!" she choked out. "It's the one he always uses in my room, when he comes to sit."

"I'll lay it over him." Norah took up the blanket, battling to keep her own voice steady. "I'm certain it will comfort him."

"More than I could?" the girl demanded, tears brimming over her lashes and running free.

Norah was certain she'd never forget the look on Cassandra Kane's face as Cadagon shut the door, barring the girl from her beloved father.

Darkness clawed at Aidan as he desperately clung to his horse's mane, plunging deeper into a nightmarish world of wind and rain and the sinister laughter of death.

Death. He held his old enemy at bay with a wild resolve as the demons peeled the skin from his body, a knife's width at a time, flaying away sanity, hope, leaving him stripped bare of everything save the pulsing need to reach her, to save her.

Cassandra.

His child. His baby. She was somewhere in this hell, lost without him.

Aidan roared out his rage, tearing at the wild trees that seemed alive, in league with the witch who had stolen

Cassandra away. With every beat of his horse's hooves, every searing breath Aidan sucked into the torturous cavities that were his lungs, he felt his strength fading, felt his life ebbing away.

Let go! the demons whispered in his ears. *You can't go on!*

But Aidan dashed them away, saying her name again and again, in a litany of love and guilt and madness.

Cassandra . . .

Oh, God, why hadn't he seen? Why hadn't he realized what was afoot? She must be terrified—terrified—unless in her innocence his angel had no idea she was stumbling closer, ever closer to the abyss.

No, he would find her, had to find her. And when he did, he'd kill the one who had tried to hurt her. Crush that lying throat with his bare hands.

Flames were licking his skin, hellish laughter like shattered crystal ground into his night-blinded eyes. His hand reached out, brushed the cool silk of Cassandra's hair, his senses filled with the scent of sweet milk and innocence that was his daughter.

Papa! Cassandra's scream of terror rent his vitals as the demons snatched her away. *Papa, help me! Frightened! I'm frightened!*

An animal cry tore from Aidan's throat, and he flung himself into the darkness where he had touched her so briefly, hurtling through emptiness, eternal emptiness.

Cass! Sweet God, where are you?

His cries were lost in that hideous jeering laugh.

Take me! he raged at the demons. *Take me instead of her!*

But the laughter went on and on, crushing his soul, shattering his heart.

I'll see her dead before I leave her to you, the voice sneered, gloating over his anguish. *She's mine . . . mine . . . forever!*

Aidan struggled after that voice, his daughter's fading screams, even as he felt the demons snap white-hot manacles about his wrists and his ankles, chaining him forever to the gates of hell.

He battled with the last strength inside him, felt it sucked away and drained. But as he sobbed out his rage, his terror, his love for the child he had lost, he suddenly felt coolness touch his torture-seared brow, heard another voice, soft and gentle, reaching through the madness of his pain.

Don't be afraid.

Tenderness? In this prison of eternal pain? No, it must be a dream, the insane delusion of a man driven into the very depths of hell.

Then why did he feel the velvety touch on his face, why did the slightest wisp of peace find its way into his battered soul, as if one of the fairy folk Cassandra so loved to dream of had suddenly reached out for him with one ethereal hand?

I'll take care of her, that magical voice whispered in the accents of England. English fairies? Aidan puzzled as the worst of his torment drained away.

She'll take care of her. Aidan clung to that certainty, surrendering himself to oblivion.

He was resting at last. Whether out of sheer exhaustion or because God had granted him some sliver of peace, Norah could not guess.

She whispered a prayer of thanks, stroking a cool cloth over features so pale, so tormented, it didn't seem possible they belonged to the same man who had kissed her in the ruins of Caislean Alainn. For five days she had kept her vigil by Sir Aidan's bedside, knowing that the only way she could help his daughter was to make certain this man would not die—a quest even the doctor had doubted would be successful.

The gypsy women had vanished into the Irish mists from whence they'd come, and the purgatives the doctor had forced down Sir Aidan's throat had done nothing to assuage the madness that held the knight in its brutal grasp.

In desperation, the physician had begun administering remedy after remedy, trying to guess at what the potions might have contained, until Norah began to believe that if the gypsy possets didn't kill Sir Aidan, the doctor's cures most definitely would.

In the end, the medical man had merely shaken his head and said that Sir Aidan's fate was in God's hands. That he could only hope the Creator would not decide to take his vengeance now for the Irish knight's myriad sins.

The words had infuriated Norah, and she'd raged at the doctor, saying that if his God could be so cruel as to destroy such a wonderful father, to shatter an innocent girl with guilt over his death, then his God could go straight to blazes! She'd save Sir Aidan herself.

Channeling her own fury, her own terror for this man and his child, she had never left Sir Aidan's bedside. She had slept in the chair beside him, let him crush her fingers in his desperate grip when the pain came, listened to his wild ramblings, his tortured cries, until her tears mingled with his own.

She had been racked with regret but had resolutely tightened the silk cords that bound his wrists and ankles, tying him to the bed in an effort to keep him from hurting himself during the worst of his torment. And when he'd finally slipped into unconsciousness, exhausted from fighting enemies that seemed to cluster about him like malevolent phantoms, Norah had loosed the bindings, smoothing healing salves upon the raw marks he'd torn in his own skin, stunning herself by raising those limp fingers to her lips.

Oh God, what was making him suffer so horribly? The barely intelligible words torn from his throat hinted at unspeakable acts and nightmares Norah feared had once been all too real. Threats of murder, whisperings of poison, and always his desperate struggle to find the little girl who was now almost a woman.

The woebegone waif who had sobbed herself sick. The girl who had raged at Norah, hated her when Norah had given the order that Cassandra be barred from her father's room unless she had express permission to be there. Mrs. Brindle, her wise eyes holding the same fright as Norah's own, had seen to it that the order was obeyed.

Yet Norah saw the consequences of her actions every time Cassandra was allowed to come to her father's side. She heard the confusion, the pain in the girl's voice, as she told her father again and again, *Papa, she won't let me stay. She makes me leave you, or I would never, never go. Papa, I'm so sorry I ever brought her here.*

As Norah watched Cassandra, her heart ached for the girl. And as she washed the sweat of agony from Sir Aidan's muscled body, and stroked his tumbled hair, she wished she could have found a way to spare both father and daughter their pain. And to spare herself the pain of knowing that, whatever the outcome of Sir Aidan's ordeal, she would still have to leave Rathcannon.

It had been inevitable from the first, and yet, with each passing day, the knowledge weighed more heavily within her. With each moonlit night, it was more difficult to deny the truth. That in the hidden depths of her soul, she didn't want to leave anymore. She wanted to reach into the vulnerable places Sir Aidan had betrayed during this grueling siege. She wanted to heal those gaping wounds she'd heard in his half-crazed cries, his broken pleas, his wild, desperate rages.

She wanted to discover the truth about what had battered his spirit so deeply, to solve the enigma of how he could seem to be two men so different from each other. To find out which was the real Aidan Kane.

Exhausted, Norah stroked that harsh, pale face, assuring herself that he was resting, for however brief a time. With gentle fingers, she tugged the sleeves of his nightshirt down to conceal the bruises on his wrists from the times she'd had to bind him to keep him from hurting himself as he thrashed in the grip of the fever.

Then she dragged herself wearily to her feet, smoothing her rumpled skirts with her palms. At the doorway, she found Calvy Sipes, the young footman who had risen to her defense what seemed an eternity before. The loyal youth was stationed there, always at her disposal.

"You may tell Miss Cassandra that she can see her father now," Norah said softly.

"She's been leading Mrs. Brindle a merry chase today. Looked ready to throttle her." With that, the footman hurried off. Norah leaned against the wall, letting the coolness of it seep into the knotted ache that was her back.

It seemed barely a moment had passed before she heard slippered feet running down the hall and saw Cassandra, her eyes filled with worry and hurt and anger, racing toward the room in which her father lay. Norah knew instinctively she didn't want to waste one precious second.

The girl who had fought so valiantly to keep Norah at Rathcannon only cast her one scathing look as she brushed past into the chamber.

"When my papa wakes up, I'm going to tell him what you've done," Cassandra vowed.

"I'm so sorry that you're hurting, Cassandra," Norah said, wishing for the thousandth time that she could reach out to the girl and hold her while Cassandra sobbed out her guilt and fear. But she had surrendered that right the moment she had made the decision to shield her from her father's nightmares.

"I hate you," Cassandra snapped. "I wish you'd never come to Rathcannon."

"I know," Norah said wearily, watching with burning eyes as Cassandra went to catch up her beloved papa's hand.

Norah felt old and totally drained as she stood in the doorway. She didn't even realize the footman had returned until she heard his voice, low, for her ears alone.

"The little missy, she doesn't understand," he said with such gentleness and respect it astonished her. "Sir Aidan will bless you a hundred thousand times for what you've done. Even if he does so from his grave."

"He's not going to die," Norah vowed to the servant. "I won't let him die."

How many times had she sworn to herself she wouldn't allow Aidan to die and leave his daughter to suffer? How many times had she sworn she wouldn't let Sir Aidan Kane destroy himself? But now, as she stared into her reflection in the looking glass that hung in Rathcannon's hallway, she saw the truth in the bruised hollows of her eyes.

She couldn't let him die because somehow, in that bleak chamber, she had lost her heart to a man who didn't want her. A man who would never let her—let anyone—see the demons that drove him, the past that haunted him.

Norah raised one hand to her face, wondering why the fates had brought her to Rathcannon.

It seemed as if they'd lured her here to break her heart.

How long she had stood there, she didn't know. But her body stiffened as she heard the first signs of restlessness emanating from the bed.

Her stomach churned with the knowledge that Sir Aidan was falling into the demon claws again, and that Cassandra would have to leave him.

Still, she turned to confront the girl who was even now trying desperately to calm Sir Aidan, to hide the plucking of his fingers at the coverlets, the jerky movements of his long legs beneath the bedclothes.

"You have to leave," Norah said, her gaze taking in the telltale signs that another nightmare was coming: the crinkling at the corners of his eyes, the twisting of that mouth carved with such carnal beauty.

"No! It's too soon!" Cassandra cried. "Let me stay with him! He needs me!"

Norah's eyes stung with tears as the footman gently led his mistress away.

Steeling herself, Norah walked back into Sir Aidan's chamber, and she wondered if the only thing she would carry away from Rathcannon would be her own nightmares. Nightmares filled with Sir Aidan's secret agony, Cassandra's anguished cries, and her desperate need to reach them both.

* * *

Warmth. Light. They tantalized Aidan with silken fingers, whispered to him from tranquil glades in his own imagination. He drank them into his starved spirit, reached for them with what little strength remained inside him. Soft, silken strands wove a gossamer snare about his fingers. Something warm and moist stirred against his arm. Something that made him feel safe for the first time in an eternity.

He marveled at it, like a man who had been adrift in raging seas but had finally reached a sheltered cove.

Not reached it, Aidan realized with a sudden insight, been drawn there. Inexorably drawn there by something . . . someone.

With grinding effort, he dragged his eyelids open, his bleary gaze fixing on pale brown hair tangled over a face gray with exhaustion, dark lashes only accenting the circles worry had painted on the fragile skin beneath a woman's eyes.

A woman, her head pillowed on his bed, her breath feathering against him with the shallow, measured rhythm of sleep.

Heaven knew, he'd wakened more than once to the discomfort of finding himself in bed with a woman whose name he wasn't certain of, whose face he doubted he'd recognize if he were ever to run across it in a crowd. But this was not his bed in the chamber above the Ball and Claw. His fingers stole out to touch the carvings that some Jacobean craftsman had created for one of Aidan's Kane ancestors.

This was Rathcannon, Aidan thought numbly. But how could it be?

He tried to shake free of the thick layer of silt that seemed to shroud his brain. He never brought his women here. From the day he had brought Cassandra to the castle, he'd spent his nights alone in this solitary bed.

Yet this was definitely a woman here beside him. And there was something oddly familiar about her, something about the vulnerable curve of her cheek, dappled by the watery morning sun that streamed through the window. He struggled to get a better look at her face.

Who the devil was she? A shiver of unease rippled through him, shaking that astonishing sense of peace. More disturbing still, what was she doing here? Aidan bloody well would have asked her, if he could just summon the strength.

But his throat felt like a white-hot poker had been rammed through it a hundred times. His arms and legs throbbed as if he'd run to Dublin and back.

With eyes still rimmed with the sandy grit of fever, he tried to focus on the figure resting on his bed.

One hand stole out with the greatest of care to brush back the web of brown locks that veiled that feminine face as delicately as the fine-woven lace of the mantillas he'd seen so often on the Peninsula. As the tumbled curls fell away, Aidan stilled.

Norah.

Why was the mere echo of her name an empty, aching place inside him?

She was supposed to be gone. He'd arranged for the coach to take her to Dublin. He'd placed three hundred pounds in an envelope and instructed the coachman to slip it into her trunk without her knowledge, to make certain she had enough to get by on until she could get settled somewhere.

Norah was going to leave. Wasn't that why he had . . . what? Drunk far more brandy than he should have to drown out the memory of Cassandra running from the room, hurling accusations? Hadn't he used the fiery liquor to obliterate the memory of Norah, her face so fragile, her eyes so soft and wounded, it had been all Aidan could do not to go to her and take her in his arms, to kiss her until she could never go away?

No. He'd wanted the brandy—craved the oblivion it promised—but he'd never taken more than a sip. He had felt so damned strange. Sick, weak down deep in his very bones. And he'd feared . . . what? That the brandy would loosen what hold he still had on himself, that under its influence he would open the door that joined his bedchamber to Norah's, that he would take her into his bed, force her to see that she could find the passion she was searching for there? That he could make her feel . . . beautiful?

Raw, shuddering terror of his own vulnerability doused what little remnants of peace still lingered in his soul, flooding him instead with an uncertainty that made his palms damp, his jaw tighten.

Oh God, Norah . . .

Had he breathed her name aloud? She stirred, as if accustomed to hearing the slightest sound, being aware of the most subtle movement. As if she were attuned to every pulsebeat of his heart.

"Hush, it's all right. You're safe. Safe." The words echoed from her lips as if she said them a hundred times. Her fingertips, cool and soothing, groped for his hand.

She raised her head, blinking her eyes as if to clear them. Never had Aidan seen a woman in such a state of disrepair. Her hair was a tangled mess, robbed of all luster, the color gone from cheeks always far too pale. The bodice of her gown was limp and crumpled, lines from his rumpled bedsheets pressed into her breasts. But in the instant those great, dark-ringed eyes met his, Aidan doubted he had ever seen anything more beautiful.

"Aidan?" she choked out his name, disbelief snagging on a broken sob. "Aidan . . . oh, thank God! I can't believe you—you are . . ."

"What I am is . . . insane. You look like . . . the devil," he managed to croak out.

Her hand fluttered to her hair. Tears trickled down her cheeks. But she was laughing. Laughing. "I must look a sight."

"You do. Why the blazes is it . . . I want to . . . kiss you?"

A raw laugh tore from her throat, and she placed her lips on his brow, cool satin, seeping in to calm the troubled waters of his mind.

"What the hell . . . has been . . . going on here?"

Her gaze dipped down to a fold of coverlet. "You were ill," she allowed, catching her lip with her teeth. "Poisoned."

"Poisoned?" A cold blade slipped into Aidan's vitals, and he struggled to lever himself upright. "What the—"

"No! Don't strain yourself!" Norah cried in alarm, forcing him back onto the mound of pillows. "It was an accident. She slipped the potions into your—"

"The brandy! Sweet Jesus, but she's dead!"

"No! Cassandra is fine! Just worried to distraction about you. I'll send for her at once." With that the woman bounded to her feet and exchanged a few words with someone just outside his door. Aidan heard a whoop of triumph, then the sound of someone running down the corridor, bellowing in a way that made his head feel as if it were about to blast apart.

When Norah returned there were pink stains on her cheeks, and she caught at her lower lip with her teeth like a nervous child.

"I think you should know that—that Cassandra is none too pleased with me at the moment. In fact, I doubt you'll have any trouble now convincing her to give up her notion of having me for a mother." She smiled, but the corner of her mouth trembled. "In fact, she's informed me on multiple occasions she quite dislikes me now."

"Dislikes you?"

"Yes. You see, I—I wouldn't let her in, when—"

She never got the chance to finish the sentence. Cassandra barreled in, a whirlwind of rose-pink gown and fluttering hair ribbons, her blue eyes seething with anger, puffy from crying. The sight of her wrenched at a place where Aidan's heart was still raw.

"Papa! Papa, I can't believe you're well!" The girl landed on him with such wild joy she drove the breath from Aidan's lungs. "I'm so sorry, Papa! I didn't mean to!"

Aidan still felt damned weak, but he held his daughter

with all his strength, stroking her golden curls, burying his face against the sweetness of her hair. "Of course I'm well. You must know nothing could ever make me leave you."

"Me either. You, I mean." The girl's voice crackled with unshed tears. "Except that *she* made me leave." Cassandra cast Norah a vitriolic glare. "She wouldn't let me stay with you."

Aidan raised his gaze to Norah's, the woman's face suddenly very still, very pale, stoic.

"Papa, I tried to send her away, just like you wanted. I hate her!"

"Hate?" Aidan echoed, stunned.

"I hate her," Cassandra sobbed. "I thought I killed you, and she would barely ever let me come into your room!"

"Cass, hush." He clasped the girl close, his brow lowering as he peered over at Norah Linton. The woman's face seemed cast in the most fragile crystal, as if the slightest jarring would shatter her. Without a word, she slipped from his bedchamber into her own.

"Norah?" he called out, wanting to stop her, but she only shut the door, gently but firmly, behind her.

CHAPTER

12

Aidan grasped his daughter's chin, raising it until he could look into her tear-reddened face. "Cassandra, what the blazes is this all about?"

Words tumbled out, anguished confessions of gypsy potions and desperate attempts to gain entry into his room, horrible tales that let Aidan know exactly how close he had come to letting go of life forever. While the villainess who reigned over all was the tyrannical Norah Linton, who allowed no one else to tend him in his illness, the dictatorial woman who had taken perverse delight in having Cassandra hauled bodily from the room on the merest whim.

Cassandra's revelations confused and unnerved him. Why would the Englishwoman stay with him when he had a whole castle full of retainers at Rathcannon? Servants who were in Kane employ? And why the devil wouldn't she let Cassandra sit with him, if it could have given the girl some comfort? Worst of all, why had she looked so damned fragile as she had slipped away?

He raked the whole maddening incident over and over in

185

his mind, while he held the crying Cassandra, soothing her, until at last she drifted off to sleep.

After summoning the footman to carry her back to her own room and put her in Mrs. Brindle's capable hands, Aidan ordered the youth to bid Norah to return to the chamber.

She entered the room a quarter of an hour later, her face scrubbed, her hair caught up in a prim knot atop her head. The rumpled gown had been exchanged for one of India muslin, printed with sprays of violets, a purple sash beneath her breasts, long sleeves skimming down to overlap pale kid gloves.

Only her eyes were the same. Tired. Resigned. Filled with quiet yearning. For what? The question nagged at Aidan.

She was fingering the brim of a particularly fetching bonnet, of white straw with cream lace and a cluster of silk violets. "I hope you don't object, but I asked Sean to ready the coach to take me to Dublin. You had given the orders before you were ill, so I was relatively certain you'd have no objections."

Aidan was surprised to feel her words thud in his chest, and he hated himself for feeling so off balance, so strange. Damn the woman anyway. "Of one thing I can be certain," he said levelly. "Cassandra won't be enacting any Cheltenham tragedies over your departure now. I was anticipating —or should I say, dreading—quite a performance before."

"No. I'm certain her ladyship won't even bestir herself to say goodbye."

Her ladyship. It could have been mockery, it could have been scornful; instead, the all-too-fitting sobriquet sounded tender, more than a little sad.

"Norah, what the devil happened between you two?" Aidan demanded, his tone more gruff than he'd intended. "Hellfire and damnation, the night of Cassandra's Curse, the two of you were bosom friends. Now I think the girl could serve you up a helping of her poisonous raspberry syrup with a smile. She claims to hate you."

He regretted the careless words the instant he saw Norah wince, her fingers tightening on the brim of the bonnet. "Does it really matter why? I should think you'd be grateful for the change. Better for the girl to rid herself of any romantic notions about me, about what it would've been like had I stayed."

"Which notions are those? Nonsensical ones like you wearing yourself to a shade while nursing me back to health?"

She flushed.

"Cass is damned determined to convince me that the reason you kept her from my room during my bout with the gypsy potion was because you were struck with a wave of pure meanness. That you are a tyrant of the worst order."

"It must have seemed so to her. It was horrible for her, not being able to be with you."

"All that considered, you must have had some reason to bar her from the room."

"You were so sick, in hideous pain. I didn't think you would want her to—to hear when you . . ." The words trailed off, fragments of memories spinning through Aidan in their wake.

A taloned beast trying to tear its way out of his belly, agony, terror welling in the slashes it made. Norah barging into his chamber, her hair tumbled over her shoulders, her dressing gown flowing over soft breasts, the primrose hem skimming her feet. Her eyes wide and a little frightened.

He could picture himself trying desperately to drive her from the room, before she could see . . . see what? That he was in agony? That he was losing himself a piece at a time to a pain he'd felt once before? To nightmares he'd experienced again and again and again?

Nightmares . . .

Ice water poured through his veins, rattled him with uncertainty, flooded him with humiliation. "Oh my God," he breathed. "I wasn't—she didn't hear—Delia, she didn't hear about Delia!"

"No. No." Norah crossed to him, one hand instinctively reaching out to his. She caught herself just before their fingers brushed, and her lashes dipped over eyes suddenly filled with shyness. "I promise you, she heard nothing."

Cassandra hadn't heard him raving like a maniac, fighting things that didn't exist except in his own tortured mind. She hadn't heard his cries, his rage, his desperation, Aidan realized with a relief so thick it made his stomach churn. Cassandra hadn't, a voice inside him mocked, but this woman had.

He could see the reflection of his own horror imprinted in that exhausted face, could see it in the empathy that shone from those dark eyes.

A sick wave of shame all but choked him. It made him lash out in a desperate effort to resurrect boundaries between the two of them and regain his footing. "Sean was to have put three hundred pounds in your trunk. Inform him I ordered that amount to be doubled, for your services as nurse."

Hurt darted into her eyes, her chin tipping up a whisper. "I don't want your money. You can't pay me for what I did. I chose to—"

"You'll damn well take it! What are you going to do, go begging in Dublin for your supper? For God's sake!"

He saw the glint in her eyes, knew the instant she was going to spin away and stalk from the room. His hand flashed out, and he manacled her wrist none too gently with his hand. A cry escaped her lips, despite the fact he could see she was battling to suppress it.

It was a cry not of astonishment, Aidan realized, but of pain. She tried to pull away, but he gently hauled her toward him. Clasping her upper arm, he stripped back her sleeve and peeled away the glove. What he saw forced a sickened gasp from his lungs.

Bruises, from fresh purple to wild discolorations days old, darkened that ivory skin, finger marks Aidan knew had been imprinted into Norah's hands by his own. What the devil had he done to her during those hours he couldn't remember? Why the hell had she let him? . . . Let him hurt her?

The notion that he had caused her this kind of pain made Aidan cringe, so stricken that when she tugged again, he let her hand slip away. She buried it in her skirts.

"It's nothing," she claimed. "I have always bruised easily."

As Aidan stared into her face, he could see it was the truth. Not only her delicate skin, but deeper; there were countless bruises far deeper in Norah Linton's spirit, where the careless and the cruel had hurt her.

"Please, Sir Aidan, it's already forgotten."

"I won't forget." Aidan's gaze swept up to hers. "What you did for me. What you did for Cassandra." He shifted against the mound of pillows. "Norah, why did you stay?"

"You were so terribly sick."

"Why should you have cared? I've been nothing short of a bastard since the first moment you arrived at Rathcannon. What if it hadn't been the gypsy potions? What if I'd been stricken with some kind of sickness, something contagious?"

"I couldn't just leave you."

Why did these simple words stun Aidan to his core? Even early on in his marriage to Delia, his wife wouldn't have so much as handed him the basin if he were ill. No, it would've been too vulgar, too distasteful. And as for the idea of Delia letting him clutch at her hands, claw at her until her skin was marred—she wouldn't have caught his hand to keep him from falling into an abyss if she were in danger of chipping one of her nails.

Loyalty. Steadfastness. Unselfishness. Courage. Aidan knew enough of the world—and enough of women—to realize how rare these treasures of the spirit were. If Norah hadn't left him when he'd needed her, he was certain she would never abandon his daughter.

Even so, would he be able to bear looking into those eyes, knowing all they had seen? She had glimpsed the darkest corners of Aidan's own soul and seen his vulnerability—a vulnerability he'd sworn no woman would ever see after Delia had left him scarred.

He raised his gaze from the coverlet to Norah's features, features not dazzling the way that Delia's had been, but rather soft, kind, caring. She possessed a quiet loveliness that made him want to reach out and curve his hand over her cheek, with the same tenderness that he would cup a mountain flower nestled in a storm-swept hollow. And he would shelter her, keep her safe from storms forever, if she would let him.

"Norah." His pulse beat erratically in his throat. "Don't."

"Don't what?"

"Don't go."

"I suppose I can postpone my departure for however long you need me here. I'm certain it won't be long before—"

"I don't want you to postpone leaving Rathcannon. I want you to stay here. Permanently."

"Permanently? But I thought we'd agreed—"

"I want you to be my wife. I need you. Cassandra needs you. And I think that you need us."

The bonnet slipped from her hands, and in her haste to pick it up she stepped on part of the brim. "This is . . . I mean, I'm astonished you . . ." She made a wounded little sound.

"Astonished I what? That I've finally had the wit to realize what a gem has been dumped on my doorstep? Norah, I still can't promise you hearts and flowers. Love. But I can take care of you, shield you so you'll never be at your stepfather's mercy again. I can give you the home you long for, and . . . a family of your own. A husband. A daughter."

"But you said . . ."

"I said a damned sight too much." He grimaced. "Truth is, I was doing my damnedest to get you to run screaming from Rathcannon of your own free will. I'm not proud to say that I would've just as soon avoided one of Cass's temper tantrums. Then, in the castle ruins, I was determined to use you for Cass's sake."

"And now? You're going to tell me things have miraculously changed?"

Aidan raked one hand through his hair. "Do you know, in all the years I've had Cass to myself, I've never been able to name a guardian for her? Oh, financially, she's well taken care of. There is enough money in trust that she can live like a princess for the rest of her life. Her affairs are in the hands of the most honorable solicitors in Christendom. The staff here at Rathcannon would walk through fire for her."

"You've taken wonderful care of her."

"The only thing I could never quite bring myself to do is to name someone to take care of her if I died. Her guardian. . . . No matter who I considered, I could find some flaw in them, something that held me back."

"It would be hard to imagine entrusting such a treasure to anyone else. She is . . . magnificent."

"Even though she hates you at the moment?"

Norah smiled a little. "Yes. Even so."

"Norah, if I could choose anyone to trust Cassandra to, anyone who would care for her, love her, understand her, it would be you."

She looked taken aback, and one hand fluttered to her throat. "You barely know me."

"I know enough. When a man spends as many hours over a gaming table as I have, he develops a sixth sense, an ability to peel back the facades people create and see what lurks beneath. I can pick out a liar and a cheater from across a room. I can guess which patrons of an establishment will be willing to cast their whole fortunes onto a dicing table. And I can tell when a person is honest. Honorable. Even though I am not."

"Sir Aidan, I—"

"I want you to be mother to my daughter, Norah Linton. Believe me, it is a relationship that would require far more of my esteem, my trust, than merely making you my wife."

She stared at him for long seconds. "But Cassandra . . ."

"The girl can take her damn moodiness and cast it to the devil. You'll be the best thing that ever happened to her. I know it."

"But she—"

"Norah, this is my decision, not Cassandra's. And I'm damned certain that if I spent a dozen years scouring all of Europe for a woman to fill this position, you would still be the one I would choose."

Was there a kind of fragile joy in those eyes? A shimmering of hope? He saw the instant a cloud of unease swept over them.

"If I married you," she said, stumbling over the words, "there would have to be . . . honesty between us. I would have to know—" She stopped, swallowed hard, then her eyes met his. "While you were delirious, you . . . you said things—about Cassandra and Delia."

Aidan's hand knotted in the coverlet. "What exactly did I say?"

"You were . . . chasing Cassandra, trying to find her. Someone had stolen her away. You kept saying something about poison, and that you—you would kill whoever had taken Cassandra away from you. From your cries I'm certain that person was Delia. Aidan, did—did you . . ."

"Murder my wife?"

He saw Norah flinch at the cold words, saw the truth in those guileless brown eyes, that somehow she had heard the rumors that had circled around him like vultures the past eight years.

"I wondered how long it would be before you overheard the whispers." No denial, no anger; he felt as if his voice were dead. "You can't imagine how many times in my nightmares I've crushed Delia's lying throat with my hands, killed her for what she did, what she tried to do to Cass. But by the time I found them . . ." Fighting back waves of dizziness, he grabbed the dressing gown the footman had left him and drew it across his broad shoulders. The restlessness seething inside him stronger than the weakness left in the poison's wake, he rose and paced to the window.

"Delia, Cassandra, and I had been at Rathcannon almost two years. Delia hated it. Almost as much as she hated me. I knew it, but in my damned arrogance I didn't care. Cass was safe, sheltered from scandal here. Nothing could hurt her. No one could."

Norah listened as she saw a brooding light drift over Aidan's emerald eyes.

"From what I could piece together from Cassandra and the servants, I underestimated Delia's determination and how far she would go to destroy me. The night Delia died, it had been storming. One of those hellish storms that sweep in from the sea. She came into the study for a little while under some crazed pretense that one of the serving maids had stolen a ribbon from her room. I was drinking brandy. Heavily, I'm afraid. It was the panacea that got me through the night once Cass was asleep. Delia took my snifter and refilled it while we argued." He gave a bitter laugh. "I must admit, I was stunned by such wifely attention, but I'm afraid my suspicions as to Delia's motives didn't stretch quite so far as to imagining she'd slip poison into the draught."

Poison . . . The word echoed in Norah's mind, raking back memories of Aidan's agonized cries, that dark cloud of fear that had swept over him when she'd said that word. *"She* wanted to murder *you?"*

"I would assume that was her ultimate goal, wouldn't you? I mean, as someone who just finished going through the singularly unpleasant experience of being half poisoned, I would imagine any such bumbling would tend to make an already estranged husband decidedly unamused."

He was making a scathing mockery of the fact his wife had attempted to kill him, Norah thought, her heart breaking. That sensual mouth was curled in self-derision, as if his life meant nothing, except where it touched his daughter.

"What . . . happened?"

"When we'd first arrived at Rathcannon, Cadagon gave

me a wolfhound pup with a taste for spirits. As Delia slipped from the room, Finn came bounding in and knocked the glass out of my hand. It was the damnedest habit—the dog could lick up the spilled wine without ever so much as nicking his tongue on the glass shards." Aidan leaned an arm against the window and rested his head on his clenched fist. Regret. There was far more regret in the man's voice over his dog than himself.

"Did the dog . . ."

"About forty-five minutes later he went into convulsions. He died just as the poison took hold of me."

"Oh my God."

"The instant I knew what was happening, I stumbled up to Cass's room."

"You couldn't have thought that Delia would murder her own child."

"Delia had always known that if she wanted to hurt me, the child was the place to strike. She used to say all kinds of wild things—that Cassandra wasn't my daughter, that she was the bastard of one of a dozen lovers. As if I would've given a damn. She was my child, Norah, in my heart. That was all that mattered. Delia had once threatened to tell Cass she was a bastard, an unwanted child that she had tried to get a witch woman to rip from her womb. Half of Rathcannon heard me vow that if she ever breathed a word to the girl, I would kill her."

Norah's gaze skated over Aidan's features, pale and yet so dazzlingly handsome, his eyes dark and intense. And she was certain he would have done anything to protect his daughter from this woman who had threatened to hurt her.

"I told her to leave, to get the hell out, but she said she'd never leave Cass. The girl was hers. *Hers.* Property. As if Cass were a goddamn dog Delia could drag around on a string. Delia didn't want Cassandra, didn't love her. She only wanted to make my life hell. In the end, she made the one threat that I couldn't fight. She vowed that if I banished her from Rathcannon, she'd find Cass when she was grown

194

up and tell her I was the one who had so cruelly separated them."

"Cassandra adores you." Norah jumped to his defense, aching for him. "She would never have believed such a lie."

"I believed Delia, didn't I? All those years ago when I went to the altar like a blasted beast to the slaughter. The woman was a consummate actress. One who took the hearts of half the men in London and twisted them to her will. Made them believe she was an angel, all the while she laughingly led them to hell. Tell me, Norah: What chance would an innocent like Cassandra have against that kind of evil?"

Norah shivered; the scene Aidan had painted in her imagination was all too vivid, the consequences of such a revelation to the proud sheltered girl in the tower room all too easy to imagine.

"When I reached Cass's room, her bed was empty. Mrs. Brindle had been Delia's nurse when she was small. I thought—thought she might have been in league with Delia, but the old woman was as shocked and scared as I was. That was when I knew that Delia had taken Cass and run. Cass was so damned brave, but the one thing that frightened her was storms. And she was lost in one far more dangerous than anything she could imagine. To make matters worse, I didn't know how much time I had before the poison . . . finished me. I didn't know which way they'd gone. I dragged myself up on a horse and rode. Thank God I passed a man who had seen a coach, hellbent for leather, heading toward the coast. The coast, and, I was certain, a ship that would take Cassandra away from me forever, hide her where I could never find her."

Norah closed her eyes against the image: Aidan, lashed by the storm, death snapping at his vitals, his daughter just beyond his grasp. If there was indeed a devil, he could not have fashioned a more hideous hell for this man.

"The whole sky was shattered with lightning, and torrents of rain were lashing down. It was the worst storm I'd ever seen, like something alive, malevolent. Delia must have seen me, or her lover did. All I know is that they veered up onto the road that snaked along the edge of the cliff. Sweet Jesus, I couldn't believe it. They were insane. On a clear day, a lone rider traveling at that speed would have been in peril. They were in a coach, and that night I doubt the angels themselves could have traversed that road without plunging to the rocks below."

His gait still unsteady, he made his way to the hearth and stared into the writhing flames, his face shadowed with that decade-old horror. "I could hear Cassandra screaming for me. Screaming." Norah saw his throat constrict in a paroxysm of remembered anguish. "If I had had Delia in my grasp at that moment, I could have killed her. Of that I'm certain. I was only a horse's length from the back of the coach when one of its wheels disintegrated in front of my eyes. The coach rolled, teetering on the brink of that cliff."

"Cassandra . . . she was—"

"Cass was inside the coach, the whole thing threatening to fall. I reached in to grab her. I remember . . . remember Delia clawing at my arms, trying to shove Cass aside so she could escape. I remember Cass screaming and screaming, her face . . . her face covered with blood. I don't know how I got the two of us onto my horse. Whatever poison Delia had used was working its way through me with a vengeance. The last thing I remember was riding like a madman, Cass in my arms, trying to get her to the doctor's house. They say I collapsed outside the man's door."

"How in God's name did you survive?"

"Cassandra kept calling for me. I had to hold her hand."

A simple admission of fact. Norah wondered if she fell in love with Aidan Kane in that instant.

"Thank God you're both safe. I can't believe you escaped unscathed."

"Not completely. Cass has a scar still on her forehead, and I'm terrified there are others as well, buried where I can never see them. And as for me . . ." He grimaced. "Delia's legacy will haunt me forever. The moment I regained consciousness, I sent a search party out to find her and the bastard who was driving the coach, but by the time they reached the accident site Delia was dead. The only thing they found of her lover was a gold-handled walking stick, with a head in the shape of a hawk."

"Had he run away?"

"After an accident like that? It would've taken a miracle. No. The cliffs claimed him, and the sea pulled him under before the search party could find the body."

"But if that's so, then why would anyone think that you murdered Delia? Everyone involved must have known the truth. The staff at Rathcannon, the people who searched. And the doctor whose aid you sought must have known as well. You must have been half dead when you arrived at his house."

"When they found Delia, her throat was crushed. They believed she had been strangled."

"She could have been injured any one of a hundred ways when the carriage overturned," Norah said firmly. "Or it could have been the man who—"

"There were plenty who claimed her 'lover' was a figment of my imagination. Someone I'd invented to cover up my heinous deed."

"You didn't kill her."

Those incredible green eyes widened in astonishment and bemusement. "Are you so certain, Norah?" he queried softly. "Sometimes I still wonder if I did it, maddened by the poison and my own rage. God knows, there were a dozen times when I thought if she made one more threat against Cassandra, if she . . ." His voice snagged. "Isn't it possible I crushed her throat in my hands and I just don't remember?"

Norah crossed to him, and her fingertips cupped his beard-stubbled cheeks, forcing him to face her, her eyes capturing his troubled gaze. "If Cassandra was in danger, you would never have wasted precious time attacking Delia. Never. No matter how much you hated her. No matter how much agony you were in. Aidan, I know you. Nothing would matter to you except getting help for your daughter."

Was it possible for those eyes that had been filled with such mockery, such self-loathing, to suddenly seem defenseless, stripped of everything save a dawning wonder? It was an astonished wonder that made Norah think she would sell her soul to have seen that green gaze in the years before Delia Kane had poisoned not only Aidan Kane's body but his soul.

He smiled, just a little, and Norah's heart wrenched for him. "I had never thought of it that way before. Christ, Norah, I . . . maybe I didn't." He raked one trembling hand through his dark hair, then gave a brittle laugh. "Not that it would matter a damn to most people whether I'd been pardoned by a band of holy angels. In the end, what I did or didn't do mattered a helluva lot less to the folks hereabouts than who I was. A Kane of Rathcannon. Most of them relished the idea that I'd murdered my own wife. One more diabolical legacy to add to the castle's illustrious history. Wife murder is a creative mode of villainy which none of my ancestors had thought to indulge in before."

Norah shivered, unsettled by the notion of so many people clinging delightedly to such tales of supposed wickedness, embroidering them with lies as great ladies would embellish their fancy work. Saints only knew how twisted the stories had become. And, Norah thought with chilling clarity, what would happen if such stories ever reached the wrong ears?

"Has Cassandra ever heard these lies?"

"God, no. I have enemies aplenty, but they know that if they dared breathe a word to my daughter, I *would* commit murder." There was an underlying savagery in his tones that made Norah almost believe him. "The one mercy about the whole affair is that Cassandra doesn't remember much about that night, or about her mother. I thank God for that much.

"So there you have it, Norah Linton. The hideous truth.

Not a pretty tale." He hesitated a heartbeat, and Norah felt as if she might drown in that stormy green gaze. "Your eyes," he breathed on a husky whisper. "They're . . . oh, God, Norah. Tears?"

She couldn't stop them, didn't try. He reached up to cup one hand on the soft curve of her cheek, his thumb sweeping along the ridge of her cheekbone, gathering up the droplets.

"Are these for my little girl?" he asked softly.

"No. They're for you."

His breath caught in his throat and his gaze was unguarded for just an instant. She wondered if anyone had ever cried for Aidan Kane. For the hidden pain in him, for the scars left by the most brutal of betrayals. For the courage he had somehow found inside himself to build a new life for his daughter.

No wonder he had walled his daughter up in a fairy-tale castle, protected from the rest of the world. And yet, wasn't it a futile quest? For someday Cassandra would have to walk through the castle gates.

What must it be like for this man to see that future ahead, knowing the tales his daughter might hear, the heartache that would almost certainly await her? Tales that could poison Cassandra's vibrant spirit with more virulence than Delia had infected into Aidan's own?

Of their own volition, Norah's fingers came up, cupping over Aidan's long strong ones. She turned her face until her lips touched that callused palm in a kiss that was burning with tenderness, trembling with a soul-deep need to heal wounds she could taste upon his skin.

She raised her tear-streaked face to Aidan Kane's, her voice clear and certain. If only her heart could be.

"Yes," she said, peering straight into his eyes. "I will marry you."

His eyes hypnotized her, mesmerized her—like those of a broken knight, led astray by an evil enchantress. A knight trying to find his way back to the path of some abandoned quest.

The bright Irish green shimmered, filled with gratitude, soul-deep gratitude, and a wondrous burgeoning of hope. Norah ached with the beauty of it and tried to ruthlessly cling to reality: The reason he rejoiced was because of his daughter—only his daughter. Not because he wanted Norah Linton as his wife.

She swallowed hard, wondering what it would be like to see those eyes glow with the love a man had for a woman.

"You could do far better than a man like me, Norah," he said, his tones roughened with emotion. "I wish to God that I could promise you . . . give you more. Give you what you dreamt of the day you sailed for Ireland."

Regret. Tenderness. Both were in the beguiling lines of his face.

"If I were a noble man, an honorable one, I would send you back to England and give you a chance to find a man who warrants what you have to offer. But I . . . I'm not." He cleared his throat. "I'd like the marriage to take place as expediently as possible. As soon as things can be arranged. I already have a special license. I purchased it before you were awake, the morning of the gypsy fair." He had the grace to blush. "If I had managed to coerce you into saying yes, I wasn't about to give you time to change your mind."

She flushed, feeling raw and frightened, more alive than she'd ever felt before. Every nerve in her body sang with the sensations. "We can wed whenever you wish. After all, it's not as if there needs to be any fuss. It's not as if it were a—a real wedding, with gowns and guests and . . . and all that madness."

Did he hear a slight hint of wistfulness in her voice? If so, the need to have the marriage ceremony accomplished must have outweighed it. "I'll send word to Reverend Rhoades. As soon as he can steal away from his other duties, we'll meet him in Rathcannon Church. He can execute the deed swiftly and quietly."

Norah tried not to let it hurt her that Aidan made the "deed" sound more like an assassination than a wedding. Her heart raced, and she was suddenly more anxious than she cared to admit to postpone such a momentous step for just a little while.

"Surely you'll want to wait until you—" she stammered. "I mean, you're hardly well enough to—"

To what? she thought a little wildly. Well enough to hold a madly passionate wedding night? To withstand the rush of emotion, the dizzying ardor of introducing her to lovemaking? The mere idea made fiery heat wash from the base of her throat to the very roots of her dusky curls.

"I want this settled, Norah. You, my wife, in the eyes of God, my solicitors, and everyone who dwells about Rathcannon. And to introduce you, we'll give a ball."

"A ball? Oh, Aidan, I don't think—I mean, I'm not certain—"

"Don't worry. It's nothing as grandiose as it sounds— simply a gathering of a few trusted neighbors, families of Cassandra's friends. A little music, a touch of dancing, and a light supper. The girl has been plaguing me for months to have this kind of an entertainment, and Mrs. Brindle assures me it will be safe enough—a good way to let the girl dip her toes into the social stream to test the waters a bit before the overwhelming crush of London. This way the whole county can know you as Lady Kane, and that unruly little chit of mine can plan and plot and rig things up to her heart's content."

"I doubt Cassandra will be in a festive mood," Norah interjected quietly.

"I'll handle Cassandra. I'll explain—" He stopped, his own cheeks tinging scarlet. Norah was certain he'd realized it would be impossible to explain to his daughter that the reason she had been barred from his room was that he had been delirious, crying out secrets she must never, ever, learn.

"I'll handle Cassandra," he repeated stubbornly. "She can be a most reasonable little soul."

Norah nodded, then turned away so that he couldn't see her eyes haunted by the memory of a teary-faced girl, blue eyes spitting hatred, broken sobs of helplessness and fury echoing from her throat. Why was it that she found it impossible to believe that this same girl would suddenly be brought to see "reason," with all of Norah's supposed injustices still stinging her pride, with all her fears still rippling through her, and with the chafing burden of guilt raking at her nerves?

No, Norah assured herself, now *she* was the one being overly dramatic. Surely with time and effort, she and Cassandra could regain the closeness that had begun to develop between them during that disastrous supper which seemed an eternity ago.

Surely Cassandra would find it in her heart to forgive Norah for barring her from her father during his illness.

If she did not, Norah knew with sudden insight that the pain of the past few days might be only a taste of a more formidable anguish than she had ever known.

CHAPTER
13

Norah sat, rigid, upon the carved pew, her back as stiff as if a rod of iron had replaced her spine, her eyes hot and searingly dry, as the Reverend Mr. Chubbiston Rhoades ranged the sanctuary, his gold pocket watch never far from his hand. With each tick of the timepiece, the cleric grew more uncomfortable, marking each quarter hour that slipped past the time the ceremony had been slated to begin with a throaty *harumph* of displeasure.

But then, Norah thought with crushing pressure in her breast, it was incredibly difficult to hold a wedding when the bridegroom was nowhere in sight.

Had he changed his mind sometime after Norah had left the house in the carriage with Mrs. Cadagon, the Irishwoman assuring her that the master and young Miss Cass would soon follow? Had he been so tormented with ghosts of his last marriage that he'd been unable to lay himself open to such vulnerability again?

Or had Cassandra snatched the horse's reins and sent the team racing off in the opposite direction from the woman she had decided to hate with the same determined absolutism she had once given to adoring Norah?

Norah's nervous fingers crumpled the gown she had chosen with such care early that morning—a simple ice-blue muslin, with lilies of the valley embroidered about the hem.

Her stomach lurched at the memory of how long she had lingered in rose-scented bath water, how many strokes she had brushed her hair, until it shone with unaccustomed luster. Most foolhardy of all were the tender white rosebuds she had plucked from Rathcannon's garden to tuck into the dark curls of her hair.

She had wanted to believe she was almost beautiful—for just a moment. But a glance in the mirror had ended any such delusions. She would have gladly plucked the silly blossoms from her hair and donned her serviceable gray gown if there had only been time. But Aidan had made it clear that the Reverend Mr. Rhoades barely had time to pop into the church and fling out the wedding vows before the holy man had to bolt off on another errand. So she had rushed downstairs, to find, not her bridegroom, but only Mrs. Cadagon waiting there for her, the apple-cheeked Irishwoman's face framed in a stiff green bonnet, her bright eyes troubled.

"Sir Aidan said that we were to go on to the church. That he'll meet us there directly. Had a bit of a snag to untangle, he did, before he could break away."

"Nothing serious, I hope?" Norah had asked, worried. "He's not grown sick again?"

"No, no, nothin' of the kind! 'Tis nothing to worry your sweet head about, Miss Norah. You wait an' see, he'll be at the church lookin' handsome enough to charm the keys to heaven right out o' St. Peter's hands."

Wait and see . . . Mrs. Cadagon's words echoed through Norah's mind. It seemed as if she had been waiting an eternity.

"Miss Linton?" The minister had gnawed at one finger-nail until it bled. "I'm most distressed, but as I informed Sir Aidan, I have a baptism to officiate at two o'clock, several miles away, and from thence I've many more miles I must travel to preside over another wedding. Much as I regret it, I fear I shall have to leave."

Norah closed her eyes for a heartbeat, sickened at the debacle this wedding had become. "Of course you must go, Reverend. I'm sorry for your trouble in racing all this way for nothing."

The cleric's withered cheeks reddened as sympathy welled up in his ageless eyes. Norah feared she would retch if she was the recipient of so much as another drop of sympathy. "I suppose I could delay a bit longer, if I knew that Sir Aidan . . ." He stopped to clear his throat. "Was not going to be further delayed."

Was going to show up at all was more like it, Norah thought.

"There is no way to be certain when Sir Aidan will be able to tear himself away from—from whatever is occupying him. I shall look forward to seeing you at a more propitious time for all concerned."

The little clergyman bustled over to retrieve his greatcoat, dragging it onto his ample frame. "I still feel most distressed to leave like this. I pray nothing is amiss with Sir Aidan."

"I am certain it is—is just some trifle that can easily be managed. At least I have worked my way through the worst of my wedding jitters."

The clergyman caught both her hands in his, and she battled to fashion her lips into some semblance of a smile. "Your bridegroom is most fortunate in his choice of a life-mate. Most brides I know would be wailing fit to bring down the rafters."

Norah grimaced. "I've found that such assaults upon the carpentry don't solve difficulties but only leave one with a raw throat and reddened eyes. Safe journey."

The little man started to walk past her, toward the rear door, but he squawked when a bellowing voice snapped out, "Where the devil do you think you're going, Chubbiston?"

Both wheeled, to see Sir Aidan storming in, his hair windblown, his eyes stormy, his jaw rock-hard with stubbornness and irritation.

"Sir Aidan! I was just—I mean, you knew from the beginning that—that I fear I have to leave!"

"You can leave the instant this wedding is complete."

"But—but—"

"Aidan," Norah began, her heart beating in a stricken rhythm. She had no idea what she had expected of this man on their wedding day. She had pictured him a hundred different ways, a score of shifting expressions on those handsome features. But never had she pictured him thus: harried and irate, confused and perhaps a little hurt, uncertain and yet wreathed with a stubborn resolve that would have made a far more formidable foe back down.

"Is everything all right?" she asked, swallowing hard. "Cassandra—"

"Cassandra has a bit of a headache," he snapped in steely accents. "She sends her regrets."

Norah's heart sank. "I know how much it means to you to have her present," Norah offered, stunned to find herself groping for any reprieve. "Perhaps we should postpone the ceremony until she is well."

"Cassandra wouldn't hear of it," Aidan said, his voice tinged with bitterness. "And I wouldn't hear of inconveniencing the Reverend Mr. Rhoades any more than we have already done so. The man's damned hard to corner."

"But Aidan, he—"

"We won't detain him long." Aidan turned to the cleric, steely determination in his face. "Don't waste time with fancy words, Chubbiston. Cut to the chase, and you can be on your way in ten minutes, I'll wager."

"You can't whip out a marriage ceremony the way you—"

you cast out cards before a table is to be closed! These are solemn vows, Sir Aidan."

"Fine. Make them solemn, *short* vows, and we can get this the devil over with."

Norah started to object, but he was already clasping her hand, pulling her toward the altar, the Cadagons stumbling up in their wake. It didn't matter that she'd placed roses in her hair, because Aidan barely looked at her, his green eyes distant and distracted, his hand clutching hers a little too tightly, as if he were afraid she would turn away and bolt.

Norah was half tempted to do so.

Many times had she listened to marriage vows being exchanged between others, husbands intoning solemn promises to cherish and to protect, while brides, their eyes shining, promised to love, to honor and obey the men who would share their lives, their beds, father the babes that would beat their way into life beneath their mother's hearts.

It was a ritual as old as time, the mating of one soul with another, a time when life renewed itself in the promise of a future. But as Chubbiston Rhoades hastily stumbled over the lines of the ceremony, it seemed as if all the magic of this ceremony, all its majesty and mysticism, only jeered at her, mocked her from this sanctuary where so many other lives had been thus joined.

Every time her gaze strayed to her impatient bridegroom —his black coat rumpled, the knot of his cravat mangled beyond recognition beneath the strong jut of his chin—she couldn't help but imagine how different he must have appeared the day he wed Delia March.

A youth, fire-hot with passion, his gaze devouring the beauty he would soon take to his bed. No suspicion would have darkened his face; that hard shell of cynicism, that faint curve of mockery that clung to his features now would have been absent. And he would have sought out his lover's eyes time and again, clutched her hands with fingers that were hungry to touch other more secret places he could soon claim as his own.

It was as if the phantom of that other wedding ceremony painted cold shadows between Norah and the man standing so rigidly at her side. And as if another shadow, that of a fairy-tressed hurting girl, whispered subtle warnings to Norah from the emptiness she felt inside.

"Do you, Sir Aidan Kane, take this woman to—"

"I do." He snapped it out so hastily that the reverend's jaw fell open. "I've done this once before," Aidan said. "I'm somewhat familiar with the rigmarole. I take her for my wife, to have from this day forward. To love and honor and cherish until death do us part."

Norah's eyes stung as the reverend turned to her. "Do you, Eleanorah Linton, take this man to . . ." He paused, almost expectantly, and Norah felt her cheeks burn.

"I *haven't* done this before," she said, trying to keep the quiver of rebelliousness from her voice. "I am not familiar with the . . . what did Sir Aidan call it? Rigmarole?"

She felt Aidan stiffen beside her, saw that handsome face jerk toward her, that intense gaze seeming to penetrate her very skin, but she kept her eyes resolutely trained on a stone-carved seraph that decorated one of the pillars supporting the roof beyond the altar.

"Oh," the Reverend Rhoades blustered, searching again for his place in the prayer book. "Do you, Eleanorah Linton, take this man to be your lawfully wedded husband? To have and to hold from this day forward?"

Norah's knees trembled, and in that instant she wanted nothing more than to bolt toward the door that led out into the warm morning sunshine. But where would she be bolting *to?* There was nothing waiting for her in the world beyond, nothing save this haven Sir Aidan Kane had offered.

"Miss Linton," the reverend began, but Aidan cut in.

"She heard you. Norah, will you have me?" he asked, looking down at her so fiercely she could barely breathe.

"I—I do. I mean, I will, I . . ." she stammered, but the minister seemed satisfied, so he rushed on.

"Do you promise to love, honor, comfort, and obey him, in sickness and in health, until death do you part?"

Love him? Norah's heart ached. She already did. But what would it be like, living forever in this empty charade of a marriage, knowing she had given him all she'd promised here this day, while he did not love her?

"I do," she said, so softly the minister had to lean forward to catch the words.

"Do you have a ring?"

Aidan snatched it from his coat pocket and slipped it onto Norah's finger. "With this ring, I thee wed."

Sacrificing yourself for your daughter, Norah thought, her eyes burning. *To protect her, keep her safe.*

"With my body I thee worship."

You'll come to my bed, show me—what was it you claimed? That passion is far sweeter than love and far less painful. But what if I've already surrendered love to you, Aidan? What if I cannot help myself?

"With all my worldly goods I thee endow."

You will give me a home, gowns, all the things I could ever want. But will you ever be able to give me the only thing I truly want? Your heart, in return for my own?

What would Aidan even think if he could hear her secret thoughts? Norah wondered, a tightness in her chest. Would he be horrified? Faintly disgusted? Would his eyes fill with hated sympathy? Surely it was only in her wildest dreams that they would fill with that awed expression that had illuminated them when he'd touched the tears running down her cheeks.

"I now pronounce you man and wife," Rhoades said, slapping shut his prayer book and making haste to where the license lay, quill and ink at the ready. "Sign, and all is official." He scrawled his own name while glancing at his watch, then cast the pen down and started to bustle from the room.

At the door he stopped, flinging over his shoulder the words, "You may kiss the bride."

Aidan had signed his name with a flourish, then handed the pen to Norah. The instant she was done, he caught her in his arms, brushing a quick kiss across her lips.

The haste of that gesture made Norah's eyes sting.

"Norah, forgive me, but I need to—to go, to try to talk some sense into Cass—" As if suddenly aware he had betrayed something, Aidan's cheeks reddened. Norah felt a little sick.

"What do you mean? Talk sense into her? You said she had a headache."

"Ahem, well, she does—one caused by being the most infernally stubborn little wretch in Christendom."

"You led me to believe that she had agreed to the marriage," Norah said, raw with a rare flash of temper. "Do you mean to tell me that she is unhappy?"

Aidan glowered. "She'll get over this mad fit of bullheadedness. I'm certain she—"

"How could you?" Norah blazed. "How could you lie to me? Make me think that all was well, when she—"

"If I had told you the blasted chit had locked herself in her room, what would you have done?"

"I would never have married you. Not until she had reconciled herself to the wedding!"

"Exactly. Reverend Rhoades is a busy man. God knew how long it might be before I was able to collar the infernal fool again. And I won't be staying at Rathcannon forever. I told you I wanted us wed as soon as possible. I did what was necessary to make certain we were."

"You lied to me, before we were even wed. Of all the insensitive, selfish—"

Something flared in Aidan's eyes—hurt, and the same stubbornness Norah was certain now seethed in his daughter's eyes. "I told you the first night you arrived that I change rules to suit me. I cheat when I have to. Now I have a girl barricaded in a tower room, an irate bride railing at me when she'd been warned of my nature, and a splitting headache from racing around to get this damned marriage taken care of. It's finished. Let's get back to Rathcannon before—"

Norah's chin bumped up a notch as what few webbings of romantic dreams she'd managed to cling to crumbled away into dust. "I would rather walk all the way to Rathcannon than to share a carriage with you."

"Fine. I suggest you return to Rathcannon in the carriage with Mrs. Cadagon. She'd be much more likely to lend a sympathetic ear." Aidan's lips twisted in a grim sneer. "You and Cassandra plot and conspire to get me leg-shackled, then the minute the noose is around my neck you both change your mind. Then, somehow, this whole mess is *my* goddamned fault."

Every word bit Norah like a lash, searing deep into places hidden and raw. "No," she said, each word a sliver of ice. "This mess is doubtless my fault. After all, I'm the bride you are saddled with."

Her words penetrated past the haze of frustration that seemed to hold Aidan in his grip. She could see him battle to rein in his anger. "Norah, listen to me. I didn't mean to begin this way."

"How does one begin a charade of a marriage? I'm certain I don't know."

"Norah—"

"Go to your daughter, Aidan. See if you can soothe the hurt we have both caused her."

"Tonight I'll make it up to you. I promise."

"No." The sting of humiliation made the denial sharp. "I would as soon spend tonight alone."

Was it hurt that flashed in his eyes at her rejection? In a heartbeat he shuttered it away. He sketched her a curt bow. "As you wish."

"Until you choose to change the rules, at least," she said. She fought the tears as he turned and stalked from the church. Norah chafed under the woeful gaze of the Cadagons, who hovered at the rear of the sanctuary.

Mrs. Cadagon came bustling up, catching Norah's cold

hands in warm, comforting ones. "Never you mind Miss Cass's temper tantrums, dearie. The girl will be over it soon enough, and then you can forget all this unpleasantness."

Norah looked down at her hand, the wedding band Aidan had slipped onto her finger glinting in the light streaming through the window. The only way she could forget this unpleasantness would be to forget her wedding. Her wedding that was not a wedding, she thought, emotionally exhausted. A broken little laugh escaped her as she glanced down at the ring.

A simple band with the mellow sheen of gold long worn next to someone's skin. Norah's throat constricted. Had this belonged to another woman, the way Aidan's heart had? The way his daughter had? Was it possible that it had belonged to . . . her? To Delia Kane? The woman who had tried to murder Aidan, steal his child.

I change the rules to suit me, his words echoed through her. *I cheat.*

Was it possible that he had lied about Delia's death as well? Norah brought herself up sharply. No, he couldn't have been lying to her. He looked so solemn, his pain still all too evident in his eyes. Why would he have fabricated such a hideous tale when she'd asked him for nothing save the truth?

What would you have done if you'd known the truth? His hard demand seemed to haunt her from the shadows pooling on the stone walls.

I would never have married you.

Exactly.

She could still see the resolute jut of that hard, masculine jaw, the fierce determination in his eyes.

She was still shivering long after the Cadagons had brought her out into the sweet Irish sunshine.

Rathcannon's gardens were a wonderland, every blossom and vine, every statue and path woven to delight a little princess. Norah wandered through the flower-spangled beauty, running her fingertips over child-sized benches and sculptures fashioned to intrigue the imagination.

A stunning Pegasus spread stone wings in flight, his magnificent equine head tossing, his eyes fixed upon the heavens. Three unobtrusive stone steps led up to where a celestial saddle spanned the mythical creature's broad back. Fading scuff marks, not worn away by rain or time, made Norah wonder how many times a far younger Cassandra had clambered up upon the delightful beast to go off adventuring.

A dragon with deliciously sharp teeth peeked about a flowering hedge, its fierce stone claws extended as if to devour any child who dared challenge its wrath.

At the far end of the garden, an orangery filled the air with citrus smells, and Norah knew instinctively that it had been put there because a girl with golden curls had a penchant for the sour sweetness of the fruit.

Her throat tightened with the knowledge that Aidan had crafted this garden in a desperate effort to make his daughter want to remain a child forever. To build a world for just the two of them—father and daughter, walled off from hurt and pain and betrayal. Safe from the madness Delia Kane had spun about them both.

There was no real room for anyone else in this ancient castle, no room for anyone else in their hearts. She had been a fool to believe otherwise, even for such a brief moment in time.

Norah rounded a shrub and discovered an elegant stone chair very like a queen's throne situated beneath the quiet shade of an arch of roses. She sank down into it, exhausted, drained, more confused than ever before.

She had barely finished her vows when Aidan had made it clear that she was still an outsider. He had offered her protection when she desperately wanted acceptance. He had offered her passion when her soul had craved love. His wedding gift to her had not been some cherished family heirloom or even words of love, far more precious than any gems could be. Rather, his gift had been heartache, more savage than any Norah had ever felt before. Now he was somewhere in the castle, attempting to reason with his daughter, a quest he had made certain Norah knew she was not welcome to participate in.

She plucked the white rose from her hair, her fingers tearing the delicate petals, her throat aching. Tears splashed her fingers, tears she would never let Aidan or Cassandra see. Tears for something that never really was, would never really be.

"Miss Linton?" the respectful query echoed along the path. Calvy, the footman she had come to like so much, was heading toward her.

She scrubbed at her cheeks with the backs of her hands and climbed to her feet, hurrying over to a patch of shade she hoped would hide the reddened state of her eyes. Who had sent him to find her? she wondered. Aidan, perhaps? Or Cassandra?

"Calvy, I'm over here. By the roses."

He stepped into her line of sight, and one look at his features let Norah know that he had heard about the fiasco that had been her wedding. She cringed inwardly, infusing her voice with a regalness she prayed would hide the fact that she felt as if her heart were breaking into little pieces.

"Does someone require my presence?"

"Yes, miss . . . I mean, my lady. There is a—an English gentleman here to see you."

Norah's heart plunged to her toes. "But—but who on earth could it be?"

Calvy extended a gilt-edged card, a name scrolled across it in elegant print. "I told him 'twas your wedding day, but he insisted. He seemed most distressed."

"Norah?"

The card dropped from her numb fingers. She didn't need it to recognize the identity of her visitor. She needed only to hear the impeccable and elegant tones of Lord Philip Montgomery's voice.

She stumbled back a step, feeling like an awkward girl again, wishing she could spin around and run headlong into the tangle of trees behind her. But it was too late, for Philip had followed the footman and was striding into sight, his brown-gold hair glinting in the sun, his tall-crown beaver hat in his exquisitely gloved hands.

Norah's stomach gave a sick lurch as she desperately attempted to paste a smile on her face.

"Philip!" she said, her tone so bright it hurt her own ears. "What a surprise! Whatever are you doing here?"

"Richard assured me he'd informed you I would pay a visit. He—" Philip stopped, his aristocratic brow creased in puzzlement.

"I—I suppose he did. I just didn't expect you quite so—so soon."

"Not soon enough, by the looks of it." Philip's blue eyes traced her features—features she was certain were blotchy and red from her recent bout of tears.

Norah's cheeks flamed, and she was certain he could tell she had been weeping. The knowledge was humiliating beyond belief.

"Norah, tell me it isn't too late to—" Philip stopped and seemed to shake himself, as if suddenly aware of the footman still hovering there, watching with mistrustful eyes. "You are dismissed," Philip bit out in a clipped voice.

Calvy merely stood there stolidly, looking to Norah. "My lady?"

"It's all right, Calvy. Lord Montgomery and I are old friends."

The footman still looked distrustful of the Englishman, but he bowed and retreated down the path.

Philip watched him go, his classically handsome features clouded with concern, his shoulders, beneath the impeccable cut of his Weston-tailored coat, set at a curiously challenging angle.

When he turned back to Norah, she was stunned by the expression in the man's eyes. "It's true, isn't it?"

"True? What?"

"Dear God, I had hoped I could stop you before it was too late! But that servant claims you are already Kane's wife."

Norah gaped at him, stunned and confused. Why would it matter to Philip if she had wed Aidan? What could the odd light in his eyes possibly mean? "We were married this morning," she said, a little unsteadily.

Philip's mouth twisted, as if she'd suddenly caused him pain. He turned his back toward her, his voice tight. "Norah, you must believe me, I had no idea what madness Richard had stirred up, involving you in such a crazed affair. Sending you off to wed a stranger."

"But Richard said that you knew—that he told you."

"Before you left, he told me that you were marrying a widower in Ireland with whom you'd been corresponding for months. He damned well didn't tell me it was Aidan Kane! *Aidan Kane!*" Philip all but spat the name. "Norah, I . . . when I got Richard's letter revealing the name of your betrothed, I . . . God, it drove me mad."

Norah felt as if her nerves were raw, frayed first by Cassandra's rejection, then Aidan's lies, and now the obvious concern of a man she had once believed herself to be in love with. Had Philip come all this way because he cared for her, at least a little?

There was a time when that knowledge would have been heavenly, as unbelievable as any fairy tale. Now it only cinched tighter the crushing weight of sadness that held Norah in its grasp.

"Philip, I—" She couldn't squeeze the words through her aching throat.

"I hold myself responsible for this. I should have looked into it further. Pushed Richard to tell me more. I should have come to you and . . . and told you—"

"I'm not your responsibility, Philip, regardless of our past friendship. And it was my decision to marry Sir Aidan. No one else's."

"You were desperate. That bastard of a stepfather, plotting to give your hand to that asinine child! It must have seemed so . . . so hopeless to you. And what did I do? The fine and noble Lord Philip Montgomery? Did I help you? Did I tell you how I . . ." He broke off the words, capturing her hands in his own. "Maybe it's not to late to dissolve this . . . this travesty you've entered into with Kane. It can be annulled. I'm certain Kane cannot have any true affection for you—the man is incapable of realizing what a treasure you are. And you—you are far too fine a woman to fall in love with such a villain."

Norah looked down to where Philip's hands clutched her own, the wedding ring Aidan had slipped onto her finger glinting in the sunlight streaming into the garden.

"Philip, I—"

The sound of footsteps made Norah jump, and she tugged against Philip's hands in alarm, but the aristocrat only drew her into the protective circle of one arm, turning to face whoever approached with a challenging glare.

Norah's heart fell when her own gaze collided with the tall, muscular form of Aidan, his wedding garb disheveled, his hair tousled by the impatient raking of his fingers. He looked as if he'd fought a dozen battles in the hours since they had left the small stone church. But it seemed he had won the war, for behind him, her steps dragging, came Cassandra, sullen-eyed and somewhat repentant.

The instant Aidan saw her with Philip, Norah saw something flare with white-hot intensity in the Irish knight's eyes, something that made her struggle free of the Englishman's grasp, her cheeks flaming as if her new husband had caught her in some flagrant tryst with a lover.

Wanting desperately to drive that expression from Aidan's eyes, she hastened toward him and linked her arm with the rigid curve of Aidan's own. "Aidan, I'm so—so glad that you have found us," she said with a wobbly smile.

"That is a new twist to such . . . garden visitations at

Rathcannon," he observed, the jeering bitterness that laced his voice making Norah wince.

She was painfully aware of Cassandra's eyes regarding the whole scene intently.

"Aidan, this is an old friend of mine from England. Lord Philip Montgomery."

"Lord Montgomery?" Cassandra repeated the name with such sterling innocence that Norah's nape prickled with apprehension. "Oh, Papa, this is the dashing hero who rescued our Norah at that dreadful party in London! Norah, isn't he the one who danced with you?"

Norah wished the garden path would open up and swallow her. "That was only one example of Lord Montgomery's kindness to me. He—he is on his way to his family's estates in Sligo."

"Then he's going in the wrong direction." Aidan's stormy gaze clashed with Philip's. "Sligo is a good deal farther north. I know you English landlords rarely visit your holdings. But if you'll follow the coast, I'm certain you'll stumble across it eventually."

"Aidan!" Norah gasped. "That was hardly necessary. He merely came to—to wish me joy in our . . . marriage." She tried to forget the stricken expression on Philip's noble face, the sound of his desperate denial.

But she felt as if the whole scene was branded on her face. Aidan flashed those green eyes in her direction, and she saw a muscle in his jaw knot. He looked as sullen as his daughter for a moment, then his shoulders slouched into that position of lazy arrogance she'd grown to know so well. "I suppose I must apologize for being a trifle uncivil, Montgomery, but it is disconcerting to come in search of one's bride, to find her in the arms of another man."

"And I suppose I might apologize as well," Philip allowed with palpable hostility. "But surely you cannot blame me for wanting you to know that Norah is not completely friendless in this godforsaken land."

Norah worried her lower lip. If they exchanged many

more apologies like these, the two men would likely be on a dueling field before nightfall.

"I have made a good many friends since I arrived here," she interjected hastily. "Mrs. Brindle is delightful, and the Cadagons are absolute treasures. And Cassandra . . ." She stopped, glancing at the girl she already loved nearly as much as she loved Cassandra's reckless father. But she much doubted Cassandra would welcome any claims of affection at the moment.

"The Cadagons?" Philip demanded. "Not Lord and Lady Cadagon of Finnsbar?"

Cassandra broke into silvery laughter, batting her long lashes at the nobleman. "No, Lord and Lady Cadagon of Groom's Cottage. Gibbon rules over our stables, and Mrs. Cadagon is the most delightful housekeeper in all Ireland."

"You have befriended the household staff?" Philip gaped at Norah with well-bred horror.

"Norah hasn't been here a month, you know," Aidan said, more than a little defensively. "Cass and I have kept her quite to ourselves."

Philip's lip curled. "I'd wager you would, Kane. A *gentleman* must protect a lady like Norah from wagging tongues. One wouldn't want to risk a prospective bride hearing anything unsuitable."

Norah felt the subtle shift in Aidan, the slight tensing of his arm, the lift of that strong-carved jaw. "Oh, I have no fear of Norah overhearing anything, Lord Montgomery. She has already heard all from my own lips."

"I don't believe it. If she had, Norah would never tolerate such—"

"Philip! Please! Aidan has been most—most forthcoming, and—and surely it is a matter between husband and—and wife," she stammered, unsettled once again by the trickery he'd used to get her to the altar, unnerved by the knowledge that Philip must be aware of the scandals that had sullied Aidan's past.

If Philip knew, Norah thought with a chill, then most of

London must remember as well. And if that were true, the danger of Cassandra being told of her parents' sins was greater than Norah had even suspected.

Norah raised a hand to her hair, the last white rose bruising at the touch of her fingers. "Philip, I thank you for your concern. And for your kindness in visiting Rathcannon on my behalf. But I know you must be anxious to reach Sligo. Perhaps I can summon up a bit of tea before you continue on your journey."

"Oh, but he must stay at least until the ball," Cassandra piped up, sweeping over to clutch at the handsome nobleman's sleeve, her eyes all sweet supplication. "We are having the most lovely party to introduce Norah to our neighbors. There is to be music, and dancing, and a delightful supper party."

"Cass, Lord Montgomery is in Ireland on business," Aidan said in hard accents. "I'm certain he has far more important things to occupy him than our insignificant rustic entertainment."

"But Papa, Lord Montgomery obviously has such great affection for Norah. And, Your Lordship, you know how painfully shy Norah is at such affairs."

"Cassandra!" Norah protested, her cheeks afire. "I—I am hardly a bashful girl any longer. There is no need for Lord Montgomery to inconvenience himself further."

Cassandra turned her brightest smile on the Englishman. "Of course, Norah would never admit it, but you know what I say is true. It would make her so much more comfortable, I'm certain, to have you there. That way if no one asks her to dance, you can rescue her again!"

"And why would my bride need rescuing?" Aidan demanded, in a surly tone. "You think I would leave her hiding behind a pillar?"

Norah glanced at him, unable to stifle an acid thought. Perhaps not a pillar—but he'd certainly left her standing at the church where they were wed.

"Papa," Cassandra said, drawing out the syllables and

making a moue of long-suffering adolescent displeasure, "you can be most careless at affairs like this. Besides, it will be quite a feather in Norah's cap if she parades an English lord about at her first party as mistress of Rathcannon."

"You are a most astute young lady," Philip Montgomery said. "And so considerate, thinking of Norah's feelings. I shall deem it a privilege to remain."

"It's not necessary, Montgomery," Aidan said stonily. "I can tend to my own wife."

"Can you? I suppose I shall see for myself." Philip turned to Norah, those steady eyes holding hers for long moments. "I shall look forward to waltzing with you once more." He raised her gloved hand to his lips, holding it there for long seconds.

"Norah," he said, low, husky. "You look . . . more beautiful than I've ever seen you with roses in your hair." His fingertips brushed the fading bud.

"Now if you'll forgive me, I shall need to procure lodging for the night. I believe I passed an inn some miles back."

"Don't be absurd," Cassandra insisted. "We have dozens and dozens of rooms no one uses! Papa, surely Norah's friend must stay with us?"

Aidan looked as if he could easily throttle his daughter, but the girl had trapped him.

"Of course, Montgomery may stay if he wishes. But often bachelors of his sort prefer the privacy of an inn to a household running half mad with preparations for this kind of an affair. I'd not blame his lordship a bit if he sought refuge in the inn."

Philip's eyes met Aidan's, and Norah sensed that the Englishman had grown more determined with each barely veiled challenge that had come from Aidan's mouth.

"You mistake me, sir," Philip said. "There is nothing I would enjoy more than the opportunity to spend time with a lady I hold so dear. If you will excuse me, I shall go inform my servants that we shall be remaining here for a brief stay."

With a curt bow, he strode away.

Norah turned back to Aidan and Cassandra, her hands trembling, her stomach lurching at the expression in Aidan's eyes. It was glittering, hard, cynical. She could see the anger in him, hear it as he turned on his daughter.

"Blast it, Cass, why the devil did you do that?" he demanded. "Invite that cursed Englishman to that infernal ball! As if it wasn't going to be bad enough already!"

Cassandra gazed up at him, all bewildered innocence. "I thought Norah would like it. You said I was to be kind to her, to try to mend things between us because the wedding is over and there is nothing else to be done." She regarded Norah warily. "Norah, won't you like for him to be at your ball? Won't it be ever so much more comfortable?"

Sir Aidan Kane and Lord Philip Montgomery circling the same ballroom? Norah thought grimly. It would be about as comfortable as being locked in a stable with two raging stallions fighting for a mare. For there could be no mistaking the hot possessiveness that had flared in Aidan's eyes, and the cold loathing, the disgust that had shone in Philip's.

Dear God, as if things weren't bad enough! Now to have Philip here, to witness what? The disaster that this marriage had already become? Her fumbling attempts to regain Cassandra's affection? The stinging humiliation and stark uncertainty of her relationship with her new husband on this, their wedding night?

Their wedding night . . .

Norah cringed. Oh God, what if Philip somehow discovered that she would be spending this night in her own bedchamber, alone?

No. There was no way Philip could know that—no way anyone could. Or could they?

She caught her lip between her teeth, a bank of blossoms blurring before her eyes.

"Norah?"

She looked up into Cassandra's face and saw triumph there. The sad triumph of a hurting child, who had managed to wound someone back. And the uncertainty of a girl, nearly a woman, who was suddenly, reluctantly, ashamed.

"Perhaps I could come to your chamber, help you with your gown and hair for the ball. You'll want to make the grandest impression, and . . ."

Norah barely heard the girl's chatter. She wanted nothing more than to bar herself in the Blue Room and stay there forever, forget about ballrooms full of strangers and a reluctant bridegroom who had barely taken the time to say his vows. Forget about Cassandra, the pain and hurt in her eyes, and forget long-forgotten dreams about a youth with golden-brown hair who danced with an agonizingly shy girl.

"Cassandra, go inform the servants to install Lord Montgomery in the chambers across from mine." Aidan's hard voice shook her to the core.

"But—but I . . ." Norah started to protest, but Cassandra had already bolted off.

"Why?" she demanded, glaring at him in fury. "There are a dozen other places he could be."

"But he will be here at Rathcannon tonight, won't he, my dear? On our bridal night."

"I didn't invite him! You must know that!" Norah insisted, her voice quivering.

"You don't want him here? Strange, when I first saw you with him here in the garden, you seemed quite pleased that your girlhood hero had come . . . to what, my love? Rescue you once again?"

The memory of Philip's words made Norah squirm. "I—I don't deserve this. I married you, Aidan."

"No, you don't deserve this. For marrying me, you most likely deserve a medal for bravery or else keys to your own cell in Bedlam. Of course, you married me and then you told me I was not welcome in your bed."

"I . . . after what happened, I . . ."

"Don't distress yourself. I'm quite certain I will get over my disappointment. It's not the first time my *wife* has

223

denied me her favors. And you will have your so-dear friend Lord Montgomery to console you. After all, you are not completely friendless in this godforsaken land."

With that, he turned and stalked away.

Dear God, Norah thought. How had everything gone so hideously wrong? She had run away from London to escape this: the grinding humiliation, the brutal sense of awkwardness that had tormented her from the first moment she had stepped into a society ballroom. But as she recalled Philip's outrage and her husband's stormy countenance, she feared that this bridal night and the morrow's impending ball might well be the most horrendous ordeal she'd ever endured.

CHAPTER

14

The bastard couldn't keep his eyes off of Norah, thought Aidan as he brooded, his eyes following Lord Montgomery's every movement with a lethal negligence that would have sent any of his gaming opponents diving from their chairs.

Every flutter of those gentle hands that had soothed Aidan in his sickness, every nervous tug of those soft lips into a smile or a tremulous frown, every glint of gold or amber in those liquid dark eyes were captured by Montgomery's arrogant aristocratic gaze.

Aidan shouldn't have given a damn. Yes, Norah was now officially his wife, but it wasn't as if he were in love with the woman—infected by that poisonous emotion that had once set his veins afire with the need to hold on to something that was as deadly as it was beautiful, addictive as it was venomous.

He was no longer prisoner to emotions that had run white-hot knives through his vitals with every laugh, every smile Delia had bestowed on another man. He'd buried that part of himself on a dawn-kissed dueling field the third year of his marriage. Even now, he could still feel the agonized struggles of the last opponent he'd faced because of Delia's unfaithfulness. The eighteen-year-old boy's only sin had been being seduced into sipping the maddening poison that was Delia. Aidan had held the boy down as the surgeon had extracted the pistol ball from his shoulder, disgusted with himself, loathing the woman who had brought them both to this pass.

Time and again, Aidan's gaze had tracked from the wound to where the boy's heart was beating, horrified at the notion that if he'd moved his shot but five inches to the left, the lad would be gasping out his final breath.

For what? For a woman who would forget him before the week was out? For a harlot in lady's garb who would likely not remember his name in a dozen weeks' time?

And Aidan—hadn't Delia triumphed over him as well? She had turned him into something repulsive, something that stung and burned and twisted in an agony of the soul that matched this wounded boy's pain.

Couldn't he extract that part of him that Delia had infected? Rip it free, the way the surgeon ripped free the lead bullet?

In that frozen moment, Aidan had done so. He had deadened that besotted fool that had been Delia's pawn until he didn't give a damn about her—about any woman, except to gain pure animal pleasure in the silken sheath of their bodies.

He shouldn't have cared that Montgomery monopolized what few forays Norah had made into the conversation held around the bridal supper's table. Or that the Englishman had rushed to pull out her chair, to compliment her gown, to ramble on ad nauseam about boyhood antics of the stepbrother Aidan had never met, the crack-brained, careless youth who had precipitated Norah's flight to Ireland.

Even Cass had bestirred herself to be charming after the long and grueling "discussion" he had had with her after the wedding. Not that he entirely trusted the chit's sudden turnabout. He was uncertain whether she was testing her budding feminine wiles on a peer of the realm, or merely trying to drive her father to distraction by prattling more questions about the infernal social whirl of London society until Aidan thought his head would explode.

It had been all he could do to remain civil in the hours since he'd stalked from Rathcannon's gardens. But he'd vowed then and there that he'd be damned before he'd let any of them know the strange, pulsing restlessness that possessed him, the hunger that had nothing to do with cakes or feasts or even the brandy he'd drunk far too much of in the hours since they'd left the table for the drawing room.

Yet with every minute that ticked by, Aidan felt the coils of tension inside him wrench tighter. With every glance of revulsion Philip Montgomery shot at him down that perfect patrician nose, Aidan became more and more tempted to break it.

"Papa, you're being dull as a stone." Cassandra's voice shook him from that attractive contemplation. "Norah has asked you three times if you would care to play a game."

Aidan shifted his gaze to his bride, letting her see the seething recklessness in his eyes.

Hers widened, like some helpless woodland creature caught in the predatory gaze of a wolf. "I—I just thought that . . . that you must be weary of enduring tales of—of childish nonsense. That perhaps a game would be diverting."

Aidan couldn't stop himself from purring, "I cannot tell you how I've been anticipating playing games upon my bridal night." His brow lifted with a suggestiveness that made color flood into those porcelain smooth cheeks, and he cursed himself as a bastard.

"I meant faro, or whist, or—" Norah's gaze locked with his, reproachful, hurt, yet glossed with an anger that made her eyes shimmer hotly. She rose and paced to the mantel, and Aidan wondered if she was trying to decide whether to break down in a bout of feminine tears or whack him on the head with the fire iron. He devoutly hoped she chose the latter. Perhaps such a blow would drive this strange fever from his brain. Obliterate this pulsing, driving need to take her in his arms, strip away her proper clothes, force cries of ecstasy from those lips that were so tempting.

"I truly am not in the mood for *that* type of . . . entertainment," Aidan said with a wave of his hand. "But if you and Philip would care to indulge . . ."

The double entendre made her back stiffen and her chin tilt at that angle that always wrenched at Aidan's heart. She wasn't beautiful, damn her, Aidan thought. Then why the hell was he crazed with the need to grind his mouth down onto the pliant curves of her lips, possess them in a way that would drive the memory of every other man in the world from her mind.

She faced him with the dignity of a captive princess. "I find myself reluctant to play any more games today. If you'll excuse me, I think I shall retire to bed."

"My dear, it's early yet," Montgomery objected, sweeping up from his chair to prevent her. "I will be here but a few days. Surely you can bear to stay with me a little longer." The Englishman looked as if the idea of her sharing a bed with Aidan Kane sickened him. Aidan wished to God he could blame the man, dismiss his scorn. Yet it was true that he wasn't fit to kiss the hem of Norah's gown.

"She said she is tired, Montgomery," Aidan bit out, furious with Montgomery, furious with his own chafing doubts. "Since your visit was totally unexpected, you can hardly expect my wife to sit up until all hours entertaining you. Especially since this is her wedding night."

The Englishman blanched. "I should think that a gentleman would not mention—"

"I doubt you would accord me the title of gentleman, my lord. Now bid my wife goodnight." Aidan unfolded his long frame out of his chair. "Cassandra, it is time for you to retire as well."

"But I don't want to—"

"You'll have a long enough night tomorrow at the ball," Aidan said in a tone that brooked no argument. "That is, unless I decide to forbid you to go because you're behaving like a fractious child."

"Papa!" Cassandra hissed, with a painful, pointed glance at their guest. The girl paled, her eyes flooding with surprise and hurt, and Aidan wondered when his relationship with his daughter had grown so infernally complicated. His throat tightened at the flash of betrayal in those eyes that heretofore had always sparkled at him with delight and complete confidence.

He wanted to call Cassandra back as the girl bid Philip Montgomery a reluctant farewell and Norah a stilted, brusque one. He felt a twinge, deep in his chest, as Cassandra glared at him and then turned stiffly and exited the room.

Not a word—no Goodnight, Papa. Not one of those exuberant kisses he treasured. If the girl had sought a weapon to wound him with, she could have found none better.

And as if Cassandra's antics weren't grating enough, his new bride now stood, her gaze shifting between him and Montgomery, as if she suspected that the minute she stepped from the room they would fling themselves at each other's throats like snarling wolves.

"Perhaps I am not so tired as I thought," she said, crossing to where the teapot sat upon a chinoiserie table.

"You look tired to death," Aidan said quietly, and he meant it. "Go to bed, Norah."

Her fingers fidgeted with the lace at her bodice. Aidan tried not to notice the soft, pale swells of her breasts above the delicately webbed trimming, the fragile cords of her throat shifting as she swallowed hard.

"Aidan, will you . . . will you join me?"

Why did the plea irritate him beyond imagining? What

did the woman hope to do? Lure him away from Lord Montgomery by promising her new husband entry to the bed she had earlier denied him? Perhaps her attachment to this Philip person must be more intense than he'd guessed. The fact that Aidan wanted her, was tempted to take what she offered in spite of that—made him furious.

"Please, Aidan." She came to him, laying one hand on his chest.

He glimpsed the gold of his mother's wedding ring upon her finger, the symbol of his right to claim her.

That warm, feminine hand pressed against his heart. He wanted it to burrow past his waistcoat, through the slit in the front of his shirt. He wanted that hand eager, seeking out the ridges that marked his rib cage. He wanted them threading through the gilding of dark hair with indescribable delicacy. He wanted those feminine fingertips to discover the dark disk of his nipple, circle it, before he taught her shy, soft lips to kiss him there the first time.

But wasn't it possible Norah had dreamed of another man teaching her the ways of pleasure? Was it possible that she had dreamed of being taken to Philip Montgomery's bed, having him worship her body?

Aidan's jaw knotted. He'd already been chained to one wife who had hungered for another man when he'd come to her bed. There was no way he would put himself through that hellish experience again. Would he?

"Aidan?" Her voice was pleading, when he'd already taken so much from her, hurt her, lied to her.

Her accusations in the church rippled through him again, chafing him. Reminding him that when he'd dragged Cass out to the gardens earlier that day, it had been with the best intentions, with a hundred resolutions to apologize to Norah for the debacle of the marriage ceremony, and his callous disregard for her feelings.

"I'll join you later," he said, his voice harsher than he'd intended.

He might have been able to recapture his good intentions were it not for the fact that he caught her glancing once again at the polished English aristocrat who stood with belligerent elegance beside the drawing-room window.

Was it relief Aidan saw in Norah's great dark eyes? Why? Because she had averted more conflict between the two men? Or was it something else?

Throughout his marriage with Delia and the many sexual affairs he had had since, he'd learned to regard women with a healthy dose of suspicion. Call it an attitude of stark self-preservation, but he'd done his damnedest to unravel their motives, uncover their plots, before he found himself neck deep in one of them again. But Norah . . . Norah had baffled him from the first moment, confused him, unsettled him.

There was something so blasted genuine about the woman. Honest, open. No wonder she'd been a target of ridicule to the haute ton. No wonder she had suffered such embarrassment.

Embarrassment.

The word lodged in Aidan's chest. Was that the reason his bride had experienced such a sudden change of heart? It would be one thing to bar a bridegroom from one's bedchamber with no one but servants to witness it. But to spend a solitary wedding night, when the gentleman of one's childhood dreams was residing just across the hall, would be painfully humiliating, would it not? And considering Montgomery's obvious disapproval of Norah's choice of husband, wasn't it possible that he would breach the gentlemanly code and discuss Aidan's reprehensible behavior with Norah's stepbrother? And perhaps even others?

Aidan's jaw hardened as Norah left the room, the scent of fading roses teasing him in her wake.

"Kane." Montgomery's voice made Aidan wheel to face him. "You're not fit to touch the sole of her slipper."

Aidan met the Englishman's glare with his own, filled

with mockery, and a hard challenge no man could ever mistake. A possessiveness so intense it shook Aidan to his core.

"I'll be touching a great deal more than her slipper tonight, Montgomery. Whether you deem me . . . *fit* to do so or not."

"You libertine bastard, taking advantage of her! If it were in my power, I'd—"

"It seems to me that Norah's future might have been within your power some years ago. All these pretty protestations of your devotion come a trifle too late. Where were you when Norah was betrothed to that simpering child her stepfather attempted to saddle her with? Where were you when she was so desperately unhappy that she chose to run away, into the arms of a stranger? Promise to share his bed? Bear his children? Though she had never looked on his face."

"I care about Norah! I—"

"You danced one goddamned waltz with her at some society affair and you expect to be nominated for sainthood. What did you spare her from? A half hour's agony in an entire season of hell? Perhaps my daughter believes you to be Norah's hero. I have more stringent standards than that."

"Standards? You have no standards at all! You think I don't remember all the scandal that swirled around you and your first wife? You, a gamester without honor; your wife, playing the harlot to so many men, even the most dedicated gossip mongers couldn't keep count."

Aidan struggled to maintain the lazy air that had always been his defense during such confrontations. "At last count, I believe the number was thirty-six—that is if you include a brace of brawny stable lads and Lady Redmond's head groom."

Montgomery paled. "You repulse me."

Aidan let a dangerous smile spread across his lips. "And yet here you are, a guest in my home. I can only hope I

repulse you so deeply you cannot bear to remain at Rathcannon overlong."

Montgomery turned stiffly and stalked toward the door.

"My lord."

The Englishman stilled, his back to Aidan.

"I would advise you against making any allusions to my
first wife's . . . appetites to my daughter. I promise you, you
would regret it for the rest of your life."

"Are you threatening me, Kane?"

"I prefer to think of it as saving your linens from
unnecessary violence. You would most assuredly end up on
a dueling field with a nasty hole blown through your
shirtfront."

"Nothing would please me more than ridding the world of
one of your ilk, Kane, and ridding Norah of this loathsome
marriage in the process. But if you think I would stoop to
filling the ears of a child with such vulgar rubbish, you are
mistaken."

"I am much relieved."

"Don't be. There are dozens of others who would delight
in nothing more. If you think you can protect her forever,
you're wrong. Someone will tell her, Kane—tell her everything."

The words struck Aidan like a verbal death blow from
which there was no escape, against which there was no
defense. Montgomery knew he had won. He strode from the
chamber, leaving Aidan alone with the truth.

For an hour, he paced back and forth through the drawing
room, trying to gain control of the beast Montgomery had
unleashed inside him. Jealousy. Self-doubt. Terror for his
daughter, and terror of the fever Norah had fired in his
blood.

When Calvy, the footman, entered the chamber, Aidan all
but snapped off the youth's head. "What the blazes do you
want?"

"I just wanted to wish you all happiness with my lady,"

the boy said, undaunted. "And also to let you know that . . . well, sir, the maids have just left her bedchamber."

The corner of Aidan's mouth tightened. "Is that one of your duties now? Carrying servants' gossip?"

"No sir. I just thought . . . well, I—"

"Goodnight." Aidan bit out the dismissal and watched as the footman made his way from the room. He felt like a surly bastard.

Damnation, was the entire household going to be peeping about corners to see when Aidan deigned to bed his bride? His jaw set, grimly. Blast the woman to hell. He wasn't about to tolerate her sacrificing herself to his lust in order to quiet gossip, and yet neither did he want any whisperings, any hint of ridicule to hurt her.

He would damn well have to join his bride in the bedchamber, Aidan admitted to himself. The only question was what the devil was he going to do with the infernal woman once he got there?

Norah paced the confines of the Blue Room, excruciatingly aware of every sound that echoed on the other side of the carved oak door: the giggles of upstairs maids as they carried away Norah's bathwater, or the low voices of footmen in the chamber across the hall, helping ready it for Philip Montgomery.

But Aidan's room remained deathly quiet, and no matter how Norah strained to hear the purposeful booted stride that she had grown so familiar with, she heard nothing but the erratic beat of her own heart.

She pressed her fingertips against the delicate bodice of her nightgown, as if she could somehow still that tell-tale rhythm, and paced once again to where the looking glass hung, suspended over Delia Kane's dressing table. The woman who stared back at Norah seemed like a stranger.

Delicate shades of rose had been buffed into her cheeks by the crisp Irish air, and the dark skeins of hair that tumbled onto the pristine whiteness of the fragile gown glowed with unaccustomed richness. Her lips seemed fuller, softer some-how, and her eyes . . . they were uncertain, wary, and yet shining, alive in a way they had never been before.

She had invited—no, she had all but pleaded for Aidan to come to her room tonight, so desperate had she been to prevent further clashes between her new husband and the old friend who had come to display such belated concern for her welfare. It had been a faint hope that Aidan would find the invitation to her bed intriguing enough to dissuade him from continuing to match verbal swords with Montgomery. But Aidan had answered her plea with a probing look in those green eyes, one that peeled back all pretenses, seemed to be searching for something in her eyes.

He had promised to come to her. Yet she had already marked the militant click of Philip's heels in the corridor, the sharp tones of his voice as the door closed behind him; there had been not a whisper from her husband.

Had he chosen not to come to her this night, remembering her angry words in the church what seemed an eternity ago? Or was he merely draining another decanter of brandy, in no particular hurry to claim her?

Norah winced, astonished at the power such thoughts had to hurt her.

At that instant she heard it: Aidan, none too quietly coming down the hall. Her pulse tried to beat its way out of her throat, and her fingers tugged ineffectually at the lace-edged collar of her bridal nightgown. When his footsteps stopped outside her door, her breath froze in her breast.

She jumped a foot when he banged his fist upon the door. God in heaven, Norah thought, rushing to open it, did he intend to awaken the whole county and alert them all to his arrival?

She jerked the door open just as he struck the panel again.

Her cheeks were afire with stark embarrassment as she stared into that devastatingly handsome face. "Do you want the whole house to hear you?"

"No, my dear. Only our guest, and any servants that still

happen to be lurking about," he said, entering the chamber and shutting the door behind him with one splayed hand. "That was the idea, wasn't it? The purpose behind your unexpected invitation?"

Norah drew back, chilled by his words. His smile was hard and reckless, dangerous and silky with a kind of sensual menace that made her skin burn. "I don't know what you mean."

"It would be rather awkward to explain, I would imagine. A newly wed husband not visiting his bride's chamber. But here I am, at your service."

Norah's eyes stung, and her knees trembled. "I only wanted for you and Philip to quit—quit behaving like . . ."

"Like what? Rutting stags with only one doe between us? You must forgive the man—I fear he has delusions of heroism where you are concerned. Conveniently timed, I might add. Now he can stalk about like some Byronic hero, gnashing his teeth and beating his breast in righteous fury, but without the inconvenience of having to pay any forfeit for his gallantry."

"Forfeit?"

"Marrying you himself, my dear. Interposing his bared chest between your vulnerable breast and my villainy."

"You're being ridiculous. Philip is a friend, Aidan. Someone who was once kind to me."

"And I am not kind." It was a statement. A challenge. "Or perhaps I am. At least I'm not as vile as Montgomery would have me be. After all, I'm here, am I not?"

With painful deliberation, those long fingers went to his jacket and began unbuttoning it, the muscles beneath flexing and rippling as he stripped it from his broad shoulders. Norah caught her lips between her teeth, nervousness running wild through her veins. She had already seen every part of Aidan Kane: the perfectly sculpted muscles of his chest, the long, powerful lengths of his thighs, the flat plane of his stomach, and that most intimate part of him nested in coarse, dark hair.

She had run her fingertips over his sleek, bronzed skin when it was damp with the sweat of his fever, had pressed her body against his in an effort to still his wild thrashings when the nightmares had grown too fierce. She had fallen in love with that wounded, pain-filled man, the earnest, battered hero who had confided to her the betrayal that had crippled his heart and changed his life.

But now, as she stared into those emerald eyes, Aidan Kane unnerved her, a man as elusive and enigmatic as the sea mist scudding into Rathcannon before a storm.

He tossed his jacket with studied negligence onto a tiny gilt chair, and his fingers went to the buttons of his cuffs. Norah couldn't watch another instant, unable to bear the heat stealing through her, the embarrassment and terrifying attraction, overlaid with a pulsing hurt that rippled from the places he'd left raw at their hurried wedding. *Not like this,* a voice inside her cried. She didn't want him to take her to bed like this, with that hard light in his eye, that almost belligerent set to his jaw, those lips so sensual, whose warm magic she had tasted so briefly in Caislean Alainn, hot and demanding, yet without the shading of tenderness that she craved with every fiber of her soul.

She turned her back to him and clutched her fingers together so tightly her wedding ring cut into her skin. "I—I think I'll just . . . I . . ." she started to stammer, then fled headlong for the bed. She climbed beneath the coverlets, as if they could somehow shield her, hide the emotions that were too painfully sensitive to endure that hard green gaze.

"What the devil?" Aidan's gaze slashed to her, and he frowned. "Oh no, my love. You mistake my intentions. You made it quite plain earlier today that you did not want me in your bed."

"But I . . . I thought you . . ." Her gaze shifted from his jacket to his unfastened cuffs, but he was merely rolling them up over his sinewy forearms. "I thought you came here to—"

"To make wild, passionate love to my bride?" Why was

there such sudden bitterness in his tone? "No. I came for another reason."

"What's that?"

His hand delved into the pocket of his jacket, his mouth twisting into a smile. "I came to play a game of wagers, my love," he said, casting a deck of cards onto the bed.

"Wagers?" She gaped at him as if he'd run mad.

"We have a deal of time to kill, to make certain all concerned believe we had a wedding night. I thought a game might be diverting. Of course, in my opinion, the interest in the game is determined by the value of what lays wagered on the table."

"I don't have any money," Norah said warily. He paced toward the bed, then strung his long, lean body across it with the grace of a jungle cat.

"Money is tedious in comparison to . . . say, buttons."

"B—Buttons?"

A smile spread across his face, dark and secretive as the lushest black velvet, as his deft fingers began dealing the cards. "Let me demonstrate."

Norah stared at him, certain he had taken leave of his senses. But whatever he had in mind, it would be far easier to placate him by playing cards than risk him deciding to indulge in other, more traditional bridal night pursuits. With unsteady fingers, she took up the cards he had dealt her.

She had always considered herself fairly accomplished at faro, but she was so unnerved by Aidan's strange behavior that she played like the rankest amateur, bumbling over her cards, tipping her hand, while Aidan played with consummate skill.

When she flung out her last card, her eyes flashed up to his, wide and a little bit shaken. "I . . . lost."

"Only this hand, my love. Now I shall claim my forfeit." A shuddering breath racked her as those supple fingers reached across the space between them, the callused warmth hooking beneath the tiny mother-of-pearl button at the neck of her nightgown. His gaze held hers, hot, taunting, as he flicked the button through the hole with practiced ease. The fabric gaped open just enough to expose the wild beat of Norah's pulse in the hollow of her throat. One finger dipped into that hollow, lingering, caressing, until Norah had to trap a moan that was rising in her throat.

"I'm not . . . certain about wagering buttons. I—"

"Surely a glimpse of your soft, secret places is not too much to ask on my wedding night. Is it, Norah?"

She nibbled at her lip. "I . . . Aidan, this is—is insane. We can't . . . this can't be . . ."

"Proper? I suppose not. But I'm your husband. If I hunger for such delights, should they be forbidden me?"

There was a primitive allure in the beautifully chiseled planes of his face, a latent sexuality that mesmerized her.

"It's just a game, Norah. I give you my word that I won't ravish you." He flashed a wicked smile. "That is, unless you beg me to."

The words stung and goaded, firing Norah with a surge of determination. "That, sir, I will never do."

He laughed, rich and deep, so loud Norah was certain everyone in that wing of the house could hear it. She was half tempted to dive across the coverlets and stop up his mouth with her hand. "Norah, Norah, a word of warning: Never dare me. From the time I was a grubby-faced boy I could never resist one."

"Then perhaps we'd best not play at all."

"Play," he said, with a meltingly carnal smile. "I cannot win every hand. Unless, of course, you are too timid. Afraid of being beaten. Ladies are often regrettably poor at games that require so much . . . er, intellect. That is doubtless why the poor dears are not allowed within the sacrosanct halls of White's."

He was baiting her on purpose. She could see it in every harsh, mocking line of that face, the subtle twist of lips whose relentless allure kept tugging her gaze back to them again and again, haunting her memory with the way they had tasted, the consummate skill with which they had initiated her own mouth into the dark flow of passion.

But despite the fact that she knew what trick he was about, she couldn't seem to resist rising to that challenge.

She held her head up high. "I prefer to think of White's as a haven where men can cower together, unwilling to match their wits with the *superior* intellect of women."

"An interesting premise. One you and I shall test tonight. If you have the nerve to do so."

"Deal the cards," Norah said through gritted teeth.

She played with steely determination, not allowing herself to become distracted by his beguiling masculine smile. She forced herself to ignore the shadings of pain that clung in ghostly whispers about his mouth, the self-doubt that wove a subtle pattern along with the restlessness in his eyes.

In minutes, she flung down a winning card, triumphant. "There. You are bested."

He looked for all the world like a thwarted boy, and he grimaced sullenly. "I suppose that means I shall have to surrender . . . my boot, perhaps? However, I'll need your aid to remove the blasted thing."

"I don't want your boot! I—"

"But that was my wager. Gaming debts are debts of honor." Green devils danced in his eyes. "Help me, Norah, else my soul be blackened by such a heinous crime. Believe me, when it comes to honor, I have very little left. You'd not want to rob me of the last of it, would you?" His eyes were smokey and seductive. "Help me, angel."

There was something fiendishly compelling in his eyes, and she climbed from beneath the coverlets, nervously eyeing the glossy Hessian he extended toward her. Gripping it tightly, she tugged and pulled at it until her hair tumbled over her flushed face. Yet she'd rather have died the most torturous of deaths than admit defeat to this arrogant, mocking man.

It was that flash of grin she caught from the corner of her eye that did it. Brilliant white teeth in a rogue's smile that could have bewitched any feminine heart from a dozen paces. The smile made her give a savage tug on the boot. It came free and tumbled her backward. She fell in a heap on the bedroom floor.

The corners of Aidan's eyes crinkled, and she could see him make a manful effort not to burst into gales of laughter. Instead, he said in tones of the most tender concern, "Did you wound yourself, my love, landing on your . . . er, delicate parts? Poor angel, may I kiss it and make it better?"

"You're impossible!" Norah said, flinging the boot at him. "From now on, any item you care to wager you may remove yourself. Now play!"

It was scandalous. It was embarrassing. It was treacherously exciting, matching wits with Aidan at cards. Tricks were won and lost, games disputed as if the safety of the throne depended on them.

But as Aidan's rein-toughened fingers dipped again and again into the bodice of Norah's nightgown, the vee of silky bared skin growing alarmingly wide, Aidan's cynical banter and Norah's bouts of outrage faded into something more subtle, more dangerous, more enticing.

Time and again Norah caught those green eyes clinging to the wedge of her skin, tracing the curves of her breasts, visible through the gap. Twice she saw his tongue steal out, to moisten lips that seemed parched, thirsting for something other than brandy or wine.

When he won yet another trick, Norah's voice was unsteady as she said, "We cannot play anymore. I—I have run out of buttons."

Dark lashes, thick and curling, dipped to half mast over those relentlessly masculine eyes. "Then I rest my case. Men are superior to females in games that require higher intellect. Of course, we *could* raise the stakes."

Norah wondered how far he could push this game. What wager would he demand of her after they had played three or four more hands of cards?

"This time," he said, fingering his own half-opened shirt,

where the crisp mat of dark hair was visible against the stark white linen. "This time I shall be magnanimous. I shall let your forfeit be my shirt."

"Your shirt? But I don't—don't want you to—"

"To strip my shirt off?" He looked at her with demonic guilelessness. "As you wish, my sweet. I was only attempting to do you a kindness. I was quite certain you would rather have me strip off my shirt than slip your nightgown down your shoulders, across your breasts."

Those hot words made her feel as if her skin were already bare to his gaze. She could picture all too clearly those big hands unveiling her breasts, those intense green eyes devouring the velvety pale mounds, lingering on the vulnerable coral tips of her nipples with earthy delight. Most horrifying of all, she was entranced by the idea, compelled by it, appalled because he had made her such a wanton that some secret part of her actually wanted to reveal herself to his uncompromisingly sensual gaze. That knowledge drew a choked reply in a passion-thickened voice she didn't recognize as her own.

"Your shirt. I accept that wager."

She played like the veriest fool, distracted as Aidan lounged against a mound of pillows, the muscles of his chest flexing, the iron-hard sinews pulling his shirt open further, ghosting over the burnt-sugar planes of muscle, tantalizing with a forbidden glimpse of his nipple against the edge of linen.

Norah was certain she would lose. She tried to take comfort in the fact that if she did, Aidan would be the one to surrender a garment. Yet the mere idea of this sulky, sensual man naked to the waist made Norah's fingers so unsteady, she could barely hold her cards.

When the last card was played, she looked up at Aidan in dismay. "I—I lost. . . ." Tension coiled low in her stomach, a prickling heat in her breasts. His hands—beautiful sculptor's hands—skimmed the fabric from the exquisite musculature of his upper body, revealing glistening muscle, silky dark webbings of hair, dauntingly broad shoulders. His black breeches were slung low on narrow hips, and Norah could glimpse the shadowy indentation of his navel just above the waistband of the garment.

He tossed the shirt aside, one arm outstretched, the dusky wisp of hair just visible under his arm, the sleek cords of muscles playing beneath his skin, starting a shuddering need deep inside Norah.

When he dealt the cards again, it was all she could do to recognize which was a king and which an ace. No matter which cards she glanced at, all she saw was sun-browned skin, rippling muscle. With every erratic breath she took, her head was filled with the scent of wind and rain and horses, that wild, mysterious essence that was Aidan's own.

Worse still, he wasn't making jests any longer. He was watching her, intent as a jungle cat about to pounce on its prey, anticipating the sweet taste of its flesh on his tongue.

Flesh . . . tongue . . . Why was it that when she closed her eyes, she could picture so clearly Aidan's mouth making a sensual foray along the path where her buttons had once been, the point of his tongue testing the pliant curve of her breast, the cords of her throat, the hollow where he had first touched her?

She all but jumped out of her skin when the callused tips of his fingers brushed her cheek. "Do you want to stop the game?" His voice was low, rough and full of desire. Norah remembered a hundred dreams she'd spun, of a man who would speak to her in that husky, need-filled voice, a man who would look at her with that lambent heat simmering in his eyes. But never had she imagined that man would be as magnificently virile, as devastatingly handsome as the man who now lounged upon her bed.

"We don't have to continue, Norah, unless you want to."

He was making her decide. Offering her a chance to retreat from what he'd begun in a fit of pure devilment. Why? Because he was beset by some errant twinge of guilt about the day's events? Or because he was as shaken as she was by the emotions he'd unwittingly unleashed between them, this sizzling heat that pounded in her blood?

He had hurt her, confused her, trampled over the hidden, vulnerable places in her soul. He had taken their wedding day and cast it aside as if it had meant little more to him than the sheaf of cards strewn across the bed. And yet, after all that had happened, he had come to her tonight because she had asked him to. He had come in order to spare her further humiliation.

If she turned him away, what purpose would it serve? To hurt him, when he was already so filled with emotional scars? To maintain a grasp on her pride?

Her pride was a cold bedfellow. One that had shared her nights for twenty-some years. Now this man, with his hot hands, his sulky, sensual mouth, his green eyes that lit fire beneath her skin, was offering her a night far different. Perhaps he could not give her the love she craved with all her heart, but he was offering her the sweet intoxication of his mouth, the skilled play of his hands, the carnal promise that shimmered in every dark strand of his hair, every sinew of thigh and chest and shoulder.

To surrender her virginity to a man she was in love with. To have him guide her into rivers of passion for the first time, delve into places that had never been touched, spill his seed deep into her womb. Had she ever truly believed such a miracle could happen to her?

It was a dizzying gift, one Norah hungered for in the deepest reaches of her battered heart. If she only had the courage to reach out and take it.

Mustering all her courage, she reached for the cards. Those unfathomable green eyes mated with hers, an almost physical possession that left her aching.

"Norah." Just her name. Ragged. Hungry, a fine sheen of sweat glistening on his half-bared body. But that wasn't enough for her now.

"I want to raise the stakes," she breathed, feeling as if she were a stranger to herself.

"Name your wager."

She couldn't look at him, her pulse so wild for a heartbeat she couldn't speak. "That if I lose, we . . . I mean that you will—will . . ."

"Will what, sweetheart?"

She raised her gaze to his. "Ravish me, Aidan."

CHAPTER
15

Silence gathered up a thousand threads of desire the game had woven between them into a crushing fist of need. Norah watched as Aidan's eyes darkened, until they were almost black, his nostrils flaring. Hunger. Primitive, raw masculine hunger. It shivered in his eyes, deepening, intensifying, compelling response from the most feminine parts of Norah's being.

She dealt the cards, fumbling, but at that instant Aidan caught her hand, engulfing it in long, hot fingers. "I forfeit."

"What?"

"I admit defeat. No. I embrace defeat."

"But you haven't even looked at your cards."

"You've beaten me with weapons I doubt you can even understand. Or do you understand more than I think, my sweet, solemn little bride? Do you know exactly what you're doing to me with those wide, wondering eyes of yours, and those velvet lips?"

A tiny cry escaped her as he dashed the cards off the bed, letting them flutter to the floor. He levered himself onto his hands and knees, shifting until he was so close to her she was engulfed by his shadow, overwhelmed by the latent power of his body.

"Are you sure, Norah? That you want this? I'll be damned if I'll let you string yourself out across this bed like some virgin sacrifice because Montgomery is lodging across the hall. Do you want this? Do you want . . . me?"

His voice was so hard, roughened with need, and yet there was vulnerability underneath.

Do you want me?

There were shadows of another woman's rejections still in Aidan Kane's eyes—a rejection that the arms of countless other lovers had not managed to cleanse. Women far more beautiful than she had tried it, Norah was certain. Women with boundless skill in the bedchamber, who would know what a man wanted and needed to satisfy his carnal hungers.

But she loved Aidan, Norah thought, her throat aching. Not the reckless scoundrel, bent on his own destruction. But the battered knight who had somehow lost his way. Surely that love should count for something.

His breath teased her tingling lips. His heat seeped through the thin layer of her nightgown. The musky-hot scent of male arousal filled her head, intoxicating her. She wanted him to reach out to her, but he kept still, waiting for her to answer.

She did so the only way she knew how. She lifted her face until the pliant curves of her lips brushed the hard lines of Aidan's own. With a groan of need, Aidan delved one hand into the thickness of her hair, opening his mouth over hers in a kiss that was all fiery hunger and fierce possession.

The powerful weight of his body was lowered atop hers, the coarse hair spanning his chest abrading the fragile skin revealed by the gaping bodice of her nightgown. His thighs tangled with hers, impatient with the fine layers of cloth that formed a barrier between them.

But it was Aidan's lean hips that seduced her, rubbing with a delicious pressure in a seductive rhythm against the subtle swell of her belly. Norah knew painfully little about the rites she was about to be initiated into, but she knew enough to recognize the rigid length of Aidan's sex for what it was as it branded its imprint into her flesh.

She gasped at the melting sensation it caused between the trembling columns of her own thighs, a primal throbbing that tore a soft moan from her lips.

"Aidan," she breathed, as he trailed sweet kisses across her cheeks, her eyelids, her throat. "Aidan . . ."

"Do you want me, Norah? Then tell me. Tell me you want me."

"Yes. I want you. I already told you that I—"

"Do you want me to touch you? Underneath your nightgown, Norah? Where your skin is all silky and soft?"

Her cheeks stung, her body trembled. She'd asked him to ravish her, to ravish her because she hadn't had the courage to ask him to love her, that plea too painful in its impossibility. But why was he goading her? Why was he forcing the words from her, when all she wanted was for him to kiss her and to hold her?

But she forced the words from her lips. "Yes. Touch me, Aidan."

"Where?"

"Under my—my nightgown."

"Do you want me to taste you?"

"T—Taste me?" He made her sound like some pagan banquet, laid out for his delight.

"Take off your gown, Norah. I need to see you, angel, see you all over."

She nodded, more embarrassed than she'd ever been in her life, and yet so intrigued it was like a fire pulsing in every part of her. He rolled to one side, his eyes clinging to her with a feverish light. Her skin felt as if it were on fire with shame—shame because she was not beautiful. Shame because of her own wantonness.

She closed her eyes, unwilling to see Aidan's reaction when he first saw her, fearful that it would wound her someplace she would never, ever heal. Then she wriggled out of the flimsy garment that veiled her from his eyes.

The silence was painful; the darkness behind her tightly closed lids failed to block out her awareness that he was watching her. The cool drafts teased the burning rosettes of her nipples, stirring the soft dusky down between her trembling thighs. She clenched them together, covering her breasts instinctively with her arms.

Dear God, what did he want from her? *Tell me that you want me . . .* His words echoed inside her. *Tell me . . .* Is that what this man needed from her? To hear the words, to believe it was true?

"Aidan," she breathed. "Touch me."

"Where, Norah? Where do you want me to touch you? Do you want me to touch your lovely breasts? Those tight little buds that are throbbing? Or should I kiss them to soothe away the ache?"

"I—I don't know!" she cried helplessly. "I just . . . I told you I want you. I don't know—know anything more. Why are you making me—"

"Because I'm a scoundrel, Norah. A blackguard. Because I have to know that you want this, or I swear by the devil himself I'll get up right now and leave your bed. I had one wife who tolerated my caresses. I won't endure that again."

"I told you I want you! How can I help it, with you lying there . . . your chest all bare, your face . . . smiling that smile. It could seduce the very angels in heaven."

"I don't want to seduce any angel tonight but the one I just made my wife," he purred. "But be warned: I intend to seduce you most thoroughly, my lady. Until you know what it is to be possessed completely by a man—even down to your very soul. Until no other man can ever touch you so deeply, so fiercely, no matter how many times you allow them to try."

"I don't want anyone else . . . could never—" Norah's anguished protest ended in a gasp she felt clear to her toes as Aidan's warm, callused palm cupped the fluid weight of one breast. He lowered his dark head, and in a heartbeat his mouth had fastened on the throbbing point of her nipple with an almost savage hunger. No tender wooing, no gentle urgings, no awkward fumblings. Just passion, in its most potent form. Desire without boundaries. Hunger that did not assuage but consumed.

Hot and wet, blessed with a fiendish skill, he suckled her, teased her, taunting the hardened bud with the tip of his tongue until she arched into his moist caress, urging him to draw harder, deeper.

Sensation speared down to Norah's womb, tightening it in tiny, pulsing contractions, dampening its entrance with dewy moisture, making her crave things only this man could offer her: fulfillment, after an eternity of emptiness; the surging power of Aidan Kane's passion after too many nights alone.

His hands were everywhere—tracing her rib cage, splaying in ardent wonder over her belly, tracing maddening patterns on the painfully sensitive flesh of her inner thighs. He nibbled gently on the underside of her breast, traced his tongue in a sizzling path down the delicate ridges of her ribs. Norah writhed, ragged moans breaching her lips, her own hands clinging to Aidan's powerful shoulders, threading through the thick, dark waves of his hair as he trailed hot kisses to places she never dreamed a man's lips would dare find.

And when he buried his face against the swell of her stomach, edged heated kisses downward until his feverish breath stirred the dewy cleft between her thighs, Norah all but screamed at the shattering sensation.

"Tell me what you want, Norah. Do you want me to stop?" He dared her, taunted her, insufferably certain of her answer. "Or do you want me to kiss you here, sweetheart?" he asked, leaving the moist print of his kiss on the inside of her thigh. "And other places if you'll let me."

At that instant she thought she'd let him do anything, as

long as he didn't stop this slow immersion in an unforgettable fire.

"I want you to—to . . . do whatever you want. I—oh!" She gasped as his finger dipped to the quivering pink bud hidden shyly beneath the dusky thatch of down.

He chuckled, the husky, satisfied sound of a lover well pleased. "Open up for me, Norah. I want to make you feel . . . delicious."

Her muscles instinctively clenched tighter. He was luring her down forbidden pathways, dark labyrinths she was certain most women had never explored. But the callused tip of his finger danced with indescribable delicacy on a pulsing-point of sensation, where every pleasure nerve of her body seemed centered.

"Open, Norah, or I'll stop." It was a teasing threat, one that infuriated her, that stung color into her cheeks. If she'd had the slightest scrap of willpower left, she would have rolled away from him, closed herself to him.

But the thought of him ending this before she reached that shimmering cloud of fulfillment that glistened just beyond her reach was unthinkable.

"You're despicable," Norah breathed, her voice catching on a half sob. But she forced her legs to relax, edging them apart beneath Aidan's burningly intense gaze.

She was rewarded by a shuddering masculine groan. His hand cupped her womanhood with a firm mastery that made her quake, and his mouth fastened on hers with an ardor that swept away everything but the mind-numbing madness that was Aidan Kane's kiss.

Her lips parted of their own volition, and his tongue swept inside the dark cavern of her mouth, possessing, stroking, imprinting the taste of him until she was certain if she lived a hundred years she would never forget the wild sweetness of this Irish knight.

Deep and sure, his tongue thrust in a rhythm that matched the movements of his hips against her, the friction of his breeches against her skin making her want to tear away the elegant fabric, until there was nothing between that throbbing, hard length of Aidan's manhood and her own fevered flesh.

She tugged ineffectually at the skin-tight garment, unable to budge it, yet able to feel the flexing of powerful muscles, the heat of him, tempting her fingers.

With a muttered oath, Aidan gained enough room between them to reach his breech flap, but instead of undoing it, he grasped Norah's hand and flattened it there, against straining fabric and rigid male arousal.

"Is this what you want, sweeting?" he murmured, arching into her hand. "To touch me? Hold me? I want it too. Your fingers tracing me, so soft. Open my breeches, angel."

She struggled with the fastenings, scarce believing her own boldness—no, not hers, but Aidan's boldness—goading her, enticing her to hazard things she never would have, try things she'd not have dared even consider. The fastenings popped free, and the straining fabric peeled back. Norah burrowed beneath it, touching velvet-sheathed steel, the length of him astonishingly hard and dauntingly large.

She had wanted to curse him a dozen times for his subtle goading, but now she had her vengeance as her fingers curled delicately around his shaft.

His hips bucked, his head arched back, his lips twisting in a grimace as if trying to control sensations sweeping through him. His jaw knotted as she stroked him, learned the feel of his most intimate mystery.

A harsh animal sound hissed between his gritted teeth as she cupped him with exquisite gentleness. Then he swore, levering himself away from her, shedding the tight garment with almost savage haste and casting it upon the floor. When he turned back to Norah he was magnificently naked, the candlelight illuminating every sinewy plane; the powerful length of thigh, impressive width of his gleaming shoulders, his hips narrow and taut, and that part of him straining, swollen, where her fingers had just explored.

Her husband . . . Norah thought, still dazed by all that had happened. This magnificent, rugged, reckless man, with his intense green eyes and his devil's smile, would come to her bed whenever he willed it, possess her body whenever he desired it, plant his seed in her womb with fierce, dizzying sensuality that made her wild and wanton, helpless and yet more powerful than she'd ever felt in her life.

It was terrifying. Miraculous. It left her feeling raw and vulnerable, and aching with need for him. She opened her arms, and Aidan covered her body with the steely hardness of his own. She had overheard horrible tales of wedding nights before—tales of excruciating pain, when the husband turned into some rutting beast, possessed by animal urges he could not control.

But as Aidan's mouth closed on hers for a hungry, melting kiss, his thighs parting the trembling columns of her own, Norah's own eagerness for the consummation raged so fiercely she arched and writhed against him, her hands clutching at him, her own tongue making increasingly bold forays to tangle with his in his mouth.

He pulled away, gasping, his eyes devouring her, his breath rasping, as he hooked his hard hands under her knees and spread them farther apart, opening her like an exotic flower. His fingers quested downward, to the most tender part of her, that part that was damp and throbbing, nearly wild to be caressed by those long, bronzed fingers. Three times he circled the throbbing nub, then dipped into the entryway that was afire with the need to be pierced by him. Three times Norah quaked and gasped, arching into his hand. Dear God, what was he doing to her? Torturing her? Teasing her?

"Please, Aidan . . ." she said breathlessly, desperately. "I . . . oh, please . . ."

"Tell me, Norah," he grated, the words a throaty rasp, those green devil's eyes dancing like twin flames of desire. "What do you want me to do?"

"I want you to—to finish it. I want you . . ." She swallowed hard, but she didn't care anymore. She didn't care if he thought her wanton. He was the one who had made her this way. "I want you to come inside me. Fill me, Aidan. I want—"

With a snarl of pure triumph, he bracketed her hips in his hands and fastened his mouth on hers in a kiss so deep, so savagely possessive, she was certain she would never be the same. At that instant, his hips settled deep in the cradle between her thighs.

The blunt tip of him probed the entrance moistened by his loving, and Norah caught her breath in anticipation.

"You're mine, Norah. Mine. May God damn me to hell if I ever let you forget it." He rasped the words as his hips surged forward. A cry of pain escaped Norah's lips as he embedded himself deep inside her body, but the pain shimmered into glittering wonder at the feel of him—hard, hot, proud, gloved by the very essence of her woman's body.

She expected skilled seduction, the teasing he must have perfected in countless other beds. She expected him to continue whatever game he'd been playing since he'd entered her bedroom an hour before.

But there was no dark amusement in Aidan's eyes now. No mockery—of himself, nor of the wildfire he'd created between them.

Fury—stark, wild, terrifying in its power—shone in every line in his face. Fury and dizzying passion. Desperation and an unexpected darting of what could have been fear.

As if he could see the reflections of his own emotions in Norah's passion-flushed face, Aidan's jaw knotted. He set himself against her with steely determination, thrusting deep, hard, every muscle in his body whipcord taut, as rough-edged sounds of pleasure and of pain escaped between his clenched teeth.

Sweat dampened his skin, fusing them together. She had not expected gentleness from this man, no tender words of loving. But it was as if something had changed, shifted in the moment he drove his sex deep into her body. As if everything had changed.

Carnal mastery disappeared in the wake of feral need, teasing gave way to astonishment. Wariness seeped into that fallen-angel face. It was as if he had suddenly stared into an enchanted mirror and seen something that had shaken him to the last hidden corners of his soul.

Aidan delved deeper, stroked harder, as if by force of will alone he could drive away whatever had so unnerved him. Norah kissed him, touched him, reveling in the stark contrast between feminine silk and throbbing male steel. She closed her eyes, dreaming of possessing not only Aidan's surging passion but his heart. And when the wave of pleasure broke over her, crashing through her in shuddering pulses of madness, she cried, her tears dampening Aidan's shoulder as he thrust into her once, twice, then gave a hoarse groan of surrender as he filled her with his seed.

Norah trembled, listening to the sudden stillness, broken only by the soft rasping of their breath in their lungs, the marrow-deep shudders of fulfillment that still coursed their bodies. He was still joined to her, buried deep, and Norah wished that she could hold him there forever.

She didn't know what to say to him, this man who now knew her body so intimately, this man who had shattered every rein she'd held on the unexpected well of sensuality deep inside her and turned her into a maddened, desperate creature of the flesh with his kisses and his caresses.

Instead she kissed him, infusing that caress with all the tenderness, all the wonder, all the love that still vibrated in her soul.

When he pulled away from her, Norah felt as if he'd torn her heart from her breast and carried it with him. His eyes were shuttered, green pools of secrets beneath the dark hair her fingers had tousled; that mouth that had devoured every inch of her with such wild hunger was tight now, curled into a frown. Why? Had she disappointed him somehow? Disgusted him with the magnitude of the response he'd drawn from her? Or was there something else that had so disturbed him?

Norah caught her lips between her teeth and groped for the coverlets to draw over her body, now so ruthlessly exposed to his glare. His eyes grew even darker.

"Aidan?" His name was the softest query. It was all she could manage to squeeze between her kiss-reddened lips. "What—what are you thinking?"

"Thinking?" A brittle smile flashed across his face, one of seething recklessness and danger. Yet it didn't reach his eyes. "That if all my gambling losses were so . . . pleasurable, I would be the most fortunate man in Christendom."

The cool words hurt the fragile places in Norah's spirit he had just opened.

"Don't look so downcast, my love. Perhaps this marriage bargain we have reached won't be so painful after all," he said, climbing from the bed. He grabbed up his breeches, putting them on with a laziness that sizzled along Norah's nerves. "In fact, any time you . . . desire me, you need only tell me you want me, and I shall be happy to accommodate you."

Mockery? After what they had just shared? It was a subtle sting of cruelty, as if he were attempting to drive her away. Norah reeled from it, her cheeks burning with humiliation. Her eyes stung. But she would not let him see her cry.

Why was it that, despite the insensitivity of his words, her gaze clung to wide masculine shoulders suddenly stiffened as if they had been dealt some kind of blow, a face filled with swirling clouds of some emotion she couldn't name.

"Why, Aidan? Why are you saying such things to me? Acting this way?"

"What way is that?"

"As if you—you want to hurt me?" She met his gaze levelly.

Something flickered in his gaze for a heartbeat—regret and bitter self-contempt. Then it was gone.

"On the contrary, it was my intention to congratulate you," he observed, tugging on his rumpled shirt. The fleeting regret shifted, a grim satisfaction clinging to those lips that had kissed her to madness.

"You have a decidedly well-loved look about you, Norah mine. Every kiss, every touch, every cry of pleasure we shared is now captured in your face. Not a person at the ball tomorrow night will doubt that you surrendered everything to me. No, not even your champion, Montgomery."

The words were like a dagger thrust, wounding Norah, piercing that fragile sense of wonder, that delicate wisp of hope his kisses and caresses had brought to life inside her. Philip. This was about Philip. Aidan's visit to her room, his passion-hazed caresses, his kisses. His voice had been so loud when he'd tormented her, his laughter rumbling out during the card game. Even when he'd entered her bed-chamber, he had knocked loud enough to alert every servant in Rathcannon that he had come to bed his new bride.

To possess her. To mark her as his own. Not because he loved her, but because of the unreasonable enmity that had sprung up between her new husband and the man she had once fancied herself in love with.

The certainty was more painful than anything she'd ever known. She raised her chin, casting Aidan a glare filled with outrage and with pain.

"Perhaps you would like me to share this night's experience with Lord Montgomery? Expound upon your prowess?"

Those broad shoulders stiffened, that rugged face stilled. "What the devil?"

"I'm your bride. You have bedded me. Consummated the marriage. From what you say, it is important that the world be made aware that I am now your . . . your what, Sir Aidan? Possession?"

"My wife," he bit out. "You'll have to forgive me for wanting to make that clear to Montgomery. The man seemed most disbelieving of my claim to you, despite the

KIMBERLY CATES

ring on your finger. But you can be certain I won't leave any
room for further misunderstandings. You are mine, Norah.
Now. Forever. There will never be another man in your
heart. . . . *Or* in your bed."

With those words the rage flowed out of Norah, leaving
only a yawning emptiness where all her dreams had been.

No, she thought with wrenching pain, there would never
be another man in her heart. Being wed to Aidan Kane,
loving him, when he could never return that love, would be
more painful than any trial she had ever known.

258

CHAPTER

16

It was ten years since the ballroom at Rathcannon had been alive with the chatter of guests. Ten years since Delia Kane had reigned here like a beautiful sorceress.

Hundreds of candles cast light through crystal, turning the chandeliers into sculptures of fire and ice. The music of a string quartet wafted across Rathcannon's ballroom, while the scent of rhododendrons banked in beribboned baskets about the floor filled the air.

Thirty-some members of Irish rural society—squires and country gentlemen, landholders and a smattering of nobility—had brought their wives and daughters to be introduced to the new Lady Kane.

Aidan should have been at Norah's side, introducing her, drawing her into conversation with the gaggle of gawking fools. He should have danced with her, and told her she looked like a fairy queen garbed in green satin, with a delicate silver netting draped like gossamer wings about her.

But all he could do was stand here, isolated by memories

that would give him no peace. He saw himself as he'd been what seemed an eternity ago, watching men surrounding Delia like some kind of unholy aura.

From beneath slitted lids, he had observed this squire and that youth, just up from Trinity College, wondering if they were plotting a tryst with Sir Aidan's woman, or if they had already lain with her to satiate her greedy desires. He had watched his neighbors dance with her, touching her hand, devouring her carnal beauty with eyes that stripped away the glistening angel-faced woman, until only the harlot remained, eager for the hands of a man on her skin—every man's hands, any man's hands—except for those of the husband who had planted his babe in her womb and then been bastard enough to insist that she bear it.

Not because he'd felt any mad desire to become a father, brainless young fool that he'd been. Rather because he'd been unwilling to let his wife fall beneath the filthy knives of some back-street butcher who would likely kill her.

Aidan leaned against a stone pillar where shadows clung, his evening attire impeccable, his eyes as hard and bright and filled with hidden fire as the emerald stickpin that glinted in the snowy folds of his cravat.

He should have been able to dismiss his memories of Delia. He might have succeeded, had it not been for the woman who glided about the ballroom now, her dusky locks caught up in a wreath of gardenias, her eyes dark pools in which a man could lose himself forever.

He knew her, every soft curve and velvety hollow, every pleasure place that made her sigh and moan. When he'd left her last night in that passion-tumbled bed, he had been certain he'd possessed her so thoroughly she would never stray. But it seemed he was cursed to repeat the past with yet a second Kane bride—for as he watched Philip Montgomery hovering about Norah, a thousand long-buried doubts shivered to life inside him.

Doubts fired by the hot, pulsing fever Aidan's new bride had afflicted him with last night in her bed.

God, how had it happened? He raged inwardly, cursing the fates that had brought this woman here. How had he lost that devil-may-care attitude with which he'd bedded every woman since Delia barred him from her chambers? He had made it a game—had even teasingly labeled bed games as sexual fencing matches, making certain that the foils were tipped so that they could not pierce the lady in question's heart, nor his own. It had been an amusement fraught with challenge and pleasure, yet one in which both parties knew the rules, and could walk away after the match was over with laughter on their lips.

But somehow, between the time Aidan had tossed the first card out upon Norah's bed and the time he had pierced the tender veil of her maidenhead, everything had changed. The practice weapons had shifted into blade-sharp points, and Aidan had felt those terrifying emotions drive deep into his chest, far deeper than even Delia had ever stabbed him.

He had thrust into the soft haven of Norah's body, felt her very essence melting into his spirit, felt those tightly guarded pieces of his soul Delia had not managed to destroy starting to slip into Norah's hands.

Felt himself . . . what? Starting to . . . *love her?*

The mere words sent terror racing through Aidan's vitals, making him feel naked, vulnerable. No. He'd vowed he would never let another woman have that kind of power over him again. He would never allow soft kisses and feminine wiles to deceive him, lure him to believe in happily ever afters, in passions that would endure beyond the realm of time.

A fool's dream. A poet's realm of blissful insanity. A draught of nectar-sweet poison served up by the same feminine hands that would one day betray the man foolish enough to drink it.

Aidan shuddered, remembering the desperate craving to be touched by Delia's hands, to be loved by her, the wild rages of jealousy that had tormented him until he feared he *would* go mad. And laughter . . . always Delia's laughter, mocking him, daring him to be man enough to take what he wanted, until he'd nearly surrendered what remained of his soul to meet that twisted challenge. Sickened himself by coming far too close to forcing her to give what she denied him, what she dangled before him, like tempting sweetmeats before a starving man's eyes.

That single memory still had the power to make Aidan's stomach churn, his nerves coil with revulsion. He had vowed never to allow another woman to make such a beast of him again, to strip away everything decent inside him, leaving nothing but rage and lust and cravings that could never be satisfied.

But here he stood, watching the bride he had taken to his bed one night before, and the hunger in his spirit was raging more fiercely than it ever had for beautiful, shallow Delia. White-hot blades of jealousy carved with exquisite torment every nerve in his body, cleaving away the illusion of self-control he had clung to since the day he had left his faithless wife's bedchamber for the last time.

He was possessed by the need to stalk across the ballroom, scoop Norah up into his arms, and carry her through the crowd up the broad staircase and into his bedchamber. He was afire with the need to fling her onto his massive bed, strip away the layers of satin from her ivory skin, to kiss and caress and suckle every part of her, until she begged him for release. To tease her to even wilder heights with his mouth, his hands, his tongue, until he was buried so deep inside her she would never forget how desperately she wanted him. Him. Only him.

He wanted to wring cries of pulsing hunger from that slender throat, hear her tell him that she loved him. Love—not born of a moment's passion, fading away when dawn's light trickled through the bedchamber window. But the love of a lady for her knight of old, transcending death itself.

If only he truly believed such love was possible at all.

He gave a bitter laugh. Considering the way he'd hurt her

in those raw minutes before he'd stormed from her chamber, he'd be lucky if his bride didn't loathe him.

"Papa!"

Cassandra's voice startled him, and he turned to peer down into his daughter's face, the mere sight of her tonight inflicting yet another blow to his already battered heart.

Cassandra—his little scrape-kneed princess—had somehow been magically transformed into a beautiful young woman, the living image of the willful girl Aidan himself had fallen in love with in that far-away ballroom in London so many years before.

But the facial likeness was the only thing that whispered of Delia in the daughter they had created together. Instead of eyes that begged a man to come hither, Cassandra's eyes were bright and eager, her mouth sweet instead of seductive, without a thousand pretty lies at the tip of her tongue. Had Aidan suffered seeing Cass thus transfigured a month ago— her gown that of a lady, her hair a woman's shining coronet—the mere sight of her would have shattered Aidan's heart. But tonight, even his cherished daughter could not seem to break the invisible chains that had been forged between him and the woman now gliding across the castle ballroom's floor in the arms of Philip Montgomery.

"Papa, you are being the biggest blockhead in all Ireland!" Cassandra accused. "Standing here as if you were hiding, when the whole assembly is fairly perishing to talk to you."

"Don't you mean pry into the strange broth that is my marriage, Cassandra?" he said with a tinge of bitterness. "God knows, even here they've given me no peace, hounding me for any scrap of scandal they can carry back to share with some other gossiping fiend. Perhaps I should stop the orchestra for a moment and make an announcement to the blasted bunch of them. *I'm sure you are all most astonished at my precipitous marriage, but you see, my daughter found me a bride and gave her to me for my birthday. And since Miss Linton had no other more attractive prospects for her future, she deigned to wed me,*" he mocked. "I can just imagine what a delightful time these old dragons would have with that tidbit of information."

Cassandra's hurt glance made him feel like a bastard, but at that moment he saw Montgomery draw Norah a whisper closer to his body, Aidan's bride tipping her head, as if eager to capture something his lordship had said.

"Papa, even if you detest everyone else here, you could at least pay some attention to Norah."

"It seems she's doing quite fine without me." Aidan's jaw clenched, his eyes seething beneath half-closed lids.

Montgomery had whisked Norah to the far edge of the dance floor, and Aidan saw Norah lean close to him, whisper something in Montgomery's ear. A fist seemed to slam into Aidan's gut as he watched the Englishman move out of the bevy of dancers and tuck Norah's hand possessively in the crook of his elbow. With a hasty glance to make certain they were unseen, Philip Montgomery led Aidan's wife out the doors that led down to Rathcannon's gardens.

How many times had Aidan watched the same scene unfolding? Delia and her lovers stealing away for thirty minutes, an hour or longer, while Aidan and every other guest in attendance pictured all too clearly the lusty exchange that was going on behind the yew hedge or a bank of roses. Delia not caring if she were discovered—actually delighting in it—then returning, licking those passion-ripe lips like a cat who had sampled forbidden cream.

Yet never, in all his years with Delia, had the pain been this brutal, this consuming.

"Oh, Papa," Cassandra said, as if realization had just dawned on her. "You are upset because she has danced with his lordship? If you ask me, *you* are the one who owes *her* an apology."

"Owe her?"

"I don't see why you should act like the maligned hero of some melodrama since you didn't offer to dance with her yourself! You could hardly expect her to stand by the wall with the buck-toothed Misses Baldrey, could you?"

"Cassandra, I—" Aidan stopped, grimaced. She was right. He was sulking in the corner with all the finesse of the confused, hurting, betrayed youth he'd been when Delia held his heart. He was acting for all the world like a lovesick fool. The knowledge enraged him, terrified him, spurring him to straighten, to draw away from the pillar upon which he'd been leaning. He had watched his first wife parade countless lovers before his face, but Norah . . . No, he'd not allow any man—especially a pompous ass like Philip Montgomery—to touch so much as the hem of her gown.

"Just a blasted minute," he said, pausing to scowl down at his daughter in confusion. "Why this sudden concern on Norah's behalf when you had decided to hate her?"

Cassandra squirmed, flushed. "I suppose I saw the sadness in her eyes. The loneliness—as if . . . as if she were pressed up against the window of a shop filled with wonderful treasures but no one had ever invited her inside."

The insight wrenched at Aidan's gut.

"In her letters and when she first arrived, she was so kind and funny and so—so good. Angry as I was at the way she acted while you were sick, well, I just couldn't believe she could be the lady in the letters and a tyrant at the same time. I don't know why I acted the way I did."

"Blast, you're a confusing little baggage. I think you females conspire to drive men mad."

"I don't want you to be mad, Papa. I want you to go find Norah. Dance with her."

"I'll find her."

With that, he stalked away, winding through the assemblage, ignoring greetings and queries, ignoring everything except the wild clamoring in his veins, the throbbing in his temples, the hot, aching hole that had once been his heart.

The garden was lit with paper lanterns that glowed in pinks and lavenders and greens. Stone benches gleamed, silvery in the moonlight, while statues born of myth and legend reared up in the uncertain light, as if enchanted by some strange magic that had made them shiver to life.

Aidan swallowed hard, the echoing of his bootheels upon the path seeming like cannon fire, his fists clenched at his sides, as if their grasp on nothingness could somehow contain the emotions tearing through him with such excruciating power.

When he heard the soft murmur of voices in a tiny arbor, hidden from the eyes of any who would stray down the pathways, he was tempted to call out. But to what purpose? To warn Norah so she could spring out of her lover's arms? Aidan grimaced, disgusted with himself. Norah was not Delia. They were as different as the silvery moon from the most dazzling sunlight, as different as a dove from a peregrine with a thirst for blood.

Trying to get the jealousy tormenting him under control, Aidan strode around the corner. What he saw all but drove him to his knees.

A lithe feminine figure was clasped in a man's embrace, her rosy arms twined about his neck in ecstasy. Laughter, silvery, ethereal, echoed from lips that Aidan had kissed the night before.

"Philip! Oh, Philip, you are the most wonderful man in the world! I knew I could depend upon you to help me! How can I ever, *ever* thank you?"

"Shall I tell you, Norah? Shall I show you?" That noble head lowered, capturing her mouth in a kiss.

"Philip!" she gasped, a vision of maidenly protest— exactly the kind men could never resist. Montgomery tangled his hands in her hair.

"You cannot love that beast you call a husband!" he grated. "No one could blame you for seeking comfort from a better man. Norah, let me love you."

The words coiled whip cords of madness around Aidan's throat, blinding him with a red haze of fury and betrayal.

"Philip, I—I don't know what to say." Shaken, she sounded so shaken. Hadn't he heard such tones a dozen times before? Women tempting their suitors to greater lengths, more grandiose vows of adoration. "I am wed to Sir Aidan."

Aidan strode into the pool of light, his voice steel sheathed in ice. "Oh, please, don't let such minuscule concerns as wedding vows interfere in your pleasure, madam."

Norah gave a tiny cry as she wrenched out of Montgomery's embrace.

"Kane, you sneaking bastard!" the nobleman snarled. "I should have known you'd be skulking in the bushes, following us."

"On the contrary, I was merely coming to claim my bride for a dance. I had not fulfilled my husbandly duty to do so, as my daughter none too gently pointed out. As for any attempt to . . . *skulk,* you are mistaken. I made a great deal of noise when I approached, my lord, but I doubt either of you would have heard the blast of a cannon if it were fired from this hedge. You were . . . otherwise occupied."

Norah pressed one hand to her chest, those delicate, gloved fingers silhouetted against the breasts Aidan had lavished with kisses the night before. He was fired with the need to drag her into his arms, force her down into the hidden bower of the arbor, and take her again, hard and fast and furious, until Philip Montgomery's kiss was nothing but a crumbling ash of memory in the wake of Aidan's own onslaught of passion.

"Aidan, please." Her voice trembled, so soft and musical, so uncertain. Aidan clenched his jaw against its dangerous persuasion. "This is not what it appears."

"You forget I have had some experience in such matters. It has always been a Kane family tradition to dismiss wedding vows as soon as they become inconvenient. However, I must say, I cannot recall any bride doing so quite this soon—a mere day after her wedding."

"You are the one who said our vows were meaningless. I never—"

"Don't bother scrambling to explain," he said, cutting her off with a wave of his hand. "You were the picture of maidenly protestations, my sweet. I suppose that you flung your arms about this man's neck because—what? He'd taken a troublesome speck of dust out of your eye? I'm quite certain that would qualify him as—how did you say it? The most wonderful man in the world."

Bitter, biting, he echoed her words of moments before, amazed at the jagged hole they tore in his chest. He expected her to wince, to flush, readily trapped in a snare of her own words. But instead of growing teary eyed, or letting that wounded-doe expression of hurt fill her eyes, the dark depths filled with outrage.

"Why don't you be honest for once, Aidan?" she said. "Say, Don't bother to explain because I don't want to hear the truth. I'd much rather leap to brainless conclusions about things I don't understand."

"A man with his hands all over you, begging you to let him love you, doesn't need much translation, in my experience."

"Why should it bother you if she did let me love her?" Montgomery raged. "Before a sennight, you'll be in some other woman's bed. Or will you have a pair of them, Kane? A brace of pretty harlots playing bed games with you? From what I hear, you have carnal appetites that could scarce be fulfilled by a decent woman. Or do you plan to debase Norah by teaching her your lecherous tricks?"

Aidan felt the blood drain from his face, fury and pain and betrayal clawing inside him. Scenes flashed before his eyes: the bed littered with playing cards, the wildly sensual wagers that had fired his blood driving him to heights of desire he'd never reached before. He could see Norah, her lips glossy, parted in a breathy gasp, as he unfastened her nightgown one button at a time, daring to touch her, taste her, tease her.

Lecherous tricks . . .

There were those who would claim it was so—the game

he had played with her in their bridal bed. But it had shifted into something so stunningly powerful, so wrenchingly beautiful, it still awed him, terrified him.

The idea that Norah might have confided such happenings to Montgomery poured acid on nerve endings already sizzling with tension.

His hard gaze flashed to Norah's face. "Did you follow through on your threat, my lady?" he asked in silky menace. "Did you tell your hero what transpired between us on our bridal night?"

"No! Of course I—I did not!"

"You didn't tell him about our diverting little game of wagers, then?"

"Aidan, please—"

"Montgomery, this I can tell you: You are wrong in your judgment of my bride. Norah may appear the gentle virgin, the quintessential lady, but I assure you, last night she was most—ahem—eager to place herself in my jaded hands."

"You bastard!" Montgomery raged. "I will do everything I can to rescue her from your clutches!"

"Philip, stop! I—"

"Montgomery." Aidan's voice was deadly steel. "If you ever come near my wife again, I vow you will regret it."

"Brave words, Kane. You didn't turn a hair the entire time your first wife was whoring her way through half the king's regiments! You think it will be long before Norah rejects you just as the Lady Delia did?"

Years of rage, beaten down by force of will, suddenly burst their dam, roaring through Aidan like wildfire. His lips curled in a feral snarl, Aidan drove his fist into Philip Montgomery's patrician face. Fire shot through Aidan's right hand at the impact, but he barely felt it, the sensation lost in the surging satisfaction of Montgomery roaring in pain.

The nobleman staggered backward with the force of the blow. One hand covered his face as a crimson stain spread beneath his impeccable glove.

"Stop this! Both of you!" Norah glared at them. The face Aidan had seen wreathed in wonder was now sick with horror.

"Norah, you see what he's capable of!" Montgomery warned. "Violence. Lechery! Surely you cannot want to chain yourself to such an animal."

"She's already chained, Montgomery."

"Chained?" Norah blustered. "What do you plan to do? Keep me locked in a tower like you have Cassandra?"

"You're mine, Norah." He snarled an icy warning.

Norah wheeled on him. "I'm not your property, you stubborn, brainless fool! Was that what this madness was about? Jealousy?"

"The bastard had his hands all over you!"

"And you just assumed I was welcoming his advances."

His fury stumbled in the wake of her outrage. "You were embracing him."

"I embraced him because he'd agreed to petition his grandmother, the duchess of Ware, to ease Cassandra's way into society."

"But he wanted you to run away with him. I heard him!"

"But you didn't wait to see if I would go, did you? No, you were so certain I'd betray you. Why do you think I wed you?"

"You had nowhere else to go."

"I wouldn't sell myself so cheaply!"

"Norah!" Montgomery cut in. "You don't owe this bastard any explanation."

She paid no notice to the nobleman. "Aidan, there is a whole wide world out there beyond the Irish coast! I'm certain I could find a corner of it for myself if I desire to. I wed you for one reason." Her chin tipped upward. "One reason only."

"What the devil is that?" Aidan demanded, hands planted on lean hips, as if daring her . . . daring her to what? Tell him things that could never be?

"I married you because I—" She stopped as her eyes

shimmered with unshed tears, her whole body trembling. "No. Only a fool would cast out her heart to be trampled over yet again!"

He stood frozen as she spun away and ran down the path, away from Montgomery, away from the arbor, away from the ballroom. But most certainly of all, away from him.

"Norah . . ." He breathed her name, his head reeling with memories of how she'd offered herself to him last night, her eyes huge and wanting, her voice breathless with little cries, shy and innocent, and yet eager, generous, opening herself to his lovemaking with a tender ferocity that had astonished him.

What could it possibly mean?

Only a fool would cast her heart out to be trampled over again. Her heart . . . her heart . . .

Was it possible that Norah had given him a treasure more precious than mere vows within the old stone church?

That she . . .

Aidan couldn't even form the thought, couldn't fathom anything so astonishing, so terrifyingly wonderful.

Too stunned to follow as Norah melted into the darkness, Aidan stared after his bride, wary and disbelieving, bewildered and more shaken than he'd ever been in his life.

CHAPTER

17

Mists swirled around Norah as she stumbled blindly through the maze of hillocks and gorse, guided by the intrepid rays of moonlight that managed to pierce the haze.

She wasn't certain where she was going, she only knew she had to escape the ballroom filled with gawking gossip mongers, Philip Montgomery's pleas, and most of all Sir Aidan Kane's fallen-angel eyes, eyes still haunted with anger and betrayal, worlds away from love—the emotion Norah would have sold her soul to see flickering in their emerald depths.

She had almost told him she loved him.

The knowledge lanced through her, making her cheeks burn, her eyes sting. She had flung out words in fury and hurt and pain, and had all but bared her heart to him, there in Rathcannon's garden, with Philip, bleeding from the blow from Aidan's fist, and the harsh words of Aidan's jealous rage still reverberating in her ears.

But she had caught herself just in time, cut off the

admission that would have made her completely vulnerable to this man who had already won far too much of her soul. He had stared at her as if she had run mad, her unfinished sentence pulsing between them, her pain and frustration doubtless branded in her face.

Madness . . . Hadn't she been possessed by it since she'd first set foot on Irish shores? Since she'd nursed Aidan's fever, let him slip his wedding ring upon her finger? Since she'd taken up playing cards upon her bridal bed, and let him seduce her with a sensuality, a wild, pulsing passion that had branded the magic of his lovemaking forever in her heart?

He had taken not only her virginity in that tumbled, passion-hot bed. He had taken her very soul. And then he had shown her exactly how little the night meant to him by making a bitter jest of what had happened between them.

He had warned her, the night she had arrived at his castle by the sea, that he had no heart to give any woman. No love to give anyone save his daughter. And she had seen the truth in his eyes. Yet, even knowing that, even knowing his trust had been so shattered by the heartless Delia, Norah had not been able to keep from making the most costly mistake of her life.

She'd been a fool. A romantic, dreamy-eyed fool when it came to Sir Aidan Kane, weaving fantasies, reaching for the most impossible hopes, believing—actually believing—they were almost within her reach.

But the truth was that only a fool would cast her heart into Aidan's reckless hands. Only a woman fairly begging to be hurt and devastated would allow herself to love him. Delia Kane had made certain no other woman would ever gain entry into Sir Aidan's battered heart. She had forced him to build that wall of recklessness and carelessness about the tender places inside him brick by brick, shutting out light, shutting out hope, leaving only a hard, brittle shell of cynicism.

Norah stumbled, catching a glimpse of something pale against the night sky: the mystery-shrouded ruins of Caislean Alainn. It seemed to be floating in the mist—a castle of enchantment, wreathed in a pearly glow, a fairy bower more mystically beautiful than anything Norah had seen before.

Awed, hurting, she sought haven there, wading through moonlight and a hundred dreams far too ephemeral to hold onto in the harsh light of day.

Her hair had tumbled from its pins, the gardenias she had woven in with such care still caught amongst her dark curls. The sea breeze chilled her arms, and the wet tears coursed down her cheeks as she stepped through the fairy ring of ancient stone, into the shadow of the castle ruins.

It sheltered her, as if the souls of those who had lived here, loved here, had reached out their hands to comfort her. But could there be any comfort in the truth that Aidan Kane could never love her?

She curled up on the ledge where he had lounged the day he had first kissed her and listened to the wind sigh, as if an echo of legendary Maire's ten thousand tears. Slowly, the sounds reached inside Norah, ever so gently untangling the wild knots of her emotions, leaving only one—despair—in its place.

It was a night of fairy moons and dark enchantments, when souls of the unwary were stolen off and mortals were lured down to the Land of the Ever Young by kisses from the fey lips of the Tuatha de Daanan.

As long as Aidan could remember, he had heard the tales, spun out by the crofter folk by the light of peat fires, tidbits of wondrous stories that had fascinated the boy he had been, mesmerized him with a hundred possibilities until he'd grown to be a man.

A man who'd dismissed such wild imaginings, with the same scorn he'd cast away tales of knights and heroes. Yet as Aidan rode his stallion through the mist this night, he felt as if he were passing through a silken veil that separated the world of reason from the one that legends wove.

As if he were being drawn into some sweet madness he was powerless to deny.

Norah.

She was waiting for him somewhere in the mist. He knew it, not with his mind, but in his heart.

For an hour after she'd fled the garden, he had tried to get a grip on the emotions racing through him. Had tried to sift through her words, her touch, her kisses, to discover whatever mysteries had whispered to him behind those dark-lashed eyes.

He had searched Rathcannon for her, tried to cling to rage, to crush sensations so strange, so new, they terrified him.

But as he wandered the hallways, the library, the tangled paths of the garden, all he could see was her face of soft ivory, like the finest cameo by the light of the paper lanterns, her eyes wide and soft and wondering as he made love to her last night.

He had heard the pleasure sounds of countless women he had bedded in the years since he'd shed his own virginity. He had made it his personal quest to bring his partners to shattering climaxes, as if by that skill alone he could rid himself of the self-doubt Delia had left to fester inside him.

Yet never, in the eager embraces of all his amours, had he ever known the excruciating sweetness that had been in Norah's touch, the agonizing healing in her kiss. Never had he felt as if he hadn't taken a woman's body but had somehow cradled the very essence of her being in his hands, a treasure beyond imagining.

Dear God, what was happening to him? Aidan thought, leaning low over the neck of his stallion. It was as if he were being drawn to Norah, linked to her by some invisible thread. A thread that drew him over the hillock, where moonlight spilled over the ruins of another man's dreams.

Caislean Alainn.

How many times had he heard the claim that the tragic castle was possessed by the Tuatha de Daanan? On certain nights, it was said, it could be found floating in a sea of mist, as if those ancient spirits were bearing it away to become a fairy bower.

He had dismissed the tales as he had so many others. But as he slowed his stallion and stared at the ruins, a primal rhythm caught his heart, a crushing sense of fate possessed him. For the castle did seem to drift, apart from the world of mortal men, as distant from cruel reality as the pale, ghostly figure silhouetted against rough-hewn ashlar that had been shattered two hundred years before.

Aidan reined his stallion to a halt just beyond the ring of stones and dismounted, his heart threatening to beat its way out of his chest.

He felt for all the world like some poor mortal glimpsing a fairy queen in her hidden bower. A being so impossibly beautiful it made his eyes ache to look on her.

She was curled upon the stone ledge, moonlight flickering over the blossoms caught in her hair. Silvery rays flowed in mystic streams down the elegant line of her cheek, the graceful curve of her throat, as she lay curled on the ledge, her head pillowed upon one pale hand.

Why had she come here? Aidan wondered, a fist seeming to crush his heart. To this place where he'd first used his kiss to chain her to him, to capture her, to hold her?

Why had he followed her here?

He started toward her tentatively, as if she were a creature of moonlight and mist that would vanish at a touch. But the snap of a twig beneath his bootheel made her stir and raise her head to peer out into the night.

He knew the moment he stepped from the mist into her searching gaze. Heard her sharp intake of breath as she hastily sat up, her face luminous, otherworldly.

Wary.

Oh, God, that she should be afraid of him, this woman of light and tenderness, courage and such inner beauty.

She said nothing, just watched him, her lips parted, her face still, so still.

And he felt like a clumsy fool who was trampling in a world where he didn't belong, could never belong. He groped for words—a hundred pleas for her to understand, to forgive him, to *love* him. But he couldn't form the words. Mist swirled up around his boots as he approached her, like a penitent approaching the holiest of shrines.

"Have you ever heard the legend of the fairy kiss?" he asked softly, as if a mere whisper could make her vanish from his sight.

She shook her head, saying nothing.

"I first heard it when I was a boy. On a night like this, the fairy folk come wandering about the Irish hills, seeking lovers amongst the mortals there. If a man should stray into a fairy ring, it's said he'll find a maiden there. One of such indescribable beauty, no man can resist her power. She'll lead him to the fairy dancing grounds, and if the man should kiss her, she steals his soul, and he will forevermore be her captive, craving the sweetness of that enchanted kiss. From that moment on, he will have fairy-kissed eyes, a dreamy, otherworldly look clinging about him, as if he is forever waiting for his lover to return."

A tiny sound came from Norah's throat, a sad, broken laugh. "There is no fairy maid here."

"Isn't there?" Aidan asked, his voice rasping in his throat. "I never believed there was truth in that tale until tonight."

"Aidan, don't."

"Don't what?"

"You don't need to spin out pretty lies or ply me with fairy stories. We both know I'm not—not beautiful. And a plain woman is not the sort to enchant a man with a kiss."

"Then why do I feel this way? This sweet, pulsing madness? Why did I feel myself drawn here? Why is it that I suddenly believe . . ." He sounded like a fool—a lovesick fool—with his heart in his hands, offering it up to a woman. Heat spilled into his cheeks.

"Believe in what?" Norah's voice prodded softly.

"In magic potions that make hunger for a woman boil like a fever in a man's blood. In fairy rings and castle legends and enchantresses in sea-green satin."

"Not two hours ago you were far from enchanted. You were in a jealous rage, striking out at Philip, striking out at me."

"I never raised a hand to you."

"No. You used words, Aidan. Scorn and mockery. Condemning me without even attempting to listen to the truth."

"I'm listening now."

"Until when? The next time you see me with a man—any man? If a footman hands me a posy, or a neighboring squire takes my hand to help me down from a carriage? Or if I dance with someone else, will you listen then, Aidan? Or will it be Delia's face you see? Delia's betrayal that cuts you so deeply you lash out at me?"

"Norah, I . . ."

"I wouldn't betray you. I could never betray you. But it won't matter, will it? I'll be forever wading through the pain Delia left in you. You managed to open your heart to Cassandra because it is safe, Aidan. She can never hurt you in the way that Delia did. But you will never open your heart to me."

He paced away from her, leaning one hand against the stone wall, feeling the pulse of pain generations past, bewitchings that had brought ecstasy and then destruction.

"Knowing that, Norah, why did you marry me?" He turned to face her.

She slid from the ledge of stone, restless, the gardenias tumbling from her hair, her body slender, supple, eminently touchable, glossed in moonlight.

"I—I am not going to discuss this. Why should it matter? You have what you want, what you needed of me: an honorable name to ease Cassandra's entry into society."

"But what did you gain? And it wasn't a home, security. No, I could see in your eyes in the garden, feel in your touch when I bedded you, that it wasn't such a simple, practical reason that you swore to be my wife."

"Aidan, I'm very tired, worn down. The wedding disaster, the ball, the scene with Philip. I—I haven't the strength to drag all this out now."

"You will tell me, Norah. The truth of it. Now. God in heaven, lady, I need to know."

"So you can chain me completely? Cassandra and I, the pair of us barred in your castle by the sea? You already hold every trump card in our relationship. And you change the rules to suit your will. Why should I surrender the only card I still hold? It's a paltry thing, far beneath your notice."

"I think not. Tell me, Norah. I ask of you. Please. Surely such secrets, shared in a place like this, must hold their own enchantment."

He came to where she stood, grasped her shoulders, and turned her to face him. She peered up at him, the most winsome, beautiful creature he'd ever seen. As he stared into the dark pools of her eyes, he saw there a loveliness that transcended the curve of her lips, the shape of her cheeks, a loveliness of the spirit that awed him.

"Tell me, Norah. Give me that gift."

She was trembling, her eyes glistening, her voice beset by a tiny quaver. "I married you because I—I love you. There, you have the truth. I was foolish enough to fall in love with a man who doesn't want me. Never wanted me. A man who can never love me back."

The words pierced Aidan's soul, shimmering there in luminescent wonder. His throat constricted, his hands catching hers, so fiercely he feared he would bruise them, but he was terrified that if he released her she would slip away, one with the mist and the madness throbbing in his soul.

She loved him. What gift could a man give in return for such a treasure? A man with no heart to offer her in return.

Swept up in the magic, Aidan looked deep into her eyes, then slowly sank to one knee. "Though I cannot give my heart, this I can vow to you: You will never regret entrusting yours to my care. I swear it, Norah, by what little honor still remains in my soul."

A tiny sound came from her throat, those delicate fingers slipping from his grasp, touching his cheek, smoothing back an errant lock of dark hair. "I want to—to believe—"

"In what? Fairy-kissed eyes and love potions that bind souls for eternity? Believe in this, then, if you can believe in no other."

He rose to his feet and drew her into his arms, his mouth seeking hers, supplicant instead of hungry, reverent instead of carnal, asking for response instead of demanding it.

She gave him her very soul.

A cry of surrender shuddered through her, and she clung to him as he kissed her cheeks, her eyelids, her throat. He threaded his fingers through her hair, crushing the gardenia petals in his fingers, releasing their rich scent to mingle with the light tang of mist, the slight salt whisper of the sea.

"I want you, Norah," he groaned, low in his throat. "Want you more than I've ever wanted any woman. I need you to touch me, angel." She could never know what that admission had cost him. "Let me take you back to Rathcannon, to my bed. Let me love you."

"No," she breathed, her fingers tunneling beneath his cloak, trailing up the hard plane of his chest.

Aidan winced, her words stinging places still raw from Delia's rejections. His jaw knotted, and he started to draw away, but she caught at him with pleading hands, her eyes making him captive. "Aidan, please. I want you here . . . here with the magic all around us."

Her words seduced him, bewitched him, setting him adrift in a world of witchery eons old, tempting him beyond bearing. Wordlessly, he unfastened his cloak, his fingers unsteady as he swirled the layered garment onto the ground to make a bed for his lady.

His lady.

He came to her, disrobing her, not in a jesting game, but

this time as if he were carefully unveiling some treasure far too fragile and precious to be touched by mortal hands. The gown that had clung to her willowy curves slid through his hands, the satin still warm from her skin, her scent clinging, elusive, enticing, to the cloth.

He praised her, rasped words against her ivory skin, as he eased her high-waisted corset from her breasts, until the lush mounds were shielded from him by only the thin, crumpled fabric of the chemise beneath.

Aidan's chest squeezed at the sight of her—the pale wisp of fabric that hugged her curves, begging for the touch of his hands, the cascade of dark silk that was her hair. And her incredible angel's eyes—God, would he ever stop hungering to peer into their depths, to see love, that tender, most elusive of emotions, shimmering out at him from beneath her lashes.

Ever so gently, he slipped the chemise from her shoulders, pressing the fabric between his palms and her body as he slid the garment past her waist, her hips, down the length of her legs, until it pooled over her dainty slippered feet. She stepped out of the ring of lace and muslin, and Aidan knelt once more, taking her foot in his hands, removing her slippers as if they were made of the finest crystal.

If there was such a thing as sorcery, he was entrapped in it this night. For as he stripped the stockings from her legs, trailing kisses upon the flesh he bared, he was certain that he would never be the same again.

When Norah was garbed in nothing but mist and moonlight, Aidan rose to his feet, his mouth dry with wanting her. He wanted to imprint the sight of her forever in his mind, to remember when life's light was fading in his eyes. He grasped her arms gently, turning her in a slow circle in the liquid silver of the rays streaming down from the heavens, his gaze caressing the firm swell of breast tipped in delectable coral, the flare of hips, the pale curve of her buttocks. Shadows dipped low, to skim her belly, and glimmers of light snagged on the dark down between her thighs.

That she should offer herself to him thus, here, in this place of magic, wrenched at Aidan's heart. And he wanted this loving to be everything she had dreamed of before she'd crossed the sea to a man who was nothing like those cherished fantasies.

His fingers went to the fastenings of his jacket, but she reached out, stopping him. Her tongue crept out, moistening her lips, as she began the task of undressing him. Awkward, fumbling slightly, she struggled with buttons and neckcloth, waistcoat and breeches, while Aidan stood, rigid, waves of arousal all but driving him to his knees. And when he was naked as she, he eased her down onto the mound of garments, covering her moon-washed body with his own.

"Norah." He breathed her name, kissing her, stroking her. "Sweet, sweet Norah. Was it some benevolent spirit who brought you here to save me from myself?"

She whimpered, her fingertips learning the landscape of his body, her thighs opening to him as naturally as a flower to the kiss of the sun.

And as Aidan mounted her, thrusting with exquisite gentleness inside the sheath of her body, he felt himself slipping into realms far more fantastical, more beautiful, than any fairy land could ever be.

A place where love was real and lasted for all time. A place where miracles touched the most jaded heart and healed betrayal. A place where Norah waited for him in a castle of beauty, with flowers in her hair and forever in her eyes.

"Tell me, Norah," he rasped, as the madness whirled up inside him. "Tell me again."

"Wh—what?"

"That you . . . love me." The words were a grated plea, a surrender.

Her hands tangled in his hair, her mouth raining damp kisses wherever she could reach his bare skin. "I love you, Aidan," she said against his fevered flesh. "I love you . . . I love you . . . I love you."

He didn't know how many times she said the words, a

sensual litany as he filled her time and time again. But if she said them forever, he knew he would still never get enough of hearing them on her tongue, tasting her passion for him, like nectar upon her skin.

He caught her nipple in his mouth, suckling with fearsome tenderness on the hardened bud, drawing wild little cries from her. Her hands were desperate on his back, his buttocks, his shoulders, as if she were battling to find something . . . something Aidan knew he could give her.

He eased one hand between their joined bodies, finding silky petals, a pearl of sensation hooded within. She jerked when he skimmed his callused finger across it, circled it, teased it.

"Norah, love, come with me, angel. Fly with me."

She cried out, and Aidan felt the pulsing of her release against the white-hot hardness of his shaft. He thrust, wild, hard, desperate. And in a heartbeat, his own climax shattered him, stunned him, rocked him until he was gasping and shaken.

He rolled slowly to one side, drawing Norah atop him, covering her with the folds of his cloak. Her hair tumbled across his chest, her face silhouetted against the moon-kissed sky.

"Norah," he breathed, as she stared down at him, a shy aura wreathing her face. "Tell me one more time."

"I love you," she said, cupping his stubborn jaw in one soft palm. "Aidan, I—"

The words died as she stiffened against him, his own nerve endings snapping taut at a sound out of sync with the night.

Hoofbeats.

"Sir Aidan!" the rider bellowed into the night. "Sir Aidan, for the love of God, where are you?"

Aidan swore and scrambled up, shoving Norah's clothes into her arms and guiding her behind a shattered outcropping of wall. Thunderation, what the blazes could be amiss now? Had that infernally meddling daughter of his noticed that he and Norah were missing and struck up a search party?

Whoever it was, there was no choice but to answer.

"Here," Aidan shouted above the wind. "In the ruins."

He had barely thrust his legs into his breeches and yanked them up into place when the rider came into view.

Stunned, Aidan glimpsed the troll-like countenance of Gibbon Cadagon. The old groom's face was stricken. "Thank God that I found you, sir. I vow I never thought the bastards would be so bold."

"What is it?" Aidan demanded, yanking on his shirt, a coil of panic unfurling in his gut.

"It's Miss Cassandra. After that Montgomery fellow left in such a state, she went into the garden, looking for you and your lady, and someone . . . someone tried to steal her away."

"Steal her away? What the hell do you mean? One of the guests was making improper advances to her?"

"Nay, sir. It was something far darker than that. I'm thinkin' they meant to kidnap her, hold her for ransom. And your bride, sir, she—she's gone as well. We fear that—"

"Norah is with me," Aidan said, and Cadagon stared as the love-tousled figure in crumpled green satin stepped from behind the wall of stone.

"Thank God you're all right, my lady," the groom said, his aged voice cracking. "Thank God."

"Tell me what happened, old man. You can't mean to say someone attempted to harm Cassandra at Rathcannon in the middle of a ball? I can't believe it."

"Take a peek at poor Calvy Sipes's leg and you'll believe it right enough. He foiled the skulduggery. Took on three of the villainous bastards and got a pistol ball in his thigh for his troubles."

"My God." Raw terror rioted in Aidan's veins at images of masked curs brandishing weapons at his daughter. "Cassandra? She's safe?"

"She's safe enough now. The lads and me fairly barricaded her in her chamber, with every burly servant in the whole castle keeping guard over her. Scared the blazes out of her, though. And she's right terrified that whoever attempted to steal her had got their hands on the lady. Kept saying she heard them say Lady Kane's name."

Was it possible for fear to cinch any tighter? Instinctively, Aidan's arm swept out, drawing Norah's trembling form against him. Feral protectiveness clawed in his vitals, seared through every nerve in his body. Whoever had dared this would regret it for the rest of their lives.

"Has the surgeon been sent for?" Norah asked. "To tend to Calvy?"

"The doctor is with him now. The boy's a hearty lad, and a brave one. Didn't even mention the wound till we had Miss Cass settled and safe. The instant she was in her room and the other guests were bustled out of the castle, the boy-o fainted dead away. Only then did we see the blood on his breeches. Sir Aidan, if it hadn't been for his courage, I vow we'd be tearing apart the countryside, searching for the little missy."

"I owe that boy more than I can ever repay him. Who the devil would dare such a thing? Attacking Cassandra in Rathcannon's garden walls? Threatening my wife?"

"Not certain, sir. They wore grain sacks over their faces, only the eyes showing through. It was dark. Calvy said it all happened so fast. The only thing he did note was the voices. They were Irish, sure enough, and full o' loathing for you."

Aidan's jaw knotted. "Irish and they hate me? That narrows it down to half the county. Damn. Damn it to hell." He felt violated to the very core of his soul at the idea that anyone should attack his family, breach the safe haven he had provided for his little girl, and now for this woman who had given him her heart. He felt helpless—the same rage, frustration, desperation, and wild, pounding agony he had during that hideous ride he had made years ago, chasing after that coach into a stormy night.

Without a word, he stalked to where his stallion was

tethered and unfastened the reins. He mounted the restive animal, then pulled Norah up in front of him, his arms surrounding her. Spurring the horse to a gallop, he raced down the dark road along which he had found such unexpected enchantment, enchantment now shadowed by dark happenings that shivered through his soul in frigid wisps of foreboding, secret dangers that reached out skeletal fingers to clutch at him from the night.

No, Aidan resolved, tamping down his panic with savage resolve. He would find the bastards who did this. And when he did . . .

A feral snarl spread across his face. When he did, hell would not be a dark enough place for them to hide from his vengeance.

CHAPTER

18

Cassandra was sleeping at last. Aidan sat beside her bed, her fingers linked in his, clinging with quiet desperation, despite her closed eyes and even breathing. The candles beside the bed flickered, picking out the bruised circles of exhaustion beneath her eyes, the tiny scratch that had marred one babe-soft cheek during the scuffle with whoever had attempted to carry her away.

She had been so shaken, his brave little Cass, all but flinging herself at Aidan, and clutching Norah, murmuring again and again that she was sorry; sorry for being angry, sorry for her temper, sorry she hadn't come to the wedding the day before.

She had been racked with guilt and fear, shaken so badly that Aidan had been beset by his own grim self-recriminations.

She had the face of an angel who had suddenly crashed to earth, battered by the hard realities he had tried so hard to shield her from. She realized, perhaps for the first time, that chilling truth. Papa might slay imaginary dragons, or send her soaring on a stone-carved Pegasus. He could love her to desperation. But even though he would give the last drop of his heart's blood to keep her safe and protected, it was possible that sacrifice would not be enough to shield her from pain, from danger, from men like those who had charged into Cassandra's world tonight and left fear and uncertainty in their wake.

Regret crushed his throat at his own helplessness in the face of the world's wickedness. Aidan reached out to stroke his daughter's hair. The candlelight glistened on the delicate necklace she had worn since that long-ago night when another mysterious man had attempted to steal her away from Aidan—that man aided by Cassandra's own mother.

The thought that someone would dare attempt such villainy again seethed inside Aidan, eating him alive with rage and terror, hate and the fierce resolve that they would never, ever, touch her.

He started at the soft sound of footsteps entering the tower room, the scent of roses wafting over him, subtle, soothing. Norah. He didn't turn, didn't move. Just waited for her to touch him, secure in the certainty that she would.

Her fingers curved tenderly against the tousled darkness of his hair, stroking his rigid shoulders. He wanted to turn in the chair, to bury his face against her body, to drive away the nightmare that had shattered this night.

Instead, he stared at his daughter, reminding himself how close she had come to being hurt, reminding himself that once again he had been helpless to shield her.

Norah said nothing, giving him the gift of her silence, her touch, until the fingers of emotion crushing his chest drove him to speak.

His finger stole out to touch the heart-shaped locket that gleamed in the candlelight. "Do you know that this never leaves Cassandra's throat?"

"It's beautiful," Norah said softly. "Strange, I never really looked at it closely before. My mother had one like it a long, long time ago, with her miniature inside it, and my father's.

It broke my heart when she hid it away after my father died."

"I'm sorry."

"It was a long time ago. Cassandra's locket is lovely. Was it a gift from you?"

"No. It was Delia's, doubtless a gift from one of her lovers," he said, his finger running over the bent gold clasp. "They were always giving her trinkets—diamond bracelets, rings, and ropes of pearls for her hair. The night Delia died, she gave this to Cass to distract her, to keep her quiet as they made their escape. I hate this damn piece of gold. Every time I see it—every time—I remember what it was like to come so close to losing Cassandra forever. I imagine her little forehead cut and bleeding, the feel of her so limp in my arms, sobbing. I wonder if this locket was a present from the bastard who was driving the coach that night. It drove me crazy, the way Cass cherished the damned thing, so crazy I thought . . . I thought if I got rid of it, she'd find it easier to forget—Delia, the accident, everything. *I'd* find it easier to forget."

He ran a thumb over the lilies engraved on the gold, his chest tight. "Eight months after Delia died, I sneaked into Cass's room and unfastened the necklace while she slept and took the damn thing away. I wanted to destroy it, crush it, shatter it with a blasted hammer, obliterate it from my sight. I still don't know why I didn't do so the instant I left her room. It was a symbol of my failure, Norah. My failure to protect Cassandra. My failure with Delia."

He paused to suck in a shuddering breath. "I hid the infernal trinket away. Hell, maybe I didn't have the courage to destroy the thing after all. When Cass found the locket was missing, she was hysterical. I'd never seen her so—so . . . wild. So do you know what I did? Sir Aidan the Noble, bastard extraordinaire? I miraculously found the thing. Restored it to Cass as if I'd returned with the Holy Grail. She thought I was a goddamned hero."

"You are a hero to her. Everything good and strong and

brave. Once I realized she had written the letters I received in England, it was so clear how much she adored you."

"Not me, Norah. Some fantasy figure. A father who rides into Rathcannon girded up with all the decency he possesses, then the instant he fears he'll slip from his pedestal, he flees like the most reprehensible coward."

"You are a hero, Aidan. To her. And to me."

"Why? I've been a bastard to you from the beginning."

"You were honest with me, and fair, even if you were a trifle rough tempered. You adore your daughter, you show nothing but consideration for everyone here in Rathcannon. And even when you didn't want anything to do with me, you didn't pack me back to Dublin at once, you didn't hurl me into the streets. You cared for me too, Aidan, though you didn't want to."

"Damn it, Norah, you don't understand what I am any more than Cass does. You're just as blasted innocent, your eyes all full of fairy dust and magic."

"You were the one who drifted fairy dust into my eyes, Aidan Kane. First, when I was in England, just the idea of you made me want to believe. Tonight, at Caislean Alainn, you took the magic in your hands and poured it over me, like water from a mystic well."

Her hushed admission was heaven, hell. "And while I was doing that, my daughter was terrified, a pistol pointed at her, while those bastards tried to drag her away."

"Aidan, you cannot guard her every moment. This was not your fault."

He released Cassandra's fingers and stood up, pacing to where the first rays of dawn were staining the horizon, the vast, green sweep of Irish coast that now hid his daughter's attackers.

"I'm her father, damn it," he snarled. "I should have—"

"Should have what? Guessed that masked strangers would attempt to kidnap her from the midst of a ball? It makes no sense. I still cannot fathom why anyone would attempt such a crazed scheme with so many witnesses about. The child runs wild over the hills unattended all the time."

The stark vulnerability of Cassandra during her rovings struck at Aidan like a dagger in his heart. "Until I find whoever was responsible for this, the girl won't so much as fetch an apple from the kitchen without someone to guard her. And neither will you."

"I suppose it's only wise to be cautious. But surely, after being thwarted tonight, whoever did this thing won't dare try it again."

"I suppose that depends," Aidan said grimly.

"Depends?"

"On how much they hate me. How hungry they are for revenge. It's a poison that can rob one of reason, until a man will take any risk to reach his goal."

"And you think that these people want to—to hurt you?" There was fear in her voice, but he knew instinctively it was not because of her own danger, it was for Cassandra, and for Aidan himself. "Aidan, promise me you won't take any crazed risks. Report this to the authorities."

"And they'll laugh in my goddamn face. They hate me as much as the crofters do, Norah."

"Surely that shouldn't matter in a case like this. It's their duty—"

"They would gloss past the barest minimum possible, calling it duty, and they would laugh behind their hands as they let the bastards slip away. No. I'll find whoever did this myself." But how? The only clue he had to their identity was that they had spoken in Gaelic, and that they were bold enough to charge into a castle full of revelers in their determination to get to his daughter.

The soft whisper of Norah's skirts rustling drifted toward him, and she slipped her arms about his waist. "You will find them. I know you will. But now you need to rest. Surely there's nothing more you can do until Calvy awakens from the sleeping draught the surgeon gave him. Rest, and then when he awakens . . ."

"No. I'll search the area where it happened, question anyone who might have seen—"

"You look half dead with exhaustion, and it's such a short time since you were sick abed yourself. Please, come with me."

"Damn it, I'm not some weakling child. Don't interfere."

"All right. All right. I—I'm sorry."

"No, I'm sorry. I just—Oh, God, Norah, I can't even describe what this is doing to me. It's tearing me apart inside. I thought that she was safe. Believed nothing else could ever touch her, hurt her. And now . . ." His voice cracked, and he buried his face in one hand. "I have to find whoever this is. Do you understand?"

"Yes." She kissed him gently on one rigid shoulder, then turned to leave the room. He heard her hesitate when she reached the door. "Aidan?" she said softly.

"What is it?"

"I love you."

Aidan's throat constricted, his chest felt afire. He waited until her footsteps faded down the stairway and he had heard the quiet greeting of the armed footman standing guard upon the stairs. Then he turned and stalked from Cassandra's room, with savage determination surging through his heart.

He fought back panic and rage and focused on stark resolve. He would find whoever had attempted to do this terrible thing. He would find them before they could harm Cassandra, before they could endanger Norah.

He would find them. And when he did, he'd make certain they could never stalk his daughter or his wife again.

Norah entered her bedchamber and shivered. There was no fire burning in the grate, most certainly forgotten due to the commotion that had followed the attempt to abduct Cassandra. It made the room seem strange, somehow, more unwelcoming than ever before, as if ghostly fingers had brushed against the bed curtains and soundless footsteps padded across the carpets.

But then, Norah thought, setting a lit taper on a candlestand, it was not surprising that she should feel so odd, considering what had almost happened tonight.

Abduction. Kidnapping. Hideous images rose in her mind, her stomach churning as she mused what kind of beast would attempt such a horrible crime on an innocent girl. More frightening still, what had they planned to do with Cassandra once they had her at their mercy? Mercy . . . Norah was certain that was something those who had stalked the girl had not intended to offer.

She paced to the dressing table, littered with the bottles and creams, scents and combs Cassandra and a pert little maid had used to transform Norah into a creature unrecognizable as herself, a creature of rose-kissed cheeks and velvety flowers, of shimmering green satin that flowed about her like mist over the Irish Sea.

It seemed as if an eternity had passed in the hours since she had let Cassandra twine flowers in the dark masses of her hair.

Norah winced, recalling how she'd been sick with nervousness, dropping her fan, fumbling with her gloves, catching her lower lip between her teeth so many times it felt raw. The thought of facing Aidan again after the intimacies they'd shared the night before had taken embarrassment to excruciating new heights. She'd been certain that whenever those intense green eyes skimmed over her body, he would be remembering every gasp, every kiss, every stroke he had made inside her. And he would let those memories show in his irreverent grin, taking pleasure in tormenting her, the way he had when he'd thrown out last night's first wager.

As she had stood before the looking glass, staring into her already flushed face, she had decided that allowing Aidan Kane to see how deeply he had moved her, to show him the tender feelings that had sprung up in her heart, would be the most dangerous mistake she could make. For he would look on her with pity or disgust, cynicism or mockery, never with love.

Yet the night had been nothing like she had imagined it. Aidan had been surly and distant, only his eyes were hot as brands whenever he watched her. He had unnerved her, unsettled her, that discomfort mingling with her own dread of crowds, the inquisitive stares, the whispered speculations. She had all but fled into Philip's arms, seeking security, friendship, help for Cassandra. But she had never expected passionate protestations, insistent kisses that had bruised more than seduced, repulsed her instead of filled her with the heady wonder she had often imagined would follow such a miraculous happening as the kiss of Lord Philip Montgomery upon her lips.

And then Aidan had stormed into the garden, looking like a pagan warlord whose bride had been stolen by some rival warrior. The civilized veneer of immaculate evening clothes had done nothing to disguise the raw power and potent masculinity that seared through his rage.

He had hurt her. Badly. With his words, with his accusations. But then he had knelt to her in a mist-washed castle of dreams, a knight weary from questing alone too long, battered, so exquisitely human in all his flaws and fears. And she spilled her love into his hands, to heal the wounds inside him if she could.

It had been magic, as if those who had lived and loved in Caislean Alainn had drifted down their own blessings on their union, as if the skies and the sea and the wind had smiled.

But there were no more whisperings of enchantment in Aidan's eyes now, only a reflection of terror eight years old, a desperation and rage that his daughter had almost been stolen from him again. And guilt. Guilt Norah sensed the source of. If he'd not been distracted by her, if he'd not followed her to Caislean Alainn, if he'd not taken the time to make love to her there, then somehow he could have protected Cassandra, kept her from being afraid.

He was blaming himself for what had happened when it was no fault of his own. He was expecting the impossible— no, demanding it of himself. Had he been doing so all his life?

Norah reached out her fingers to touch the silver box that had belonged to Delia Kane, hating the woman for what she had done to him. She'd left a legacy that still twisted and scarred and maimed.

One Aidan would never escape.

Almost by instinct, she righted a scent bottle overturned in her haste and swept up the few fragrant gardenia buds Cassandra had not managed to twine in her curls. The creamy petals were wilting, a few falling free, as she lifted them to throw them away.

She had barely moved them when she suddenly stilled, her gaze captured by what had lain unnoticed beneath Cassandra's mound of flowers.

A folded bit of paper, scribed in a handwriting chillingly familiar. The same writing that had been contained in the note she'd discovered her first night at Rathcannon, the missive that had filled her head with suspicions, lies, that Aidan Kane had murdered his wife.

The nape of Norah's neck prickled, gooseflesh crawling down her arms as the flowers fell from her hand. She glanced over her shoulder to where the draperies rippled in shadow, the quiet of the room suddenly ominous. Gibbon Cadagon had said the villains had wanted not only Cassandra but herself as well. Calvy had heard them say her name.

Was it possible in all the confusion that . . . that what? Someone was lurking here? Waiting for her? That was madness. Who would be crazed enough to do such a thing in a house already in an uproar?

Swallowing hard, she picked up the note and opened it with fingers that trembled.

Three dangers has Rathcannon—
A girl child, straying toward traps she cannot see,
A lady whose heart a blackguard now possesses,
Three wagers that shall draw them both into a
long-past hell.
You failed to heed my warning last time. Do not
be so foolhardy again. Do not let the girl out of your
sight this night.

Norah stared at the words, the warning, feeling as if the floor were shifting beneath her feet. Was it possible that this missive had been on the dressing table before the ball? That when Cassandra and her maid had bustled in to help Norah prepare, they had tossed the accoutrements they had brought on the table, burying the message beneath them?

If that were so, it meant that someone had crept into Norah's room and attempted to warn her that some plot was afoot before the ball. Someone had known . . . had known the danger. . . .

Perhaps if Aidan could find this person, he could discover who was responsible for what had happened in the garden.

Quickly, she slipped the lid off the silver box, retrieving the missive she had hidden there the first night she'd arrived at Aidan's home. Then she hurried from the room, winding through the corridors, searching for Aidan.

She heard him first, his rough, impatient voice emanating from the study, in counterpoint to Gibbon Cadagon's. Norah paused at the door and knocked.

"Who the devil is it?" Aidan bellowed.

Norah opened the door and stepped inside.

"Norah." He attempted to gentle his voice, but nothing could soften the torment carved in every line of his face. He was bending over a desktop littered with scrawled papers and notes. She glanced down, seeing that they were accounts of what different servants had seen throughout the night. It was a search for some tiny clue in a labyrinth of information.

296

"I told you to go to bed," he said, meeting her gaze with hard green eyes.

"I tried. I was just starting to get undressed when I . . ." She cast a glance at Gibbon, her cheeks heating. "Aidan, I need to speak with you. Alone."

"I'm damned busy right now tracking down whoever meant to hurt Cass. I don't have time—"

"This is about Cassandra. It's important. Please."

Aidan cursed, low, then motioned the others from the room. When the door had shut behind them, he turned, hands on hips. "Make it quick. What the blazes is this about?"

"These." Norah extended the notes. Aidan took them, his brow furrowing. "I found the first one the night I arrived here. The second one was buried beneath some flowers on the dressing table in my bedchamber. I just found it now, but I think I was meant to discover it earlier, before the ball."

Aidan stalked to where a branch of candles spilled over the papers littering his desk. He shoved the first note toward the flame, his gaze scanning the script. The planes of his face hardened, stilled. Murder . . . Even though he knew he was innocent, what must it be like to see that epitaph scrawled above your name? He gave a bitter laugh. "So someone designated themselves as your guardian angel. I wondered from the first how long it would be before you heard the rumors. I never suspected it would be the first night. No wonder you looked so damned scared of me."

"Aidan, the other one is far more frightening."

He cast the first note onto the desk, then unfolded the other. She caught the slightest tremor in the hands that clutched the bit of paper. "My God. Who the devil—"

"I don't know. I just found them propped on the table. I saw no one, heard nothing."

"Someone was in your bedchamber," he grated, "someone who knew what those bastards were going to try to do to Cassandra. To you." His eyes glinted, like a wolf hungering to tear out an adversary's throat. "There must be someone in the house, someone at Rathcannon who knows where these came from. I vow, I'll drag the truth from them if I have to."

"It could have happened a hundred ways. The castle is so large. Someone could have stolen in from outside, they could have entered the window, or—heaven only knows what. But I don't think they're evil. Whoever wrote the notes was trying to warn me."

"That you were about to marry a murderer? That my daughter was about to be kidnapped? Sonofabitch. Excuse me if I don't see them as some blasted benevolent spirit! If they knew this much, they must know more."

At that moment Rose entered, the maid carrying a hod with peat for the fire. She hesitated, her gaze flicking to the notes. Norah saw the girl pale. "Your pardon, sir, my lady. In all the fuss, I forgot to stir up the fires, but I'll nip back later to tend to—"

"Stand where you are, Rose," Aidan commanded.

The girl swallowed hard, her white cap quivering. "Aye, sir."

"You tend the fires in the bedchambers as well, don't you, girl?"

"Aye, sir."

"I suppose you've never seen these bits of paper Lady Kane has just brought me?" He extended them toward her, catching a dart of fear in the girl's eyes.

"N—Nay, sir," she stammered. "What would I be doin' with such things? I can't even read."

"But if that is so, why do you look so pale?" Aidan demanded with silky menace. "Why are your hands shaking?"

The girl set down the hod, clasping work-roughened hands in her apron as if to hide them. "Sir, I—"

"You have a mam and five brothers and sisters to care for, don't you, Rose? They're tucked away in the cottage near the Hill of Night Voices."

"Aye, sir."

He was aware of Norah's eyes on him, watching him. "If you were not employed at Rathcannon, there would be most unpleasant consequences for your family, would there not?"

"Please, sir! I—I know nothing—"

"I've made a fortune reading peoples' faces over a deck of cards, Rose. I know when someone is lying. Tell me the truth, now, or I vow you'll be cast out of here without a shilling."

The girl's mouth trembled as tears crested in her eyes. "Oh, sir, nay! I didn't mean no harm! It was just . . . he'd done such kindnesses for me mam and the young ones, and it seemed such a simple thing he was askin'."

"Who was asking? Damn it, who?"

"I cannot tell you, or he'll . . . they'll . . . Horrible things happen to those that betray him. None in the valley would dare—"

"Gilpatrick!" Aidan rasped, his voice hoarse with disbelief.

The girl let out a piercing wail. "I didn't tell ye! I never would! I—"

Stunned by the truth evident in the girl's eyes, Aidan fought for balance. The nemesis he'd thought he'd understood seemed to shape-change, like some Druid priest of old, shedding the honor that had been a part of Gilpatrick despite his ragged clothes and starveling body, the princely arrogance that a hundred years of subjugation by Aidan's ancestors hadn't managed to beat from his features.

And yet, difficult as it was for Aidan to believe the girl's words were true, he could see it in her face: genuine terror of Gilpatrick's retribution, dismay that she had betrayed this champion of her people, and anguish that she had not been a better liar to shield the Irish rebel.

Something snapped in Aidan, and he grabbed Rose by her plump arms, shaking her. "It was Gilpatrick, wasn't it? He sent the notes, and you smuggled them into Lady Kane's chamber!"

"Aidan!" Norah cried, rushing over. "You're frightening her."

"If she doesn't tell me the whole truth—all of it, damn you—she'll be worlds more than frightened!" He was savage, savage with fear for his daughter and with a strange, crippling sense of betrayal—betrayal by a man he'd known as an enemy so long. They were absurd, ridiculous, these twisted emotions that drove the breath from his lungs. And yet the memory assailed him of the night he had encountered the English troop, the night he led them away from Gilpatrick and the rebel's wounded comrade. Had he, by his rash interference in English "justice," allowed the man responsible for Cassandra's terror to go free? The soldiers had claimed Gilpatrick was planning some sort of skulduggery, some dark mission. Was it possible that that mission could have been kidnapping Aidan's daughter? Yet the notes had held warning, not a threat.

"Why?" he blazed. "Why would Gilpatrick write these notes? It makes no damn sense."

"Donal feared for the lady," Rose cried. "He only wanted to warn her."

"That I was a murderer? That she should refuse to wed me?"

"Aye! It was that."

"But the note was in the chamber the night she arrived," Aidan raged, trying to piece together the madness that was this crazed tangle. "How did Gilpatrick know she was coming here? And to be my bride, no less? Even I had no idea."

"I don't know, sir! I don't know!"

"And tonight—the bastard knew what was afoot. What was this damned note supposed to be about? A sinister game, to pleasure himself before he stole my daughter?"

"Donal wouldn't hurt a child!"

There had been a time Aidan would have believed that, deep in his gut, despite the enmity he and the heir of the

Gilpatricks had borne each other for so long. And yet how could he doubt it now, with the evidence staring him in the face? The attempted abduction must be related to Gilpatrick somehow.

"If Gilpatrick wouldn't hurt a child, then who came into the garden tonight? Who terrified Cassandra? Who put that pistol ball in Calvy's leg?" Aidan was shaking the girl, his fingers bruising her arms, primitive fury rending him with images of what might have happened—stark tragedy he couldn't even comprehend.

The maid was crying, great, hiccoughing sobs. "Please, sir—I don't know . . . I only put the notes in the chamber."

"Aidan, you're hurting her!"

He felt Norah's hand on the rigid muscles of his arm, her voice urgent, rippling through him like cool water over a blazing fire.

"Look at her face, Aidan. She knows nothing!"

"Then I'll find out the truth from Gilpatrick himself," Aidan snarled. "Rose, you tell me where to find him."

The maid's eyes rounded with horror. "Nay. If I betray him—"

"Tell me where to find him, or your services at Rathcannon are no longer required." He watched his threat wash over the girl's features, and what he saw sickened him, but he was too desperate to let her see his flicker of weakness.

"But me earnings are the only money we have, the lot of us. Without it, the wee ones would starve."

Aidan's face felt cast in stone, his gut afire with thirst for vengeance. "Some sonofabitch put a pistol in my daughter's face tonight. I'm not over-full of mercy. Tell me."

A war waged in the girl's face, but in the end, she sobbed out, "There's to be a gatherin' at the standing stones on the Hill of Night Voices."

The standing stones. It was strangely fitting that Donal Gilpatrick would choose that site for his rebel meetings, a location filled with dark powers and mystic secrets. A place most crofters would shun in superstitious fear once night fell.

"When is this meeting to take place?" Aidan saw the slightest flicker in the maid's eyes, as if she were torn with indecision, plotting to find some lie to save not only her employment at Rathcannon but the rebel Gilpatrick's skin.

"Lie to me, and it will be the last lie you tell at Castle Rathcannon."

The girl stared at him, with the fascinated horror of a mouse caught in the gaze of a hunting peregrine. In the end, her fear of Aidan overawed her loyalty to Gilpatrick.

"When?" Aidan demanded.

"Tonight. At the rising of the moon."

The moon.

Aidan gritted his teeth, thoughts of his blood enemy fading in the memory of the silvery beauty of its rays melting down upon Caislean Alainn, Norah making love to him in a world of such magic he had forgotten all else—dark legacies of hatred, his vulnerable daughter, the lies that tripped so easily from a woman's tongue. Norah had never told him about the note, the warning, never told him that someone had come into her chamber, whispering of murder.

If he had known that, wouldn't he have been more wary, more watchful? Wouldn't he have guarded his daughter with more care?

He shook himself as betrayal sluiced through him, anger building, surging in to fill spaces where helplessness and guilt had churned inside him. He glared down into Rose's round, frightened face.

"If you're lying to me, I will make certain every person in your family, down to the tiniest babe, will suffer for it."

Keeping hold of the girl, he hauled her into the corridor, where two alert footmen stood guard before the door. The menacing gleam of pistols shone at their waists. "Rose will be spending the rest of the day and all night in her chambers," he said. "Lock her in, and God help the man who lets her escape."

One of the footmen looked as if he were about to argue, but he obviously thought better of it once he glimpsed the fire in his master's eyes.

"I'll see to it myself, sir."

He watched the two lead the crying girl away. His jaw clenched. The rising of the moon was hours away, but the restless blaze that was in his blood, the hunger for vengeance, for answers, was already driving him half mad. The knowledge that Norah had not been honest with him ate like poison inside him.

"Aidan." He heard Norah say his name, felt her touch him, tentative, so tentative. "Aidan, what are you going to do?"

He jerked away from her and stalked to the fireplace, staring into the flames as if they were the gateway to hell.

"I'm going to hunt down Gilpatrick. Make him tell me who is behind this madness."

"You can't ride into the midst of a band of rebels all alone."

"So what would you have me do? Make an appointment to meet him at White's? Or wait until the rebel bastard writes another cryptic message to my wife? Not that she'd bother to show it to me until it's too late."

Norah paled. "I didn't find the note until after the ball."

"You found the first one a helluva lot earlier than that, but you didn't feel compelled to show it to me!"

"What was I supposed to do? Pound on your bedchamber door and say *Excuse me, but did you murder your wife?* You were already furious, intending to pack me off to Dublin at first light. There seemed no reason—"

"No reason to mention it to me? Why? Because you were afraid it was true?"

The expression on her face was answer enough. It hurt Aidan, more than he dared admit.

"I did ask you about Delia. When you awoke from your sickness. I asked you and you told me what had happened. I believed you. Why would I present the note to you, knowing that it would only cause you pain?"

"Because if you had, I would have known something was afoot. I would never have consented to this infernal ball." He swore, slamming his fist into the mantel.

"I see," Norah said, so quietly it stunned him. "This is my fault, then."

"I didn't say that."

"You might as well have. Of course, I understand it must be so. That way you don't have to face the truth."

"And what truth is that?" he demanded, stung by her words.

"That you can't protect Cassandra from the world, no matter how much you want to. That there are things you cannot control. That someday, she's going to be hurt, just like the rest of us—by cruel words or cruel deeds—and you are going to be helpless to stop her pain."

"If I hadn't been chasing over the countryside searching for you, I would have been here when she needed me."

He was wounding her. He could feel her pain throbbing in his own chest, reminding him with excruciating clarity how damn good it had felt not to care. About Delia. About any woman. Especially this woman, with her soft eyes and her healing hands.

He swore. "Go back to your room, Norah. I have more important things to do than argue with a woman."

He expected her to run, flee in a bout of tears. God knew, any other woman he'd ever encountered would have. Instead, she asked in a tight voice, "What are you going to do?"

"I'm going to confront the rebel lord of Rathcannon," he said. "To see if the blackguard has the courage to face a man instead of terrorizing a child."

"Aidan, he hates you."

"Then perhaps the bastard will have the courage to put a pistol ball through my heart. God knows, he's been hungering to do so for the last twenty years."

With that, he spun on his heels and stalked from the chamber, racked with his own hunger—for the coming of the night.

CHAPTER

19

The circle at the Hill of Night Voices had imprisoned
secrets long before the first bard touched fingers to a harp
made of bog oak. Gray stone thrust up from the clearing in
mystic contortions, like arms reaching for some treasure lost
in the heavens—or, Aidan thought grimly, like the forever
damned clawing at night in a wild attempt to escape from
hell.

It was a place of mystic power, rooted deep in the Irish
hills. One that had intrigued countless throngs of the
curious, including Aidan himself when he'd been a boy.
He'd not been able to resist the tales of human sacrifice and
strange pagan rituals that had been practiced within the
cryptic monument. He'd followed with interest scholars'
efforts to unlock the riddle of the stones. And he'd understood the fascination of those who hungered to release the
dark magic centered there, seeking the entryway to other
worlds they believed existed beneath the hillocks on which
the stones held their vigil.

It seemed somehow fitting that Donal Gilpatrick should choose the mystic circle as his meeting place this night.

Gilpatrick.

Never had Aidan been able to hear that name without the stirring of a memory that still had the power to make his jaw clench in a wash of shame and frustration decades old. They had been born to hate each other, schooled in it as boys by a master of such emotions. And they both still bore the scars from that encounter: Gilpatrick's on his face, Aidan's hidden from any eyes but his own.

Yes, Gilpatrick was his old adversary, dangerous, and yet one he thought he'd understood—until now.

Aidan held his stallion to a walk along the narrow path that carved its way up the stone-scarred hill, aware of the hot press of eyes boring into his back, the hair on the back of his neck prickling, as if it could feel the nudge of cold invisible pistol barrels against his skin.

Gilpatrick was no fool. The Irish renegade was cunning and careful, or he'd have dangled from a traitor's gallows years before. Aidan was certain that the tangle of gorse and blackthorn concealed any number of Gilpatrick's sentries— men bred from the cradle to hate Aidan like Donal Gilpatrick himself, served up the thirst to shed Kane blood with his first taste of mother's milk.

It was madness to range the night, searching for those who would rejoice at his death. Of that much Aidan was certain. He was courting a rebel pistol ball through his heart with the same dark fervor he had lavished on Norah at Caislean Alainn.

But he couldn't stop himself now, any more than he'd been able to keep himself from laying Norah down upon his cloak in the moonlight and making love to her until he was raw inside, and aching and unsure.

For he was one with the darkness. One with the sin-blackened souls who were the lords of night. Hadn't he always been? Condemned even before his mother had

307

brought him into a world that despised him because of the Kane blood that flowed through his veins?

He was a villain whom the angels had chosen, in a cruel twist of fate, to entrust with a child of light. He had tried so damned hard to guard her, protect her, keep her safe from the evil swirling all around, even the dark places in his own soul.

Yet last night, those jeering angels had shown him how futile his quest had been, how helpless he was to shield her.

Someone had tried to harm his daughter.

Why? There could be only one reason. To use Cassandra as a weapon against him—the only weapon that could give his enemies ultimate power over his soul and destroy him completely.

No, a voice inside Aidan whispered, mocking him with a vision of soft brown eyes, so earnest, so filled with wonder in the shadow of Caislean Alainn. Cassandra was not the only weapon an enemy could wield against Aidan Kane's heart. Not anymore.

The stark vulnerability slayed Aidan. His fingers gripped the reins of his stallion as if they were the slenderest of threads keeping him from falling through the entrance to Hades.

Norah. How had she breached his defenses? She had managed to slip past his guard with the same subtle warmth as a ray of sunlight through a crack in a thick stone wall. She had warmed him in places he didn't want warmed, had touched him in ways his raw and weary heart had never expected. She had made him hunger for her hands on his body, her mouth under his, so he could catch her breathy whispers, hold onto the words she had spoken time and time again at his command: *I love you.*

Love. From the instant the words had first fallen, so shy, so reluctantly from her lips, he'd been starving for the sound of them.

Even when he had stridden into Rathcannon's stable at dusk and found her waiting outside his stallion's stall, he had wanted to draw her into his arms and kiss her. Promise her that everything would be all right. He had expected anger, pleading, raging.

But she had merely stood there, in the first light of the lantern suspended from an iron hook in the stable rafter. She had been quiet, so quiet, while Sean O'Day and Gibbon Cadagon had demanded to be allowed to follow their master into this den of rebels. Two guns to watch his back, Cadagon had claimed.

Two men—innocent, good men with families dependent on them—volunteering to take a bullet for Aidan Kane. The notion had raked mercilessly across his nerves, unsettling him in ways he couldn't begin to understand.

He'd been surly as hell with the two, telling them he'd be in more danger that they'd shoot him by accident than that Gilpatrick's men would manage to gun him down. But at the hurt in those puckish Irish faces, he had softened, clasping first Cadagon's hand, then Sean O'Day's. He had gazed into the eyes of these two men he trusted and told them that he needed to know Cassandra was guarded, safe; and with the two of them at Rathcannon, Aidan said he doubted the devil himself could steal Cassandra away.

At that rough confession, he'd seen the determination melt out of the Irishmen's eyes and sorrowful acceptance take its place. Cassandra, the treasure that must be guarded, kept safe at all costs. Cassandra, the child that these two loved nearly as much as Aidan himself did.

But it had been Norah who had lanced his soul with her huge, fear-filled eyes, far more eloquent in their aching silence than the Irishmen's pleas. She had crossed to him, laying her fingertips against his lips, soft, so soft. "Revenge can't hold your daughter while she cries, or rejoice when she laughs. Cassandra needs a father far more than she needs to be avenged." The words had twisted deeply into his heart and lodged there.

He'd been furious at the sensation that she was able to reach him, cripple him in a way no woman had for eight long years. He had wanted to shake her, to kiss her, to beg her to understand. But he had clenched his jaw and turned away from her. He hadn't spoken. He couldn't trust himself to.

Instead, he had stripped down to shirtsleeves, then swung astride his stallion and rode into the night.

He'd welcomed the chill night air, biting through the thin fabric, cooling the fires of confusion and rage inside him. And he had hoped that his unorthodox plan would serve as some kind of shield against Gilpatrick's hatred, and that somewhere, in the rebel's heart, there remained a scrap of the oak-tough code of honor Aidan had once believed to be unbreakable, the one quality in the one man he had come close to envying.

The white of Aidan's shirt would stand out starkly against the backdrop of night, announcing his presence to Gilpatrick's watch. He wanted the bastards to see him. He wanted them to know he didn't give a damn if the whole county knew he was coming to confront the bastards who had dared terrorize his daughter.

If there was anything Gilpatrick could understand, and grudgingly respect, it would be bold-faced courage, a foe who dared face him down, outnumbered a score to one. Besides which, Aidan was certain it was the only way he could get close enough to the rebel to demand the answers he needed.

The stallion tossed its magnificent head, whickering nervously, and Aidan tightened his knees around the animal as it sidestepped, dancing away from a clump of underbrush. Survival instinct raged inside him, demanding he turn toward the brush, tear back the veil of darkness with his eyes. But he rode on, his features impassive, his mount under iron control.

His heart thundered in his chest, as if realizing that each beat could well be its last.

In the moonlight, he could see the first glimpse of the Stone of Truth, which legend said had sent Eremon

O'Caighan to hell for his crimes against his chieftain's wife. Orange-gold tongues of flame from a torch or lantern licked hellish reflections onto the towering slab.

Every muscle in Aidan's body was coiled, as if expecting the fiery lash of a whip, every nerve ending sparked and tingled.

Soon. It would happen soon now, whatever greeting Gilpatrick's men intended to give to him.

The thought had barely formed in his head when a blur of shadow catapulted down on Aidan from the overhanging branch of a tree, a blood-chilling Gaelic war cry cleaving the silence of night like a broadsword of old.

Something hard slammed into him, driving him from his stallion's back as the horse reared and plunged in terror.

Pain radiated through Aidan's shoulder as he crashed to the turf, his attacker landing atop him. The rebel, his face masked, drove his fist into Aidan's jaw, snapping his head back until stars exploded before his eyes.

He shook himself, trying to regain his bearings through the swirling darkness of night and the sick, dizzy circlings inside his head. With an oath he rolled the guard over, wrestling the bastard with all the pent-up fury that had been boiling inside him since he'd first learned his daughter was in danger.

But before he could land his first punch, another hand grabbed his hair from behind, yanking his head back so savagely his neck seemed likely to snap, and the blade of a knife snaked around until that silvery kiss of death was pressed against his throat.

"I wouldn't be rearrangin' anybody's face, lest you want us to carve up yours, ye Kane bastard," a muffled voice warned from behind a crude mask of sacking. "Though nothin' would give me greater pleasure, I vow."

"I have no quarrel with you. My business is with Gilpatrick."

The brigand chuckled, low. "The master is real particular about who he conducts business with. And from past

311

experience, I doubt he'd be fool enough to do so with a thievin' traitor who bears the name Kane. Last time a Kane entertained a Gilpatrick, Rathcannon fell into your bastard hands, and Donal's great-grandda and uncles decorated an English gallows."

Aidan's jaw knotted as the knife bit deeper. "Can't you recall the rest of the tale? His brothers, his father—their fates?" Despite his peril, Aidan's stomach turned at the memory of his own father regaling him with pride about his grandsire's quest to complete the destruction of the once-noble Catholic lords, the Gilpatricks. How Crevan Kane had made it his personal quest to obliterate the family that had held prior claim to Rathcannon, sparing no one—even cutting the tiniest Gilpatrick heir from his mother's womb.

Aidan gritted his teeth, wondering if he was baiting this rebel into slitting his throat, daring him to.

"You bastard." The man's voice was silky with hate. The other rogue climbed to his feet, while Aidan was still on his knees, helpless. The Irishman kicked him full in the ribs.

Agony seared him, his chest seeming to cave in, his lungs screaming for air. But it was a miracle the other assailant had kept the knife from gouging deep. Aidan fought to stay conscious, to squeeze the words from his strangled throat.

"You want me dead—all of you. I full intend to give your leader a chance to show how courageous he is when pitted against a Kane."

"What the devil?"

"I come to issue a challenge to Donal Gilpatrick."

"He's run mad," the other man said. "We should just kill him and serve him up before Donal like a slaughtered sheep."

"What?" Aidan jeered in a desperate gambit for his life. "You fear your leader hasn't the mettle to meet me man to man? It's no wonder. The world over knows that any man with a drop of English blood in his veins can crush a lowly Irishman. I suppose your fear is understandable."

"Lord Donal could carve the meat from your bones an

312

inch at a time, if he'd a mind to," the man welding the knife declared.

"I dare him to try. No, I'll do better than that. I'll wager him a thousand pounds I can best him. Of course, if Gilpatrick is a coward . . ." He let the word hang between them, goading, chafing, knowing his very survival dangled in the balance. An eternity seemed to pass in the seconds before the man who held the knife cursed.

"We'll take ye up to Gilpatrick, Kane, and cheer when he spills your life blood into the dirt. Tully, bind the bastard's hands."

The man who had kicked him in the gut jerked Aidan's arms behind his back, nearly wrenching them from the sockets as he tied them with a strip of leather. Aidan bit back a groan at the pressure against his throbbing shoulder as the two men half dragged, half shoved him the rest of the way up the hill.

He heard the rise and fall of voices, then silence as his two captors shoved him from the shadows into the ring of torchlight. Aidan stumbled, going down on one knee. He gritted his teeth against the pain and levered himself upright. Steel poured into his spine as his gaze searched the circle of faces until he found that of his enemy. Gilpatrick's scar gleamed in a twisted rope down the side of his face, his eyelid pulled down at a gruesome angle beneath the clear blue of his left eye.

Aidan remembered how smooth that same face had been the first time he'd seen it: grinning at him in pure devilment as he stole an apple from Squire Donbea's orchard, despite the fact that the squire kept a fractious bull fenced therein. Aidan remembered the boy running, barely reaching the fence. He was certain Gilpatrick would have been skewered by one of the bull's horns if Aidan hadn't reached over the fence and yanked the Irish lad away from those tossing points.

A dozen wild adventures had followed, the two boys never knowing each other by any name other than Donal and

Aidan, never knowing they were sworn enemies, until the day Aidan's father had discovered them together.

"What the hell?" Gilpatrick demanded, his overly thin body fairly radiating fury and surprise.

"He was ridin' up, bold as ye please," the knife wielder said. "Said he'd come searchin' to offer you a challenge."

Gilpatrick's eyes shimmered in the torchlight. "A challenge, Kane?"

"Man to man, Gilpatrick. You and me. With your guard dogs here under orders not to interfere."

The Irishman stared at him with the air of a king. "To what would I owe this unexpected pleasure? There must be a reason you've decided to confront me after all this time."

"You must have hungered to repay me for that little decoration carved on your cheek. I come to grant you your heart's desire. To strike a wager with you."

"You think I would make a wager with a cur like you? To do that, I'd have to trust a Kane to keep his word. We Gilpatricks have far too long a memory to make such a mistake again. The last time we believed in what your kinsmen told us, they barred nearly our whole family within a castle hall and slaughtered them down to the last babe."

Aidan's mouth tightened. "My ancestors were hell-spawned bastards, is that it? Making war on women and children? But what of you, Gilpatrick? That false honor you wear like a mantle over your rags?"

"What the divil are you implying, Kane?"

"I'm not implying anything. I'm accusing you, straight out, of being a coward, the worst kind of villain. And when we duel, if I get my blade against your throat, your forfeit will be to answer whatever questions I choose to put to you."

"Questions about what?"

"About the happenings at Rathcannon last night. About animals who put pistols into the faces of innocent girls. But then, you know all about that, Gilpatrick, don't you?"

Gilpatrick paled, a flicker of emotion tightening his

mouth. "About terrorized children? Murderers with pistols stalking the innocent? I'm acquainted well enough with those." Gilpatrick's fist knotted. "Am I to assume that whoever put the pistol into your daughter's face did not pull the trigger?" The words were cool, so cool Aidan might have been deceived, had it not been for the flame eating inside his adversary's eyes.

"Cassandra is safe. But the mystery of her attackers has yet to be solved. They left no trace except a pistol ball in one of my footmen's legs. That, and two letters, secretly tucked in my wife's bedchamber."

Gilpatrick regarded him with steely, cold eyes. "Are you quite certain they were not from the previous Lady Kane's former lovers? I would imagine she had to keep up the devil of a lot of correspondence."

Aidan jerked against his captors' arms, a savage twist to his mouth. "You know damn well they were sent to Norah. You had them smuggled in to terrify her."

"That was never my intent. I merely wanted to warn the lady that she was straying into the dragon's den."

"Then you admit that you're responsible?"

"For the notes? I admit that most readily, though how you discovered that truth is most puzzling."

"It doesn't matter how I discovered it. Let's just say that when my daughter is threatened, I can be as ruthless as any man whose veins are filled with Kane blood. Imagine my surprise when I discovered you were involved in the plot to kidnap my daughter."

"And that is what your . . . informant told you? That I had plotted this kidnapping?"

"Who else could it be? The hatred between our families is as old as these stones. The note that said Cassandra was in danger was penned in your hand. You knew the attack was going to happen before the men fell upon Cassandra. How could you be privy to such an attack if you weren't neck deep in it?"

"How, indeed? Surely, I couldn't be giving you a warning to keep your daughter safe. Only the worst kind of fool would do that for his darkest enemy."

"Don't bait me, Gilpatrick. You knew about the attack. You knew about the fact that a bride was coming to Rathcannon. You knew even before I did."

"Perhaps I have the second sight. Perhaps I can predict your future, Kane, since because of you and your accursed family I have no future."

"What the hell is your game, Gilpatrick?" Aidan raged, fury surging through him.

"To see Ireland free." Simple words, quiet ones, but his face was filled with a passion Aidan hadn't felt for anyone, anything, save his daughter, and now a dark-eyed Englishwoman who loved him.

Gilpatrick's mouth curved into a smile. "What is wrong, Kane? Feeling helpless? The sensation chafes at a man, doesn't it? In time, it eats away at him until he's half mad."

"Is that what this is about, then? Driving me to madness? I offer you a quicker, sweeter victory. Match swords, Gilpatrick, or pistols, unless you are a coward."

Gilpatrick laughed. "You think that you can bait me into fighting you by casting slurs upon my honor? I don't give a damn about your opinion of me, Kane. I know what I am. A patriot. An Irishman, down to my last drop of blood. Lord of these lands in a way that you can never be. By right, Kane. By right. I don't have to prove anything to you."

Rage and something like envy bit into Aidan's chest as he was stricken by the knowledge that this ragged outlaw spoke the truth. Gilpatrick would be able to look his child square in the eyes, like the warrior king in a hero tale. He would never have to fear the look of horror and revulsion Aidan was certain would mar Cassandra's eyes when she discovered the truth about her father.

"Fight me, Gilpatrick," Aidan raged, wishing to God he could grapple with more insubstantial enemies as well. "Fight me, damn you."

"Teach the Kane scum a lesson, me lor'," one of the masked rebels begged Gilpatrick.

"Aye, Donal! Show him what mettle true-born Irishmen are made of."

"Made of?" Aidan spat the words. "You're made of madmen's dreams and wild impossibilities, clinging to glory centuries old so fiercely you don't even realize your throats are crushed beneath the muddy boots of your conquerors. The men who have bound you like slaves in your own land." He sneered, unadulterated mockery obscuring the desperation pulsing deeper inside him, as he attempted to latch onto something, anything, that might goad the implacable Gilpatrick to fight him. "No, you're all descended from kings and heroes, aren't you? Down to the lowest rag-picker amongst you. In fact, I'd wager that fool boy I saw you with that night a week past was a goddamn prince, Gilpatrick. Spilling more royal Irish blood upon the soil when he fell beneath superior English firepower."

As Aidan's verbal thrust rammed home, he felt the same sickening reverberations he'd experienced when, in the midst of a battle, his sword pierced flesh.

In the torchlight, Gilpatrick's features turned white, the men encircling him snarling in horror and outrage.

"Cut Kane free." The rebel leader's voice was cold and deadly.

One of Aidan's captors slid the knife blade between his hands, slicing the thong none too gently. Aidan winced at the burning cut it left in his skin, but then he felt nothing but the surge of blood back into his numb fingers, the searing path of pain that set his hands afire.

He curled his fingers into fists, flexing and releasing them in an effort to work some suppleness back into them, but they were awkward and clumsy feeling, as if they weren't firmly knitted to his wrists.

Considering how he'd baited Gilpatrick, Aidan had no delusions that the rebel would give him the concession of waiting until Aidan could work the feeling back into his

317

fingertips. Even still, Aidan welcomed the chance to release his frustrations by battling his age-old enemy.

"What's it to be, Gilpatrick? Swords? Pistols?" Aidan asked, rubbing his wrist with the fingers of his other hand.

"We could recapture the pleasure of our first battle, Kane. No blades, no pistols, just hand to hand, me against you. Of course, you might be reluctant. Especially since your da isn't here to interfere with the outcome."

Humiliation ate in Aidan's chest, the image of his father as clear as if it had happened yesterday. And as he stared into the ruined face of the Irishman, he felt a wrenching in his gut—not at the memory of two boys rolling on the turf in murderous fury, but rather playing at Robin Hood upon Aidan's beloved pony, kicking up mischief in the squire's dovecote, splashing naked, like the little savages they were, in a burbling stream. Naked not only of their clothes but also of anger, of prejudice, of all the ugliness that surrounded this most enchanted, most tragic of isles.

They had understood each other in the most elemental way possible. They were kindred spirits, wild with the need to fling themselves into life's adventures.

Until Aidan's father had found them together. Enraged, he had demanded that Aidan give the "bastard Gilpatrick" a beating he'd never forget. When Aidan had refused, his father had pulled out his pistol and put the barrel to Aidan's pony's silky head. Aidan could still remember standing there, his gut churning, his eyes burning with tears, unable to throw the first punch. Gilpatrick had done it for him.

Aidan forced the thoughts from his mind ruthlessly. Whatever those two naive boys had shared had been wiped away long ago. Gilpatrick was rebel scum, with enough blood on his hands to justify a hanging. If it hadn't been for the bravery of Calvy Sipes, Cassandra's blood might have been shed as well. If not by Gilpatrick himself, then by whoever's leashes he held, these rebels with their faces lost in masks.

It didn't matter whether or not Gilpatrick had been

directly involved. If a man had a savage dog he'd trained to attack, and that dog tried to tear out an innocent's throat, the master would still be responsible.

Just the same way Aidan had been responsible for the scar that writhed its ugly path down Gilpatrick's face.

Aidan met the Irishman's glare. "I'll fight you any way you name."

The rebel's lip curled in a snarl, his dirt-encrusted fingers beckoning to a brace of his men. "We'll use a crofter's weapon then, Kane. Instead of one of those elegant weapons you arrogant curs have been usin' to slit our throats for so long."

Gilpatrick's compatriots returned to the torchlit circle, and Aidan's gaze snagged on the wicked hook of a scythe. The silver metal glowed like the fang of some demon creature come to hunt in the night.

Gilpatrick's hands closed on the thick wooden staff on which the blade was mounted, fondling the weapon as if it were the throat of a familiar lover. The bastard smiled, a smile designed to scrape like a jagged knife on Aidan's pride.

"What say you, thief of Rathcannon? Have you the courage to best me without a troop of murderin' Sassenach soldiers at your back?"

The cluster of rebels roared with surly laughter, and the man holding the other scythe flung it at Aidan with a calculated savagery. Aidan glimpsed it hurtling toward him and leapt out of the way, attempting to catch the handle in fingers still half deadened from the bindings that had held them.

The wooden staff collided with his hands, and spikes of pain drove through his wrists. His face burned with fury and humiliation as the scythe clattered to the turf at his booted feet.

"Our fine knight can't even hold a weapon wi' out sixteen servants to polish it up an' stick it in his hands," a scraggle-haired man of about fifty jeered, skittering with a spry gait to retrieve the scythe. "Here, Sir Aidan." He sketched a bow with mocking solemnity, dusting off the wood with a soiled kerchief. "Take this real careful like. We'd not be wantin' ye to rub any blisters on yer palms."

Aidan spat an oath and snatched the scythe from the rebel's hands, forcing his own burning fingers to close on the smooth wood. Heavy, cumbersome, hopelessly awkward, the scythe undermined his shaken equilibrium further, exacerbating the dizziness that spiraled up from his cracked ribs.

He planted his feet apart, attempting to brace himself, his jaw clenched, as he looked from the wicked blade to Gilpatrick's scarred face. There could be no doubt of the Irishman's intentions. No man would select such a hideous, brutal weapon unless he intended to carve away his pound of flesh.

Aidan's jaw clenched. This was a game in which Gilpatrick would hold all the advantages. Aidan was crippled, not only by the ache in his hands and the unfamiliarity of the weapon he wielded, but also by the knowledge that he didn't dare to unleash all his fury and his power against Gilpatrick. A dead rebel could answer no questions.

As if Gilpatrick had read his mind, the rebel's lips curled into a sneer, the Irishman flicking the blade of the scythe in a hellish rhythm, until the torchlight painted it, seeming to tip it with blood.

"Come ahead, Kane," Gilpatrick goaded. "If you dare."

Aidan gritted his teeth, resolving to use the thick handle against his foe instead of the blade. He swept the wooden length hard toward Gilpatrick, but the Irishman leapt out of its path, laughing.

"You'll have to do better than that, boy-o."

The jeer made Aidan strike out again, harder, faster, but Gilpatrick deflected the blow with his own weapon, while Aidan's bruised wrists threatened to shatter at the impact. He barely had time to register that pain when the butt of Gilpatrick's scythe drove into the pit of Aidan's stomach,

320

driving the breath from his body, draining the strength from his knees. Aidan stumbled, crashing to the turf, battling not to lose the contents of his stomach, as the thick length of oak cracked down on the back of his head.

Waves of dizziness threatened to drag him into unconsciousness, but he struggled to get up, to escape the slashing bite of the blade he anticipated with every ragged breath he sucked into burning lungs.

It never came. Aidan jammed the butt of his own scythe into the turf. Using it to lever himself upright, Aidan staggered to his feet. He raised his head to see Gilpatrick standing a dozen steps away, leaning with infuriating nonchalance upon his weapon.

"Seems I won't be answerin' any questions, Kane," the rebel taunted. "That is, unless you beg me real pretty like."

Aidan's muscles coiled, and he lashed out with his own weapon, the thick length of wood slashing toward Gilpatrick's middle. It caught the rebel in mid-laugh, hammering a grunted oath from the man's throat and driving the lazy insolence from his features.

Aidan swung his weapon at Gilpatrick's ribs in a savage, crippling arc, but the Irishman deflected it with a brutal thrust of his scythe. The ugly blade slashed Aidan's shoulder with delicate precision.

It should have left a gaping wound in its wake, severed muscles and tendons, rendering Aidan's arm useless. But the blade bit just deep enough to trail agony through his flesh. Aidan was stunned, confused by the knowledge that one flick of the rebel lord's wrist could have defeated him, maimed him forever.

Why in God's name would Donal Gilpatrick not press his advantage? It was as if the man didn't want to kill him, didn't want to leave him in a crumpled, bloody ball on the sacred earth encircled by enigmatic stones.

How could that be possible?

It wasn't. The bastard was just toying with him, taunting him before he closed in for the kill.

Aidan gripped the handle of the scythe tighter, circling Gilpatrick, fighting for balance as the rebel stalked him with eyes as unfathomable as the secrets locked in the Druid ring.

"Donal, ye goat-kissin' fool!" a man in a filthy jerkin brayed. "Ye could'a cleaved him from gizzard t' man stones a dozen times by now! Ye've got 'is traitorous Kane neck on our own choppin' block after so long! Finish it!"

"Kill 'im!" a bloodthirsty lad of about thirteen warbled. "See if the bastard bleeds red like the rest o' us."

Aidan heard the hiss of metal blades, knives being drawn, pistols being cocked. If the lord of the Gilpatricks was reluctant to stain his hands with Kane blood, his underlings obviously were not. Even if by some miracle Aidan was able to defeat Gilpatrick, it was obvious the rabble led by the brigand would not honor the bargain struck between the hated enemy and their leader.

In that frozen instant, Aidan knew there was only one chance to ride away from the circle of stones alive. The only chance was to get the blade of his scythe pressed against the neck of Donal Gilpatrick, have the dread rebel at his mercy. A hostage—the key to escape, the key to the answers he sought.

"Keep your filthy hands off him, all of you." Donal's command cleaved the night, a chorus of gruff protests rising in its wake. Gilpatrick wheeled on his men, exposing the back of his head, leaving himself vulnerable.

Aidan poised to strike, to lunge at Gilpatrick, certain in a heartbeat he could have the rebel lord in his power. God knew it wouldn't be the first time he'd pressed his advantage, traded honor for victory.

But invisible chains held him motionless—chains forged of dark, love-swept eyes and sparkling blue ones, believing in him, trusting him, innocent eyes that had spun out a hero where there was only a flawed, jaded rogue.

That moment's hesitation was enough to rob him of his chance. Gilpatrick swung around, his twisted face seething with some emotion Aidan didn't understand. Then the wiry Irish rebel hefted the scythe again.

Aidan ground his teeth, certain no altruistic motives had been behind Gilpatrick's orders to his rabble. The bastard merely wanted to toy with his prey longer. Enjoy the moment of a Kane's ultimate defeat, so that years later Gilpatrick could savor the tale as he spun it out in the glow of a peat fire.

Fury surged through Aidan, that he'd been fool enough to surrender his chance to have Gilpatrick at his mercy—a mistake that could cost him his life, further endanger his daughter, his wife.

With a roar of animal rage, Aidan flew at his adversary, fighting with every fiber of strength he possessed.

He heard Gilpatrick's guttural oaths as the oaken staff caught him twice, three times, saw the man's face whiten with concentration and a kind of grudging respect. A blur of silver blade and dark brown wood danced before Aidan, the rebel leader handling the scythe with the same dangerous grace as a master swordsman would his most cherished rapier.

In a heartbeat it was over. Aidan lay sprawled on his back against a cushion of turf, his unfocused eyes on the standing stones that seemed to be writhing like Druid dancers about a pulsing pearl of moon. The faces of the rebels were sickening blurs, distorted, inhuman.

The point of the blade indented the fragile skin at the pulsebeat of Aidan's throat. Images flashed before his eyes: Cassandra chasing rainbows across a dew-kissed meadow, Norah, vulnerable in moonlight, loving him with her hands, her mouth . . . her heart. Sweet, savage grief cut him more deeply than any blade could have. Grief for years they would never share, grief for a future that had existed so bright, so tantalizing for the merest whisper of time.

Aidan faced his enemy with fierce determination.

"Kill me," Aidan rasped out, his eyes clinging to

Gilpatrick's hooded ones. "You've . . . earned the . . . right. Just swear you'll . . . leave my daughter and my wife alone. Swear . . . it, on the . . . Stone of . . . Truth that killed my ancestor, and I'll go to hell gladly."

Silence spun out into eternity as he waited for the movement of Gilpatrick's wrist, the cut of the blade into flesh. And in that instant, he knew that Norah's face would be in his heart, his mind, even when his life blood spilled free to stain the ancient holy soil.

CHAPTER

20

The night was alive, rasping its claws against the window, peering with its mocking moon-eye into the tower chamber where Aidan Kane's most treasured dreams lived. Norah could feel the demon breath against her neck, see the gleam of fate's greedy fangs ready to snatch away every hope that had taken flight on butterfly wings in the ruin of Caislean Alainn.

She was helpless against the dark spirits that roved this night. And yet she would rather have been wandering the darkness herself than be trapped in this tower room, helpless to do anything except pace before Cassandra's exquisite bed, while the girl lay oblivious in sleep.

It was what Aidan would want her to do, Norah knew. The reason he'd wed her—to guard his child, to comfort her should any ill befall him. And yet how could she offer comfort when she was half wild with fear, inconsolable at the mere thought that Aidan might never return?

How could she calm Cassandra when each tick of the whimsical clock on the mantel flayed away another piece of her sanity, until the only thing that offered her anchor in this maelstrom of uncertainty was the crumpled wisp of linen she pressed to her face time and again, drinking in the scent of bay rum buffed from an iron-honed jaw, the fragrance of heather blossoms crushed beneath passion-hungry skin.

Aidan's cravat.

She had found it on the spiral stairs leading to Cassandra's room and felt as if a hundred half-answered prayers twisted claws into her heart. She remembered her own fingers tearing the knot of the garment free, remembered it tangling with Aidan's shirt as he stripped it away from the taut sinews of his body, eager to feel every fiber of her nakedness with his own.

They had both forgotten the neckcloth in the alarming ride from Caislean Alainn to Rathcannon, yet it had somehow clung to the collar of Aidan's shirt until he'd bolted up these stairs to make certain his Princess was safe.

Now Norah clung to that wisp of linen as if it were a talisman, shattered by the knowledge that it might be the only treasure she would be allowed to keep from a night that had promised heaven, then snatched it away, taunting her with the cruel possibility that Aidan might never hold her in his arms again or steal her sanity away with his kiss.

All her life, Norah had prided herself on being strong, practical, controlled. She had faced adversity stoically—not out of any strength of character, but rather because she knew it was futile to rail against the inevitable. Letting her anguish break free would change nothing, except that it would expose her vulnerabilities to those who would use them against her.

And yet this was an agony so deep that it was impossible to deny it, impossible to bury it, no matter how much she might struggle to do so. Impossible because of the emotions she had seen in Aidan's face when he had laid her down in the castle ruins and stripped away not only the clothing that had shielded her body from his eyes and his hands, but also his own closely guarded defenses, exposing something buried deep inside him. Emotions Aidan could not yet confess. After tonight, Norah thought with a savage twist of loss, he might never have the chance.

Norah couldn't stifle a ragged cry of denial, burying her face against the folds of Aidan's cravat.

No. He was alive. She had to believe that.

She would know if he fell beneath a rebel pistol or sword. She would feel his death vibrate through the very core of her. If a giant hand reached out to snatch the heart from her breast, she would feel it tearing free. Wouldn't she?

"Blast you, Aidan, don't die!" She breathed her plea into the night, but only the call of nightbirds answered, their mournful strains clinging to the air like the final harp notes from a dying bard's hands.

"N—Norah?" Cassandra's voice was sleep-blurred and uncertain.

With her back toward the bed, Norah hastily scrubbed the hot tears from her face with Aidan's cravat, wishing it were as easy to gather up the fragments of her shattered strength. Fighting to hide her bounding terror and heartsick fear from the girl, Norah turned to where Cassandra was struggling to sit up among the tousled coverlets.

The sight of Aidan's daughter was enough to undo her. She felt overwhelmed by the all too real possibility that the girl might never hear her father's loving laughter again, that Aidan might never know the bittersweet and soaring triumph of leading his daughter into a ballroom and watching her change, before his eyes, into a woman.

Yet most heartbreaking of all was the splinter of envy that pierced Norah's heart at the knowledge that she might never know the wonder of carrying Aidan's child in her own womb, of laying a babe they had created together into his arms.

"So you're awake at last, sweeting," Norah said aloud, her voice that of a stranger, raw with all the things she couldn't say. "Cook has been working so hard to stir up your favorite dishes. Shall I ring for her?"

"No. I don't want anything except Papa." The girl's soft plea made Norah's heart ache. "Can you fetch him for me?"

"Your papa . . . isn't here. While you were sleeping he . . ." Norah sat down on the bed, catching one of the girl's hands, wondering how many times Aidan had done so, banishing his child's fears, while he was beset by the relentless darkness of his own. "He'll be back soon. I . . . I'm certain of it."

The lovely planes of Cassandra's face blurred through the veil of tears that filmed Norah's eyes, her throat a searing wound. Clutching Aidan's neckcloth so tightly her hands trembled, she started to rise from the bed, intending to seek haven in the shadowy section of the room, to hide herself from Cassandra's too-wise eyes.

"Norah, what is it? What's wrong?" Cassandra demanded, scrambling from beneath her coverlets.

Norah sucked in a steadying breath, bracing herself for the tide of terror and pain and uncertainty her next words would unleash in the girl.

"Your papa discovered something that might lead to whoever was responsible for what happened in the garden, sweeting. He's gone to stop them from hurting you again."

No storm of tears broke over the chamber, no wailing or raging. Instead, Cassandra gave a sigh of pure relief. "Is that all? For a moment you had me quite frightened."

Norah wheeled to face the girl, stunned. Absolute trust and blind faith shone in the fresh ivory contours of Cassandra's face. Her eyes glistened, not with dread, but rather with a hero worship as unbreachable as the walls of the castle tower.

"Papa is the smartest, bravest man in the world. He'll make those villains sorry they were ever born!"

"But he—he went alone. There is no telling how many men he has to face, how desperate they might be." Norah hated herself for allowing the words to tumble from her mouth, aware at once that they could only unnerve the girl who was being so brave, so blind in her belief in her father.

"Papa fought off a score of men at Badajoz, and a dozen other battles too. He was knighted for bravery."

Norah turned away, wanting to shake the girl for her naiveté, wishing to God she could steal some of that blessed ignorance away for herself.

She chewed at her lip, struggling to keep from screaming. She pressed Aidan's cravat to her face, trying to drink strength from its folds.

Suddenly she was aware of a light touch on her shoulder, and she raised her face from the cloth to see Cassandra regarding her with solemn, knowing eyes. The girl touched the white ripple of cloth draped over Norah's fingers.

"Papa's," Cassandra said, with an understanding far beyond her fifteen years.

The sobs were pushing against Norah's throat, battering her. She bit her lip so hard it bled. Traitorous tears welled up at the corners of her eyes spilling free in silent grief.

"Oh, Norah," Cassandra said, catching it with her fingertips. "You . . . you *do* love him."

Quiet, simple words. They ripped savagely through Norah's breast, releasing a flood of pain, of desperation. She couldn't speak, could only nod in abject misery.

"You're afraid Papa won't come back, aren't you?" Cassandra asked. "You think he might . . ."

"Don't say it," Norah pleaded. "I can't—can't bear—"

"Papa isn't going to die," Cassandra said with utter conviction. "You have to believe in him."

"But how can I believe when he . . . he's out there alone somewhere. When anything could happen—"

Norah's voice broke. Soft arms, garbed in a soft nightgown, encircled her, Cassandra comforting Norah with a gentle faith that drifted over Norah's heart.

"I want to believe. But it is so—so hard."

Cassandra smiled. "When I was a little girl, I almost stopped believing. I wanted to believe in magic, but the other children, they teased me, because I still chased fairies and looked for unicorns and elves. Papa found me crying, and I told him I was giving them up forever. That fairies were stupid and only babies believed."

Cassandra led her to the window, and Norah sank down onto a bench, listening, aching.

"Late that night, Papa got me out of bed to go on an adventure. He took me to Caislean Alainn, in the fairy ring, and said that we were going to find out if there were fairies once and for all."

Norah's throat closed, her heart aching in her chest at the vision her imagination conjured of Aidan indulging his little girl's dreams, guarding her sense of wonder as vigilantly as he was now guarding her safety. "What happened?" she managed to squeeze from her throat.

"He was up on a ledge, climbing, when suddenly he let out this—this whoop. I ran over, and his hands were cupped together so careful. He told me to hold out my hands and slipped something into them. I could feel wings beating against my palms, fluttering and magical. Fairies. I knew they were fairies. Papa told me so."

Norah's heart was shattering, a tiny piece at a time. So much love inside Aidan, so little he dared believe in. Yet he showered magic on his little girl.

"How?" Norah asked. "How did he make the magic?"

"He crept out earlier and caught butterflies in a crystal box, then he hid them, and . . ." Cassandra gave a soft laugh, filled with memories more precious than any treasure Norah could ever touch. "The next morning I went to find the boys who had been teasing me, told them they were wrong. That I'd held a fairy in my hand. They said I couldn't prove it."

She stopped, the wonder of it all still evident in her eyes. "Papa was coming in from the stables and heard them. He said they were right, he supposed. The only way to prove you'd touched a fairy was if you could see fairy dust on your skin. He held up my hand to the sunshine, and there were flecks of gold, sparkling, glittering on my skin."

"How? How did he . . ."

"He'd scraped some gilding off the leg of a chair and sprinkled it on my hand while I was sleeping. It wasn't until Mrs. Brindle told me what he'd done years later that I knew."

The girl gave Norah a smile that trembled just a little. "Papa still insists they were fairies."

Fairies and unicorns, Pegasus wings and cascades of shimmering stars. Dreams Aidan never dared for himself but lavished on his daughter. Love welled up in Norah, so fierce it was the sweetest agony she'd ever known. She closed her eyes, imagining other children, with dark hair and mischievous green eyes, fairies cupped in their hands.

She imagined placing wonder in Aidan's grasp, somehow making him see. See what Cassandra saw when she looked into his eyes, touch what Norah touched when she delved into his soul. Find all the beauty life had stripped away from him.

Please, Aidan. She cast her desperate plea out into the night. *Please come home safe, so we can make you believe. . . .*

In happily ever afters and fairy-tale princes saved by a maiden's kiss. In quests that ended not in glory but in forever joy.

Where was he now? Her husband, her love?

Her gaze clung to the mystic swirlings of the wild Irish night, and she prayed that the fairies Aidan Kane believed in would shield him from the evil he'd ridden out to confront like some battered knight of old.

Silence pulsed against a thousand secrets caught in the ring of stone, echoing back the agonized words that had torn from Aidan's throat.

Kill me . . . just swear you'll leave my daughter and wife alone.

He'd sworn he'd face hell gladly, in return for such a vow,

but none of Lucifer's torments could be as hideous as plunging into death knowing that Cassandra and Norah were still in danger.

Aidan focused on Gilpatrick's face, on the knotted scar that had haunted his nightmares for so many years. He willed the rebel leader to speak.

"I don't make war on children, Kane," Gilpatrick rasped, his lungs straining for air every bit as badly as were Aidan's. "And I'm not going to kill you. Not this time."

A roar of protest welled up from his men, but Gilpatrick silenced them, flinging his weapon to the turf. "A life for a life," he bellowed, his gaze lashing the ranks of his followers with the force of a cat-o'-nine-tails.

"But what life has a Kane ever spared?" a banty rooster of a man demanded.

"My son's." The words slammed into Aidan, paralyzing him. Gilpatrick's *son?* Aidan could picture all too clearly the Irishman's desperate face the night he'd stumbled across them on his wild night ride, the lad cradled against Gilpatrick's chest as English wolves in red coats hunted them.

"Yer son is dead!"

"Because of Kane, he died in his mother's arms, with his sisters all around, instead of in an English gaol. He died in peace, instead of suffering the hell of those Sassenach bastards trying to beat your names out of him before he slipped beyond their grasp."

Aidan winced at the cruel mockery of fate—the strange, twisted patterns that had always interwoven his life with that of Gilpatrick. While Aidan had been warring for England in the Peninsular War, Gilpatrick had been fighting for Irish freedom. While Gilpatrick had been a fugitive rebel, Aidan had been a fugitive as well, running from himself. And in this very cycle of the moon, both their children had been in danger. Gilpatrick's was dead, Aidan's own saved only by the grace of God and the courage of a footman. Aidan shuddered, imagining all too clearly the pistol ball that had pierced Calvy's leg finding another target, blood blossoming on Cassandra's breast, Aidan cradling her, knowing he was helpless. . . .

Gilpatrick had tried to prevent such a horror from overtaking a man he hated.

Aidan levered himself upright, his head still spinning, sick with confusion and regret.

"I'm sorry," Aidan grated. "About the boy."

Gilpatrick reached out, his callused, hoary hand closing on Aidan's and pulling him to his feet. Aidan could feel the pulse of agony in the rebel leader, an anguish Aidan understood far too well.

"The blood of kings did flow through his veins," Gilpatrick said softly. "And he died like a king—brave beyond his years, fighting for a patch of ground that was the life blood of his heart. Ever since he was a wee babe in my arms, I dreamed of giving it back to him. Scooping up a handful of Rathcannon turf, closing his fingers about it, and . . ."

Gilpatrick turned away, as if suddenly aware of how much he'd revealed to Aidan, his most hated enemy. Aidan knew the savage ache vulnerability could be. He spared Gilpatrick the only way he knew how, by shifting the subject to one that would cause the rebel no pain.

"Then you didn't hurt my daughter," Aidan said. "I'm sure of that now. Tell me who did."

Aidan could see Gilpatrick fold away the anguish that had savaged his features, a dark light of gratitude filling the rebel's eyes as he once again donned the mantle of leader. "I don't know who was responsible. It was pure chance that I got wind of a plot while buying powder from an English bastard who knew we'd hated each other from birth."

"A plot?" A dark shudder wrenched through Aidan's gut, the word diabolical, terrifying.

"The Sassenach thought I would rejoice in your downfall," Gilpatrick said. "God knows, I thought I would too. Until I saw what lengths this animal would go to to see you destroyed. You have a powerful enemy, Kane. That is all I know."

An enemy who would stalk Cassandra, who would spill poison into the safe world he'd fought so hard to create for his daughter. Of all the darkest fears that had preyed on Aidan in the night, this was the most chilling. That his child should pay for his sins.

"Tell me everything you know."

"The attempt to abduct the girl is part of three wagers struck in some devil's bargain to destroy you."

"Three wagers?"

"You blue-blooded devils are always striking the blasted things. It's a game, Kane, and somebody is delighting in the sport of running you to ground."

"What are they, these blasted wagers? And who the hell made them?"

"I don't know. One had to do with your daughter being taken. Another . . . there was something about your wife."

"Norah?" Aidan felt as if Gilpatrick had jammed the scythe blade into his gut. "Think, man. You must have heard something, anything . . . some clue to help me unravel this."

"Not so much as a whisper."

"If it's an official wager, it would be recorded somewhere," Aidan said, groping for something to stem the tide of panic engulfing him, the wild, shattering helplessness. "Damn, it must be—"

"What, Kane? You think this villain strolled into your high-brow White's and scribbled it in the betting book?" Gilpatrick shook his head. "Only a madman would write such a thing down, leave evidence that could fall into careless hands."

"A madman," Aidan said between gritted teeth, "or someone so arrogant, so certain of victory, they delighted in their own boldness."

An arrogant madman, plotting vengeance against a child

334

—pressing his blade of uncertainty against his foe's most devastating vulnerability. A man who would joyfully tear out Cassandra's throat to cause Aidan pain. And Norah . . . Now she was in danger as well.

Aidan swore, his gut churning so viciously he feared he'd spill the contents of his stomach on the turf.

"As if that twisted pleasure were not enough, there is also gold to consider."

"Gold?"

"The payment for your destruction is enough to ransom a king."

"But who?" Aidan demanded, as much of himself as of Gilpatrick. "God knows, it could be any one of a dozen men in England. And in Ireland." Aidan gave a bitter, agonized laugh. "It would be easier to name who would *not* be willing to aid in my destruction."

"For your daughter's sake, I wish I could tell you who is responsible. But I don't know. All I am certain of is that there are two types of men when it comes to a mission of vengeance. Those in whom passion and fury rage out of control until they do something reckless, rash—who fling themselves openly and honestly at their nemesis." Gilpatrick's smile was twisted by his scar. "You and I are men of that kind, Kane. And then there are those who caress their vengeance as if it were a whore, planning every pleasure, savoring every press of their fingertips on the points that will spill agony into their enemy's soul. That is the kind of opponent you face now, Kane. May God have mercy on your soul."

The words insinuated themselves like knife blades beneath Aidan's skin, exquisite torture honed with truth.

Sickened, he battled to picture faces across gaming tables, over dueling fields, faces from battles on blood-soaked Spanish soil. Hatred, malevolent, lurking like some beast sprung from hell. Hell, or the wicked reaches of the netherworld that had so long shrouded Aidan's soul.

No. He wouldn't let that evil drown the only two decent treasures in his life. His daughter. And—the knowledge clawed at the vulnerable places inside him—his wife.

"They'll try it again. Your only hope is to keep your wife and daughter well guarded until you uncover whatever wickedness is afoot."

"No. My chance is in finding the bastard who told you about this plot in the first place. Where can I find him?"

"In the graveyard of St. Colmcille's. When I arrived for our last meeting, I found him rottin' in his own blood, his throat slit." Gilpatrick's features went grim. "The powder and lead he was to sell was still layin' there. One of the crate boards loosened, bloody fingerprints on the wood. Somehow he'd managed to slip a letter he'd been carryin' into the crate before he died. A letter intended for you, demanding payment for warning you there was a plot against your daughter."

Aidan's blood ran cold. Was it possible this man had died because he'd known of the scheme against Aidan? What kind of ruthless beast was stalking those Aidan loved? And what, in God's name, could he do to protect them?

"So you took the note?" Aidan asked numbly.

"I merely passed on the information it held, without the demand for Kane gold."

Aidan looked with glazed eyes into Gilpatrick's face, his chest aching with gratitude as well as raw, numbing terror. The Irishman had discovered the truth and put aside generations of hatred in an attempt to warn him. Gilpatrick had known what was to befall Aidan's daughter and had chosen honor instead of vengeance.

But how had he known other things? That Norah was coming to Rathcannon? "You knew Cassandra was in danger because you stumbled on the note. But the first message was to Norah, warning her not to wed me—it was delivered before I even knew a bride was to arrive."

Gilpatrick shrugged. "There has been a Gilpatrick spy at Rathcannon since before your great-grandfather was born,

336

Kane. When your daughter wrote letters huntin' you a bride, they were intercepted, read, then passed on their way. I figured that if this Norah Linton were my daughter, my sister, I'd want her to be aware what she was stumbling into."

"The arms of a man who murdered his wife?"

Gilpatrick's mouth hardened. "If ever a woman needed killin', it was that one. Even so, lookin' at you here, now, I doubt you could've stomached snuffing out her life."

Wary respect, exchanged despite years of hate, despite the hideous scar, the stolen lands. Despite everything.

"What the devil am I supposed to do to find the bastard who made the accursed wager? Where am I to start?"

"By hiding the girl," Gilpatrick said. "If she were my daughter, I'd keep her locked up tighter than the Regent's crown. The slightest signal to these men would see you dead. And there are more around every corner, choked up with hate and poverty, needin' someone to blame for their children's empty bellies. Your enemy wouldn't have to flip them more than tuppence for them to bloody a dirk in your chest."

"Calvy said Cass's attacker spoke Gaelic."

"That narrows the field to half the crofter folk in the west country, trying to keep the words alive. None of my men came after your daughter, Kane. But someone did. And if I were a wagering man, I'd guess they were hungering for a tale about how they'd breached the walls of Rathcannon and stolen away your princess. Hungering for the gold of whoever is thirsting for your pain." Gilpatrick's jaw hardened. "Be certain of this, Kane: If I do learn any more about who stalks you, I'll get word to you as fast as I can."

"I don't understand—why . . . why you are doing this."

"Because even when your da would'a shot your pony, you wouldn't fight me, Kane. Not 'til I struck the first blow."

With that Gilpatrick signaled, and a raw-boned man with a pronounced limp came forward, leading a skittish Hazard by his reins.

Aidan mounted, bewildered as if the cudgel end of the scythe had yet again slammed into his skull.

"If I catch wind of anything more, I'll send word to you," Gilpatrick said, turning to stride away.

"Donal?"

It was almost thirty years since Aidan had used that name. An eternity. Yet only yesterday. Gilpatrick turned, meeting Aidan's gaze with a quiet intensity, a certainty that he was remembering too.

"Give your son a piece of Rathcannon he can keep for all eternity," Aidan said, his throat tight.

"What?"

"The Gilpatrick crypt is untouched. I'll leave orders that you are to be allowed on Rathcannon land whenever you wish to visit him."

The rebel's eyes widened. "You would . . . offer that? Why?"

"Because he belongs there," Aidan said softly. "Bring the boy home, so he can sleep with kings."

CHAPTER

21

The Thorned Paw Inn reeked of neglect, stale liquor, and intrigue. A haven for the dregs of humanity, poison seemed to seep through its walls, its floors, along with the stains water sent oozing down the walls.

It was a place most sane men would shun—especially a man like the one even now pacing the confines of the cramped room. His immaculate breeches and exquisitely tailored coat were as out of place as a handful of glittering sapphires would be on the splintered oak table. But momentary discomfort was a small price to pay when vengeance was nearly in a man's grasp.

Richard Farnsworth paced the room, impatience flashing in his eyes.

Even so, he could wait however long was necessary. Patience was the one virtue Richard had attained the hard way. It had been a long time to have to hide the poison in his soul, but the waiting would soon be over.

They should return any moment now, the men he'd hired

to abduct the prize he had plotted so long and hard to make his own.

Cassandra Kane, Aidan Kane's cherished daughter, an heiress in her own right, the perfect tool to exact his revenge.

She would be frightened, no doubt—the proud little beauty stolen away from her papa's castle. But she could hardly expect pity from him. It was ironic justice that she be as terrified as he had been when his path first clashed with that of Aidan Kane.

Richard downed another mug of wine. Vengeance. That was the only thing left to him. The goal he would go to any lengths to achieve—even if it meant taking a young girl into his bed. Distaste drew a shudder from him at the prospect. But there was no escaping the necessity.

A drunken vicar lolled in the inn's chimney corner, his slack flesh so permeated with gin that a pinprick might burst him like a rotted wineskin. Gin and a heavy purse would assure his cooperation in performing the wedding rites, the license in Richard's coatpocket would see that it was legally binding. And the consummation would be a masterpiece of hellish vengeance beyond Satan's own imaginings. But the purest pleasure of all would be the instant Kane realized that he'd been betrayed by yet another wife—that his mousy little bride was the one who had flung wide the gate to his castle, allowing his enemy in.

Richard rubbed his fingers together in anticipation, greedy for the moment he saw destruction in Kane's eyes. The same blazing humiliation, the utter desolation the Irish knight had left in Richard's own.

The sound of horsemen riding up made Farnsworth straighten, and he all but bolted down the stairs to greet his reluctant bride.

But when the door opened, no terrified beauty spilled in, only the curs he had hired to abduct her, the three looking bewildered, shaken, and chagrined.

"Where is the girl?" Richard snapped.

"She was too close guarded! A bleedin' army couldn't a taken her!" a bald man whined.

"We had 'er in hand, and some damned fool servant dodged betwixt us. We shot him, certain sure, but it gave the girl time to get away."

"Aye, an' the shot brought a score of people runnin' from the ball. We were lucky to get away with our very skins."

Frustration and rage raced like venom through Richard's veins, the emotions all the more potent because they had seethed inside him, hidden for so long. The thought that Kane had bested him again was acid in old wounds. The knowledge that he'd been thwarted when he'd been so close to his goal was infuriating.

"You fools! You incompetent fools! I should shoot you myself!"

One of the men eyed him warily, a hand flicking to the hilt of a knife.

"Damnation, you're not worth bloodying the floorboards," Richard raged. "Get out, all of you. If I ever see your faces again, or if you ever breathe a word of this night's work, I swear I'll shoot you where you stand."

The men bolted out, and Richard turned to see the vicar staring at him owlishly, a damn annoying smile on his vacuous face.

"Whatcher goin' t' do now, friend? Yer ladybird seems to have slipped the net."

"I'm going to snare her myself. And when I do . . ." Richard's jaw set grimly. "I shall repay her a hundredfold for the inconvenience she has caused me."

"I suppose you're goin' t' walk right up t' Sir Aidan's doorstep an' say how d'ye do?"

"Exactly. It's time I made a most concerned call upon my beloved stepsister. She will be delighted to see me. She always was."

With that, Richard stalked to the chamber in which he'd planned to bed his bride. He flung his clothes into a portmanteau. If he hurried, he could reach Rathcannon before nightfall.

Exhausted, Aidan made his way up the castle stairs. How many times had he passed by the crests knitted into the very bones of Castle Rathcannon, ornamenting doorways and mantels, turrets and grand ballrooms?

More often than he'd admitted, even to himself, he'd felt the subtle rasp of guilt against him, the excruciating sensitivity a thief must feel when taking out a stolen treasure, breathless because of its beauty, while his hands felt soiled by the knowledge that he had no right to touch it, to hold it.

It was the same clumsy awe he'd felt for Cassandra. An awe that reached new heights in the wife who waited for him in the bedchamber that had been the scene of Delia's darkest betrayals—and that now, with biting irony, held his own most fragile hopes.

He clamped his good arm around ribs that throbbed and ached from the blows he'd taken from the butt of Gilpatrick's scythe, the pain exacerbated from the jolting ride along dark byways. The gash cleaved into his shoulder arced a ribbon of liquid fire from his collarbone to midbicep, his legs dragging like lead weights of pure exhaustion. But neither the beating he'd suffered, nor the wounds he'd sustained could match the battering he'd received in places far deeper, where fists and cudgels and blades could never reach.

Nothing was what it seemed. Gilpatrick, his sworn enemy, had attempted to save Aidan's daughter. Rathcannon, the bastion of safety built to protect Cassandra, had almost been the scene of her abduction. Delia with her poisonous beauty had made Aidan swear never to trust another woman. Yet now, half broken, bleeding from wounds no one else could see, Aidan had brushed aside the worried queries of Sean and Gibbon, Mrs. Cadagon and Mrs. Brindle, and instead of going up to Cassandra's tower, was rushing as fast as he could toward the one person he needed to see, to touch, to tell.

Norah.

Never, from the time he'd been a boy, had he allowed himself this shattering need to pour all that he was into another person's hands. His father had taught him young to mock such tender feelings, that nobility and honor were only disguises for weakness and stupidity, that to reveal the vulnerabilities in one's heart was like baring a jugular to a ravening wolf.

God knew, Delia had seared the truth of his father's words into every fiber of Aidan's being during the storm-tossed night he had raced after the coach, poison spreading through his body as he clung to sanity by the frayed thread of his child's cries of terror.

Yet in the midst of the standing stones on the Hill of Night Voices, Aidan had bared his throat to his enemy and received, not the expected death blow, but a hand, offering to aid him. In the child whose birth had destroyed his first marriage, Aidan had found his own salvation.

In the marriage bed with a bride he had never wanted, he had found not lust, not even something so simple as passion, but rather a mystic elixir that had pushed him beyond the mere limitations of flesh and need and desire, into a realm so wondrous he was still shaken by the power his solemn-eyed bride had unleashed in him. A power, a beauty that had been magnified a thousandfold in the enchanted reaches of Caislean Alainn.

Miracles—they were all miracles he didn't deserve. Chances to make things right, where he had failed for so very long. Hope—or, a voice inside Aidan whispered, the final torment of hell itself, dangling salvation before his eyes, something decent and good after so many years lost in darkness. Salvation he could glimpse, grasp with his unworthy hand, for the merest heartbeat, before the jeering fates ripped it away.

He turned down the corridor that had once mocked him with Delia's recriminations, to the bedchamber that had once echoed with the groans and pleasure sounds of his wife with another man, and realized that now there was only a kind of quiet peace, a soft expectation. Welcome.

At Norah's door, he released his ribs long enough to turn the latch and steal into the chamber quietly, so quietly. What he saw in the guttering light of the candles stole his breath away.

Half hidden by the bedcurtains, Norah lay on the bed where Delia had betrayed him, her fingers pressing something soft and white against her cheek. His cravat, Aidan realized with a jolt as he took a step toward her. She'd been crying against it; salty tracks of tears were dried upon her cheeks.

The knowledge that this woman had wept for him was more humbling than anything Aidan had ever faced in his life. The certainty that he was unworthy of even one of her tears raked through him, leaving more pain in its wake than the scoring tip of Gilpatrick's scythe when it had cut into his shoulder.

He crossed to the bed and reached out his fingertips to feel the petal softness of her cheek, so warm and alive.

He needed her. The knowledge ate like acid inside him, the raw vulnerability the most terrifying emotion he'd ever faced in his life. The trust he placed in her—this woman of gentle dignity, sweet, quiet courage—was the most delicate spindle of spun glass, indescribably beautiful, bright, and yet so fragile, it seemed it must shatter with the merest brush of his hand.

"Norah." He breathed her name, watched her come awake with a start. Her eyes flashed open, disoriented, tear-reddened, and shadowed with desperation and pain, and he knew in that instant what she had suffered for him. She cried out, a choked sound of joy, flinging herself against him with a sob. White-hot pinwheels radiated out from his ribs, the wound in his shoulder igniting afresh, but he didn't care. He wrapped his arms around her, pulling her tight against him, drinking in the warmth, the vibrancy, the sweet, sweet honesty that was his new bride.

She was touching him everywhere, his hair, his face, as if she didn't believe her eyes. "Aidan! Sweet God in heaven, you're alive!"

Had anyone ever greeted him thus? Emotion crushed his throat. "Hush, ladylight," he whispered, stroking her dusky curls with his bruised hand. "I'm fine."

"Did you find the—the men who tried to hurt Cassandra? You were gone so long, I was certain you must have found the rebel—"

"I found Gilpatrick. He isn't responsible for the attack. He is the one who tried to warn us."

Norah gazed up at him, her arms still clinging, her eyes shimmering, soft. "But I thought you were enemies."

"We were bred to be. And yet . . . he's a good man, Norah. One I would want at my side if I were charging into battle. One I would trust with my life. He already did his best to save my daughter's."

"Oh, Aidan." Her palm curved about his jaw, tenderness and understanding seeping through him.

He felt so unsettled, off balance. "It isn't over. I have to find whoever did plot against Cass. Gilpatrick gave me some information to begin with, and he promised to send me word if he learned anything more. Whoever is stalking me is a cunning bastard, one making a game of my destruction. There are wagers involved. One regarding Cassandra. And . . . another about you."

"Wagers? What kind of wagers?"

"I don't know. The only thing I'm certain of is this: He wants to toy with me before he closes in for the kill."

"He must—must hate you. Is there an enemy you can think of? Someone so villainous—"

"I've spent my life neck-deep in villains, Norah. Libertine

345

blackguards who would joyfully slit a throat over the turn of a card. I've done things I'm not proud of, more than I can even remember."

"Aidan, I don't believe—"

"That I'm every bit the sonofabitch I told you I was the night you arrived here?" A ragged sound tore from his throat, rife with self-contempt. "Believe it, Norah. When I inherited Rathcannon, it was in ruins. I found it vaguely amusing at first. I was a bold rakehell with London at my feet. I didn't give a damn about the estate, my inheritance, anything. I was a soldier, but I'd had a belly full of killing. The only other skill I possessed was at the gaming table. I used it. Ruthlessly. To survive. God knows how many of my opponents I could have ruined. We Kanes have always had an overdeveloped sense of self-preservation, the devil take the price to anyone else."

"I don't care about that Kane legacy. I know you."

Her belief in him should have healed, should have comforted. Instead, it ripped away the fragile coverings of scars long buried.

"You don't know me at all," he grated. "I pray God you never do." Shuddering need raced through him, that blend of desperation, panic, and love—God, oh, not love—that he'd felt for his daughter, yet worlds different, somehow agonizingly new, the emotions sharpened, honed even more intensely when he looked into Norah's eyes. The need to protect her from himself was fierce, and yet there was a part of him that wanted nothing more than to pour the truth into Norah's hands, to take that final risk—that, by some miracle, she could love him. In spite of the ugliness. In spite of what he had been, the past from which he could never be free.

But the hideous possibility of seeing her love for him change to revulsion, the chance of feeling those hands that had been so magical, the most beautiful things that had ever touched him, changing, shifting, shrinking away from him as if he were something dirty, loathsome . . . God, the courage it would take to hazard such a risk . . .

He drew away from her, feeling as if he'd somehow tainted her, sickened by all that he was, all that he stood for. He meant only to put distance between them, so that he could drag the tattered remains of his guard about him, cover up the places she'd bared in his soul with those exquisitely gentle hands.

He raised his fingers to rake his hair back from his eyes, and he heard her breath catch in her throat. Her face paled, her eyes widened, locked on his shirt. "Aidan, you're hurt!" she gasped, staring at the blood-soaked tear in his shirt.

"It's nothing. The tiniest scratch." He attempted to brush her concern away, but Norah scrambled out of the bed, her brows crashing together in such stormy anger he almost smiled.

"I barely get you healthy after your bout with the gypsy love potion, and you charge out and get yourself injured again!" She attacked his buttons, stripping the ruined garment from him. The cloth clung to the wound, and he saw her catch her lip between her teeth as she tried to gently pull it free. She flinched as she saw the eight-inch gash.

"It looks far worse than it is, Norah," he said gently. "Trust me. It's not as if I've never been wounded before."

Her mouth trembled, and her eyes filled as they skated from the cut to a chest covered with darkening bruises.

"The fête at the standing stones was a private party. Some of Gilpatrick's men took exception to my arriving without an invitation," he said, attempting to jest. "I just need to wash the cut, and then bind a tight cloth about my ribs."

"Aidan, they hurt you. I thought you said Gilpatrick had tried to help."

"His men didn't have their leader's philanthropic impulses. And as for the fight with Gilpatrick, I goaded him into it. I wanted so damn bad to gain control of something again, anything. To fight some foe besides this—this phantom that melted out of the night to try to steal Cassandra and then disappeared again."

He crossed to the washbowl and lifted the pitcher to pour water into the bowl. A spike of pain jolted from his collarbone through his ribs, and he winced. Norah snatched the china pitcher away and filled the bowl herself. Then she took him by the arm and settled him in a chair.

Aidan sank down into the cushions, exhaustion seeping through his body, pulling him down into emotions he couldn't conquer, couldn't hide. And as Norah's hands began gently swabbing his wound, Aidan let his head sag onto the chair back, his eyelids slipping closed.

God, it was so beautiful, feeling her fingertips glide across the wounded places on his body, tending him with such infinite tenderness. Love . . .

Belief in him, when he didn't deserve it. Love, when he had none to give her in return. Magic, where there had only been darkness and dread and self-loathing.

She was a treasure that should be cherished, framed in a backdrop of love worthy of her devotion. She should be forever safe, in the care of a far better man than he.

Aidan's heart tore with the pulsing terror that he would somehow fail her. His jaw knotted, his fingers clenching on the arms of the chair. He welcomed the pain of his hands throbbing, wishing it could drive away the deeper pain in his heart.

"Aidan, what—what are you thinking? Feeling?" Her breath wisped over him as she bandaged his wound.

"Damn it, Norah."

"You say I don't know you. I want to. Need to. Tell me."

Aidan wanted to shake her, rage at her, tell her that the truth would destroy her. She should pull away from him, not try to peel back the layers of his soul, because what she'd find there . . . oh, God, what she'd find there . . .

And yet there was a pull in those remarkable dark eyes of hers he couldn't deny, a kind of dignity, courage, love that reached inside him, cupping about his pain, drawing it to the surface, until for the first time in his life Aidan felt words spilling free, memories rising inside him, things he'd never talked about coming out in the rasping voice of a man imprisoned for an eternity, speaking for the very first time.

"I feel like the first time I stepped onto a battlefield, being swept under by bloody currents, flailing in the darkness, my lungs screaming for air. My hands grappling for purchase on something, anything to drag myself out of the gore, to stop from hearing the shrieks of men dying. Knowing I was helpless to save them. Sweet Christ, what if I can't save you or Cassandra? What if—"

"You were knighted for bravery. You did save as many men as you could. Cassandra wrote—"

"Cassandra wrote a damned fairy story, rigged out in laurels I never earned. Yes, I saved my men. But I saved the accursed major as well—a pompous ass, hungry for his own glory, greedy for promotions. I was knighted for saving that bastard. I should have let him die. Hell, I should have put a bullet in him myself."

"I don't understand."

"While I was being knighted for bravery," Aidan all but spat, "the sonofabitch was sending my men in to be slaughtered as cannon fodder so that he could climb over their bloody backs and rise among the officers' ranks."

He'd fought so damned hard to dismiss his past, layer it in devil-may-care scorn. But he could hear the pain in his own voice, see its reflection in Norah's meltingly dark eyes.

"I'm sorry. So sorry. But Aidan, you couldn't have known."

"They labeled me a hero. Hero. For saving that bastard's life. But I wasn't any goddamn hero. I was a reckless fool who had plunged in without knowing or thinking. Just as I did in every other facet of my life."

A bitter smile twisted his lips. "War was a nightmare, but I thought I could escape it, cleanse myself of what I'd seen, done, as I had washed away the blood on my hands. When I got back to England, hell, my marriage made war seem like a cursed musicale by comparison. When Delia discovered she was pregnant . . . God, the joy I felt. For just a moment, I believed the fates had given me the chance to start over, to make things right with this new life we'd created."

"It was a new chance, Aidan. One you've taken advantage of. You have made something beautiful in Cassandra."

Her praise was an acid-soaked whiplash against the raw places in his soul. "You see Cass as she is now," he insisted. "Here. Safe. You wouldn't be handing me any hero crowns if you had known me during those first years of her life, Norah. You'd be as sickened, as disgusted as I am with myself, every time I remember."

Those soft lips firmed, her chin tipping up with a stubbornness that wrenched his heart. "I don't believe you were ever a bad father. Ever."

"I wasn't a father at all, damn it. I didn't even exist in Cass's world. Delia hated me for burdening her with a child, made me feel as if I'd raped her, forced my baby inside her. I all but begged her to let us make a new beginning, but it was too late. She said that after what I'd done to her, I owed it to her to leave her in peace. I could only destroy the baby, the way I'd destroyed Delia's life, the way I'd destroyed the troop of soldiers, the way I'd destroyed everything I ever touched."

Tears welled in Norah's eyes, and Aidan saw them fall free. She knelt down at his feet, so he had to look into that lovely angel's face. "You didn't destroy Cassandra, Aidan. You made her . . . magnificent."

"I didn't *make* Cassandra anything. She survived because of her own strength, her own courage, her own blasted stubborn will. I only saw her once in the first five years of her life. I'd stayed away, like Delia demanded. I didn't even know when she had the baby. God knows, no one at the March household thought it important to notify me that I was a father. I was cheating at a game of hazard when one of the Marches' acquaintances congratulated me on the birth of my daughter. Cass was three weeks old."

"It must have hurt so badly," Norah said, her hand stroking his. "To find out about your child that way."

Aidan bit back that remembered pain, too raw to be examined, and went on. "I rode all night to reach Delia's parents' estate. My wife had already gone off to Bath to take the waters, and, I don't doubt, to renew her acquaintance with her former admirers."

"She'd left the baby?" Disbelief echoed in the soft query.

"She cast Cassandra aside the instant she was up from childbed, with no more thought than if my baby had been a wilted posy from some forgotten beau." Aidan sucked in a steadying breath, his lungs burning at the memory.

"I went upstairs to the nursery and saw Cass cuddled in this elegant cradle that had been in the March family for a hundred years. She had this little lace bonnet on, and her knees tucked under her, her little rump in the air. She was . . . so damned beautiful, lost in rose-satin coverlets, so innocent, so helpless. I was afraid . . . afraid she'd break if I touched her. I was afraid I would hurt her."

"You loved her even then," Norah said gently. "How could you leave her?"

His voice roughened on the pain of the man he had been, so young himself, without the hard core of cynicism to protect him. "I left to save her from myself."

"Aidan . . ."

"Since the night I first waltzed with Delia, her mother had hated me, seen me as her daughter's despoiler. God, how could I blame her? Yet that day, when she came to me, the proud Lady March stooped to plead with me. She begged me to leave Cassandra in her care."

"But Cassandra was *your* daughter. You loved her and wanted her."

Aidan raised an unsteady hand to his eyes, rubbing away the burning sensation that had little to do with exhaustion. "Lady March promised me that if I gave my daughter into her care, Cassandra would have everything she ever wanted or needed. That she'd have love, security, a home. The kind of stable life I could never give her."

His lips twisted in mockery. "Hell, I could hardly have dragged a baby with me to my apartments over a tavern or gaming hell, could I? The blasted old dragon was right about that. With the kind of life Delia and I led . . ." He stopped, swallowed hard. "I thought about changing—casting aside my life, making a place for Cassandra and me. But even if I had, what did I have to give her? Nothing but a crumbling castle in Ireland. I remember standing there over Cassandra's cradle, staring down at her, memorizing . . . memorizing the way her lashes curled on those plump little cheeks, the way she crinkled up her nose. I stored up images of the little shuddering sigh of contentment she gave when she got her tiny fingers in her mouth and sucked on them."

Something hot and wet splashed his bruised hand. Norah's tears. Would God Aidan could shed some himself, for the confused, hurting youth he had been, standing over his daughter's cradle.

"I couldn't even touch Cassandra because I knew that if I did, I would never be able to leave her. And I had to. For her sake, I had to let her go. I'd been through a war, the destruction of my marriage, but I never understood the depths pain could reach until I rode away from my daughter."

Norah's hand slipped up to curl her fingers around his, the way this woman had somehow managed to curl herself deep in the battered reaches of his heart.

"Don't cry for me, angel. I don't deserve it," he said roughly. "I'm not proud of the life I lived after I left Cassandra in that cradle. I drowned myself in brandy, gambled like a lunatic. And there were women—I don't even know how many, Norah, can't even remember their faces. I was so damned broken inside, trying to prove to myself that I could make some woman . . . any woman . . . want me when my wife did not. I didn't care if I lived or died. Hell, I wanted to die. I believed Cass would be better off if I did.

"Five years I stayed away. Delia was playing harlot to half the men in London. I'd quit playing the jealous fool after I almost killed a raw lad in a duel over Delia. I suppose I'd finally realized she wasn't worth another death on my conscience. I turned everything into a game then, a game of wagers—bed sport, gambling, drink. The amazing thing was that suddenly I couldn't lose at the gaming tables. I knew that Rathcannon was Cassandra's legacy. I poured every shilling of my ill-gotten gains fashioning it into something she could be proud of. I even created the perfect room for her. It was the only way I could think of to let her know that I loved her, wanted her, that every day she was in my mind . . . in my heart. One day I was racing my curricle near the March estate when a wheel shattered."

He paused, blessing that broken wheel and the brainless wager that had ended in his getting his daughter back.

"I knew I should just go on to an inn, hire out another carriage, see to the fixing of my own. But instead, I went to Lord March's door. Suffice it to say they were not thrilled to see me. I demanded to see Cassandra . . . to just see her. I didn't want to upset her life, intrude. I just—just wanted to look at her and to make certain that she was all right."

Aidan smiled, an aching, brittle smile. "Mrs. Brindle was there. She had loathed me, like the rest of the Marches, for defiling Delia—but she led me into the garden, let me wander through it, searching. . . .

"They say children are innocent. But they can also be incredibly cruel. I found Cassandra on a stone bench, crying her eyes out because the cousins she'd been playing with had taunted her about her mama and papa and the fact that we didn't want her. She didn't even know who I was, Norah, when I tried to comfort her."

His jaw set, hard. "I decided then and there that my child's life was going to change. I hauled Delia away from her lovers, cast my gaming aside, took every shilling I'd won, and went to Rathcannon with a bewildered little girl in tow. You know the rest. Delia's hatred, the poison, her death. I know you can't choose your parents, but whatever angel delivered Cassandra into the hands of Delia and me had made a terrible mistake. I'm still sick when I think of the years I lost. . . . The time she first walked, smiled, her first skinned knee. I wonder what scars those years left inside her, in places I will never see."

"You've done wonders with her, Aidan."

"Have I? Or have I just made things worse? Left her unprepared for the future? I've given her eight years of fairy tales when she has to face a reality that's harsh and ugly. She's so brave, so damned innocent, so open. But someday she's going to stumble into the truth—about Delia, about me. And when she does . . ."

"I think you underestimate your daughter's love for you and her faith in you. Yes, it will be a shock. And painful. But she knows you love her, Aidan, and even when she discovers things about the past, she'll still have fairy dust to hold."

"Fairy dust?"

"She told me about Caislean Alainn, and butterflies and gold flecks that clung to her little hand."

"One more of my accursed lies. God, I was so good at them."

"You made magic."

"No. I painted her illusions, while her real legacy waited outside these castle walls. Shame, because of what her parents were; revulsion when she hears the truth; and now, worst of all, some kind of animal who intends to use her against me, to hurt her so he can destroy me. Most terrifying of all, I don't know if I can protect her."

"You'll do what you have to do, Aidan. Cassandra believes in you." Her voice dropped low. *"I* believe in you. You have so much love inside you, I know you'll find the strength to get through this. You'll find a way."

It was a gift, the most precious one Aidan had ever received. "You almost make me believe in myself," he said in a ragged whisper. "I haven't for a very long time. Maybe . . . maybe I never have."

Norah reached out to him, and he felt her arms close about him, her cheek pressed soft against his bare chest.

He felt as though he had bared his soul, and the need to bury himself in her love became an obsession fiercer than he had ever known. Yet within that precious gift lay the possibility of his own damnation. For if he failed Norah, failed Cassandra this time, Aidan knew it would destroy him for all eternity.

"Aidan?" She breathed his name, then paused for a heartbeat. "I love you."

The words trembled between them, Aidan's throat parched with the need to whisper them back to her, tell her. But all he could do was lower his mouth to hers, trying with all that was in him to let his kiss reveal to her the words he could not say.

When he pulled away, she looked up into his face, so full of faith and hope and determination and quiet courage. "Aidan, we'll find a way. Tell me where to begin."

"Begin? Christ, if I only knew. There are dozens of possibilities, and somehow I'm going to have to look into every one. I'm going to try to track down any information about the bastard Gilpatrick told me of. He may be dead, but there might be some clue, some hint, some trail leading back to whoever told him about the wagers. Then I intend to rake through my memory, list the worst enemies I might have made. Men bested at the gaming table or on the dueling field. Maybe a few I knew back in the war. The problem is, it will take time. And time may be the one thing Cassandra doesn't have. There's no telling when this sadistic bastard might strike again. No telling how desperate he might be. It makes me insane, staring into every face, wondering . . . wondering if they might be the one stalking Cass, stalking you."

The sound of a knock at the bedchamber door made Aidan straighten and Norah pull away.

"Lady Kane and I are not to be disturbed," Aidan bit out roughly.

"Your pardon, sir, but the gentleman insists on seeing Lady Kane. He says he'll not leave until he does."

"Who the devil—"

"It's an English gentleman, sir. A fine one."

"Blast it, if Montgomery is sniffing about again, I'll bloody his chin this time."

"I can't imagine it's Philip. He left for his estate in Sligo when the rest of the guests departed last night." Norah rose, tidying her hair with distracted hands, smoothing her gown. "I'll just run down for a moment."

"Like hell." Aidan dragged on his shirt, then looped his arm protectively about his wife, his eyes simmering with distrust, his muscles tense and wary, and they both walked down the stairs toward the drawing room the servant had settled the guest in.

Norah opened the door, then stepped into the room. She stiffened and shrieked with joy. In a heartbeat, she tore away from Aidan's grasp and flung herself into the Englishman's arms.

"Richard!" she cried out. "Thank God you have come!"

CHAPTER

22

Aidan stiffened as the stranger let out a ragged laugh, the sound grating against already frayed nerves.

"I couldn't stay away another moment," the man said, swirling her around in his embrace. "I've been insane with worry, cursing myself a hundred times a day for a fool because I ever let you go. *God,* Norah—"

"*Another* heartbroken suitor?" Aidan bit out.

Norah turned a glowing face back to him, and he felt a crippling jab of jealousy.

"Aidan, this is the person I love and trust most in the whole wide world." She flushed. "After you and Cassandra, of course. My brother, Richard."

The instinctive dislike he'd felt the moment he'd laid eyes on the man intensified. Aidan's shoulders squared, his jaw hardening. "I see. So this is the man who sent you off to wed a complete stranger."

"Aidan!" Norah's soft protest was lost as color spilled up Farnsworth's neck onto his handsome cheeks.

Fires of shame and anger simmered in bright eyes. "No one is more ashamed of that day's work than I am. I've blamed myself a dozen times a day, wondered if she was safe . . . happy."

"I am!" Norah insisted. "Oh, Richard, I—"

But the man warmed to his diatribe, with all the passion of a parliamentarian pleading a cause destined to swell his bank account. "When I discovered your reputation, Kane— God, I all but went insane."

"It seems to me my . . . reputation . . . should have been easy enough to unearth. The mere mention of my name should have drowned you in tales of scandal and debauchery."

"Aidan, please! Richard did his best to help me. He only stumbled across tales of your bravery in the war, and—"

Aidan regarded the Englishman through narrowed lids, his voice soft. "I'm certain tales of my heroism would be the first thing off the lips of the society dragons. We all know how charitable the haute ton is, determined to show everyone in the most favorable light."

Hurt welled up in Norah's chocolate eyes, her sweet mouth curving in a silent plea. Aidan felt like a bastard. Exhaustion, frustration, and very real fear left him feeling edgy, goading him to lash out. And God knew, since Norah had been dumped on his doorstep, helpless and friendless, completely at his mercy, he'd thought more than once what he'd say the first time he met the brainless idiot who was responsible for thrusting her into such possible danger.

And yet it was obvious from every curve of his wife's sweet face that she had affection for this brother, the one person in her stepfather's cursed household who had offered her even the most simple kindness. Besides, Aidan's conscience nudged him, had it not been for this heedless fool, this miraculous woman would never have come to Rathcannon to change Aidan's life.

He battled long seconds to rein in his temper, bracing himself by laying one hand on Norah's shoulder. The feel of her warmth against his palm reminded him how much he owed her. Offering this brainless stepbrother of hers a decent welcome was little enough to give her in return. Yes, Farnsworth's arrival was ill-timed: The blithering fool could hardly have chosen a more inappropriate moment to make his appearance if he'd tried. But his visit might actually cheer Norah and Cassandra. Help take their mind off the encroaching danger.

Aidan heaved a sigh, a twinge shooting through his ribs. He cursed, low. "Farnsworth, it's been a helluva night. I'm . . ." Aidan looked from Norah to her stepbrother, fully intending to apologize for his churlishness, but somehow he couldn't squeeze the words past his throat. Instead, he said gruffly, "You're Norah's family. This is her home. Of course you are welcome."

The smile on Norah's face should have dazzled him. Instead, he fought the strange urge to interpose himself between her and the man whose handsome features were now wreathed in the most forgiving of grins.

Farnsworth came toward Aidan with the slightest limp and extended his hand. Aidan gritted his teeth and took it, giving it a brisk shake.

"Apology accepted," Farnsworth said, with a sunny inflection that made Aidan want to check his pockets to see if they'd been picked. "I don't blame you for being indignant on my little sister's behalf. She was treated shamefully by my father and by me."

"No, Richard! You were so kind!" She turned to Aidan, her heart in her eyes. "Aidan, Richard even met me at the docks before I left and made me a present of trunks full of clothes, the loveliest trousseau any bride could ever have wished for."

"Bah! As if a few trinkets could obliterate the wrong I did you," Farnsworth insisted. "I was a bumbling fool who might have blithely sent you off into disaster. Norah, no matter how well intentioned I might have been, Kane is right. It's only by the grace of God that you're safe, and . . . dare I say it? Happy?" Tenderness oozed out of every scented pore as Farnsworth caught her chin between his fingers and tipped her face up to him. "A blind man could see that you've formed an attachment to your new husband. And yet I fear there are shadows in your eyes. You know, you could never hide it from me when you were troubled. Please, darling, let Richard help, if I may."

Aidan could see the moment Norah's joy at her stepbrother's surprising arrival was tainted by the memory of the tense time all at Rathcannon had suffered. She nibbled at her lower lip, looking so delicate, so uncertain.

"Aidan was just—just saying how dreadfully much he has to do. I'm certain that you will be an absolute godsend, considering all that has happened," she confided.

Aidan's hands tightened into fists. The mere thought of this polished Englishman being privy to Aidan's darkest fears made every nerve in his body sizzle. "Norah, your brother has come to visit with you. There is no need to distract him with matters that are none of his concern."

Farnsworth's brows drew down over his straight nose. "That sounds rather ominous, Kane. Is something amiss? If so, you may consider me at your service. After all, we are brothers now."

Aidan knew a swift need to snap out a denial, yet he leashed his tongue for Norah's sake. "I . . . thank you for your offer. I will be sure to consider it should I ever happen to need your aid."

"But you were just saying how much there is to be done. Surely Richard can be of use. I know he may seem a bit . . . a bit . . ." She hesitated, plucking nervously at a fold of her gown, her cheeks coloring.

But if she feared offending the fool, she needn't have. Farnsworth let out a self-deprecating laugh. "Shallow? Scatter-brained?"

"That's not what I meant to say at all!" Norah said defensively. "Perhaps . . . impulsive."

"Ah-hah. A more diplomatic way of saying scatter-brained," Farnsworth observed. "Perhaps it *would* be better if Kane didn't entrust me with this great dark secret."

"Don't be ridiculous. It's not a secret." Norah turned to her brother. "Last night Aidan's daughter, Cassandra, was nearly abducted from the castle gardens."

Farnsworth clapped one hand to his chest, his eyes widening in disbelief. "Abducted? By brigands?"

"We don't know for certain who made the attempt. We can only be glad it didn't succeed."

"My God, she's just a child!" Farnsworth exclaimed. "How old is she?"

"Fifteen," Norah supplied. "Aidan went out in search of the men who did it, but they'd vanished."

"But why would anyone strike out at an innocent girl?"

"To get to me," Aidan ground out.

Farnsworth seemed to be struggling to digest that, outrage blossoming on his face. "The villainous churls!" He groped for his cravat, shuddering. "Of course, one does hear of such . . . such abominable things happening, and yet—My God, it makes my skin crawl when I think of what the poor innocent girl might have been subjected to. She could have been murdered. Raped."

"Farnsworth!" Aidan snarled, the man's words stirring up all his own fears and nightmares, every time he thought of how close Cassandra had come to being helpless, in the power of maniacs bent on revenge. His stomach twisted, his chest constricted.

The English fool stopped, casting a horrified glance at Norah, as if suddenly realizing what had slipped from his unguarded tongue. "Forgive me. I just . . . I cannot tell you what a shock it is to hear of such a thing."

"There is more, Richard," Norah said. "It seems this monster has struck a set of wagers—one about Cassandra, and—and one about me."

Farnsworth's jaw set with determination and his arms

361

crossed over his chest. "Exactly what are you going to do about this, Kane?" There was challenge in the words, a gauntlet flung down.

"I'm going to find the bastard behind this. And then I'm going to kill him."

"You're confident of your ability to do so? That 'bastard' already practically waltzed into your very home, took your daughter. By God, he seems like a cunning devil."

"What he is, is an arrogant fool. He'll make a mistake, and when he does, I'll be waiting."

Farnsworth raked his fingers through his blond hair. "Well, I'll be damned if I'm going to sit in the infernal gardens sipping tea when my sister is in danger! You may not want my help. You may not approve of my involvement in Norah's coming here. You may not even like me very much. But you *will* accept my aid in bringing this cowardly cur to heel."

"Damn it, I have enough of a disaster on my hands without—"

"Without what? Another man to help guard your women-folk? Another pistol raised in their defense? Another set of hands to help flush this bastard out of hiding? Thundera-tion, man, think!"

"Aidan, please." Norah placed a supplicating hand on his arm. "Richard can help. I know he can. And you . . . look at you already. You need to sleep and eat. And you're injured besides."

"Injured? You mean you already had an altercation with this animal and he got away?"

"No, dammit. If I'd gotten my hands on him the devil himself couldn't have wrenched him from my grasp. I—" Aidan thought about the confrontation with Gilpatrick and his teeth ground closed. No, there was no way to explain such a thing to Farnsworth without revealing more vulnera-ble places. And the idea of exposing vulnerabilities to anyone save Norah was beyond comprehension.

"Kane, be reasonable. My sister needs me. You need me.

Your daughter needs me. You can hardly expect any decent man with a shred of honor to walk away from such a duty."

"Cassandra and Norah are mine to protect."

"And you've obviously been doing a damn fine job of it!" Sarcasm dripped from Farnsworth's voice, but he stopped with a muttered oath. "I don't mean that, Kane. I know I've begun badly here, and that you have every right to dismiss me as a heedless fool after I allowed Norah to come stumbling over here alone. But give a man credit for attempting to right his past mistakes. For owning up to them. Surely you can understand my need to make things right."

Aidan wanted to fling a bitter rejoinder back at him and stalk away. He wanted to shove the idiot bastard out Rathcannon's doors and bar them behind him. But Richard Farnsworth's words burrowed past anger and wariness, past exhaustion, frustration, and stark foreboding, touching a raw chord in Aidan's own chest.

Surely you can understand my need to make things right.

God, could any man understand that need to right past wrongs better than Aidan himself? The need to strip away a thousand regrets and feel clean again, whole again?

His gaze flicked from Richard Farnsworth's earnest features to Norah's face, the depths of her dark eyes revealing all too clearly the bruises his harsh words to her brother had caused her, the hurt, the uncertainty, the torn loyalties rending this woman Aidan would have done anything to protect from pain.

"Papa?"

The sound of Cassandra's voice in the corridor made Aidan start, the words punctuated with the staccato rhythm of her slippers tripping toward him.

"Mrs. Brindle said you'd gotten back."

He turned to see his daughter rushing through the door, fully intending, Aidan was certain, to fling herself into his arms. But at the sight of the handsome stranger, the girl slammed to a halt, one hand sweeping to smooth her skirts,

363

the other to pat a curl back from her cheek as she hastened to cloak herself in adolescent dignity.

Her eyes brightened, her cheeks stained delicate rose as if the horrors of the night before had already been swept from her mind, relegated to the status of childhood nightmares about dragons lurking under her bed.

To Aidan it seemed as if his daughter had aged five years in that single heartbeat. She was beautiful—beautiful and breathless with anticipation and yet more poised than he'd ever seen her.

"Father, why didn't you tell me we were expecting company?" she asked, favoring Richard Farnsworth with her loveliest smile. "We haven't been introduced. I'm Cassandra Kane."

Farnsworth looked as if the girl had neatly divested him of the power of speech. Aidan had always known that Cassandra was beautiful, and he should have been prepared for the effect a first glimpse of her would have on a stranger. Yet Farnsworth's gaze clung to the sweet curves of the girl a trifle too long, and Aidan suspected that as a young soldier he himself had worn the same glazed expression the first time he'd set eyes on Delia March. In a heartbeat, Farnsworth seemed to shake himself, a coolness wisping over his eyes as he adopted a more appropriate expression.

"So you are my new niece." He reached out to clasp one of Cassandra's dimpled hands in both his own. "I am . . . enchanted."

"We've had about all the 'enchantment' we can survive here of late," Aidan snapped, irritation coiling through every fiber of his tall frame. "I doubt I could survive another bout. Cassandra, this is Norah's stepbrother," he said, as if those words alone would be enough to drive the glittering interest from his daughter's eyes. If anything, her interest seemed even more marked.

"Well, I can hardly go about calling him 'Norah's brother,' can I?" Cassandra said with a breathless laugh.

"Call me 'Richard.' I would be honored, unless you think

such familiarity too bold." The embodiment of impeccable manners, Farnsworth hazarded a glance at Aidan. "I just thought that since we are family, after a fashion . . ."

Cassandra beamed. "Considering that, it would be absurd to stand on ceremony, wouldn't it, Papa?"

Aidan started to grumble something about ceremony and propriety being in place for a reason, but Cassandra was breezing on.

"I think 'Richard' is a lovely name. I shall be delighted to use it, but only if you will call me 'Cassandra.'"

"'Cassandra,' then. Did you know that you were named for a princess of Troy? They say that Helen's face launched a thousand ships, but I vow, if my charming new niece had been ensconced within the city's walls, every ship on those ancient seas would have come to pay homage not to Paris' stolen beauty, but to you."

The girl fairly shivered with delight. "What a pretty thing to say!"

Aidan grimaced. He'd wager his fortune the glib-tongued fool fairly spat rose petals every time he opened his mouth. The risk was always being cut by hidden thorns. "Cass, if you're to enter society next year, the first rule is that only a simpleton puts any store by such nonsense. It is a game. One you mustn't take too seriously."

Farnsworth's teeth flashed beneath his smile. "I would think a gambler the likes of you would know that life itself is one huge game, and the man who wins is the one willing to take the biggest risks. With the cards, or the dice, or . . . with the ladies."

"Richard, you mustn't tease so," Norah intervened, her gaze flicking to the muscle ticking in Aidan's jaw. "I'm afraid after all that has happened, we're decidedly lacking in a sense of humor."

"Forgive me." Richard spread his hands out in apology. "It's just . . . a treasure such as Cassandra must be guarded at all costs. I would deem it an honor to be allowed to serve her."

365

He sketched the girl an elegant bow. Aidan saw his daughter's cheeks dimple, her chin tip up in that age-old discovery of feminine power.

He gritted his teeth, trying his damnedest not to heave the bloody fop out the door by his breeches. Norah must have noted his thunderous glare, for she grasped his sleeve. "Aidan, please," she breathed low, for his ears alone. "It will be lovely to have Richard about. He can distract Cassandra, watch over her, leaving you free to make your search for whoever tried to harm her."

"The man is an incorrigible flirt."

"He's harmless. He will guard her every bit as carefully as he has guarded me."

Aidan looked down into that soft ivory face, remembering it the first night she'd stayed at Rathcannon, her eyes wide and frightened, her hands knotted in her nightgown as he stormed about the bedchamber, bent on terrifying her so badly she'd flee the castle with the first whisperings of dawn. She'd been so damned brave, so much at his mercy.

He will guard her every bit as carefully as he has guarded me. Norah's words echoed in Aidan's mind.

That was what he was afraid of.

No, blast it, Norah was right: He needed all the help he could get at the moment. Every pair of eyes to keep guard, every set of hands to defend. He needed the aid of every mind sharp enough to help him discover a foe so cunning it terrified him, so elusive it seemed as if the phantom figure were no more solid than a moonbeam slipping between his fingers to disappear.

Much as Aidan disliked the elegant fop who was Norah's brother, the truth was that Norah had affection for him and, what's more, believed in him with the same blind trust she had offered to Aidan himself.

Aidan had spent the years since his marriage to Delia dragging on mantles of doubt and distrust and cynicism until they were as common to don in the morning as a fresh cravat. He'd become so jaded, he could look into the

Madonna's own eyes and see there one of Satan's angels. Distrust. The wariness of a hunted animal. It had lived inside him so long, he'd nearly missed the treasure that was Norah. Wasn't it time to believe in someone? Wasn't it time to believe in *her?*

"Kane?" Farnsworth paced toward him, his gaze starkly earnest. "When your daughter is with me, I vow she'll be as safe as if she were clasped to her mother's own breast."

Claws buried deep in Aidan's gut unsheathed, dug deep into his most secret fears. Farnsworth couldn't know . . . couldn't possibly guess that such a comparison would fire Aidan's unease and rake across his nerves like the blade of an assassin's knife.

Aidan brought himself up sharply. No, the only way to assure Cassandra's safety was to begin his hunt, not stand here, bandying words with some idiot English fool.

"I have business to attend to now," Aidan said roughly.

"Of course," Farnsworth said, straightening his cravat. "You must carry on with your search. But before you leave, let me reassure you of this: You may hold me personally responsible for anything that happens to your daughter from this moment on."

Aidan barely suppressed the sarcastic twisting of his lips. The day he was rash enough to entrust Cassandra to a bumbling idiot like Richard Farnsworth was the day the earth would crumble into the sea. The bastard was there as entertainment, a mindless distraction for both Norah and Cassandra. That was all.

"I'll not lay a burden of responsibility quite that heavy upon you, Farnsworth."

Those strange eyes clung to Aidan's for a heartbeat, something unguarded in them for just a breath of time. Then it vanished as quickly as it had appeared, leaving nothing behind but bored arrogance, affable foolery. "I promise you, Sir Aidan: By the time I leave Rathcannon, you will know exactly how far you can trust me."

Oddly unsettled, Aidan turned and walked out of the

room, away from Norah's pleading gaze and Cassandra's excited one. Away from the memories Farnsworth's words had spawned, the rattle of coach wheels, the lash of thunder, the sound of Cassandra screaming from her mother's arms.

Laughter rippled through the open window as sunshine streamed down to set the stable yard a-glitter. Norah leaned out the open window to peer out at a scene as pastoral as a Gainsborough painting: serene skies, banks of flowers, and a golden-tressed little beauty in rose-hued skirts, delighting in an exquisite cream pony. And delighting in the day and in her guardian knight who lay against a backdrop of lush green grass, weaving her a crown of meadow flowers.

From the moment of his arrival, Richard Farnsworth had scarcely left Cassandra's side, watching over her with a fierce protectiveness that had touched Norah deeply. Tending her with a seriousness of purpose that had made Norah hope, believe that her scapegrace stepbrother might at last be finding his way, shedding the futile posturings and useless affectations of the ton for something better and more wholesome.

Richard had been so solicitous and tender when he'd come to her alone, saying that he wanted to help, to make certain Norah could support her new husband and care for him during this trial. That unselfish emotion was the reason he'd been so attentive to Aidan Kane's daughter. It was the least he could do, Richard had insisted, after being such an incompetent bumbler when Norah had needed him before.

Norah would have liked nothing more than to be able to ease her husband's burdens, to help him defeat this ghostly foe who darted from the shadows, then melted away to haunt only the reaches of Aidan's imagination.

But there was no room for her in Aidan's private hell. There was no room for her in his arms, in his bed. It was as if the mere sight of her or of Cassandra somehow poured subtle acid over wounds she couldn't see, as if reproach clung like some sickly-sweet perfume to their hair.

He might have been some hero of old, locked in battle with the dragon sent to destroy them, and until that dragon was defeated he felt unworthy to touch so much as the hems of their gowns.

Not so much as a whisper had come from Aidan's foe in the week since Richard's arrival. It was as if Aidan's enemy knew instinctively the agonies Aidan was suffering, as if this faceless adversary was enjoying that pain before closing in for the kill. Norah could almost feel vengeful eyes watching them and feel the cold fingertips reaching out to gouge into the most vulnerable places in Aidan's battered soul.

It was hideous, nerve shattering, this ominous quiet like the eerie calm before a tempest broke. It was as if Aidan were drowning and she couldn't reach his hand.

Norah shivered, remembering Aidan's bitter voice: The only way a Kane could ever get into heaven is to steal the keys. At the moment she would have gladly stolen them from St. Peter's own hand if by doing so she could spare her beloved pain.

But there was no escape from the darkness stalking Rathcannon. There was no haven to retreat to. Only uncertainty—the writhing, sinuous abyss that hurled back images of her own most secret fears.

"Richard! Is that for me?" Cassandra's delighted cry drifted through the window on the blossom-scented air, shaking Norah from her troubled thoughts. She looked up to see her stepbrother unfold his lanky frame, only the slightest hint of his limp still evident, as he made his way to Cassandra's side and perched the crown on her head.

Norah wondered how often Aidan had twined blossoms or ribbons in his daughter's hair, and her heart twisted, ached for the man locked away in his study, mounting a campaign to rival any general's.

She had been alone for most of her life, yet she had never understood the depths loneliness could reach until now.

"My lady?"

Rose poked her head into the drawing room. Ever since

369

the night Aidan had ridden out to meet Gilpatrick, the girl had been more devoted than ever, her loyalty fanned because Aidan had forgiven her for her transgressions. Not only forgiven her, but thanked her for her honesty in sending him to the Hill of Night Voices.

"I was wonderin' if I could—could speak frank with you about—" The girl stopped, worry creasing her brow. "You look worn to a shade. Both you and the master." Rose twisted her apron about chapped fingers.

"I'm fine. Thank you for . . . for your concern. What was it you needed to ask me about?"

"It's nothing," the girl answered too quickly, lowering her eyes.

"You came here to ask me something, Rose," Norah said, too weary to make more of an attempt to draw it out of the girl.

The girl's cheeks flushed. "It's just that Mrs. Cadagon says she's goin' to march you an' Sir Aidan into dinner at gunpoint tonight if she has to. I think I'll help her. You both need somethin' to eat, an' some sleep, if you'll pardon me saying so. Those men who wanted to kidnap Miss Cassandra won't have t' trouble themselves if y' keep this up. The both of you'll be nothing but starved skeletons, an' the villain'll be able t' walk in the front door an' blow you out of his way with a puff o' wind."

Norah tried to curve her lips into a smile. Failed. "Tell Mrs. Cadagon she's right. I'll see to it that Sir Aidan is at the table myself."

Rose cast her a respectful smile. "You're a real fine one, my lady. Gibbon and the Cadagons, Calvy an' me, we all of us think so."

Acceptance. Affection. Norah's throat constricted at such precious gifts.

"Ye're the best thing 'at ever happened t' Sir Aidan and t' Miss Cassandra. 'Tis a pure miracle you wound up on their doorstep."

A miracle, Norah echoed. She thought of the bright,

blue-eyed girl amusing herself with her pony, the dark-haired, haggard man tearing himself to shreds over the danger that was threatening his daughter. And the danger to Norah herself, she thought, with a searing memory of the pain-ravaged, desperate expression that haunted his eyes whenever they met hers.

A miracle. It truly was a miracle that had drifted her down into the arms of a man she loved, gave her a home, a daughter, a future filled with hope that someday she might win Aidan Kane's wary heart.

Norah's gaze strayed out to where Cassandra stood in the sunshine, Richard bending close. His fingertips were brushing her cheek, as if he were trying to capture a stray lash caught in one of Cassandra's expressive blue eyes.

Norah's heart squeezed. Was it possible that God would grant yet another miracle to those who lived at Rathcannon? She prayed with all her might that the angels Aidan scorned would help him find the monsters who were stalking his daughter, help him destroy them before Aidan destroyed himself.

CHAPTER

23

The dining room was redolent with the mouth-watering scents of the most delicious food that Cook could conjure up, a veritable repast spread before Aidan on glistening china. All of his favorites had been laid out to tempt him, as if he were a much-indulged boy just recovered from a nursery bout of fever.

It touched him, the solicitousness of the servants clustered around: footmen whose eyes glinted with respect and affection, Mrs. Cadagon bustling about like a mother hen whose hatchling had just been hauled back from disaster. The staff of Rathcannon had rallied about him with a loyalty that astonished Aidan. It was if they all had faith in his power to avert the calamity that had careened down on the castle the night of the marriage ball.

Most sobering of all was confronting Norah's face across the table. Seeing her, really seeing her, perhaps for the first time since he'd gone to her bedchamber a week before and poured out the most guarded secrets of his heart, the most scathing vulnerabilities he had kept locked inside him for so long.

Misery etched deep into the fragile curves of her face, tension tugging at that soft mouth he ached to kiss even now. And her eyes were filled with such empathy for his anguish and faith in his strength, those emotions overlaid by a love painful in its intensity, terrifying in its power.

In the end, it had been her anxiety that had made Aidan agree to join her and Cassandra and that brainless brother of Norah's for the first decent meal he'd eaten in a week.

Yes, it had been to ease Norah's worry that he paused in his mad search. That, and something else.

The first glimmers of hope in this morass of confusion. The first shining sliver of a clue that might lead to Aidan's enemy.

He hazarded a glance across the table's massive surface, to where Cassandra was giggling over some jest Richard Farnsworth had just drawled. Aidan knew he should be pleased that the English fop had served some kind of purpose, that he had managed to distract Cassandra from the danger that swirled in a red mist all around them.

Yet an odd sense of irritation stirred inside him as well, an impatience. God, couldn't Cass see through the slippery fop? Maybe Norah was right. He had overprotected the girl. She was innocent and trusting as a spring lamb. And the hard truth was that Farnsworth was a slick-tongued fool, unscrupulous about flirting with a child; but Cassandra was likely to encounter other men far more dangerous in a London ballroom. If Cassandra couldn't see through Farnsworth's feeble guises, how could he hope she'd be able to discern true evil when she faced it? Greedy fortune hunters, bastards who made a game out of fresh young beauties like Cassandra?

He shuddered inwardly, his mind straying to the three wagers Gilpatrick had spoken of, the tension tightening inside him.

"Aidan?" Norah's voice made him look toward her, and his breath snagged at the beauty in her uncertain smile. "I just thought I would remind you that the object to your left is a fork. You use it to scoop up the food and put it in your mouth."

Aidan grimaced. He'd felt off balance all day, a little woozy from lack of food and lack of sleep. He'd come into the dining room determined to eat so that he could stay on his horse's back when he set out later that evening to corner his quarry.

He grabbed up the utensil and took a bite of roast beef. Norah rewarded him with a smile.

"So, Sir Aidan, any new developments on your quest today?" Farnsworth queried, popping a sugarplum into his mouth. "You know, any secret codes unraveled, villain lairs discovered?"

"As a matter of fact, I may have unearthed something at last."

"Oh, Aidan!" Relief flooded Norah's features.

Aidan held up one hand in warning. "Don't get too excited. I'm not certain it will amount to anything. I can't even begin to tell you how many snippets of information I've traced to their source, only to come back empty-handed."

"But you don't think that will happen this time," Norah insisted. "I can see it in your face."

"Time will tell."

"How much time, Father?" Cassandra asked.

"I'm not certain. Tonight, if all goes well."

"So you should have the villain cornered tonight?" Farnsworth shifted in his chair, then rose to stretch his legs for a moment. "Excellent, Kane. God knows it's taken long enough."

There was something beneath the layer of bored arrogance that set Aidan's teeth on edge, a barely concealed mockery, a twisted sting of pleasure caused no doubt by

374

Aidan's own pointed criticisms about how Farnsworth had cared for Norah.

Aidan glared at the young man.

Farnsworth flashed him a guileless smile. "Pardon my ill manners," he said, patting his left breech leg. "Got a stiff leg that picks the most inopportune times to kick up a fuss. Blasted thing's been aching like the very devil today. Must mean it's going to rain."

"What happened to your leg?" Cassandra asked with big-eyed worship. "I mean, I've been wondering what happened but thought it was rude to ask. Were you injured in the war? My pa—father was a hero on the Peninsula."

"No fate quite so glorious for me, I'm afraid. I was racing about on a slick road with a green-broke team of horses and an ill-sprung carriage when it overturned. Lay on a cliffside for three full days before some fisherman found me. Knew I was heading for the devil of a spill before the thing crashed, but I had my whole fortune riding on it, don't you know. Ah, Kane, it's blasted embarrassing, isn't it? The scrapes a man can get into when he's young and foolish?"

"You must have been terribly hurt," Cassandra commiserated, nibbling on a sugary roll. "How awful for you!"

"I'm certain Richard would be delighted to tell you about his brush with death later," Norah interrupted. "I want to hear what your father has discovered."

"I've sent riders to every inn, every cottage, every hostelry within a day's ride of the castle, asking if anyone has seen something odd or suspicious. An hour ago Sean O'Day came back with the news that the innkeeper at a most disreputable place had a rather distinguished guest the night of the ball."

"Is that so? I don't mean to burst your hopes, Kane, but have you considered that the poor guest might have had his carriage break down? His horse come up lame? Or he could just have an odd taste for more rustic accommodations—a delight in bedbugs and the like."

Cassandra giggled, and Farnsworth flashed her a wink

that set Aidan's teeth on edge. As if suddenly aware of Aidan's glowering, Farnsworth flushed.

"Forgive me, old man. I don't mean to make light of your discovery." He adopted a mien of rapt attention. "Where, pray tell, is this nefarious innkeeper who entertained a mysterious guest?"

"The past three days the innkeeper has been gone. From all accounts, he's been visiting his daughter who just presented him with a grandson. I've tried my damnedest to track the blasted girl down, but to no avail. Still, the man is to return to his establishment late tonight. I intend to be there when he does."

"Wondrous exciting news. And what exactly is this place called? This den of iniquity you've discovered?"

"The Thorned Paw Inn."

Farnsworth's lips tightened over his teeth. "This guest must've been more than a little insane, as even the name of the establishment reeks of discomfort. Perhaps—just perhaps—you have stumbled onto something after all." Farnsworth's brow darkened. "But have a care, Kane. There is an ill wind blowing tonight. You may well be dicing with a devil more dangerous than you know."

Storm winds wound skeins of black clouds through the tangled branches of trees, the limbs beating out the rhythm of a macabre dance. The moonless sky was bruised a purplish blue, while chills scuttled down the castle corridors to huddle in shadowy corners and creep on tiny legs up Norah's spine.

Foreboding crackled in the air, sizzling into her skin with each flash of lightning. Each distant rumble of thunder echoed a warning.

Strange. She could only remember experiencing this breath-stealing, nerve-wracking sensation once before. A feeling as if the veil between the present and the future had thinned, hazy images of disaster dancing inside her mind.

She had lost her father that night. It had devastated her,

changed her in one ruthless sweep into a sad little ghost, certain that if she had done something, said something, pleaded with her papa not to go out that night, he would have lived.

Yet the loss she felt lurking in the shadows tonight was even more terrifying than that childhood terror. The menace that circled Rathcannon on predator's feet was far more cunning than the fever that had killed her father.

There is an ill wind blowing tonight, Richard had cautioned.

And she knew, with a cold certainty, that he was right.

She could sense it, a palpable presence in the air. And from the moment she had gazed across the dining table into Aidan's eyes, she knew he sensed it too.

Some slight discord sounded in the whispered melody of the castle walls, like invisible fingers plucking at sleeves, trying to give warning.

Norah went to the doorway joining Aidan's chamber with her own, the panel half open, the sounds of Aidan beyond it beckoning her. As she shoved the door open wider, her eyes took in broad shoulders flexing as he jammed the tails of his shirt into the waistband of a pair of doeskin riding breeches.

A burgundy-hued jacket lay on the bed, while a brace of pistols gleamed beside it, blue-black glimmers of light skating evilly up the barrels.

"Aidan?" She breathed his name, and he turned toward her. The starkly handsome planes of his face were burnished with determination, and with an aching sense of loss, as if somehow he knew, sensed . . . what? That the fates would demand some sacrifice tonight? There could be no question that he was willing to offer himself up, in his daughter's place, in Norah's place.

He smiled, the curve of his mouth shaded with a wistful longing for tomorrows that might never be. "I'm almost ready to leave, ladylight."

"Aidan, don't go." The words slipped out, absurd, futile. "Not tonight."

"You know I have to." He crossed to where she stood, one rein-calloused palm sweeping up to cup her cheek with inexpressible tenderness. "There's no need to worry. This time I'm taking every able-bodied man at Rathcannon with me. I intend to lay a net of them about the place, just to make certain no one can slip away once I arrive there. It's just a precaution—and God knows I'm probably being overly vigilant. The guest I've heard tell of might be long gone—might never have existed at all. The innkeeper might remember nothing. Hell, this might just be another path leading nowhere."

"It's not. You feel it, just as strongly as I do. This strange sense of—of something about to happen . . . I can see it in your eyes."

"Maybe something good will come of tonight, Norah. Maybe I'll finally be able to make an end to all this."

"And maybe this is the beginning of something . . ." Her voice trailed off, but the mocking voice whispered on, relentless, inside her head.

Maybe this was the beginning of something hideous, something dark, something careening toward them with the same devastating force as the runaway coach that had sent Delia Kane to her death.

Aidan's voice dropped low, gravelly with emotion. "Whatever happens, Norah Kane, I . . ." Words seemed to hang in the air between them, unspoken, ineffably sweet. Norah's heart slammed against her ribs, her whole being starved to hear what he was trying to say.

But after a heartbeat, he caught up her hand, pressed it to his lips in a fierce kiss. And Norah couldn't shake the intuition that this was the last chance she'd ever have to hear the words Aidan Kane couldn't squeeze past the knot that betrayal, cynicism, pain, and anger had left in his throat years ago. Her heart ached at the knowledge that her chance might just have slipped through her fingers forever.

"Norah, whatever happens tonight, I thank God you came to Rathcannon. I thank God you came into my life."

"You know I—I'll take care of Cassandra."

"This isn't about Cassandra," he cut in, a ragged edge to his voice. "It's about me, Norah. I thank God for you."

He framed her face in his hands, turned it up to his own hungry, anguished gaze. "Ladylight, if . . . when I come back, can we begin again? When all this is settled, will you let me—be a husband to you, believe in . . . in miracles?"

Tears spilled from her eyes. "Aidan, you are my miracle. I love you."

He kissed her, long and tender, hungry and hurting, until his lips seemed to melt into hers, his passions and pain melding with her very soul.

Then he broke away, turning to take up the pistols lying on the bed. Jaw tight, eyes like steel, he jammed the weapons into the waistband of his breeches.

Norah grabbed his coat and helped him put it on, cherishing the task of smoothing it over those strong shoulders. And she battled the urge to fling herself against the burgundy fabric, dampen it with tears that would only make it harder for him to leave.

Instead, she took his hand, determined to touch him for as long as she could, drive back the chill kiss of her own fears with the warmth in his grasp.

She wanted to cling to these final moments alone, wanted time to drive back the foreboding, label it a ridiculous bit of superstition worthy of the gypsy women at the fair.

But how could she dismiss the unease pulsing through her veins? She could find no comfort when her thoughts only reminded her of Aidan, standing with his hand clamped in the crabbed one of the old crone, mysticism wreathing her ageless face as she predicted doom, suffering, a battle waged for his very soul.

Tonight, a voice whispered inside Norah's breast. Tonight the battle would be won or lost. She was certain of it, in a secret, guarded place within her soul.

As they descended the stairs, Norah was dismayed to see an elegant figure lounging in a gilt chair in the entryway, obviously waiting for Aidan to descend. Richard Farnsworth's usually lazy eyes were glinting with a latent excitement, his mouth curved in a grin brushed with eagerness and anticipation.

"All ready to go out and tilt with dragons?" he inquired, rising stiffly to his feet.

"I suppose you could say that."

"I just wanted to speak with you before you left. Set things straight between us, don't you know."

"Farnsworth, at the moment, I don't give a damn about anything but finding whoever is stalking my daughter and my wife," Aidan snapped, signaling a footman for his cloak.

"Ah, so I am beneath the exalted notice of a hero, is that it? Of no consequence."

"Richard, please!" Norah burst out, anger sparking through her at his sudden resurgence of selfishness. "Aidan is half crazed with worry, setting out to track down this . . . this villain."

"I see. Well then, sister mine, I'll not bother to keep your bold husband from his quest a moment longer, except to tell him this: I intend to prove myself to you, brother-in-law, prove myself a worthy . . . player as you cast the dice tonight."

"It's not a goddamn game, Farnsworth."

"Indeed? Life is a game. One grand wager we make with the devil. I wonder who will win this time."

With an oath, Aidan snatched his cloak from the footman and swirled it about his shoulders. Then, without another word, he stormed out into the night.

Norah stared after him, hurting, furious. She wheeled on her stepbrother. "Why, Richard? Why bait him when you know he's nearly crazed with worry? When he's going out to face whoever this—this demon is who is tormenting him?"

"Why torment the heroic Sir Aidan Kane?" Farnsworth demanded, something disturbing sparking in his eyes. "Because he dares to act like a noble fool, when in reality he's as vile a libertine as ever breathed. But he fooled you, didn't he, my mousy, spinsterish little sister? No doubt on the night he breached your maidenhead."

She gaped at her stepbrother. Her cheeks flamed hotly, fury and confusion twisting in the pit of her stomach. "I thought this marriage is what you wanted for me."

"It was, but I never expected that you would—" He stopped, his face twisting, a curse low in his throat.

"Richard, what is the matter with you?"

"Nothing is the matter. I was in sad need of diversion when I left London. And your esteemed, rather beleaguered husband has provided me with enough to last me for a good long time. However, I find I'm becoming quite bored with rusticating in the wilds of Ireland. Perhaps it is time I departed."

Relief spilled through Norah, and she felt a vague sting of shame at the fact that she was glad her brother was leaving—leaving Rathcannon, leaving behind the all too impressionable Cassandra, who had fallen prey to his charms. And hopefully taking with him the odd sense of strain that had sprung up between him and Norah. "Richard—"

"Don't play the grieving sister, please," he said, his voice hard-edged, almost wounded. "I know you will be glad to see the last of me. Besides, Kane's daughter has been growing rather fond of me, hasn't she? Perhaps a little too fond for your liking?"

"Richard, she's a child."

"Some man will soon be making a woman of her, I can guarantee it. She's no pale fruit to go overripe on the spinster's vine. And by the time you bolster her considerable promise of beauty with her doting papa's fortune . . . I'm quite sure she will have a raft of men slavering over her hand."

"Richard, stop it!" This bitter nastiness was all too reminiscent of Winston Farnsworth's scathing cruelty. It appalled Norah. Sickened her. The shimmer of anger in him

381

left her confused and unnerved. She lifted her chin with a sense of pride Aidan had given her. "I think it's time that you did leave."

Farnsworth's mouth ticked up, his eyes glinting, dark. "Time? Yes. I think it is time indeed. After all, I've accomplished what I came here for."

"And what was that?"

"Why, to see you happy, sister dear. To share in your joy. However, there is one last obligation I must keep. I had promised Cassandra quite faithfully that I would take her out and show her the constellations tonight. She's developed quite a fascination for them. Or perhaps it's walking in the moonlight with a gentleman that intrigues her. After all, she is her papa's daughter."

"There is absolutely no way I will allow you to take Cassandra walking after all you have said."

She expected argument, that stubbornness that so often sparked in her stepbrother's eyes whenever he was foiled in his desires. She was stunned when he merely sketched her a mocking bow.

"Of course, your wishes must be obeyed, mustn't they, little sister? You're not a cast-off waif anymore. You are mistress of Rathcannon." He laughed. A laugh that made her bones chill, her nerves twitch.

With that, he strode up the stairway, leaving Norah shaken at the strange glimmer that hardened his smile.

"Richard! Richard, stop!" How many times had she seen him lash out thus, when he was thwarted or angry? Striking whoever had crossed him at their most vulnerable point? He was just upset about Aidan's dismissing him, just out of sorts because of what he saw as Norah's defection in loyalty to her husband. It was absurd, this withering unease that shot through her.

This was Richard—Richard her smiling stepbrother, who had given her Aidan's letter, bought her the beautiful trousseau so she could "bewitch" her husband. Richard who had defied his father's wrath to aid her, and who had been so kind to Cassandra that the girl was all but dazzled.

He was spoiled, self-centered, maybe a trifle heedless. But he was her stepbrother. Her stepbrother. Not something dangerous lurking in the night.

She went to her bedchamber to wash her face and calm her nerves. As soon as she collected herself, she would go to him, try to find out what had made him lash out that way and say things that were so cruel. Surely there must be some reason. She must be able to make some sort of peace.

Yet the oddest feeling stole through her, cloying as hot summer rain.

She would not feel safe until Richard was gone.

Silence blanketed the castle hallways, dampening the corridor that led to the chambers Farnsworth had been given the night he'd first arrived—so unexpectedly, so filled with worry and self-blame. Norah made her way toward his bedchamber, a dozen half-formed apologies on her lips, warring with the odd feeling of suspicion and distrust that crept beneath her skirts, chilling her skin.

She brought herself up sharply. No matter what Richard had said, he was the only real family she had left. Her mother—the mother she'd known and loved as a tiny child—had been obliterated by Winston Farnsworth years before. Corabeth Linton Farnsworth, in those early days of her second marriage, had been forced to sacrifice her daughter to the cold scorn of the man who had offered her security and wealth. Norah's stepfather had chosen to loathe her as the living evidence that his woman had spent nights in another man's bed. Only Richard had offered her the smallest sense of worth, of importance. Only Richard had acted as if the dark-eyed, sad little girl existed.

Despite her anger, her unease, this strange humor of foreboding she was experiencing, she couldn't let her stepbrother go off to England carrying memories of her anger with him.

She needed to try to understand what had driven him to be so cutting to Aidan in the moments before her husband had ridden out to face his phantom foe. She needed to know why he had lashed out at her with such savagery.

At the doorway, she paused and knocked.

Silence.

A sick sensation roiled up in the pit of her stomach. It was barely an hour since he'd left her in the entryway. Surely he couldn't have . . . what? Swept together his belongings and left before she could say goodbye?

She pushed open the door, half expecting him to be in the chamber, sulking. But as she entered the room, she saw none of the mad clutter that had always heralded Richard's presence. The few clothes he'd packed for this impromptu journey were nowhere to be seen; even his elegant portmanteau was gone.

All that was left was a slim leather volume lying on the bed, a creamy square of vellum marking a page somewhere in the middle.

Kane was scrawled across the top of the missive in Richard's careless hand.

Norah crossed to the bed, a sick churning in her stomach, her hands trembling, tears welling in her eyes at the certainty that she was too late. Relief warred with regret. Her stepbrother was already gone. Yet why had he written to Aidan? Why not spew out an angry letter to her?

Perplexed, she picked up the missive and hesitated for a moment. No, the letter was not for her. But the book . . . She reached out one hand, opening the volume to the marked page, her gaze tracing down the scribed lines.

Three Wagers to assure the Destruction of Aidan Kane . . .

Bile rose in Norah's throat, and she clung to the book with nerveless fingers.

No. It was impossible. Unthinkable. Why would Richard do such a thing? Richard, her feckless stepbrother with his careless kindnesses, his thoughtless wagers on everything from how long it took his friend to tie his cravat to how many warts would spring up on Lord Constable's nose. The stepbrother she knew couldn't possibly be involved in this vile set of wagers. Unless she didn't really know Richard at all.

She trembled, remembering the odd glint in Richard's eye . . . almost as if she'd betrayed him.

Her soul died a little as she skimmed the hellish lines, the truth searing into her with the force of a pistol ball. She had been the tool her brother had used. To get into Aidan's house. To gain access to Aidan's innocent daughter.

She alone was the weapon that had given Richard the power to destroy the man she loved.

But why? her heart screamed. Why did Richard hate Aidan? What bond could there be between the scapegrace brother she had known not at all and the man who had become her whole life?

She grabbed the letter, ripping it open, the sense of foreboding that had haunted her seeming to crush the breath from her lungs as she read:

> *Kane,*
> *By the time you read this, your daughter will be at my mercy—my wife, initiated into the joys of the bridal bed. Of course, you will try to find us, Kane, with some misguided notion of saving her from my clutches. I am cherishing that knowledge. For when you do ride in to face me, I will kill you, before your daughter's eyes.*
> *And as you're on your way to hell, you will know that I will spend the rest of my life making her pay for your sins.*
> *You will be helpless, Kane.*
> *How does it feel to be helpless?*

Norah pressed her hand against her mouth, her stomach threatening to betray her, horror a living thing inside her. Sweet Jesus, was Richard really capable of such a terrible act? Brutalizing an innocent child . . . for what? Some crazed wager? No. There were undercurrents in this letter far more grim, some hidden poison she didn't understand.

She caught her lip between her teeth. An hour had passed since she'd faced Richard in the entryway: Was it possible he had already lured the girl away?

She raced through the castle, calling Cassandra's name, desperate, so desperate, all but slamming into little Noddie, the servant's arms filled with fresh sheets.

"Noddie, have you seen Miss Cassandra?"

"She stepped out with Mr. Farnsworth."

Norah's head swam. "When? Where were they going?"

"I don't know. It was when I was tidying up the study. Maybe an hour ago."

An hour ago . . .

Sweet heaven, they could be anywhere! By now Cassandra must know something was amiss. By now the bright-faced, beautiful girl must be reliving the terror that had scarred her childhood, being torn away from the father she adored.

And Richard had ridden off leaving this note behind. Even if he had guessed Norah might find it, he was doubtless smug and certain his stepsister would be too weak to follow.

"No!" Norah breathed aloud, her heart torn asunder by visions of Aidan riding in the other direction while his daughter was being taken from him. Aidan returning too late to aid Cassandra, discovering this cruel note about his child's peril. Aidan losing his daughter to such a hellish fate forever.

God, he would never forgive himself: Norah knew this with sick certainty. He would never forgive her.

She had to try to find them, had to stop Richard from doing this terrible thing. But how? Where would she even begin to search?

Sick futility drowned her, but she shoved past the big-eyed servant and ran to Aidan's room. She dug through his clothespress, dragging on a pair of breeches, a flowing white shirt scented of sandalwood and sea spray, that wild, primal mixture that was Aidan's own. It was exquisite torture to draw it on, feel it enfold her. Then she raced into his study, where a brace of dueling pistols gleamed in a polished case. They felt huge in her hand, unwieldy.

"My lady?"

Rose's query made Norah jump, wheel, the girl's astonished gaze snagging Norah's. "My lady, what's amiss?"

"My stepbrother has taken Cassandra."

The Irish girl's face went pale, her eyes bobbing out. "What!"

"He's stolen her away, taken her—to elope with her, I think. I don't know. It's insane."

The girl looked sick, stricken. But Norah's veins iced as she realized Rose did not look surprised.

"I should have told you . . ." Tears brimmed in the girl's eyes, her face ashen. "But you were so worried about the master and all. And besides, even if I did tell, I wasn't sure you'd believe me. Feared you'd turn me out of Rathcannon, a servant sayin' such things about your brother, and—and now if anything happens to Miss Cassandra I'll never forgive myself."

"What are you babbling about?"

"He was tryin' to get beneath my skirts the first night he came here, Mr. Farnsworth was."

Norah remembered with sickening clarity the conversation she'd had with the girl earlier, the indecision in her eyes, the nervousness.

"Please, my lady, you must believe me. I never would've thought the beast would hurt Miss Cassandra! What are we going to do? Everybody except Calvy is with Sir Aidan. The rest of the men are out chasin' the horses. I was just comin' to tell you Gibbon sent word someone let 'em out from the stable yard an hour or so past. The whole lot of Sir Aidan's prize horses racing to the wind. Sweet Mary, you don't think—think yer brother did that a-purpose?"

Norah said nothing, feeling only the web of Richard's deception tightening about her in exquisite strands of betrayal and lies, a torment that would soon snare Aidan as well.

"I can go after the menfolk," Rose offered. "Try to find them."

"By then it might be too late. I'm going after Cassandra myself."

"No, my lady, you cannot! If Mr. Farnsworth is evil enough to take Miss Cass, there's no telling what he might do to you."

"I'm the one who gave Richard entry into this house. I'm the one responsible."

For what? The ultimate betrayal of Aidan Kane? The shattering of the battered yet noble knight she had discovered beneath years of anger and hurt, pain and betrayal?

A sob lodged in Norah's breast. "I don't know where to start looking for them. I don't know where—where he could have taken her. Rose, please. If you can think of somewhere, anywhere . . ."

The girl chewed at her bottom lip. "He was bent on takin' me to Noonan's abandoned cottage. Tried to lure me there. If he wanted to . . . to hide Miss Cassandra, maybe . . ."

It was the frailest hope, but it was all Norah had. "Where is it?"

"'Bout ten miles from here, to the west. Ride to the site of the gypsy fair, then head down the valley. There's an overgrown road that turns left. The cottage is at the end. But even if you want t' chase 'em, you can't. There be no horses."

"There has to be one left. Oh, God, please let there be one left!" Norah raced toward the door, then paused, turned. "Find someone to go after Sir Aidan, Rose. Give him this book." She thrust the leather volume and letter into the girl's hand. "Tell him to start searching . . . searching every road."

With that, Norah turned and ran out into the darkness. The darkness that had mocked her from the first moment it had stained the horizon this night.

A darkness that now had a name.

A menace that now had a face.

That of the stepbrother she had never known.

Richard. A man who had worn the most cunning mask of all.

A beast who had honed her into the perfect weapon to cut out Sir Aidan Kane's battered heart.

CHAPTER

24

A dozen horsemen thundered through the night, Rathcannon's strongest, bravest retainers streaming behind Aidan, all grim-faced, all ready to confront the villain who had dared endanger their little mistress.

Yet despite their presence, Aidan felt alone, imprisoned by his own fury, his own most hidden fears.

Darkness.

How many times had he embraced it like a lover, a cloak to hide all that was dark in his soul?

He should have been glad that each hoofbeat carried him closer to the Thorned Paw, eager to confront the enemy who had been tormenting him since the night his daughter had almost slipped into the hands of someone who hated him. An enemy without conscience, evil enough to embroil an innocent young girl and a beautiful, gentle woman into his cruel game.

Christ knew, Aidan's hands had been fairly burning to feel the bastard's throat beneath them, feel his fingers crushing the life out of the animal who had stalked those

Aidan Kane loved. Why was it, then, that he felt clinging fingers trying to hold him back? Why was it that he heard the faintest whisperings in the wind, a reproach in the rumble of thunder?

Why was it that he kept hearing Richard Farnsworth's mocking drawl, taunting him, slicing him with words as precisely honed as an assassin's stiletto?

It was insane, this tension biting into his gut, this pulsing instinct of danger that hovered over him, pressing on his chest more certainly than the stormy air.

Farnsworth was annoying, grating on his nerves. But he was Norah's stepbrother.

God, he had tried so hard to accept Farnsworth because of Norah. To endure him. Yet Aidan knew instinctively that if he had been at a gaming table with the man, he would have caught Farnsworth cheating or trying to stir up trouble.

What was it Farnsworth had said, with those eyes that seemed so guileless, hidden beneath their innocent mask?

Consider me responsible for anything that happens to your daughter from this moment on. . . .

I would think a gambler the likes of you would know that life itself is one huge game, and the man who wins is the one willing to take the biggest risks. . . .

When your daughter is with me, I vow she'll be as safe as if she were clasped to her mother's own breast. . . .

They were the words of a pompous popinjay, weren't they? A harmless if irritating fool. One who had bumbled, sending Norah to Rathcannon . . . and then turned up fortuitously with a stricken conscience after Cassandra had nearly been abducted.

Why? Aidan was damned certain Farnsworth hadn't come out of any devotion to his stepsister. Then why blaze his way into the wilds of Ireland? Ensconce himself in Aidan's castle? Endear himself to Aidan's daughter?

Why?

The thunder cracked, lightning shattering the sky into fragments of night.

Before half-blinded eyes, an image danced; Farnsworth rising to his feet amid dinner, stretching his stiff leg. His eyes had been hooded, something simmering beneath the lids.

How did you injure your leg? Cassandra's innocent question jolted through Aidan, followed by Farnsworth's reply.

I was racing about on a slick road with a green-broke team of horses and an ill-sprung curricle when it overturned. Lay on a cliffside for three full days.

No, this was madness, Aidan thought, leaning over his horse's neck, urging the animal to greater speed. Surely he couldn't believe . . . what? That Richard Farnsworth had more menacing reasons for coming to Rathcannon? Insinuating himself into Aidan's life? That Richard Farnsworth had had more nefarious motives for flinging his stepsister into Aidan's bed?

Aidan's mind filled with huge, dark eyes in a pale oval face, an uncertain smile tugging at lips that had never known a man's loving until he had kissed her, deeply, thoroughly, and lost his own soul. From the beginning, there had been something incongruous about Norah and the lovely bonnet that had perched on her dusky locks. What was it Aidan had thought in those frozen moments when he had seen her in the carriage circle? That she looked like a child got up in her mother's finery?

What had Norah said when she'd been attempting to smooth over Farnsworth's arrival at Rathcannon? That he had given her the gift of a trousseau. A nightgown fashioned of wispy lace and mist to tantalize a man's desires. Delicate gowns to set off Norah's quiet beauty, make a man want her.

Gowns Norah never would have chosen herself.

But Farnsworth had chosen them for her, bundled them into a trunk and sent her off to meet the husband he'd miraculously found to rescue her from the fate her stepfather had planned.

Coincidence. Aidan's fingers clenched the reins until the leather gouged into his gloved hands. This whole morass with Farnsworth was just coincidence. Just as it had been coincidence the night Aidan had sat by Cassandra's bed and told Norah the tale of Cassandra's necklace.

The necklace.

It's lovely, Norah had said, a tender wistfulness clinging in a web to her voice. *It reminds me of one my mother once had, with miniatures of her and my father inside.*

The necklace was a gift from one of Delia's lovers. . . . One of Delia's lovers . . .

A sudden shaft pierced Aidan's heart, crippling him with memories of a rain-slick road, screams—Delia's screams, Cassandra's screams . . .

What happened to the man driving the coach?

We never found him.

A carriage accident . . . I lay waiting for help for three days. . . .

Jesus, God, it had been years since that storm-tossed nightmare. Eight years. If Farnsworth was indeed the man who had taken Delia on that wild midnight ride, he must have been planning his vengeance all that time. Honing it to hellish perfection. Seeking out Aidan's jugular, to tear with fangs of agony.

Cassandra.

He closed his eyes for a heartbeat, seeing Norah flinging herself into the arms of her beloved brother. Introducing him to a bedazzled Cassandra. Farnsworth bending over Cassandra's golden curls with an attentiveness that would have bewitched any girl straight out of the schoolroom. Most painful of all was the memory of Cassandra staring up at the polished Englishman with an adoring light in her eyes.

A hideous premonition jolted through Aidan, freezing his blood, twisting his nerves into a raw knot of terror deeper than he'd ever known.

Aidan drew rein on his mount, wheeling his massive stallion around. The rest of his men struggled to halt their horses, shouts of confusion echoing through the night as they battled not to crash into the riders nearest them.

"What be amiss?" Sean O'Day bellowed, all but toppling from a gray gelding.

"I have to go back to Rathcannon."

"But—have ye gone daft, sir? The villain you seek is at the inn."

Aidan hesitated, his gut clenched. What if he was wrong? What if the man he sought was at the Thorned Paw, and this crazed goose chase would only mean that his enemy had slipped farther beyond Aidan's reach?

"You go on. I'll ride back alone."

"Sir, I—"

"Just do as I command!" Aidan bellowed. Then he slammed his heels into his stallion's sides, the powerful beast surging down the shadowed ribbon of road as if the dark demons loosed the night Delia had died had returned.

It seemed an eternity before he reined his mount to a halt outside the castle doors. An eternity of agony, of sensing disaster pressing the air from his lungs, uncertainty sizzling black poison through his veins.

Yet the first glimpse of the haven he had made for his daughter by the sea shattered him, impaling him with a soul-crushing certainty.

Tear-streaked, desperate, the chambermaid Rose was attempting to help Calvy Sipes onto a horse, the footman in obvious agony and barely clinging to the animal's mane. When the girls' eyes locked on Aidan, a shriek of relief tore from her throat and she abandoned the footman, running toward Aidan's stallion, her skirt flying, her hand rummaging in her apron pocket.

"Sir Aidan! Thank God you've come back!"

The stallion danced on its massive hooves, but the girl flung herself against Aidan's stirrup.

"Where's Norah? Cassandra?"

"You have to help her! Th—They're gone! Merciful Mary, he took . . . took the young miss!"

"Who?" Aidan snapped. "Who took Cassandra?" But he already knew.

"Mr. Farnsworth. My lady rode out after them. She left you this. Told you to hurry."

The little maid thrust something toward him with one hand.

Aidan cursed at the writing, blurred in the darkness. Guiding his mount until it danced beneath the ring of light from a lantern, he wrenched open the book to the page marked by a note, his eyes raking down the paper.

His breath stopped. His heart slammed to his toes. Bile rose in his throat as Richard Farnsworth's hideous words spilled their venom into Aidan's veins. A devil's bargain, a pact with hell.

> *Three wagers . . .*
> *Sir Aidan Kane will take a wife. . . . That wife shall take another man to her bed. . . . Kane's daughter will be abducted by a fortune hunter. . . .*

They were diabolical, fiendish in their perfection—the cleaving away of Aidan's soul a knife stroke at a time.

His memory flooded with images: Norah, his miracle, his bride, Philip Montgomery in the garden, his hands all over her, pleading with her to let him become her lover, the danger that had lurked in that same garden, a predator waiting, trying to steal Cassandra away. . . . And Farnsworth, forever smiling that sly smile, taunting Aidan with his double entendres, his mocking quips, knowing . . . knowing what he had in store for the enemy he'd come to Ireland to destroy.

God, was it possible that Norah—his Norah—had any idea what she was a party to? That she had come here, knowing—

No. The denial was swift, sharp, relentless. The mere thought that he might suffer betrayal at her hand was too hideous to contemplate. Impossible to fathom. He dashed it away.

He grabbed up the note, the book tumbling from his

hands. What he read was even more hideous than the wagers themselves. The bastard was mocking him with the fiendish glee of Satan himself.

"Where?" Aidan rasped. "Where did that bastard Farnsworth go?"

"I don't know. Maybe to Noonan's abandoned cottage."

Noonan's cottage—one more legacy of Kane treachery. The tenants had been flung out in his father's time while the wife was in an agony of labor, the young husband shot when, in his desperation, he had dared attack his lord and master. The knowledge that Cassandra's screams might even now be battering those same unfeeling walls was an irony that sickened Aidan. The knowledge that Norah—gentle, sweet Norah—had gone after his daughter wrenched his heart from his chest.

Oh, God, what chance could his ladylight have against a monster like Farnsworth if she could even manage to find him in the storm-darkened wilds that rippled out from Rathcannon?

It was as if he'd been hurled back, to the moment he realized Delia had taken Cassandra. His daughter was lost somewhere in the vast abyss of night.

Aidan cursed himself. Why hadn't he dragged Sean and the others back with him? Why? Injured, Calvy could barely cling to the horse's back, let alone wrest Cassandra from Farnsworth if he could find them. Any man who might be of use was riding hell for leather in the opposite direction.

"Rose, you have to go after Sean and the others. Bring them back to help me, damn it."

The girl trembled, her fingers knotting against her breast as she eyed Calvy's horse with fright. "I don't—don't know. About riding . . . horses . . ."

"You can do it, girl. I know you can," Aidan said. "Cass could be anywhere by now. I need Sean and the others to help me search every road and path."

With an oath, he turned and spurred his mount into the night-shrouded hills, his mind filled with agonizing images of Norah, so brave, so broken by her stepbrother's betrayal; Cassandra, frightened, helpless. Again. Just as she had been the night Richard Farnsworth had imprisoned her in a runaway carriage, hurtling toward the cliffs.

Aidan knew, with each beat of Hazard's hooves on the turf, each searing breath he dragged into his lungs, that Farnsworth's prediction at the dinner table that night would prove right. Tonight he would dice with the devil. But the wager was far greater than anything Aidan had ever risked. It was the soul of his daughter and, Aidan knew with blinding certainty, that of the woman he loved.

Lightning lashed the sky in delicate whip cords of light, yet that subtle torture was nothing in comparison to the savage raking of guilt that battered Norah with each beat of her horse's hooves. Each precious minute that slipped through her fingers was a separate agony—a minute in which her imagination tortured her with images of what Cassandra might be suffering at Richard's hands.

Every pulse of her heart shuddered through her in exquisite terror that Richard and the helpless girl she so loved might even now be racing in some other direction, to vanish until it was too late. Too late to spare Cassandra unspeakable horrors, too late to save Aidan from the diabolical destruction Richard had woven about him.

Cassandra . . . Dear God, the mere thought of the girl lost in this nightmare was agonizing beyond belief. The thought of what might be happening to that bright beautiful girl right now didn't bear thinking about, lest she go insane.

And it was Norah's fault—Norah who had stripped away Aidan's layer of protection, Norah who had brought Richard into Rathcannon, leaving Cassandra vulnerable.

Guilt battered her as she groped for the butt of Aidan's pistol, the smooth feel of the weapon reassuring her at least a little.

She reined in her horse, searching for the road Rose had spoken of, the darkness an enemy that writhed and coiled about Norah's very soul, jeering at her helplessness. She was just about to spur her mount on when a bolt of lightning picked out a narrow trace that might be a path, all but obscured by the underbrush struggling to reclaim it.

Norah hesitated for a moment, then reined her mount down the pathway, praying with every fiber of her soul that she wasn't making yet another costly mistake.

The path writhed, twisted, her horse stumbling over tangled roots that wound across the abandoned road. Panic coiled deeper into Norah's chest with the certainty that if she had taken the wrong turn, she might not be able to find her way back until daylight. Too late to aid Cassandra.

She all but sobbed with relief the instant she caught the first glimmer of light from deep in a hidden valley, the white hulk of a tumble-down cottage crouching in the crook of a hillside like a wounded beast.

Rotted, wood-framed windows peered out like empty sockets, eyes blinded to human suffering, pulsing terror, the horror that might even now be taking place in the room beyond.

Norah spurred her horse on faster, racing up to the building, flinging herself from her mount in the shadow of a dying hawthorn tree.

Splintered wood sliced her fingers as she grasped the cottage's door latch, flung the panel wide.

In a heartbeat, the scene in the chamber seared itself into her mind. Cassandra, huddled on a musty pallet, her skin painted in hellish hues by the flickering light of the oil lamp upon a rickety stool. Her golden hair tumbled about her face, bits of grass and leaves tangled in the strands, her gown a torn puddle on the dirt floor. The delicate cotton of her chemise drooped over one babe-soft shoulder. Silk cords bound her wrists, a nasty scrape on her elbow, a darkening bruise on her jaw.

While Richard, stripped to the waist, stalked her with an expression of distaste on his handsome features.

At the sound of the door crashing against the wall,

Cassandra screamed. A stunned Richard wheeled to face the door, his haughty cheek scored with the glistening tracks Cassandra's nails had cut into his skin.

His hand flashed toward the pearl-handled pistol pillowed on his cast-off clothing. But suddenly he froze, recognition and stark astonishment registering in his eyes as they slashed from Norah's wind-tousled curls to the breeches that barely clung to her waist.

"I'll be damned," he muttered, his lip curling in dark amusement. "Who would have believed—"

"Richard, have you gone mad?" Norah demanded. "Let her go!"

"N—Norah!" Cassandra's cry pierced her heart. The girl fought against her bindings, trying to dart toward her, but she was trapped by Richard's tall frame.

"Not so fast, my dear," he said, taking up the pistol and jamming it in the waistband of his breeches. "We aren't quite ready to receive felicitations as yet—even from the stepsister who made our romantic liaison possible. But as soon as we get the unpleasant business of our bridal night over with . . ."

"No, you can't be married," Norah said. "You can't—"

"I intend to bed the chit first. In fact, I would already be finished with the infernal task if she hadn't managed to lunge off my horse and nearly escape me. She led me the devil of a chase, but I caught her and dragged her back. I promise you, she'll learn obedience once she is my wife." His hand swept up to the scratches on his cheek.

"I'll never marry you!" Cassandra choked out. "Norah, please help me!"

"Norah can't help you," Richard cut in with an ugly laugh. "Even if she was tempted, it wouldn't be in her best interests to do so. Once your precious father discovers her involvement in the wagers I made, he will hate her. She'll be cast off—utterly helpless, alone in the world. But you needn't fear for Norah's future, Cassandra. She will gain complete independence as a reward for her part in my plot—enough money from your handsome dowry to set her up quite comfortably."

Norah gaped at him. He seemed for all the world like a clever boy who expected approval for some cunning trick he had played. It sickened Norah, horrified her.

"Norah," Cassandra breathed in a tiny, broken voice. "You—you knew about what he was going to do?"

"No, angel. No." Norah said, her heart shattering.

"Of course she didn't," Richard scoffed. "I was the one who came across your letter. I was in control from the very first. The only thing I couldn't predict was that she would be fool enough to fall in love with a womanizing rakehell like your father. It complicated things in a most annoying fashion."

Norah sucked in a steadying breath, groping for some way to reason with this man, this stranger before her.

"Richard, let her go. Whatever demon is driving you to this terrible thing, you must know that Cassandra is innocent. She's a child. For mercy's sake—"

"Mercy? Don't preach to me about mercy! Her father left me to rot on a cliff for three days, broken on the stones, waiting for death to claim me. If I hadn't managed to crawl up the cliff face, I would have died. That bastard Kane wanted me to die."

"No. I don't believe it." Norah shook her head, trying desperately to grasp the threads of Richard's tale. "Aidan would never do such a hideous thing. You're not making any sense. What could Aidan have possibly had to do with your accident?"

"You want to know, little sister? I'll show you." He wheeled on Cassandra, his fingers catching hold of the necklace that dangled by a thin chain from her neck. He snapped the chain and flung the trinket down upon the hard-packed floor. The heel of his Hessian crashed down on the delicate bit of jewelry; a horrible cracking sound like snapped bones echoed through the room.

He kicked the broken locket toward Norah, and she stared down at the broken pieces.

Norah reeled. "Wh— I don't understand . . ."

"A gentleman needs love tokens for his lady, and my father was such a cheap bastard, I couldn't afford anything exquisite enough out of my allowance. So I stole the necklace from your mother's jewelry box and gave it to Delia Kane the night we were running away."

Images whirled up in her head: Aidan's voice, tearing back the veil that hid his deepest agony, revealing what had happened, the night that had changed him forever, scarred his soul so brutally only his love for Cassandra had saved him.

"Richard—oh, God, it was you . . ." Norah stopped, her eyes flicking to Cassandra's tear-streaked face, desperate to shield her from the implications of Richard's confession. But it was too late.

"You were the man who—who was waiting for Mama and me that night? The night of the accident?" Cassandra asked, disbelieving.

"Delia was my whole life. She took me up when I was a callow, awkward fool and made a man of me. One to be reckoned with. My father thought I was worthless. He made me feel . . ." Old pain streaked across Richard's features. "Delia was the only one who ever gave a damn about me. I owe everything I am to her."

Norah shuddered inwardly, knowing it was true. Richard was yet another man Delia had twisted and warped and crippled forever.

"My leg was injured the night the carriage overturned. The bones broke on the rocks below. My hand . . ."

The child had already been frightened enough. To hear the ugly truth battered out this way was Aidan's worst nightmare come real. "Richard, don't—"

"Don't what? Tell Kane's proud little princess the truth? It took almost a year for me to crawl out of my sickbed, teach myself to walk once again. And the pain!" He paused, his features tight. "But I didn't give a damn. Every step I took brought me closer to the time when I could get my vengeance on Kane. But not a simple bullet through the heart. No, that would be too quick, too merciful, after all he had made me and Delia suffer. I wanted him to experience the agony I'd known, the helplessness she had felt all those years she was in his power."

A tiny whimper echoed from Cassandra, sickening Norah.

"Cass, don't listen to him. This is insanity."

"I assure you I am quite sane. No one gone in madness could have plotted such a perfect vengeance and carried it out."

"Richard, Aidan sent help back to the coach the minute he regained consciousness. He was all but dead himself by the time he got Cassandra to the surgeon."

"You expect me to believe that? He drove Delia to her death and he left me to die. He destroyed my life, and now I will make him pay the forfeit for his crime."

"By terrorizing an innocent girl?"

"It's unfortunate, but necessary. The girl is the best weapon to use against Kane, and I intend to wield that weapon without mercy."

She groped for some way to deter him and latched onto the only thing she could. "Cassandra is Delia's daughter. If you loved Delia, how can you hurt Cassandra?"

"This will be best for everyone in the end. Cassandra will be away from Kane's lecherous influence. The pain of breaching her maidenhead will be brief enough." His lip curled in distaste. "And God knows, I'll hardly be able to stomach touching her later. How could I when she is alive and Delia is dead?"

"Delia would hate you for hurting her child. I'm certain—"

"What do you know about a woman like Delia? Nothing! You can't stop me, Norah. No one can."

"Richard, let her go," she attempted one last time. His sneering smile was her answer.

It was over. Norah could see the intent in his eyes, the impatience. Hell itself couldn't bar him from working his will.

Norah grasped the cold butt of the pistol and drew the weapon out, her fingers chill, trembling. "I'm not going to let you hurt Cassandra. I'll shoot you if I have to."

Richard hurled her a pained glance. "You expect me to believe that you can pull that trigger, sister mine? That you can kill your own brother?"

The words slammed into Norah, but she tightened her grip on the pistol. "I'll do what I have to."

"You'll shoot me? You'll kill me for Aidan Kane?" Richard's bitter laugh echoed to the tumble-down rafters. "You're a bigger fool than I could have guessed. He'll be out pawing other women before he gets his first babe in your belly. He'll be laughing at you, making jest of you while he partakes of the charms of beautiful women. God knows, the man always had an eye for the most delectable tidbits of female flesh."

Norah struggled desperately to find an opening, stalling Richard the only way she could—by talking, by giving him something to bait her with. "Aidan thinks I'm beautiful."

Richard swore in disgust, pacing toward her. "Christ! I could never understand how a paltry soldier tricked Delia March into marrying him. If Kane is that good at spinning out lies to his women—"

The pistol trembled. "Cassandra, get up. Move toward me."

"She's not going anywhere," Richard said, coming closer, closer. "I've explained everything to you. Why it has to be this way."

"Richard," Norah pleaded. "Don't make me—"

"Shoot? It's the only way you're going to keep me from bedding Kane's daughter. I've been waiting a long time for vengeance, Norah. I'm not about to sacrifice it now. You've already kept me from winning my wager by refusing Montgomery your bed—a blunder that will cost me dearly, I might add. But one mustn't bewail what is already beyond repair."

"Philip? Philip knew of the wagers?"

Richard had managed to undercut her, stun her completely. "The honorable Philip Montgomery? Montgomery had wanted you long before you left England. If the man had had any stones, he would have wed you himself, but no, the illustrious Montgomerys needed brides with fortunes, and you were nearly penniless. When I thought you were married, I merely mentioned your alliance to Philip, pointing out that you were in the licentious clutches of Aidan Kane, and Montgomery did just as I expected. Came racing to Ireland to be your champion. I tried to make it good for you. To arrange your heart's desire. An affair with Philip Montgomery was to have been your reward for being such a helpful accomplice in my little game. But no. You couldn't just accept the gift that I offered you. You had to cling to your noble principles."

He was stalking her, his eyes resolute, lit with dark fire, and Norah realized then that hell itself could not stop him. She would have to pull the trigger if she was to save Cassandra.

He was so close, she could see the scar on his chin, the glint in his eyes.

"Are you going to kill me, Norah?" he demanded softly. "Do you have the courage to watch me die?"

Her mind filled with images: Aidan at Caislean Alainn, butterflies in a tiny Cassandra's hands—the fires of Richard's revenge consuming them both.

She steeled herself, tightened her finger. In a heartbeat Richard's hand flashed out. The hammer of the weapon cracked down—not on the firing pin but on his flesh, the pistol failing to fire.

Norah tried to jerk the pistol away and fire again, but Richard ripped it from her with a savagery that sent spikes of pain up her arm. Surprise and outrage surged into her stepbrother's gaze.

"You *did* pull the trigger! You would murder your own brother for a wastrel bastard like Aidan Kane? Don't you realize what I would have done for you?"

Cassandra cried out as Richard's fist arced toward Norah's face. Pain exploded in Norah's jaw. Her head snapped backward, dizziness overwhelming her, fingers of unconsciousness dragging her down. But she fixed her gaze on the tumbled curls of Aidan's daughter, clung to the agony of knowing what her destruction here would do to her father.

Norah groped for the other pistol at her waist, but Richard moved with diabolical quickness to tear it free.

"Damn it, Norah, now you've ruined everything! I'm afraid I will have to kill you. Another regrettable necessity. Not a pleasant scene for my betrothed to witness, and yet you leave me no choice."

Norah's blood chilled with the certainty that he meant what he said. Her stomach churned at the twisted air of both pleasure and regret in his features.

"You shouldn't have interfered in my game, Norah."

"No! N—Norah!" Cassandra struggled, fought against her bindings. "If you shoot her someone will hear!"

"There is no one within miles *to* hear. I made certain of that."

Norah skittered back, searching for a weapon, any weapon to use against him—seeing her death glimmering in his gaze. Desperate, she searched for words to help Aidan's daughter survive the dark fate written in Richard Farnsworth's eyes.

"Cassandra, whatever happens, your papa will find you. He'll find you and make you safe. Richard can't touch your soul, angel. Remember that."

"Farnsworth won't be touching anything at all."

Deep, vibrating with primal fury, the familiar masculine voice cut through the chamber.

"Aidan!" Norah gasped out, her gaze flicking to the open cottage door. "You found us! Thank God!"

Her glad cry was cut off as Farnsworth grasped her by the hair, yanking her back against his chest. The pistol he'd wrested from her grasp jammed against the soft cord of her throat where the fragile beat of her pulse thrummed close to the skin.

But her eyes were filled with Aidan, standing in the doorway, his hair a wind-spun tangle about his lean cheekbones, his face that of a Celtic warrior whose lady had been threatened.

His fingers gripped a pistol. His eyes simmered with violence. "I'm the one you want, Farnsworth. Not Norah. Not Cassandra. You want a sonofabitching wager? Take this one: I'll kill you for what you've done tonight. Tear you apart a piece at a time."

"You may attempt it, of course. As long as you don't mind sacrificing your bride, Kane. It's an intriguing dilemma, I must admit—one that should prove vastly entertaining. Who is to be the sacrifice? Your bride or your daughter? Either way, I win."

"Go to hell, Farnsworth."

"Undoubtedly. However, before I do, I'll see you trapped in a prison far worse than the devil's domain. Put the pistol down, Kane, or I swear I'll pull the trigger." Farnsworth yanked Norah's head back even farther, exposing the fragile curve of her throat, the sinister nudge of the gun against it.

"Don't do it, Aidan," Norah pleaded, her eyes locking with Aidan's agonized green ones. "He'll kill you anyway. And Cassandra . . . you have to help Cassandra."

"Quite a noble plea, stepsister. You attempt to kill me, but you are ready to fling yourself on the sacrificial pyre for love of this whore-chasing bastard."

Norah saw Aidan's fingers flex, white-knuckled on the

pistol butt, seconds spinning out into eternity, his mouth twisting in an agony so great it shattered her.

"What's it to be, Kane?" Farnsworth goaded. "I would as soon get this over with. I'd not want to keep your daughter waiting for our bridal night too long."

Norah felt Aidan's hell sear her own soul, knew there was only one way she could end it, force her stepbrother's hand so that he couldn't torture Aidan with this demonic choice. She braced herself to wrench against his hold, goad him to pull the trigger.

But at that instant Aidan let his pistol thud to the floor.

"No," she whimpered. "Aidan, no! Why did you—"

"I can't let him hurt you, ladylight."

"I must say this tender display astonishes even me," Farnsworth said with a sneer. "Such noble self-sacrifice and all that rot. But then, you've had a woman's blood on your hands before, haven't you, Kane?"

"That woman made her own choices."

"That woman? That's a rather vague term, isn't it? We'd not want poor Cassandra to be stumbling over the path of our conversation, would we? He's talking about your mother, beloved. And she didn't have any choices from the minute your bastard of a father jammed his wedding ring on her finger. Tell me, Kane, how did it feel to know that your wife hated you? What did you think when the poison she gave you spread through your veins? Did you realize that, Cassandra? He made your mother's life such hell that she tried to poison your father?"

"Papa—" Cassandra's voice was broken, shattered.

"She poisoned him because it was the only way she could escape him. But the bastard didn't die. He came after us, chasing us. Because of him, the coach overturned. Because of him—"

"It wasn't Papa's fault! It wasn't!"

Norah could feel the pounding tension in Aidan, see him struggling desperately to find some opening, some way to hurtle himself at Farnsworth without endangering her.

"It was his fault, damn it! He killed Delia as much as if he'd put a bullet in her breast! He was a drunken bastard, flinging away a fortune at cards. A sadistic sonofabitch, who dragged her to Ireland, chained her to his castle in the middle of nowhere, saddling her with a child she never wanted."

Despite the danger, Norah could see the welling of hurt in Cassandra. "My mother was taking me with her! That night in the coach—"

"Cassandra, don't listen to him!" Norah choked out. "Don't believe—"

"She hated you, you blind little fool!" Farnsworth raged. "Hated you because you were a part of him—a reminder of how she'd thrown herself away on Irish scum. All the nights she lay in my arms, she cursed the day you were born. When she agreed to run away with me, she said she had to take you with us—but not because she wanted you. She was taking you because she knew that you were the only thing that mattered to Kane—that by stealing you away she would rip out his heart. And Delia deserved that pleasure, that taste of vengeance for what Aidan Kane had put her through."

"Farnsworth, you . . ." Aidan nudged a step toward them, white-faced. A gasp of pain tore from Norah as the gun jabbed deeper. But Farnsworth was warming to his subject now, a feverish anticipation shuddering through him.

"Tell her, Kane. Tell your spoiled little daughter the truth about her precious father."

"What truth is that?"

"That by eloping with her, I'll be sparing her the agony of suffering the consequences of being your spawn. That for eight years, not a decent drawing room in London would taint itself with your presence. Not a single decent woman would allow you to touch so much as the hem of her gown. That you are a gambler, a cheat, who has dueled a dozen times over the cast of a dice or the favors of a pretty harlot, a drunken wastrel with a dozen mistresses clamoring for his attentions. Can you smell the stench of vice on him, Cassandra? Know that he's done things that would sicken you?"

"I don't believe you!" the girl raged.

"Tell her, Kane. Tell her it's true."

Aidan's hard gaze flashed to his daughter, his features a study in agony. Every muscle was tense, coiled, as he moved toward her. "Cass, I . . . it is true. Every word."

"Papa—"

Farnsworth's avid gaze was feasting on Aidan's destruction.

"I am everything Farnsworth says I am, girl. That's why I kept you at the castle, so you would never have to know. But you grew up, Cass." Aidan's voice cracked as he searched for some way, any way, to break Farnsworth's hold on Norah.

The bastard was so damned calm and cold with murder in his eyes. Only when he'd spoken of Delia had there been another emotion in that handsome face, one Aidan recognized all too well.

Obsession.

He could use it against Farnsworth, cripple him in ways that were all too familiar to him. And yet the cost—oh, God, the cost . . .

His eyes flicked for a moment to his daughter, crumpled on the bed, every nerve in his body screaming in denial. No. He couldn't tell her. Yet how could he compare the wounds his words would inflict on her to the fate Farnsworth had planned?

Aidan let mockery curve his lips, contempt fill his eyes. "You loved her, didn't you? Loved Delia? You poor besotted fool."

Farnsworth stiffened. "She was the most glorious woman in the world. A treasure a man like you could never understand."

Aidan laughed. "Plenty of men understood my wife. More

than I could count. She was a harlot who collected men's hearts like some women collected slippers, always hungry for some new diversion."

Farnsworth's face whitened. "Don't you dare malign her that way! She went to other men's beds because it was the only way she could escape the misery of being married to you! Once we fell in love, she didn't want anyone else, need anyone else!"

"Is that what she told you?"

"She loved me! Only me! We were going to build a life together, someplace you could never reach us."

"I wouldn't have cared if you and Delia had set up housekeeping in the next bedroom. Hell, it would've been a relief! At least I would've had some idea which man was going to come skulking out of her chamber at night. Delia knew that. She knew I wouldn't have given a damn if she'd run away to play a harlot's service to a whole regiment as long as she left Cassandra behind."

Aidan's blood chilled, dread coursing through him as something wild and frightening shivered to life in Farnsworth's eyes. Aidan knew a stark terror that the desperate gambit he was making to save Norah's life might be the impetus that made the sadistic bastard pull the trigger.

"Delia had to repay you for the misery you made her suffer. The girl belonged to her. Once we arrived in France, we were going to throw her away, Kane. Hurl her on the steps of some poorhouse so our lives wouldn't be tainted by your spawn."

The words sickened Aidan; the fact that Cassandra was hearing them nearly killed him. But he forced himself to plunge on, praying that he could goad the bastard into making a mistake, praying for the slightest opening so he could fling himself at the Englishman and kill him.

"You were willing to risk my fury in order to grant Delia this crazed revenge? Such grand passion the two of you shared, Farnsworth. It touches my heart."

Aidan's pulse raced, every muscle in his body coiled, ready as he steeled himself to fling out the words that would drive Farnsworth over the edge. That would give Aidan a chance, the slightest chance, to overpower him.

"Of course, I have one tiny question regarding this magnificent love affair of yours. If Delia . . . *loved* you so desperately," he said, contempt dripping from the word, "why was it that the very afternoon before your grand escape, I found her in the tack room with a strapping young stableboy between her thighs?"

"No!" Farnsworth's eyes were wild, his face contorted, hideous, the pistol shaking in his hand, tearing at Norah's soft skin. "You're lying! I don't believe you!"

"She was making that pretty little sound she made when she was near her peak, clawing at his shoulders. She laughed when I stumbled upon them. Now I know she wasn't laughing at me, she was laughing at you."

"I don't believe you!"

"You poor bastard. You were just another one of Delia's besotted fools."

A cry of rage ripped from Farnsworth's chest as he waved the pistol wildly in Aidan's direction. That split second was all Aidan needed.

He hurled himself headlong at Farnsworth just as Norah wrenched free of his grasp. The two men slammed into the cottage wall with a force that sent rotted thatching raining down on their backs, silting their eyes. The lamp sputtered and smoked. Cassandra's cries echoed in Aidan's ears as his fists cracked into Farnsworth again and again.

He outweighed the Englishman, yet Farnsworth fought with the strength of a madman, a man obsessed by a woman who had bewitched him, then made him her fool.

He heard Norah scrambling past them and felt her desperation, glimpsed Cassandra's face—her innocence shattered, as broken as she would have been had Farnsworth worked his will on her. But Aidan had destroyed his daughter with his words, hurt her in a way Farnsworth never could.

Aidan slammed his fist into Farnsworth's jaw, heard the bones snap. The man's jaw shifted at a stomach-wrenching angle as it broke.

There was murder in Farnsworth's eyes now, a crazed animal rage, the thirst for blood. Farnsworth's fist drove into Aidan's half-healed ribs. Agony streaked out as a sickening, cracking sound split the air.

Aidan fell back, fighting against waves of dizziness, but Farnsworth had already snatched up a thick length of board and begun swinging it toward Aidan with deadly force.

Aidan hit the dirt and rolled, but he couldn't entirely escape the blow. Solid wood connected with his shoulder. It stunned him, froze him for just a heartbeat.

In that moment Farnsworth's fingers grappled for his throat.

Aidan fought like a madman, feeling Farnsworth's hands close like a hunting beast's talons, cutting off breath, draining away his strength. Aidan clawed at the bastard's wrists, trying to break his grasp, his lungs burning, his mind tormented with images of Cass, of Norah, at Farnsworth's mercy if Aidan failed them.

Lights danced before Aidan's eyes, his throat on fire, his head swimming wildly. In a heartbeat it would be over. The bastard would win.

With the last wisp of his strength, Aidan slammed his knee up, catching Farnsworth in the groin. The Englishman gave a shriek of rage as he released Aidan's throat and staggered back.

Aidan pushed his way through the hazy web that tried to suck him into unconsciousness and struggled to gain his feet. But he slammed to a halt as something cold and hard bashed into the side of his face.

He fell, his eyes clearing enough to see Farnsworth's face making sickening circles before him, the pistol gripped in his hand.

"You're dead, Kane," Farnsworth rasped. "Dead."

Aidan glimpsed Norah's pale face, knowing it would be the last sight he saw before the pistol shot that would end his life. The most brutal regret in a lifetime of regrets would be the fact that he had never had the courage to tell Norah he loved her.

He lunged toward Farnsworth, knowing it was futile.

But at the last instant, something glaringly bright arced down over the bastard's head. It was the lamp clutched in Norah's hands.

Farnsworth jerked hard, the pistol exploding. Pain ripped the skin at Aidan's temple, the shot grazing him just as glass shattered and flames flared. Farnsworth's shrieks of agony ripped through the cottage as he was drenched in hellish waves of liquid fire.

He hurled himself at Norah as if, even in supreme agony, he was determined to drag her down to Hades with him. Desperate, Aidan lunged and grabbed his arm, flinging him away from her.

Sparks rained on Aidan's skin, burning him. Cassandra screamed, scrambling out of the way as Farnsworth crashed against the pallet. The ragged ticking stuffed with hay years old burst into flame.

"Get out!" Aidan roared. "Cassandra, Norah, get out!"

He saw the blur of his daughter running from the cottage and heard Norah's cries. But despite the flames spilling, spreading to every surface, Aidan grabbed up a tattered quilt, trying desperately to suffocate the blaze dancing such deadly patterns on Farnsworth's body. The Englishman writhed from his grasp, his skin bursting, melting, the sickly stench of roasting human flesh searing itself into Aidan's nostrils.

Heat danced onto his own sleeve as a hungry tongue of flame found new fuel to feed upon. He heard Norah's shout, felt her grabbing him, snuffing out the fire just as the quilt in his hands erupted into flame.

Aidan flung it away, his gaze snagging on Farnsworth one

last time, but Norah's stepbrother was beyond the aid of anything earthly. The Englishman fell back, eyes rolling in his head, his mouth contorted in a hideous mask of death.

Aidan's head throbbed, his lungs seared with smoke and ash. He scooped Norah into his arms and staggered out of the Englishman's den of pain.

They collapsed on the turf, Aidan clutching Norah close as Cassandra flung herself against him. Both his heart's treasures were battered and soot-stained but alive—praise God—alive.

"It's over." He drew his daughter into the crook of his other arm. "Over."

The three of them clung together as Sean O'Day and Gibbon Cadagon thundered out of the dark night.

CHAPTER

25

Rathcannon was ablaze with lantern light as the bedraggled band of horses and riders cantered up the road. Servants spilled out across the lawns, their faces drawn, their lips still mumbling half-formed prayers.

Mrs. Cadagon clutched rosary beads to her ample breasts and Maude Brindle's stoic face seemed to have aged a dozen years. Rose ran out to meet the riders, self-blame still rampant in her face.

"Miss Cassandra . . . Lady Kane . . . are they all right?" the girl cried, her gaze sweeping from where Aidan cradled his wife before him on his stallion, his arms tight about the treasure he'd come so near to losing to Delia's legacy of hate.

Norah raised her head from his shoulder, her cheeks so pale it broke Aidan's heart, her voice still carrying shadows of horror branded into her soul from the ruin of Noonan's cottage.

Yet she forced a weary smile for the girl. "We're both fine, Rose. In large part thanks to you."

"But Miss Cass—where is she?" The maid's voice choked

off as a much-worn horse nudged forward in the ranks. Sean O'Day cradled Cassandra in arms that were strong as hewn oak, steady and infinitely gentle. The cloak he'd wrapped about the girl's half-bared form in the shadow of the burning cottage engulfed Cassandra, making her seem even more fragile, more like a child.

"The little princess is asleep," Sean said, one finger smoothing back a lock of her hair as if it were spun gold. "I'll carry her to her chamber if you wish, Sir Aidan."

Aidan drew rein, then slowly lowered Norah into Gibbon's arms, the old man steadying her with gnarled hands.

"Thank you," Aidan said to the stalwart coachman, "but Cassandra and I . . . we need time to talk."

Time: Was there enough in all eternity to heal the wounds dealt his sheltered daughter this night? Talk: There were a thousand things he needed to say to her, and to the woman standing so exhausted, so drained, leaning on Gibbon's arm. But what words could he say to erase the poison he'd poured into his daughter's ears at the cottage? What pretty phrases would convey to Norah a love that was beyond all reason, beyond his power to fight? A love that had almost been consumed by his bitterness, and Richard Farnsworth's hate?

Shattered, Aidan scooped his daughter from Sean O'Day's arms and carried her into the castle in which he'd tried so desperately to keep her safe and hidden.

But there was no place to hide from the truths Richard Farnsworth had cursed the girl with. There was no way to gild the truth about what Aidan was and what he had done.

Cassandra's tower chamber was lit by candles, the fire in the grate glowing, sending the peat-flavored warmth into the exquisite room.

With all the gentleness in his battered soul, Aidan laid his daughter down in the bed ornamented with creatures of myth and fairy tales, wishing he could draw the Pegasus-spangled curtains closed, shut out the roiling tempest that had all but drowned Cassandra this night.

His throat constricted, and he wished with all his being that Cassandra could be a little golden-haired cherub again, sucking on her fingers, smiling in her sleep, dreaming such beautiful dreams there would be no room for the hideous inheritance he and Delia had chained her with.

"Papa?" Her eyes fluttered open as he drifted her head down onto the pillow, and staring down into her face was one of the most painful things Aidan Kane had ever done.

Oh, God, what did she want of him? Reassurance? A way to wipe away the ugliness, the pain? To capture dreams in his hands, the way he had when she was a child, and slip butterfly fairies between her soft fingers?

Aidan sat down on the edge of the bed, his soul shattering. He would have happily sacrificed it to the devil himself, if it could ease even a whisper of what his beloved child had to face.

"Cassandra, I'm sorry," he grated. "Sorry you found out the truth—about me, about your mother—in such a terrible way. I never wanted it to hurt you. I thought—thought I could protect you from it. But I was wrong. There's no way to erase the past. Make me into a man you can truly be proud of. The hero papa you so often called me."

"You are my hero, Papa. You always will be."

"But I . . . what Farnsworth said . . . It must have shocked you terribly, hurt you."

"It hurts to hear anyone say such ugly things about you. But as for the other things, the things about mama being . . . being a . . . having lots and lots of—of lovers . . . I already knew that. And I heard the stories about you a long, long time ago."

"You . . . knew? How could you possibly—"

"Other children. The day you found me crying over the fairies—not believing in them—I was really crying over something else. The boys had told me so many awful things, about you and Mama. They said that she—she was a whore, and that you killed her."

417

Aidan reeled at the memory of how small she had been then, how she had cried in his arms. But she had never even hinted at a far greater pain than the loss of a fragment of her childhood imagination. "God, Cass. Why didn't you tell me?"

"You always looked so strange whenever I mentioned Mama. And sometimes I'd catch you staring at my necklace and know you were remembering the night of the accident. I didn't want to hurt you, Papa. And maybe—just a little—I was afraid it might be true. I was a child, but I knew how unhappy you both were. I'd hear you shouting at each other sometimes, hear the horrible things Mama would say about you."

"All this time, you thought I might have killed her?"

"No. The night you took me to Caislean Alainn to hunt for fairies, I decided it was impossible that all those bad things they said about you were true. You were my father, and you were the most wonderful hero in the whole world. I loved you so much, Papa, and I knew you could never do the things they said you did."

Faith. Blind faith. Trust, a gift beyond measure. Aidan's eyes burned, his throat closed. All those anguished years that he'd been lost in fear that he would lose Cassandra's love had been wasted, the misery, the torment.

"Oh, God, Cass . . ."

He crushed her in his arms, burying his face in her curls. "I love you, Princess."

"I'm not a princess, Papa. And it's time I stepped out of my enchanted tower, don't you think?"

He drew back, staring down into his daughter's lovely face. "It's time, angel," he whispered, knowing in that instant how very much he'd miss her, his little girl now grown into a woman.

But she was right, his wise, cherished daughter. It was time to cast aside old chains and throw back the locks on towers of enchantment, to let go of the old life and open the way for the new. The life that Norah offered, so beautiful, so changed.

"I love you, Cassandra," Aidan told her. "We'll open the tower door together."

She stood in the window, bathed in the first glimmerings of dawn, an angel more miraculous than any Aidan could have imagined, a second chance to make right so many mistakes that had haunted his life.

He hesitated in the door that led to her chamber, as uncertain as any raw lad come to his lady love with his heart in his hands. But what could he offer her after the hell she'd faced that night? What could he give her in the wake of her brother's betrayal? Would the shadows of this night ever disappear from those dark eyes? Would she ever be able to look into Aidan's face and not see the reflection of her stepbrother's hideous death?

They had already wasted too much time by failing to grasp the full measure of happiness the capricious fates had thrust into their hands. They had almost lost it forever. Yet he wouldn't push her, wouldn't rush her, wouldn't be the cause of any more strain marring her beloved face.

"Norah?" He breathed her name.

"Richard." The name broke on her tongue. "What will happen now? My stepfather will have to be told."

"That bastard can't hurt you anymore. Your stepbrother died in a fire in an obscure cottage in Ireland. A freak accident. No one will ever have to know."

"That I killed him?"

"You didn't kill him. You kept him from killing me. And Cassandra. And yourself, Norah."

"I know. I just . . . it was so hideous. The way he died." Her voice dropped. "The way he lived. And worst of all, he made me part of his madness, twined me so tightly into his plotting that I'll never be free of it."

419

"I hope not." Aidan groped for the words to help her, to heal her.

She stiffened as if he'd struck her.

"Norah, if Farnsworth hadn't tangled you in his plans, I never would have found you. You wouldn't be my wife."

"How can you even look at me without thinking what I almost cost you? You could have died. Cassandra . . . When I think of what almost happened to her, I can't bear it. And even more painful than what Richard did is the knowledge that because of me, she had to find out in the most horrible way possible the things you'd fought a lifetime to protect her from."

Aidan's lips curved into a smile, one filled with pain and with love. "It seems you were right all along. My daughter has informed me she doesn't want to be protected. She's not a princess in a tower, no matter how much I wanted to make her one. As for the truths she heard about Delia and me tonight, she already knew the worst of it. She'd heard it years ago."

"She knew?"

"She decided that she loved me, that she didn't believe the things people were saying about me. She doesn't care about the things I've done, things I'm not proud of. It seems a hero doesn't have to be perfect. He just has to—to try his best, to make fairies out of butterflies, to read stories, to while away the hours spent sick in bed."

"I'm glad, Aidan. So glad."

"Whatever happens when she enters society in London, she'll be strong enough, secure enough, loved enough by both of us to triumph. I feel it in my gut. Cassandra wants to slay her own dragons from now on. I'm going to try my damnedest to let her."

Aidan sucked in a steadying breath, his hands trembling, his heart feeling too large for his chest. It pressed against his ribs as if the slightest brush of his hand would make it burst.

"It seems a hero just has to love his daughter," Aidan said. "It made me think . . . hope that maybe we could begin again if I . . . loved you."

She turned to him, fey as a fairy queen, fragile as any spirit who had ever wandered the battlements of Caislean Alainn. A woman of mist and magic, who had kissed him in a fairy ring and carried his heart into a realm beyond reality, one so beautiful he never wanted to return to the real world again.

"You . . . love me?"

"Ever since Cassandra was tiny, I dreaded the day she would grow up. I thought my life would be over—barren, empty. How could I have guessed that I'd have a chance to start over, Norah? To make things right? Do you remember what I told you a long time ago? That the only way a Kane could enter heaven was to steal the keys?"

"I remember."

"I didn't have to steal heaven, Norah. You came to me, ladylight, and put the keys into my hands."

Tears welled up in her eyes, spilled down her cheeks, cleansing away pain and fire, grief and guilt, leaving shining wonder.

"Marry me, Norah."

"But we're already wed."

"Marry me today, in Caislean Alainn, with the sun streaming down and the Old Ones offering us their blessing. The vows I took in the church were cast out, careless. This time I want every word to be a treasure, to take out and hold when I draw my last breath. Give me forever, Norah. Let me give you not what I am, but all I hope to be. With your help, angel. With your hope."

She flung herself into his arms, a thousand dreams in her eyes, infinite love in her heart.

With exquisite tenderness, he bathed away the traces of soot on her cheeks, in her hair, drifted a delicate gown about her slender body. Then he swept her into his arms and carried her out into the new-dawned day where his stallion was waiting.

Love shimmered in the Irish sky and kissed the Celtic wind as the horse carried them across dew-sweet hills. It wreathed a Castle of Beauty in a new magic, a new promise, as rakehell Sir Aidan Kane took his ladylight to wife, in his heart, in his soul, their union blessed in the enchanted circle of the ancient fairy ring.

**POCKET BOOKS
PROUDLY ANNOUNCES**

GATHER THE STARS

KIMBERLY CATES

**Coming Soon from
Pocket Books**

**The following is a preview of
Gather the Stars. . . .**

Rachel had never suspected that war was so uncomfortable. Hot spikes of pain screwed themselves into every joint of her body. The rough blindfold made her eyes itch. The constant jolting of the horse jarred her until her teeth threatened to chatter right out of her head.

How long she'd been trapped in this hell, she couldn't begin to guess. They'd ridden through the night at break-neck speed, and continued on until she felt the sun strike her face. After, the warming rays had vanished, but she couldn't be sure if night had fallen once again or if a cloud had merely obscured the sun.

She focused all of her effort on not allowing so much as a groan to cross her lips. And she knew she had passed beyond exhaustion into a comatose state when, no matter how hard she fought the waves of tiredness, she found herself dozing off.

Yet how could anyone fight off sleep forever?

They had been riding for an eternity. An eternity Rachel

had spent listening to every sound with excruciating intensity, trying to gauge any clue that might help her retrace the horse's steps once she escaped. She'd distinguished the rushing music of a burn spilling over stone, and tried to count the number of times her body shifted in her captor's arms as he guided his mount up sweeps of hills.

She'd congratulated herself for her genius in demanding to be allowed to answer calls of nature whenever she guessed some distinct landmark might be near. Those few moments of grudging privacy had given her time enough to sneak up the hem of the blindfold and glance at the wild highlands of Scotland engulfing her.

Terror clawed inside her, the terror Persephone must have felt as she was dragged down to hell. However, Persephone had been face to face with her nemesis from the moment of her abduction, while Rachel was left at the mercy of a too vivid imagination. To her, it seemed as if the Glen Lyon were vengeance incarnate; hints of his dark deeds had made Rachel's spine tingle with foreboding while she was safe in the garden, but here in the vast wildness her skin was icy with pure dread.

During the gruelling trek only one thing had kept her sane: the hope that she would be rescued at any moment. Sir Dunstan and the other bold men who had filled the ballroom must be, even now, riding hard in search of her.

To aid them, she had done all in her power to slow her captor's progress, dallying as long as possible during the moments he'd shown her the mercy of shoving a crumbling bannock into her hands or pressing an otterskin full of water to her lips. Yet as time ticked by, even Rachel had had to admit that it would be more and more difficult to track her in this immense wildland.

That admission left her two choices: give way to hysteria and blind panic, or screw her courage to the sticking place and confront the despised enemy of her betrothed as though she were a captive queen. Face the rebel who was almost a legend. . . .

She swallowed hard, imagining a primitive Scots warrior with tangled hair and savage eyes, lust twisting a cruel mouth—every maiden's worst nightmare in the days of the border wars.

She was just dismissing the image as one more folly when a shrill sound shattered the silence, drawing a stifled cry from her own lips.

Not even her wildest imaginings had prepared her for the barbarian war cries erupting around her as her captor slowed the horse to a halt. The Gaelic cries raked down her nerves like the blade of a claymore, leaving her knees shaking no matter how desperately she tried to stop them.

Then a high-pitched voice pierced her ears through the cacophony: "You've got her! That bastard Wells' woman!"

"I hope to hell I've got the right one," her captor called out, dragging her down off the horse with him. "It'd be damned inconvenient to have abducted the wrong woman."

He flung her over his shoulders like a sack of grain, crossing with long strides to God knew where. Rachel could feel fingers plucking at her, poking her.

"Did she scream and faint?" someone demanded to know. "I bet she cried."

"If she didn't already, the Glen Lyon'll make her wail like a pig with its tail caught in a gate," another voice insisted.

"Glen Lyon can go to hell!" Rachel snarled. "Take your hands off me, you—you traitor scum." Yet it was unnerving: the voices pounding her like battle-clubs, the chill that seemed to envelop her, the hard hand of her captor smack in the middle of her upturned rump. Without another word, he dumped her unceremoniously onto something cool and hard.

She struggled to stand up, damned if she was going to face these traitors on her knees. But before she could rise, a swarm of fiends engulfed her—crawling over her legs, tugging at her, their hands sticky . . . with blood? The gruesome possibility teased her mind.

Dear God, what had she stumbled into?

She felt as if a horde of demons had been set upon her. One of them ripped the blindfold from her head, taking a good deal of her hair with it. Light from blazing flambeaus bored to the backs of her eyes, blinding her for long seconds. When her vision began to clear, she wanted to grab the blindfold again and draw it over her eyes.

She was staring into the face of the most hideous gnome she had ever seen. It was barely a hand's length away from her nose. Thick white paste stiffened its hair into gruesome spikes; primitive, painted symbols traced grimy paths on skin dark with filth. One side of the creature's face was horribly distorted, its cheek bulging, its upper lip twisted. Claws dug hard into handfuls of her linen robe. Despite all her brave intentions, Rachel couldn't keep from shrinking back. Dear God, what was it?

"We're not going to feed you even a crumb, Sassenach!" The gnome's hate-filled voice echoed through what seemed to be a rough stone cavern. "We're going to starve you until your bones stick right out of your skin."

"The Glen Lyon will be the one meting out justice here," her captor cut in. "Of course, I'm certain he'll take your suggestion under advisement."

She turned to see the man who had carried her away from the garden—a mountain of a man with swarthy skin, ebony hair, and a flashing grin that made her want to ram his white teeth down his throat. "Now, let the lady up this instant," he commanded.

Obedient demons? Rachel wondered incredulously as the pack of gnomes scuttled off her with groans of disappointment. She scrambled to her feet, her knees all but buckling as she braced herself against a wall. She towered over her tormentors, their faces shifting into better focus as one of them plopped a grimy thumb into its mouth.

"Children," she gasped out, disbelieving. "They're . . . children." The notion horrified her beyond anything she had experienced, the threats they had spewed out far more unnerving because they had fallen from what should be innocent lips. "What kind of monster would keep children? . . . They're like animals."

"I suggested Glen Lyon drown the lot of 'em, but he says they'd spoil the drinking water." Was the man actually smiling? "Now, we don't want to keep him waiting."

He guided her through a twisted passageway that led deeper into the cave, to where a fresh-hewn door had been fitted to the stone. Was it the rebel's lair? Rachel wondered. Or a prison buried so deep in the bowels of the earth that no one would hear her scream?

The Lyon's den. . . . Rachel couldn't stifle the throb of raw fear. She felt as if she were about to be some nefarious monster's next meal. She steeled herself to confront the vile fiend who had ordered her abduction.

But as the door was shoved open, revealing the makeshift chamber beyond, Rachel froze, gaping.

A man sat at a wooden desk, a dark-gold mane of hair falling in wild disarray about a lean face. Intense gray eyes peered through the lenses of spectacles at whatever was in his hands, and there was a dark smudge of something on his jaw. He was spouting a string of words in perfect Latin. But despite the fact that she'd been educated far more thoroughly in the language than any other woman she knew, they were words she had never heard before.

"Christ's blood," the man spat. "I'm going to murder that bastard when I get my hands on him."

"On *her*, brother," interrupted her captor. "You did specify I was to bring you a woman."

The man wheeled, looking stunned, as if he'd been

clubbed from behind by one of the demon-children. He leapt to his feet, his spectacles sliding further down his nose, a bundle of garish scarlet velvet tumbling to the floor. A spool of thread careened across the room to thump into the heather-stuffed mattress crammed beside one wall.

"Blast it, if I've lost that needle again . . ."

Rachel gaped at him, more stunned than if he'd been a naked savage gnawing on human bones.

"Miss de Lacey, may I present the dread rebel lord Glen Lyon," her captor said with a grin.

The golden-maned man stopped groping for the needle, and straightened. He was tall and too thin, with the mouth of a poet, the expression of a scholar, and the eyes of a dreamer—the absolute antithesis of every raider Rachel had read about in her contraband French novels.

Strangely, she felt almost cheated—furious at this man for the imaginings that had tormented her since she'd been stolen from the garden. It was upsetting enough that she'd been abducted—but to be abducted at the order of a man like this . . .

The Glen Lyon? He looked more like a Glen *Kitten!* But couldn't a man such as this be even more dangerous? Weak men were often the cruellest to compensate for their own failings. And it was obvious that this rebel had a whole brigade of minions ready to act upon his command. The other man who had plucked her from the garden had looked strong enough to bend steel bars into coiled springs if the spirit had moved him.

"Miss Rachel de Lacey?" Glen Lyon sketched her a bow, as if they were at a soiree. "I'm—"

"You don't need to introduce yourself," Rachel shot back. "From the moment I arrived in Scotland, I heard tales of the coward of Prestonpans. But I had no idea that you were so craven you wouldn't even take your own prisoners. What kind of a man are you? Forcing others to do vile deeds for you because you lack the courage."

She'd called him a coward, taunted him in a way that would have made Dunstan violent with rage, and this man didn't even have the grace to blush! She watched him long seconds, expecting *some* reaction—an explosion of masculine outrage, a gruff denial of the charges leveled against him, or at the very least savage shame. Instead, Glen Lyon regarded her with something like amusement twinkling in his storm-cloud eyes.

"Abducting ladies isn't my strong suit, I'm afraid. I would've made a disaster of it. And there's nothing more upsetting than a botched abduction. However, I do trust that Adam saw to your every comfort?"

Her mouth hung open like a fish wife's. Sweet God, was he jesting?

No, the bastard was toying with her as a cat did with its prey. He had her in his power, and had all the time in the world to torture her. He wasn't fooling her with that solicitous smile.

"Comfort?" she sputtered. "I was snatched from the midst of a ball, slung over a saddle like a sack of grain, and hauled off to God knows where. Then I was set upon by demons."

"Demons?" He frowned, lifting off his spectacles and rubbing the bridge of his nose. Then his grin widened, as if lightning had struck his all-too-numb brain. "Ah. They aren't demons, they're Picts. An ancient barbarian tribe who swarmed into Scotland in about . . ."

"I couldn't care less about ancient civilizations!" she blustered in disbelief.

"That's obvious enough. Your . . . ahem, attire is completely wrong."

He'd just had her abducted, and he was giving her a lesson in historical costuming? The man truly *was* insane. Insane people were dangerous. . . .

"You were attempting to wear a gown of the Grecian

mode, I presume," he continued. "The beauty in classical styles comes from flowing, draped lines. The ancients believed that the gods had endowed women with their own natural beauty. They didn't believe in crushing their ladies into torture chambers of bone and steel until they couldn't breathe. So to remain true to the time period, your corset should definitely have been discarded."

"My c-corsets?" Hot blood flooded into Rachel's cheeks, the cave's coolness suddenly kissing bared skin where her robes had sagged askew. Her breasts, pushed high by the garment, were half revealed, an edge of stiff-boned silk corset visible to the Glen Lyon's eyes. Eyes that were suddenly anything but vague and distracted, clinging to swells suddenly blushed with heat.

Clenching her teeth, Rachel jerked up her robes with trembling fingers. "I suppose you're going to ravish me," she said, every fiber of her being straining to keep him from knowing the terror the thought spawned in her. "But I warn you, no matter what horrendous, savage, vile things you do to my body, sir, you cannot touch my soul."

Glen Lyon's gaze sprang away from her breasts. "Ravish you?" he echoed, blinking hard. "Miss de Lacey, I assure you, I fully intend to do everything possible to see to your comfort, but there are limits to even my hospitality."

Rachel stared at him. Was this traitorous coward telling her that she was safe from the horrors she'd been imagining? She should have been elated, relieved. Instead, fury sizzled through her.

The corner of his mouth ticked upward. Though he hadn't made a sound, the bastard was laughing at her. No one laughed at Lord General Marcus de Lacey's daughter!

"I doubt you would be man enough to take a woman. In fact, I'd not be surprised if you fancied boys." Even Rachel was shocked by what had slipped past her unguarded tongue—perversions she'd heard whispered of about the army camp. Was she insane? God in heaven, she was all but daring him to what? To prove his manhood by raping her?

Yet for the first time since that awful moment she'd been snatched from the garden, she felt as if she'd struck a blow in her own defense. The sensation was far headier than anything so somber as wisdom, far more bracing than caution. She would rather have been flayed alive than back down.

His gaze darkened. "A woman who has just been abducted might be wise to mind her tongue."

"Why else would a bastard like you keep that pack of beastly urchins? They were threatening to starve me. Where do you suppose they might have learned about such ghastly things? Perhaps I should ask them."

"Say a word to them, and I swear, it will be the last time you ever speak." The words were squeezed through bloodless lips. "If those children are not the perfect little cherubs you'd prefer, Miss de Lacey, you can thank your betrothed for that. These—little animals—are only repeating what they've seen. Their families were starved by the British army, every living thing slaughtered, every shelter destroyed. They were dying by inches. But when that wasn't expedient enough for your betrothed, he sped up the process by setting his ravening dogs on their mothers, their sisters, even their grandmothers."

Her stomach pitched, bile rising in her throat. "Soldiers can get—get out of control. Even papa admitted that. It's hardly their commander's fault if a few of the men do despicable things."

"In my opinion, the commander is responsible for every blade of grass his soldiers crush beneath their boots, but that's immaterial here. Tell me, Miss de Lacey, would the commander be responsible for what happened if he gave the order to his men to rape and slaughter women and children?"

The words pierced her like the blade of a knife, thickening her throat. "Are you even daring to hint that Sir Dunstan Wells, the most honorable officer in Cumberland's army, would do anything so—so barbaric?" She was fairly frothing with outrage.

"I'm not hinting anything. The truth is, I have an aversion to officers who believe they are God, and to spoiled generals' daughters who play nasty little games with men's lives."

"I don't play games!"

"What else do you call battles set up for your entertainment? Men breaking their necks to prove their courage to you, cutting each other down in duels?"

His accusation affected her like the nettles she'd wandered into as a child, stinging, biting until she squirmed inwardly. "How could you possibly know about . . ." She choked off the question, glaring at him, but all her resolve couldn't keep telltale heat from spilling into her cheeks.

"I've been in society enough to have heard all about you. You're quite notorious, in fact."

Rachel swallowed hard. When she had jested about her challenge with Cumberland, it had all seemed incredibly amusing, delightfully mischievous. How could this nobody —this cowardly rebel—make her feel almost ashamed?

She struck back, the only way she knew how. "Perhaps you know me, but I hadn't a clue you even existed. But then, a coward and a rebel would hardly have moved in the same circles as Lord General de Lacey's daughter."

"No. That was one misery I was spared. But for the time being, Miss de Lacey, you and I are going to have to come to an understanding. You aren't holding court among a battalion of besotted men now; you are a guest of the Glen Lyon. If you abide by my rules, you will be released not much the worse for your little adventure. But defy me, and you invite ugly consequences."

She gave a scornful laugh to cover up her disquiet at the intensity that suddenly shimmered in his hooded eyes. An intensity that made her forget first impressions of clumsiness and ineptitude, leaving behind the aura of a sleepy lion—currents of danger buried deep.

The trembling in her hands intensified, and she knotted them into fists, her nails cutting crescents deep into her soft palms. "N—Nothing you can say will ever make me bow to the will of a poltroon like you," she spat out. "My papa, the general, would rise up from his very grave if I ever resorted to such behavior."

She had meant to laugh at him, to mock him, to anger him. She had meant to drive back her own chill fear. But something stole into the man's eyes, an ember of understanding that made Rachel want to turn away from that probing gaze that seemed to see too much.

Yet in a heartbeat, that odd spark of understanding vanished, the Glen Lyon's voice cold as steel. "Your betrothed made the mistake of underestimating me once. Don't make the same mistake. In the months since Prestonpans, this coward has learned ruthlessness from a master. I'll do whatever I have to do to force you to submit while you're in captivity. *Whatever* I have to, Miss de Lacey. And as you can see, my little band of outlaws will be most creatively helpful in their suggestions."

"What kind of monster are you? They're children. *Children!*"

"I try to help them remember that." Storms whipped up in his eyes—gray and blue tempests of something like despair. Then his gaze intensified, hardened, until it felt like a dirk blade pressed against her throat.

"Miss de Lacey, your stay here can be as comfortable or as miserable as you choose to make it. But if you do anything —*anything*—to upset those children, I swear this will be the most hellish month of your life."

"I hardly expected it to be anything else! The only question is *why*. Why kidnap me? What do you expect to get in return?"

"Perhaps a king's ransom in gold. Perhaps the pleasure of humiliating your betrothed. Or perhaps the harbor at Cairnleven cleared of the bastard's soldiers."

"Why clear the harbor? So you and your loathsome rebels can skulk away with your tails between your legs?"

"Absolutely. My loathsome rebels will leave Scotland with a pocketful of Sir Dunstan Wells's gold, and the satisfaction of knowing that we've brought the bastard to his knees."

"Sir Dunstan would die a thousand deaths before he allowed a miscreant like you to bring him to his knees. You're not going to get away with this, no matter what you threaten to do to me! The British army doesn't strike deals with traitors!"

"Then I suppose we will be stuck with each other, Miss de Lacey." He looked about as pleased with the prospect as she felt. "Of course, I suppose I could dig through the Cowardly Traitor Handbook to find out the procedure for ridding one's self of an unwanted hostage."

Without another word, he spun on his heel and stalked from the makeshift chamber. The oaken door slammed shut behind him, and Rachel heard the heavy, scraping sound of a thick wooden bar being slid into place, imprisoning her in the echoing silence alone.

She stumbled to the desk where he'd been sitting, and sank down onto the chair, despair coursing through her in debilitating waves. She bit her lip, hard. She was tired, bone-weary, soul-deep.

And frightened.

The words whispered through her consciousness, despite her efforts to crush them. There had been sarcasm in his threat to research a way to rid himself of a hostage. And yet, would that bitter humor disappear when the Glen Lyon found himself thwarted? Discovered she was right?

The soldiers might rip Scotland apart searching for her, yet they had been searching for Glen Lyon for over a year and had never found his lair. There was a grave danger that they never would. In time, despite her station as general's daughter, they would have to turn their attention back to issues of more pressing national concern. They would be forced to abandon her as one more casualty of war, because their honor would never—*never*—allow them to bend to the will of someone like the Glen Lyon.

"Oh, God, Papa," she whispered, "what am I going to do?" It wasn't a whimper, but it was close enough to appall her.

She could almost see her father's thick white brows crash together in a formidable scowl, those piercing general's eyes drilling her with disapproval.

A soldier never wastes energy on fear, girl. If he is captured by the enemy, it is the soldier's duty to escape, even if it costs him his last drop of blood.

Rachel held her head high. Papa was right. Only a weakling or a fool would sob in a corner, waiting for someone else to rescue her. If the army couldn't help her, then she would bloody well find a way to save herself.

The resolution sent renewed strength surging through her aching limbs, her gaze scanning the chamber. She was about to cross to the splintered chest against the wall, to search for something to use against her captors, when she saw it, half buried among the litter upon the desk's battered surface. Blue-black metal, polished to a deadly sheen.

Her eyes widened in disbelief.

Thunder in heaven! The man *was* a complete idiot!

No, even he couldn't be stupid enough to . . . She didn't dare formulate the thought, because if she were disappointed, it would be too crushing.

She rushed over to the desk, oblivious to her aching

muscles, and plowed through sewing implements and tattered books until her fingers closed around her prize—the shimmering length of the Glen Lyon's pistol.

Look for
Capture the Stars
Wherever Paperback Books
Are Sold
Coming Soon from
Pocket Books